Something To Be Thankful For

D0104711

Carrie Carr

Yellow Rose Books

Nederland, Texas

ISBN 1-932300-04-X

First Printing 2003

9 8 7 6 5 4 3 2 1

Cover design by Mary D. Brooks

Published by:

Yellow Rose Books
PMB 210, 8691 9th Avenue
Port Arthur, Texas 77642-8025

Find us on the World Wide Web at
http://www.regalcrest.biz

Printed in the United States of America

Acknowledgments:

Lots of good folks helped bring this book about: Steph, who suggested that I try to write a "short story" for Halloween; Day, with her tireless reading and good-humored grammar corrections that made editing almost fun; Lori, a superb writer in her own right who cheered me on and helped me stay focused while working on it; my AJ, the love of my life and the woman who put up with my late-night brainstorming; and Cathy, the best damn publisher in the world, and a wonderful person to boot - for allowing me to continue to live my dream.

Dedication:

To my Mom and Dad, thank you for always being there for me, and for your living example of how love works. It's not easy, but it's definitely worth it.

To my brother Kenneth, his wife Judy, my niece Kailee, and my nephew Kennedy - thank you all for the smiles and unconditional love - I am truly blessed to have such a wonderful family.

To my daughter Karen, who shows more and more every day what a beautiful young woman she's become, I love you. Thank you for coming into my life.

And last, but most certainly not least, to my AJ. The love shining from your eyes and face every time you look at me, reminds me how lucky I am to be on this earth. Forever and always, my love.

Chapter
1

The Woodbridge City Limits sign caused several expressions to flit across Randi Meyers' face. Nervousness warred with curiosity as she slowed her yellow 1978 Corvette, mindful of the radar traps that often caught motorists unaware. *Welcome to Podunk, USA,* she thought bitterly, the old familiar feelings starting to gnaw away at her stomach. The town was also home to a large Christian university and wasn't known for being progressive. Even though she had grown up in the little town of Woodbridge, Texas, she had never felt as if she belonged. It wasn't until she had moved away and come to terms with her own sexuality that she had begun to feel like she fit in somewhere. *And it sure isn't here.*

Except for the occasional family holiday, Randi had rarely returned to her hometown since she'd graduated from high school almost eighteen years earlier. But even when she did visit, she rarely ventured far from her grandmother's home. Those who knew her back then would have been hard-pressed to recognize her now. The long, medium-brown hair that used to trail down to her waist had been cut to just above her collar and was now sprinkled with gray. Her light brown eyes were often hidden behind wire-framed glasses; and the once slender girl had become a slightly stocky, mature woman.

With a heavy sigh, she pulled her automobile into the parking lot of a roadside motel on the outskirts of the sleepy town. Unfolding herself from the car, Randi grimaced. The aches from sitting too long reminded her that she was no longer twenty years old, and she limped to the motel office on pained knees, a legacy of too many years of playing sports with the feeling of invincibility.

The garish Halloween decorations scattered around the lobby presaged the next day's holiday. A smiling Middle-Eastern gentleman behind the counter greeted her.

"Good afternoon, madam. How may I be of service to you today?"

His thick accent told of his Pakistani heritage, and it took a moment for Randi's mind to register what he had said. "Ahh, yes. I need a room for the next two days," she said, reaching into the back pocket of her jeans for a brown leather wallet that had seen better times. She thumbed through scores of old receipts and other bits of paper until she found her rarely used credit card, passing it over to the clerk with a tired smile on her face.

"Very good, madam." The middle-aged man accepted the card and slid it through a slot along the top of the computer keyboard, then handed it back to her. He studied the computer screen and looked back up at her. "Smoking or non?"

"Smoking," Randi mumbled, the long drive finally catching up to her. She accepted her key and nodded automatically as the man droned on about the room. "Right. Thanks." While the clerk continued to talk about the "new and improved" rooms, Randi turned and waved as she left the motel office. After stopping by her car long enough to pull a large duffel bag from the trunk, Randi pushed open the door to her room and tossed the bag onto the far side of the bed, dropping her exhausted body right next to it.

Waking from her short nap and deciding to unpack, the still-weary traveler sat up and rubbed her eyes. Randi unzipped the heavy duffel and pulled out her clothes. Rolled up to keep them from wrinkling, a quick snap was all that was needed to make them presentable. She hung up the black slacks and shirt, and brushed specks of lint from the matching jacket. "Looks good enough to me," she muttered, knowing that her grandmother wouldn't feel the same. The old woman was not one to let a chance to complain pass her by; and Randi knew that when Edna Meyer's youngest granddaughter appeared for the funeral dressed in something other than a black dress, there would be hell to pay.

Randi's uncle, Randolph Meyers, was being buried the following afternoon. He had lived a fast-paced and prosperous life, but due to the fact that he and her father had never gotten along, the young woman who was his namesake had only actually met him twice, once being her grandfather's funeral, years previously. Randi had vague memories of a man too busy with his many business ventures to ever get married; one who doted on his nephews while virtually ignoring his nieces. She was to be the sole representative of her branch of the family for the gathering. Her parents, who had moved to Santa Fe after they retired, were on a well-deserved cruise and couldn't make it back in time for the funeral. Randi's two older brothers were at separate ends of the country, neither one willing to take time off from their own lives to mourn the death of the man who had sent them through their respective colleges.

Bitterness brewed in her stomach at the ingratitude of her siblings. *Pricks. Uncle Randolph gave them everything, and they can't even be bothered with seeing him off.* Her uncle had never offered to pay Randi's way through school, and she was too stubborn and full of pride to ask. She had worked her way through college, taking almost twice as long to get her veterinary degree because of the scarcity of money.

She walked over to the dressing area of the motel room and looked at her reflection in the mirror. Dark circles still appeared prominently under her eyes, and tiny lines had begun to form around her mouth from years of smoking. Reaching into her shirt pocket, Randi removed a slightly crumpled red and white pack and pulled out a cigarette with her teeth. Glaring at the stranger in the mirror, she dug into her jeans and grabbed a silver lighter, flicked it open, and waved the flame at the end of the stick of tobacco. *A few more wrinkles won't hurt anything.*

Halloween afternoon turned out to be overcast and humid. Randi made her way from the car to the church, limping slightly as the damp weather aggravated her aching knees. Trying to slip into the entryway unnoticed, she cringed as the heavy door slammed behind her. She stood just inside the doorway for a moment, hesitant to remove her sunglasses in the bright artificial light.

The local funeral home wasn't large enough to accommodate the crowd that was expected at Randolph Meyers' funeral, so the services were being held at the First Baptist Church of Woodbridge. The cavernous interior could easily hold several hundred people; but from the looks of things, it would barely be large enough for today's gathering. Randi looked up at the stained-glass windows that covered three sides of the room, and sighed. She remembered being forced to attend services at this very church with her grandmother every Sunday when she was a young girl. Randi's parents were never the churchgoing types, so Edna took it upon herself to see that her granddaughter's spiritual needs were met, much to Randi's dismay.

Heads turned at her entry, and several sets of eyes narrowed as they spotted the dark-haired woman in the doorway. Two women, slightly older than Randi and clad in prim black dresses, rushed over to the newcomer and shook their heads in comic unison.

"My goodness, but you've let yourself go, Randi. How long has it been?" one of the women tittered. Amy was an inch or so shorter than Randi, and quite a few pounds heavier. Her shoulder-length blonde hair was cut in an expensive style, and her makeup looked as if it had been applied by a professional. Only three years Randi's senior, Amy and her twin, Andi, had always enjoyed taunting their cousin.

"Not long enough," Randi mumbled under her breath. She removed her sunglasses and raised an eyebrow at her two cousins. "Amy...Andi. Doesn't look like either one of you have been starving to death, yourselves." She gestured toward Amy's hair. "Decided to go lighter this year, huh?" Both were naturally brunettes, but it seemed like every time Randi saw them, they were sporting a new shade.

Two blonde heads bobbed simultaneously. "Somewhat," Amy said. "But our husbands don't seem to mind." Her insincere smile turned nasty. "I don't see a ring on your finger, cousin. Still can't find a man to put up with you?" Amy exchanged amused looks with her sibling. "Or maybe there's not even a *woman* around who'll give you the time of day."

Randi's sexuality had been a topic of conversation between the sisters ever since she'd told her family she was a lesbian, several years prior. Her two cousins rarely let an opportunity go by without getting in some sort of catty remark. *One...two...three...*Randi counted to herself before answering. "Unlike you two, I tend to be particular about who I'm with." She looked over their heads at a tiny, elderly woman who was waving a white handkerchief in their direction. "I'd love to stay and chat, but it looks like Grandma needs me." Pushing past the simpering twins, Randi straightened her back and steeled herself for Round Two.

"Good Lord, Randi Sue. What are you wearing?" Although she was in her mid-eighties, Edna Meyers had a voice like a bullhorn and loved to hear her words echo around her. Her diminutive stature was deceiving—the matriarch ruled over the Meyers clan with an iron fist. Edna loved each and every one of her grandchildren, but the woman standing in front of her had always found ways to antagonize her. She held out her arms. "Come give your grandmamma a hug, child."

Properly castigated, Randi stepped forward and allowed herself to be gathered into the frail woman's arms. She leaned down and kissed the nearest wrinkled cheek. "It's nice to see you too, Grandma," she whispered.

Randi almost winced at the harsh words that tickled her own ear. "How dare you come here in slacks! What will people think?" the old woman whispered angrily. "You always have to be different, don't you? Just this once, couldn't you have behaved like a lady?" Edna pulled back, and her wrinkled face wore a pained smile. "I see the rest of your family isn't here, as usual."

Fighting the overwhelming urge to run from the church, Randi nodded. "Mom and Dad are somewhere in the Caribbean, and I honestly have no idea about Augie or John." Randi hadn't seen either of her brothers in well over a year. Neither of them had returned her calls when she'd tried to make arrangements to meet them for the funeral. *Nothing unusual in that,* she thought. *They always were self-involved and petty.*

Edna looked around to see if anyone was listening. "Of course. I'm sure Augustus has his hands full, with his sweet wife recuperating from their last baby." She glared at her granddaughter. "That's number four, isn't it? When are *you* going to settle down? Although it's probably too late for you to have children."

Randi took a deep breath and bit back an angry response. *Why argue? She's probably right. My prospects for any sort of relationship are bleak, and I can't have children, anyway.* During her early twenties, Randi had gone to the gynecologist for severe cramps and had been diagnosed with endometriosis, necessitating a hysterectomy soon thereafter. Only her mother and father were aware of the surgery, so she quite often had to fend off backhanded inquiries like this from other family members. The sharp tones of her grandmother's accusations still hurt, and Randi struggled to keep her composure.

A man in an expensive suit stepped in and placed a gentle hand on Edna's arm. "I'm sorry to disturb you, Mrs. Meyers, but the minister said it's about time to commence the services." He looked at Randi and nodded. "Randi. I didn't think we'd see you here, today."

"That's what you get for thinking, Paul," Randi snapped. She studied her cousin Amy's husband for a moment as Edna made her way to the front of the church. Paul Whitaker was five years older than Randi and extremely arrogant. He owned a jewelry store in the town's only mall, and often gloated about his successes at family gatherings.

Tall, thin, and quickly losing what little dark hair he had left, the jeweler had gotten on Randi's bad side sixteen years earlier on the day of her grandfather's funeral. He had tried to edge his way into the family limousine with Edna, elbowing Randi in the ribs and shoving her out of the way. The older woman may have been grieving, but she caught on to him immediately and required that he called her Mrs. Meyers ever since. He met Randi's gaze, then made a show of looking behind his wife's cousin. "Alone, again?" With an ugly sneer, Paul looked her over from head to toe. "It's no wonder, the way you dress."

Before Randi could come up with a suitable retort, Amy rushed by and grabbed Paul's arm. "We have to hurry if we're going to get good seats near the front," she whined, pulling him away without even glancing at her cousin.

"Assholes," Randi grumbled, pushing her way through the crowd and slipping unobtrusively into a rear pew.

Randi winced as her car found another large pothole on the cemetery's graveled lane. "You'd think they'd join the twenty-first century and pave the road," she cursed to no one in particular. Her nerves were still on edge from the confrontation with the family at the church.

Thankful that she hadn't joined the rest of the family in the limousines, Randi parked her car at the end of the queue. She glanced at the dark clouds and shook her head as she realized that her umbrella was in her apartment, several hundred miles away. The heavy breeze brought with it a damp and eerie feeling, causing the hair on the back of her neck to stand up. "Definitely Halloween," Randi mumbled as she followed several others to the graveside. Trying to stay away from her family, she stood at the back of the crowd, not even able to hear the minister's words as they were carried away by the wind.

Bored, she glanced around at some of the other people around her. Everywhere she looked, Randi could see money and power. Her uncle had been an influential man, and she wasn't too surprised to see a senator and several congressmen on the scene.

The last time she had seen Randolph Meyers was over ten years before. The occasion was one of Edna's holiday family gatherings, for which the matriarch had harangued most of the family members until they'd agreed to attend. Although rich and powerful, Randolph was not immune to his mother's well-rehearsed guilt trips, so he had promised to come, as well.

"Randi Sue, there you are," Edna proclaimed loudly. She had left the kitchen in search of her youngest granddaughter, and

quickly grabbed the younger woman by the arm and pulled her from the living room. Slipping into an unoccupied bedroom, Edna closed the door and looked up into the surprised brown eyes. "I need you to do something for me, dear."

Confused, Randi shrugged. "Sure, Grandma, whatever you need. Do you want me to chase Amy and Andi out of the kitchen?"

"No, child, although, that's not a half-bad idea," Edna said as she let out a cackle. She sat down on the edge of the nearby bed and patted the space next to her. Waiting until Randi was beside her, she took the younger woman's hand and held it gently. "You're the only one of these idiots here I trust," she said, and as she spoke, it seemed like the wind went out of her.

"What's wrong, Grandma?" Randi was becoming increasingly concerned over her grandmother's demeanor. In seconds, she had gone from high-energy to depressed. The matriarch seemed almost defeated, and it scared her.

Edna stroked the strong hand in hers, not making eye contact. "There's something that needs doing, and it's either ask you, or do it myself and leave those morons in charge of my kitchen."

"Whatever it is, I'll do it."

"Wonderful." Edna reached into the pocket of her apron and pulled out her car keys. "Your Uncle Randolph is arriving at the airport in less than an hour, and I need you to go pick him up."

"What?" Randi stood up. "All of this secrecy, just to pick someone up at the airport? I don't understand."

"No, you wouldn't," Edna said. "My son is a very influential man. This is one of the few family gatherings he's chosen to attend, and I don't want some simpering cousin or in-law trying to get money or favors out of him between the airport and the house." She stood up and, in a rare show of emotion, touched her granddaughter's cheek. "Randi Sue, you're the only person in this family who has never asked anything of him, and I know you never would. Please, do this for me?"

Randi nodded. "If it means that much to you, I will. But why your car keys? My car runs perfectly fine."

Smiling, the older woman patted Randi's cheek. "Don't take this wrong, but he's much too important to be riding around in that old heap of yours."

Almost an hour later, Randi found herself standing at the terminal holding up a placard with Randolph's name on it. She couldn't exactly remember what her uncle looked like, and the last thing she needed was to miss him and upset her grandmother. People disembarked from the gate, and she studied the crowd for some hint of the man for whom she was waiting. Momentarily, Randi stood face-to-face with a foul-tempered man holding an unlit cigar between his teeth. His height and build reminded Randi of her father, but that's where the similarity ended.

Randolph Meyers wore his dissatisfaction with the world on his face like some people wore a favorite shirt—it looked like hell, but he was comfortable in it. Thrusting several claim checks into the young woman's face, he demanded, "Fetch my luggage, girl— and be quick about it. I don't have all day." With that, he disappeared through the outer doors of the terminal, on his way to light the cigar that he chewed on so mercilessly.

"Uh—" Randi was taken by surprise, and only moved when she was nudged by a young man wearing a dark suit and a chauffeur's cap.

Mistaking her for a driver, he said, "Better get moving. You'll never get a decent tip by standing around." A quick glance at her jeans and sweatshirt caused him to shake his head sadly. "You'd better learn to dress nicer, too. They like that." With a wink, he took off to help his elderly client with his carry-on.

Once Randi had loaded the baggage into the trunk, she efficiently maneuvered the dark Lincoln through heavy traffic. Woodbridge was a small town, but its airport was the only one for over a hundred miles in any direction, and the abundance of vehicles on the roads around it attested to that fact.

"You must be new," Randolph muttered from the backseat.

Looking into the rearview mirror, Randi frowned. "How do you mean?"

He waved an impatient hand in the air. "You drive too slow, and you dress like hell. What service are you from, anyway?"

"Service?"

"Yes, you idiot, service." Randolph sighed and leaned forward. "Who is your employer?"

Still not understanding, the young woman turned her eyes back to the road. "Actually, I'm working two different jobs right now. Why do you ask?" I don't care what Grandma says, this guy's an asshole, *Randi thought to herself.* I can't believe that he's related to my father.

Randolph fell back against the seat. "Never mind. Just get me there in one piece, and I won't have you fired," he grumbled.

The rest of the drive occurred in silence, until Randi pulled the late-model car into the driveway. She had barely put the vehicle into park when her uncle opened his door and climbed out. "Just put my bags on the porch," he ordered, tossing several bills into the backseat.

"Now wait just a damned minute." Randi barely gave the *money a second glance before she chased after him. "You can get your own damn bags."*

He turned around and glared at her, not seeing his mother open the front door. "Do you have any idea who I am?"

Randi nodded. Through gritted teeth, she said, "My father's brother," then pushed by him and into the house. As she passed her grandmother, she handed Edna the keys and continued into the living room, where some of the family sat watching a football game.

Now, standing at the rear of the jam-packed crowd, Randi shook her head. "I don't even know why I bothered to show up," she mumbled under her breath. "He was nothing to me." Her heart knew the answer. Family meant everything to Randi, and she knew that Edna had expected her attendance, no matter how distanced she was from the deceased. So, to keep the peace and appease her grandmother, here she was.

Randi was startled when a cool hand grasped hers, causing her to look down. Standing beside her was a young boy around ten years old. He wore a rumpled navy suit, the red and white striped tie knotted loosely at his unbuttoned collar. "Um, hi," Randi said quietly.

He squeezed her hand tighter and sniffled. Pale blue eyes filled with sadness looked up into hers. "I'm scared."

With a quick glance at the service in front of them, Randi squatted to place herself at eye level with the youngster. "Why are you scared? Where are your parents?"

He pointed to a clutter of headstones several yards to their left, on the final row before the fence. "Mama's over there." Large tears began to trail down his face. "Kiki doesn't feel good, either."

"Who's Kiki?" Randi looked around, assuming the child was talking about a pet, or maybe a favorite toy.

The boy pulled her hand until she stood up. "C'mon. Kiki doesn't feel good." He tried to tug her away, unnoticed by the large group of people.

Randi allowed herself to be led through a break in what used to be a wire fence, but was now just a few rotting wood posts and rusted strands of wire partially buried in the overgrowth. She found herself amongst the heavy cedar and oak trees that bordered the cemetery, marveling at how focused the youngster was on his task. *He still hasn't told me who this Kiki is.* After a few minutes of walking in silence, she spared a glance behind them and realized with surprise that they were deep in the woods. Randi stopped, causing her young guide to look up and glare at her.

"Hey! I told you that we have to go to Kiki," he chastised Randi. His young face scrunched up into a pout, and he yanked his hand away to cross his arms over his chest.

"Look, kid..." Randi returned his glare and slipped her hands into the pockets of her dark slacks, fighting the urge to light a cigarette. "I don't know you, or this Kiki. For all I know, you're leading me on a wild-goose chase."

Tears began to roll down his face again. "Kiki's my sister, and she needs help." He grabbed her arm and pulled. "Please."

The boy's fear and sorrow touched her, but she still was not completely convinced. "This isn't some Halloween prank? 'Cause if it is—" Her threat hung in the air.

"No! I promise," he pleaded. "Please. Nobody else will listen to me. She really needs you."

With a heavy sigh, Randi extended her hand. "All right." She looked up through the dying leaves that still hung on the oak trees around them. "But we'd better hurry. It looks as if it's gonna rain any time now."

After ten more minutes of walking, the boy stopped and pointed through some heavy shrubbery, which had begun to die for the winter. "Over there."

"Where? I don't see..." Randi strained her eyes until she could barely make out a crumpled form clad in a denim jacket and jeans, lying in a clearing. "Is that..." She looked down, but the boy had disappeared. She glanced around. "Hey! Where did you go? Hey! Kid!" But he was nowhere to be seen.

Fighting sharp branches, Randi finally struggled through the shrubbery and stumbled into an area about five yards in diameter. She knelt down next to the still body that was lying on its right side, turned away from her. Wet tendrils of dark blonde hair clung to the woman's face, which was pale from the cold. Reaching down, Randi gently touched a limp arm. "Miss?" Mud-covered athletic shoes indicated that the woman had been walking in the woods for some time. Her right leg was twisted beneath her, and the bits of dead leaves and smudges of dark soil made it clear that she had fallen down the slight hill that was just above their position. Randi didn't know if the woman was breathing, so she leaned close to the pale face and listened for a breath, feeling a hint of warmth touch the side of her cheek. Relief flooded through her. Just as she was about to touch the slender wrist to check for a pulse, the woman moaned.

Blinking several times, the injured woman looked up and saw the concerned face of a stranger looking down at her. "Who..."

she croaked, then cleared her throat. "Who are you?"

"My name's Randi. Do you remember what happened to you?"

"I was just out for my usual walk, when I tripped over a root and ended up down here." She struggled to sit up, then tried to straighten her legs. She cried out as she leaned down and reached for her right ankle. "Oh, God! That hurts!"

Randi pulled the other woman's hand away before it grabbed the injury. "Hold on. Let me see." She tried to push up the leg of the jeans, but they were tapered and wouldn't budge. *Unless this woman has extra-thick socks on, with all the swelling, I'd have to say it's broken.* She looked up into the brown-flecked hazel eyes filled with tears. "I'm afraid we're going to have to..." Randi pulled out the dark-handled pocketknife that had been given to her by her father when she was a teenager. She kept the blade of the old buck knife honed to razor sharpness, never knowing when she might need it. Holding it out for the injured woman to see, Randi gestured at the leg of the jeans.

"Go ahead," the blonde said in a resigned voice. She sucked in a pained breath as the sharp knife sliced through the denim, feeling the pressure slip away from the swollen skin. "Ow!" she cried, as her foot was jostled in the process.

"Sorry," Randi apologized. Still kneeling at the woman's feet, she glanced down at the ankle, which appeared quite swollen. *Definitely broken.* "We're going to have to immobilize this." She looked around the clearing, finally spying a few nearby sticks she could use as a splint. After gathering up the dead wood, Randi knelt once again by the injured woman. She cut the torn pant leg off at the knee and sliced it into strips to help secure the ankle. "Where did your little brother go?"

"My brother?"

"Yeah, your brother. The little guy who dragged me through the woods to find you." Randi looked down at the quiet face. "You're Kiki, aren't you?"

If possible, the shocked face became even paler. "No one's called me that in years. How did you know?"

"Like I said," Randi explained, exasperated, still working to brace the broken limb, "this little boy, about ten years old, came up to me while I was at my uncle's funeral. He told me that Kiki didn't feel good, and he practically dragged me God-knows-how-far to here." Randi stood up and dusted off her hands, studying the petite woman lying on the ground. *Now how am I going to handle this? I've got to get her out of here, but I don't want to leave her. I hope she's as light as she looks.* "Is there someplace close we can take you for help? I think I can piggy-back you."

"Are you sure? My house isn't too far." The injured woman cleared her throat. "Oh, I'm sorry. My name is Katherine, although my friends call me Kay." She pointed up the hill. "My house—" Her expression took on a faraway look.

Kay's glassy-eyed look caused Randi to think that she was going into shock. "Come on. Let me help." Randi reached down to help Kay up onto her good leg. "Are you going to be okay?" When the woman nodded, Randi shifted around, staying close to Kay, and presented her back in order to hoist her up. "How far?"

"I live just over that rise. It's..." Kay trailed off, dropping her head forward onto Randi's shoulder.

Great, Randi sighed. Making certain that she had a good hold on her cargo, she began the slow process of hiking up the incline.

Bright lights sifted through closed eyelids and brought Kay out of her pain-induced slumber. Blinking several times, she was able to focus on the tiled ceiling. She attempted to sit up, but a firm hand against her shoulder held her down.

"Whoa," a throaty feminine voice ordered. "Calm down."

Kay turned her head and saw the woman who had found her. "You?" Looking completely rumpled and exhausted, the woman sitting beside her was no youngster, if her salt-and-pepper hair was any indication. The tiny lines around her eyes and her mouth were another sign of her age, although Kay was hard-pressed to hazard a guess as to just how old she really was.

An embarrassed smile and a blush made the older woman appear much younger. "Yup. Me." Randi tried to subtly disentangle herself from the hand she had been holding. "um...since you were unconscious when I brought you in, they want to keep you overnight for observation." She couldn't help but notice how young Kay looked, especially with the dark blonde hair that didn't quite reach her shoulders in disarray. *She's probably in her early twenties, if that. Poor kid.*

"Overnight? But..." Kay tried again to sit up, but was promptly held down. She looked down at the foot of the bed, where her right ankle had been casted from the knee down. "Broken?"

Randi looked at her quizzically, then followed Kay's line of vision. "Oh, yeah. But it's a clean break. They said you should heal up just fine." She shifted uncomfortably in her seat.

"How long have I been out?" Kay asked.

"A few hours," Randi said. She reached down and picked up a

purse, handing it to Kay. "I found this in your car, so I brought it inside. I'm sorry I had to go through it to find your insurance card."

Kay smiled at her rescuer. "That's okay...Randi, isn't it?" She held out the hand that Randi had just relinquished and waited for the other woman to take it. "I don't know how to thank you for what you've done for me."

Randi blushed again. "um...no problem, really. I'd have never found you without your brother's help." She glanced around the room in a panic. "Oh, no! I forgot all about him! I don't know where he went—"

"Wait!" Kay squeezed the larger hand and fought back tears. "My brother is dead, Randi. He was killed by a hit-and-run driver on Halloween five years ago." She struggled to keep from crying. "There's no way he could have brought you to me." She closed her eyes and nuzzled the knuckles she held, gathering comfort from the touch.

Randi felt the hair on the back of her neck stand up again, like it had when she had first arrived at the cemetery. "But..." She glanced out the window and saw a young boy smiling back at her. He waved once, then faded off into the misty rain that had once again begun to fall. Shaken, Randi looked down at the woman who was holding her hand and crying softly. "It'll be all right, Kay. I'll take good care of you," she promised, leaning forward and kissing the top of the blonde head gently.

Chapter
2

The quiet whine of wheels on the damp street broke the stillness of the early morning. Hazel eyes stared through the side window of the old Impala, watching the passing scenery with detachment. Kay turned away from the view and stared across the car at the profile of the woman driving. "You really didn't have to drive me home, Randi." Her voice echoed in the quiet car. "I'm sure I could have gotten a ride from someone who didn't have to go so far out of their way."

Randi flicked her eyes from the road and smiled at the younger woman. "I'm sure you could have too, Kay. But since I'm the one who got you there, the least I could do was bring you back." She redirected her full attention to the slick city street. "Besides, I needed some way to go back to the cemetery and pick up my car." Unbeknownst to Kay, Randi had spent the entire night in the hospital, unwilling to leave the woman she had found in the woods.

"Oh, that's right," Kay remembered. The previous day was still a blur, but she did remember Randi telling her about coming to Woodbridge for a funeral. "I'm terribly sorry for your loss," she said quietly.

Randi shrugged. "Don't worry about it." She stopped the car at an intersection and looked around. "um...which way?" Randi's sense of direction had never been that great; and although she had grown up in Woodbridge, she barely remembered the route from Kay's house to the hospital. *Lucky I didn't get us* both *lost,* she thought ruefully. *All these damned streets look the same in the morning light.*

Kay pointed forward. "Turn right at the next light. The cemetery is only a few miles that way. If you continue past the graveyard, my house is about two miles north down the same road." She shifted slightly in her seat, trying to get comfortable. "I'm going to have to call my aunt when I get home. She's not going to be happy about this."

"What do you mean?"

"She's always griping about me living 'out in the boonies,' as she calls it. I'm only about five miles outside of town, and have lived out there just fine for a couple of years. But she'll use this as an excuse to move me back to that old tomb she calls a home." Her eyes widened when she realized what she had just spoken aloud. "Don't mind me, Randi. I think the medication they put me on has fried what few brain cells I have left."

Randi laughed. "Sounds like your family is as interesting as mine." She turned the vehicle onto the aforementioned road, grimacing as the back tires spun on the wet pavement. "Sorry about that."

Kay reached across the car and touched Randi's arm. "It's not your fault that this old car needs new tires." She looked down at her right foot, which was in a cast from the knee down. "Guess it'll just have to wait, huh?"

"Might as well. No sense in buying something you're not gonna use for a while." Without knowing why, Randi's mouth opened and she offered another solution. "Or, if you want, I can take care of it after we get you settled at your house." Brown eyes widened and darted around beneath the mirrored sunglasses. *What the hell am I doing? She obviously doesn't want—*

"I couldn't ask that of you, Randi. You've already done so much for me. Who knows how long I would have lain out in the woods if you hadn't come along."

The entire sequence of events had played over and over in Randi's mind all night, and she was no closer to finding a logical explanation for any of it. She blinked several times and took a deep breath. "Well, I'm glad I was there. And, I don't mind taking care of your car for you."

Kay sighed as the car turned onto the gravel drive that ran up to her house. The compact single-story structure was well away from the main road, and the woods that she enjoyed walking in surrounded it on three sides. Although the horizontal wooden slats that covered the house were in need of paint, the once-white home was otherwise well-kept, and sported a neat flower bed under the front windows. The five concrete steps to the covered porch that she usually jogged up without thought loomed obstructively before her. She thought about the wooden crutches that were lying across the back seat of the old car. "Damn."

"What's wrong?" Randi turned off the ignition and turned to look at Kay. "Does your ankle hurt?"

"Not too much, yet." She gestured through the windshield to her front door. "But it probably will by the time I get into the house."

Pulling her sunglasses off and placing them on top of her head, Randi frowned. She stepped out of the car and walked around to the other side, then opened the rear passenger door and pulled out the crutches. Leaning them against the car, Randi opened Kay's door. "Well, seeing as how I carried you back to your house yesterday, I think I can piggyback you up a few little steps." She extended her hand to the injured woman. "C'mon."

"Oh, I don't know. I wasn't wearing this cast yesterday," Kay argued, although she allowed Randi to help her stand beside the vehicle on her good foot. *Not to mention I was half out of my head with pain.* Being too close to the near-stranger who had helped her the day before embarrassed her, as she wasn't used to asking for help from anyone. "This thing weighs a ton."

Randi looked down at her new friend. *She probably doesn't weigh more than a hundred pounds, soaking wet. Even as out of shape as I am, it should be a piece of cake.* She shook her head. "Nah. If you'll just grab your purse, I'll come back for the crutches." With a wink, Randi turned around and bent slightly at the waist. "Your ride awaits, milady."

"You're crazy," Kay chortled. She lifted a leather strap and draped it over her head so that her purse wouldn't fall from her shoulder. Gently climbing onto the offered back, she wrapped both arms loosely around the other woman's neck and felt Randi take a shaky breath. "I'm not hurting you, am I?"

"Uh, no. I'm fine," Randi mumbled, while she struggled to get her emotions under control. No mention had been made of the kiss she had placed on Kay's head the evening before. *She was under so much medication, she probably doesn't even remember it.* As she walked slowly to the house, another thought caused her to stop momentarily. *Or maybe she does, and is embarrassed because she doesn't know what to say. Stupid, Randi. You've got to learn to control yourself.* She couldn't understand what had possessed her to be so forward with someone she had just met, but she chalked it up to being overprotective.

Kay had her eyes closed, her cheek lying at the base of the other woman's neck. *Mmm. She smells good.* When Randi suddenly stopped, Kay's eyes popped open. *I didn't say that out loud, did I?* "Is everything okay?"

Mentally shaking her head, Randi sighed. "Yeah. Sorry about that." She took a firmer grip on the legs that were draped around her hips. "Just wanted to make sure I didn't drop you." She navigated the cement steps and gritted her teeth as her knees creaked under their combined weights. *When am I gonna remember that I'm not a kid anymore?* At thirty-six, her body constantly complained to her about the abuse it had taken when she was younger. Both knees had been operated on for the wear and tear that had resulted from playing sports for over half her life, and she knew she was long overdue for the next round of surgeries.

"If you'll give me the keys, I'll unlock the door," Kay said, not realizing the strain her rescuer was under. Hearing the gasp as Randi reached the top step, she tapped one broad shoulder. "Or better yet, put me down and go get the crutches. I can make it into the house just fine, now."

Randi's sense of chivalry warred with the fear of falling flat on her face, and fear won. "Okay, but only if you're sure," she puffed. She turned and straightened up, allowing Kay to slide from her back and then grab hold of the railing. With a slightly embarrassed grin, she handed Kay the keys and jogged back to the car.

Comfortably ensconced on her sofa, Kay glanced down at the colorful quilt that covered the lower part of her body. It had taken over two hours to assure Randi that she'd be okay, although a part of her thoroughly enjoyed being fussed over. She aimed the remote control at the television set on the other side of the sparsely furnished living room, and began to surf aimlessly through the channels. *One hundred and sixty channels with this blasted satellite dish, and there's not a damned thing on that's worth watching.* Deciding on a softly narrated program about Tahiti on the Travel Channel, Kay closed her eyes and leaned back against the pillows that she was propped up on.

She felt the weight of the cordless phone in her lap and sighed. Picking up the receiver, she automatically hit a number on the speed dial and waited for an answer.

"Hello?"

"Aunt Louise? This is Katherine."

The woman on the other end of the line sniffed dramatically. "Where have you been? I called several times last night. Or is it too much to ask that you pick up the phone when I call?"

Not even the pain medication with which she had been sent home could counteract the effects of one of her aunt's tirades. Kay pinched the bridge of her nose in an attempt to ward off the impending headache. "I'm sorry. But I had an accident yesterday afternoon."

"Accident? What kind of accident? You didn't wreck my car, did you? I told you it was just a loan until Nancy comes home."

"No, Aunt Louise. Your car is just fine. While I was out walking, I fell down a hill and broke my ankle." She could just imagine the look on her aunt's face over that revelation.

"Oh, well." Louise was silent for a long moment. "You know, if you still lived here with Nancy and me, that never would have happened."

Louise's daughter was twenty-eight years old, a year older than her only cousin, Katherine. She was a bit taller, a lot heavier, and her dark hair was dyed a platinum blonde. Nancy Weatherby was a younger carbon copy of her mother, right down to the tacky makeup and superior attitude. She was presently on a missionary trip with members of her church, and had been gone for the past four months.

Kay realized that her aunt was still nattering on about the accident.

"We have sidewalks here in town, not some nasty old trails. My sweet Nancy would never be that careless, you know."

Yes, I know. She's too lazy to walk across the street, let alone go hiking. I'm sure the people she's with right now really enjoy waiting on her hand and foot. Anxious to change the subject, Kay tried another tack. "Speaking of Nancy, have you heard from her lately? When is she supposed to be coming home?"

"Hopefully, soon," Louise said. "Can you still drive? I need to go to the grocery store this afternoon, and that's why I was trying to call you yesterday." Louise had never learned to drive, but after her husband died a few years earlier, depended on Nancy to shuttle her wherever she needed to go. She even paid for Nancy's car, not wanting her daughter to have to worry about getting a job.

"Um, no, I can't. It's my right ankle that's broken." Kay braced herself for what was bound to come next.

"*What?* How on earth am I supposed to get around? I could starve to death," she wailed.

Kay almost laughed out loud. *Oh, yeah. She's stored up more fat than a bear going into hibernation. No way she'll starve.* "Now, Aunt Louise, you live two blocks from the supermarket. If worse came to worst, you could always walk."

"*Walk?* In my condition? Are you out of your mind? I'd never survive in this weather, Katherine."

"What weather? It's sixty-eight degrees out there. Aunt Louise—"

"No, no. Don't you worry about your poor aunt. After all, I took you in and raised you as my own when my only sister died tragically. But no, don't you waste another thought on me. I'll be just fine." Louise started crying and hung up the phone.

Kay looked down at the receiver that she had just pulled away from her ear. "No, other than a broken ankle, I'm fine, Aunt Louise. Thanks for asking." She pushed the "off" button and dropped the phone back into her lap. *Tragically, indeed. Mom drank herself to death after Dad ran off with that manicurist from the mall.*

Since Louise and Harold Weatherby were their nearest living relatives, fourteen-year-old Katherine and her two-year-old brother Jared were placed in the Weatherbys' custody after their mother's death. Katherine immediately clashed with her older cousin. The two girls were supposed to share a bedroom, but their vicious arguments caused Harold Weatherby to convert the one-car garage into a room for both Kay and her brother scant weeks after they moved in.

Three years later, Harold Weatherby died in his sleep of a massive coronary, leaving Kay and Jared at the mercy of their aunt and their cousin. Only a month after her uncle passed away, Kay packed up her meager belongings and moved out of the garage.

Looking around the room that had been her home for the past three years, Kay closed the old suitcase with force. Her uncle had done what he could to make the old garage comfortable for her and Jared, but living in a place without windows had nearly been her undoing.

A sniffle from the twin bed on the other side of the room caught her attention. Kay turned around and forced a smile onto her face. "C'mon, Jay Jay. It's not that bad." Wrapping one arm around his thin shoulders, she pulled him close.

"I want to go, too," Jared cried. His five-year-old mind had trouble grasping the reason his sister was moving out. All he knew was that his world had been changed, and he didn't know why.

Kay's heart broke at his tears. "You will, baby. As soon as I graduate from business school and get a decent job, I'll come for you, I promise." She had taken extra classes and graduated from high school a year early, in the hopes of bettering her and Jared's lives. "Besides, the place I'm moving into is smaller than your side of the garage," she said, reaching over and poking his ticklish ribs.

"Stop!" Jared giggled, falling back onto the bed. After his laughter faded, he sat back up and looked at up at his big sister. "Why is Louie so mean to you, Kiki?" When they first moved in with the Weatherby's, he had trouble pronouncing Louise's full name, so he'd shortened it the best he could and it had become habit.

I didn't think he was old enough to notice, *Kay worried. "I don't know, honey. Maybe she's just sad because Mama has gone to Heaven, and she misses her." She knew this was a lie. Kay knew full well why her aunt despised her so. The young girl was a favorite of her recently deceased uncle Harold, and he had always doted on her instead of paying attention to his own spiteful offspring. She had heard the couple argue many times over his preferential treatment of his niece. Now that he was no longer alive, Kay had no reason to stay.*

The above-the-garage apartment a friend found for her to rent was only a couple of blocks from Commercial College where Kay planned to attend. Living so close to the school let her save on cab fare, and most of the money she earned working at the Burger Hut could go into her savings account. She was bound and determined to make something of herself, and to be able to take her little brother with her.

Sad about where her thoughts had led her, and disgusted by the entire conversation with her aunt, Kay rubbed her forehead with one hand and closed her eyes, willing sleep to claim her.

"Shit!" Randi slipped on yet another twig and almost fell on her face. She limped along slowly, cursing her stupidity. "No, I'll just walk. It's not that far back to the cemetery," she mimicked her earlier assertion. When Kay had offered to call a cab to take her back to her car, Randi had waved off her concern. Since taking the main road would have added at least an extra mile or so to her journey, she had assured Kay that she could find the same wooded route back to the cemetery that she had taken the day before.

But now, the winding and overgrown path that she had followed with her mysterious guide seemed to have disappeared, and the exhausted woman fought branches and pools of mud as she tramped through the heavily wooded area. "Egotistical idiot. I just hope I don't stay lost."

A slow drizzling rain began to fall moments after she had left the house, and Randi pulled her suit jacket closed. "Guess I should be thankful it's not snow," she grumbled, grateful that west central Texas was not known for being too cold in early November. Light mist soon soaked her clothes completely, and the dark clouds made navigating through the woods even more difficult. With her knees aching from the activity and the damp weather, Randi reached into her jacket pocket and pulled out her cigarettes, lighting one and inhaling deeply. As she walked, to get her mind off her problems, she thought back to the day before.

Although she had not been sleeping well for the past few months, she couldn't believe that her mind had simply fabricated the young boy who'd led her to the injured Kay. The loneliness, the stresses from the office, and the feeling that something was missing from her life had kept her up more nights than she cared to admit. *Even if it was my imagination, how do I explain knowing her nickname? This is all just a bit too creepy for me. There's got to be a logical explanation for all of this, because I know for a fact I wouldn't walk through these woods on a lark.* Randi thought about her grandmother. *And leaving the services before they were through is certainly not the brightest thing I could have done. Grandma Edna is going to have my hide.* She mentally cringed when she thought about having to apologize to her grandmother, knowing the old woman would probably perpetrate one of her famous guilt trips on her.

Over an hour later, breathing heavily, Randi broke through the trees that surrounded the cemetery. She ground out her last cigarette, bent down and picked up the butt, then slipped it into her pocket with the rest. Cold, wet, and tired, she trudged over to the waiting Corvette and opened the driver's side door. Her keys still hung from the ignition, and Randi breathed a sigh of relief that the graveyard was as secluded as it was. She closed the door and turned the key.

Click.

Click-click-click.

The engine didn't turn over. Randi looked down at the light control knob. "Shit." Pushing the knob back into the "off" position, she leaned her head against the steering wheel and fought back tears of frustration.

"Finally!" Randi almost cried in relief when she spotted the old black mailbox with the letters "K. Newcombe" stenciled along the side in yellow paint. Her legs felt like rubber, and she could swear that a rock the size of her fist was lodged somewhere in her shoe. She was afraid to take the footwear off to check, because she knew her feet had swollen from the long walk. *I'm too damned old to be traipsing around in this mess.* Randi limped up the concrete steps she had left hours earlier.

The knock on the door woke Kay from a restless sleep. She had been dreaming of being whisked away to a castle in the sky by a handsome knight, only to find out that the knight was a woman with short, brown hair and light brown eyes. She opened her eyes and looked around the semi-dark room, the only light coming from the silent, flickering television. Unable to figure out what had awakened her, she ran her hands through her hair in an attempt to neaten the unruly locks. Another knock, this time more forceful, caused her to look over at the front door.

"Kay? Are you all right in there?" an anxious voice asked, pounding on the door again.

"Uh, yeah. Just a minute," Kay called, reaching for the crutches on the floor and struggling up from the sofa. Groggy from the medication and the sleep, she gracelessly worked her way to the door.

Randi was on the verge of busting the door down when it finally opened. She was greeted by the worried frown of her new friend. "I'm sorry, I—"

"Good grief! Get in here," Kay ordered, grabbing a handful of soaked blazer and pulling Randi inside. Once she had the door closed, she looked over at the clock on the wall and shook her head. "You've been gone for hours. What happened to you?" She reached for Randi again, but one crutch fell out from underneath her arm. "Damn."

"C'mon. Let's get you back down on the couch, and I'll tell you all about it." Randi picked up the crutch and handed it to the injured woman. She gently guided Kay back to the sofa and squatted down on the floor beside her. "You wouldn't happen to have any jumper cables in your trunk, would you?"

Kay winced as she propped her foot up. "Jumper cables?"

"Yeah. Did you know that if you leave your lights on all afternoon, evening, and night, the next day the battery will be dead?" She wiped the wet hair out of her eyes and then wiped her hands on the leg of her slacks, then looked up at Kay with a mixture of sheepishness and misery on her face.

"You poor thing," Kay commiserated. She suddenly remembered that Randi was soaking wet. "You need to get out of those wet clothes. Go down the hallway and take the first door on the left. There's a robe hanging on the back of the bathroom door."

Randi looked at Kay, then pointedly back down at her own body. "Uh, Kay. I don't think I could even get my arm into anything of yours." At five-eight, Randi was about four inches taller, and at least fifty pounds heavier than the other woman. "But I will borrow a towel, if you don't mind too much."

"I don't think you'll have a problem with the robe," Kay told her quietly. "It's my girlfriend's. She's a bit bigger than you, I believe."

"Girlfriend?" Randi blinked, then fell back on her rear. She scooted across the wooden floor, away from the sofa. "I'm sorry, I didn't realize..." Upset, she was trying to stand when her knee gave out on her and dumped her back onto the floor. "Shit." She struggled up and ran one hand through her wet hair. "Um, if you'll just let me use your phone, I'll call the Auto Club for a jump."

Without thinking, Kay swung her legs to the floor and tried to stand. "Wait, Randi." She put weight on her injured leg and fell back to the sofa in pain. "Dammit," she said, rolling onto her back and grabbing at the cast.

Randi hurried back over to where Kay was rocking back and forth in pain. "I'm so sorry." She squatted next to Kay and hesitantly placed one hand on the injured woman's leg. "Do you want me to get you a pain pill?"

"No," Kay whimpered, not wanting to stay drugged up all the time. "Just stay here for a while, please?"

"You got it," Randi said readily. "Whatever you need." She eased up into a standing position and pulled the quilt up over Kay.

You, Kay's mind supplied helpfully. Exhausted from the pain, she snuggled under the covering and closed her eyes. *But we can talk about that, later.*

Randi awoke to total quiet, and a glance at her watch as well as the only slight dampness to her clothes told her that she'd been asleep for a couple of hours. After Kay had dozed off, Randi sat down in the dark gold recliner near the sofa for just a moment, but the quiet of the house had easily lulled her to sleep. Randi blinked several times and, by the light of the television, studied the living room they were in. The square room was barely ten feet wide, and just about as long, with a wooden bookshelf under the window that looked out to the front porch. A few feet in front of the bookshelf sat the old sofa on which Kay was asleep. Large, blue, and overstuffed, the sofa had a crocheted blanket in hues of gold and brown resting along its top. End tables bracketed the sofa, with a reading lamp on one, and a potted ivy on the other. The house had been built in the early fifties, and the light wood paneling on the walls appeared to be original. The scratched coffee table that sat in front of the pillowed sofa was covered in magazines. *Looks like someone likes to read.* She turned her head slightly and noticed a freestanding lamp, which she turned on in order to see the room more clearly.

Kay moaned, but didn't waken. She pulled the quilt that was covering her body up higher and quieted once again.

Deciding to let Kay sleep, Randi reached into her jacket pocket and pulled out her glasses. She slipped them on and picked up a magazine to read.

Sometime later, she felt eyes watching her and glanced up. "Hey there." Randi stood up and slowly walked over to the sofa, in deference to her once-again stiff joints.

"Hi," Kay returned as she sat up. "I'm sorry I fell asleep on you like that. Guess I'm not a very good host." She patted the cushion next to her in silent invitation.

Randi smiled, placed the magazine she had been reading on the coffee table, and sat down next to the groggy woman. "No, really, I'm fine. I just woke up not too long ago, myself." Her smile widened as a hand reached over and touched the frames on her face.

"I don't remember you wearing glasses before," Kay marveled shyly. "They look really good on you."

"Uh, thanks. I don't wear them as often as I should." Embarrassed, she was about to take them off when the hand stopped her. "What?"

"Leave them. Please?"

The dark head ducked down bashfully. "Sure." After she felt the heat leave her face, Randi looked up again. "Can I ask you a question?"

"Anything."

"You said earlier that you had a girlfriend? Does she live here?" Afraid of the answer, Randi felt her heart begin to pound and lowered her head. She wasn't sure why it mattered to her, but it did. The attraction she felt for Kay surprised her, and she thought that Kay felt the same. Cool fingertips touched her chin and forced her to look into Kay's eyes.

"Actually, I said that the robe *was* my girlfriend's. She hasn't lived here for almost six months, since I asked her to leave." It was Kay's turn to be embarrassed. "I don't know why I've kept the stupid thing around." She wondered why Randi was upset at finding out she had a girlfriend. *Is she homophobic? I thought that maybe she was...Well, anyway, guess I blew that.*

Randi exhaled in relief. "You broke up?" She remembered the last thing Kay had said. "Maybe you keep the robe because you still feel something for her."

Kay snorted. "Hardly. The only thing I feel for that bitch is complete disgust." She looked up into the shocked face across from her. "I'm sorry. I guess I sound a bit hateful, huh?"

"She must have really hurt you to cause those kind of feelings," Randi said, reaching over and touching the other woman's cheek without conscious thought.

Closing her eyes at the touch, Kay nodded. She felt relief at the knowledge that she hadn't been wrong about Randi. "You could say that. I found her in bed with one of our friends. I had gone to south Texas to visit some relatives, and she thought I'd be out of town longer. Since it was our anniversary, I came home early to surprise her." Tears of anger and hurt fell from her eyes as she relived the painful memories. "We'd been together for six years," she said, falling forward into Randi's arms.

Surprised, but not unpleasantly so, Randi quietly held the younger woman while she mourned the end of the relationship, understanding the feeling all too well. She was about to say something when she heard Kay giggle. "What?"

"I'm sorry, but your stomach rumbled so loudly that I thought a plane had passed overhead," Kay teased. "When was the last time you ate anything?"

"um." Randi scratched her head with her free head. "Yesterday morning?" *That explains why I'm nauseous and have a killer headache.* "I had a few cups of coffee at the hospital last night, which pretty much filled me up. It's not that big of a deal, though. I can pick up something later."

Kay sat back. "It *is* later, Randi. Do you realize that it's almost eight o'clock in the evening? You really need to eat something." She rubbed her stomach. "And to tell you the truth, I'm starving too."

"Well, that settles it then. You have anything in your kitchen? I'll be glad to whip something up for you." Randi stood up and took off her black suit jacket, draping it over the recliner. "Just point the way."

"You can cook?" Kay cringed when she realized she was once again guilty of preconceived misconceptions about the other woman. *Just because she looks a bit butch, doesn't mean she doesn't know how to cook.*

Randi shrugged. "I'm not some master chef, if that's what you're asking. But," she winked, "you can tell by looking at me that I haven't missed many meals. I do okay around a stove." She looked over at the wide entry that obviously led to the kitchen. "If you'll give me a few minutes to figure out where everything is, I'll bring you in something to eat."

"Uh, okay," Kay said. "It should be pretty well stocked. I just went to the store a couple of days ago."

"Great!" Randi saluted and walked into the next room. "Be prepared for a culinary experience you won't soon forget."

"Uh-oh."

"I heard that!" the indignant squawk echoed from the kitchen.

Kay waved her fork around in front of her, pointing it at the woman at the other end of the sofa. "You ever going to tell me what you put in these eggs? Mine never taste like this." They were both finishing up the meal of scrambled eggs, sausage, and home-made biscuits that Randi had prepared.

"Now if I told you that, I could lose my chef's license," Randi teased. "Seriously, just a dash of garlic powder and a touch of picante sauce. No biggie."

"Whatever it is you do to them, they're great." Kay chewed for a minute and shook her head. "This is so weird."

"What is?"

"I know this may sound silly, but here we are sharing a meal in my house, and I don't know a thing about you."

Randi blushed. "Um, well, what exactly is it that you want to know?"

Placing her fork back on her plate, Kay shrugged. "Oh, I don't know. Where you live, what you do, your last name." She paused for a moment. "If you're seeing anyone," she finished quietly.

Oh! Hmm...maybe... Chuckling nervously, Randi had trouble meeting the other woman's eyes. "Vital statistics, huh? All right." She held out one hand and counted off on her fingers. "My name is Randi Meyers, I'm thirty-six years old, I live in Fort Worth, and I'm a veterinarian." She reached across the space and touched Kay's hand, looking directly into her eyes. "And, there's no one special in my life." *Yet,* Randi's mind finished for her.

"Great!" Kay exclaimed, then colored in embarrassment. "I mean, it's great that you're a vet. I've always loved animals, too. You live in Fort Worth? Then I guess that means you were only here for your uncle's funeral." She realized she was babbling, but couldn't seem to control herself.

"Yeah," Randi said. "I'm supposed to be back at work in the morning."

Kay looked at the clock. "It's almost ten o'clock now. Isn't that about a two hour drive?"

"Closer to two and a half. But I've decided to take a few more days off," Randi said. She was about to say something else when there was a knock at the front door.

"Oh! That's probably the tow truck driver," Kay told her. "I hope you don't mind, but while you were cooking, I went ahead and called the Auto Club for you."

Randi smiled as she stood up. "No, that's great, thanks. Let me go explain to him what an idiot I am." She patted Kay on the shoulder as she walked by. When Randi opened the front door, she was met by the frowning visage of a burly woman wearing jeans and a blue flannel shirt. The grimy baseball cap covered short, brown hair that, given the style, appeared to have been cut at a barbershop. She was a couple of inches taller than Randi, and easily outweighed her by forty pounds or more. Her shirtsleeves were rolled up to just below her elbows, showing off thickly muscled forearms.

"You the one that needs the jump?" the woman asked gruffly. She leaned to one side and tried to peer past Randi.

"Yeah. Let me just get my jacket." Randi stepped away from the door and grabbed her blazer from the back of the recliner. "I'm going to go get my car. Just leave the dishes and I'll take care of them when I get back, all right?"

Kay smiled at her new friend. "Okay. But I feel like such a helpless idiot, letting you do everything for me." Her back was to the door, and she couldn't see the nasty look the tow truck driver was giving Randi.

"Nah, no sense in feeling like that. I bet you'd do the same for me." Randi pulled the quilt up and tucked it around Kay's waist. "You gonna be okay while I'm gone? Shouldn't take more than fifteen minutes."

"I'll be fine, Randi. Stop fussing so much," Kay chided, but her smile softened her tone.

"All right. I'll be back before you know it," Randi said. She met the driver in the doorway. "I'm going to need a lift back to the cemetery," she explained as she closed the door behind her.

The tow truck driver pulled on a pair of worn leather gloves and started down the steps, barely looking at Randi. "Sure. Whatever." She climbed into the cab of her truck and waited until the other woman was inside with her. "So, you have car problems and just come here to use the phone?"

Randi looked across at the driver curiously. "um, not exactly." She frowned as the heavier woman grumbled something unintelligible. "What was that?"

"Oh, nothing." Stepping on the gas, she made the truck seem to fly over the old road. "You live back there?"

"No." Randi had to brace her left hand on the dash and the other against the door to keep from being tossed around in the truck. "You want to slow this thing down? I want to pick up my car at the cemetery, not move in there." The turn into the cemetery nearly threw her into the driver's lap.

The woman behind the wheel chuckled mirthlessly. *Chicken.* "Yeah, sure." She pulled the truck up beside the yellow Corvette and stopped. "I'm Beth, by the way."

Relieved to have finally stopped moving, Randi adjusted her glasses on her face and turned to hold out her hand. "My name's Randi. I really appreciate you coming out so late."

"That's what I get paid for," Beth assured her, gripping Randi's hand in a strong grasp. She looked down at the car beside them. "Corvette, huh? Seventy-eight, right?"

"Yeah. I bought it used when I graduated from high school. Had it ever since." Randi climbed out of the truck and walked around to the other side. "Temperamental as hell, but it's my baby." She opened the driver's door and pulled the latch to open the hood. "Of course, if I'd had the sense to turn off my lights yesterday, we wouldn't be here now."

Beth nodded as she gathered up what she needed. "I know what you mean. But the way I look at it, people like you are my job security." She hooked up the cables to the battery and stepped back. "You live around here?"

Randi shook her head. "No. Just down here for a funeral."

"Well, that *is* good news, then," the driver muttered happily. "Give me a minute, and you'll be ready to go."

Once her car was started, Randi thanked Beth and paid her, giving the woman a generous tip. "Thanks again for all your help, Beth. I really do appreciate it."

"No problem." As the Corvette drove down the cemetery road, Beth's smile turned to a frown when the car turned right instead of left toward town. "Only here for a funeral, huh? I'll just bet."

Hearing a car pull into the driveway, Kay couldn't help but smile as she thought of her new friend. *She's so sweet. I can't believe she's not involved with someone.* Her smile widened as the knock on the door was immediately followed by the door opening. "You made good time."

"Yep," Randi said, closing the door behind her and walking over to the sofa. She squatted next to Kay and smiled. "Feels good to have my wheels back."

"I'll just bet it does." Not thinking, Kay reached over and tried to brush the unruly hair away from Randi's eyes. Although the dark hair was only collar-length, it was thick and full of body. The strands of gray only highlighted the many shades of brown that her fingers were enjoying ruffling through. Drying without the benefit of a brush seemed to have made the natural curl go wild, and Kay thought it was beautiful.

The touch to her head was unexpected, but not unwelcome. Randi closed her eyes and enjoyed the feel of Kay's fingers combing lightly through her hair. Her enjoyment was cut short as one knee began to complain about the position it was in, and for the second time that evening, Randi found herself sprawled on the floor.

Alarmed, Kay reached down to help Randi up. "Are you all right?" Her hand was gently batted away by the embarrassed woman.

"Yeah, I'm fine," Randi grumbled as she stood up and dusted off her rear. "Sorry about that."

Kay took Randi's hand and pulled her down to sit next to her on the sofa. "Are you sure? That's twice that has happened tonight." She waited until the light brown eyes met hers. "Did you hurt yourself carrying me around?"

"No, nothing like that." Realizing that Kay was waiting for more of an explanation, she sighed. "My body is just getting back at me for all the years of abuse, I guess. Up until a couple of years ago, I played softball. But the eighteen years of playing catcher screwed up my knees, and I'm about due for the next round of surgeries."

"Surgeries? You've had them before?"

"Oh, yeah. Every few years they go in and clean things out in there. It's not that big of a deal, but I just haven't had the time to mess with it. So, my knees get cranky and give out on me at times." Randi patted the hand in hers. "Nothing to worry about, really. Just old age," she said.

Kay laughed. "Oh, yes. You're so over the hill." She shifted around until there was an empty space beside her. "Why don't you sit over here and get more comfortable? Hanging on the edge there can't be too good for your knees."

Randi accepted the offer and moved to sit next to Kay. She leaned back against the sofa and released a heavy breath. "Thanks. This is better." She turned her head and grinned. "Before I left, you got to know all about me."

"And?"

"And, don't you think that turnabout is fair play?" Brown eyebrows waggled comically.

Kay laughed. "Time to unbury all my deep, dark secrets, huh?" She looked down at their entwined hands. *This feels so right.* "All right. You asked for it." She took a deep breath before continuing. "My name is Katherine Renee Newcombe, I'm twenty-seven years old, and, up until a week ago, I was a file clerk at Reeves, Hollis, and Brown."

Eyes widened at this last revelation. "What happened a week ago? Or is it none of my business?"

"No, that's okay." Kay looked down at the quilt covering the lower part of her body. "I just got mad and quit."

Randi sat up angrily. "Why? What did they do to you?"

"Nothing sinister, Randi. Things hadn't been going well there for a while, and I finally got fed up and left." Kay squeezed the hand in hers, silently thanking the other woman for her concern.

"What are you going to do now?"

A sigh escaped from Kay's lips. "Before yesterday, I would have told you that I'd go out and put in a few applications around town. But with this broken ankle, I guess I'll just have to wait and see."

Randi squeezed the hand she was holding. "I don't want to sound nosy, but can you afford to do that? I mean, to wait until the cast comes off before looking for another job?"

Kay looked up into the concerned eyes slightly above hers. *Dear, sweet Randi. You are definitely someone special.* "Well, the rent on this house is only three hundred a month, and I do have some savings tucked away. It may get a bit tight, but I should be just fine."

Embarrassed by her sudden interest in Kay's life, Randi nodded. "Ahh, good. um, I'm really glad you'll be okay." *What am I thinking? Her life is here, and I'll be leaving in a couple of days. Get your head on straight, Randi.*

"Are you all right?"

"Huh? Oh, yeah. Sure." Randi looked at her watch and shook her head. "I had no idea it was so late. You must be exhausted." She stood up suddenly and looked around the room. "I should go so you can get some rest."

Kay looked at her in confusion. "Did I miss something here? What happened?"

"Nothing happened. I just realized how late it was, and..." Randi picked up the empty plate that Kay had set on the coffee table earlier. "I'll just take care of the dishes, and then be on my way." Her retreat from the room would have been comical if the atmosphere hadn't been so tense.

A few minutes later, Randi stepped from the kitchen and stood in front of the sofa. "Well, everything's cleaned up and put away. If you want, I'll drop by in the morning and check up on you, see if you need anything."

"No."

"What?"

"No, I don't want you to go," Kay whispered. "You said yourself it was late. It's been raining, and you don't know the area that well." Her voice had continued to rise in both pitch and volume, and she stopped for a moment to gain her composure. "I...I care about you, Randi. Please stay."

Caught flatfooted, Randi had no ready answer for Kay's plea. "um. Well, I..."

"Please." Without permission, tears begin to fill Kay's eyes.

Damn. I can't leave her like this. Randi found herself nodding. "All right. I really didn't want to go out in the rain again, anyway," she said with a smile.

Chapter
3

Streaks of sunlight danced across the lightly freckled face, causing the small nose to twitch. Kay moaned and then stretched her arms over her head as her eyes blinked open slowly. The movement caused her to twist her injured leg too far, which made her cry out in pain. She sat up and reached for the plaster-wrapped limb. "This is going to take some getting used to, I think." Remnants of a disturbing dream tickled Kay's subconscious as she looked around the room and struggled to get her wits about her.

The bedroom looked as if a tornado had torn through it. Clothes were not only scattered all over the floor, but the four-drawer dresser opposite the bed bore the weight of a large stack of clean garments that had yet to be put away. Magazines and books liberally littered every other available surface, and the computer desk in the corner opposite the closet held a fifteen-inch monitor and a tower system that was in several pieces. Kay riffled her fingers through her hair and sighed. *Nothing looks different. I wonder what woke me up?* She reached for the crutches that were propped against the wall next to the bed. A large smile graced her lovely features. *Think I'll go check on my guest.*

Kay maneuvered into the living room, expecting to see a black-clad form draped across her sofa. There had been a short argument over who should take the bed, with Randi finally getting her way. She had claimed that she was an insomniac, and that the television in the living room would be good company for her. Searching eyes widened at finding the room empty. A metallic clang coming from the front yard caused Kay to hurry over to the door and peer outside.

Randi was squatting at the right rear wheel of the Corvette, a tire iron in her hands. She fiddled with the jack for a long moment, then stood up and threw the factory-bent bar off into the nearby trees. "Stupid son of a bitch!" Randi kicked the tire and then grabbed her left foot, hopping around as she cursed.

Struggling to keep from laughing out loud, Kay stepped onto the front porch. "Randi? What's going on?"

At the sound of her friend's voice, Randi stopped hopping and turned around. "um. Hi." She gestured to the car with one hand. "I got up this morning and found out that I had a flat tire. Great time to learn that the jack that's been riding around in my trunk all these years is rusted closed, isn't it?"

"You've never had a flat before now?" Kay asked. "How long have you had the car?"

"Since I graduated from high school," Randi said, as she walked up the steps to stand next to her friend. "I've had a few low tires, but I was always able to get them to the shop without having to take them off the car." She turned around and stared at the yellow vehicle. "Mind if I use your phone? Looks like I'm going to have to call the Auto Club again."

Kay smiled sympathetically. "How about if I call them for you? Give you a chance to get cleaned up a bit, at least." She looked pointedly at her friend's legs. The dark slacks had twin circles of mud ground into the knees; and where Randi had rubbed her hands, the thighs looked almost as bad. "I'll be glad to put those in to soak."

"Uh, well..." Randi looked as if she wanted to run. "I appreciate the offer, really; but all my clothes are back at my motel. They're probably holding them hostage until I show up to pay for an extra day."

Kay was determined to get Randi into clean clothes, no matter what it took. She knew that staying in the same outfit for over two days had to be getting uncomfortable. "Okay, how about this? You take my car to get your things, and I'll wait here for the Auto Club for you."

Randi sighed. "Are you sure? That's a lot of trouble for someone you don't even know that well." But she was beginning to warm to the idea. *Spending a little more time here with her is a bonus I don't think I want to miss out on.*

Kay nodded. "I'm completely sure. Besides, it's not my car. It belongs to my cousin."

"Aha! Now I see how you are," Randi teased. She pushed the door open and motioned for Kay to go in front of her. "Ladies first."

Shaking her head, Kay did as she was told. "You are a brat, Randi Meyers."

"I aim to please, ma'am," Randi said, following her friend inside.

A heavy knock on the front door caused Kay to jump. With a deep sigh, she grabbed her crutches and hobbled over to answer it. She peeped through the blinds in the nearby window and saw a large African American man standing on the porch. "Who is it?"

"Auto Club, ma'am."

Kay opened the door and had to look up at the person in front of her. "Hi."

Over six feet tall, the man appeared to be in his early fifties, but didn't seem to have an ounce of fat on his body. He took off his hat and nodded. "Ma'am. Are you the one who requested help with a flat tire?"

"Yes." Kay pointed behind him. "It's the Corvette over there. Our jack was, um, broken." She decided that there was no sense in telling a complete stranger all the details.

"All right. Did our truck not come out last night? Our log shows that you called for help then, too." He put his hat back on and looked down at crutches and the diminutive woman with the cast on her leg. "Can you drive like that?"

Kay gritted her teeth to keep her comment to herself. She looked at the name that was embroidered over his right pocket. "No, John, I can't drive like this. But it's not my car. And yes, your truck did come out last night. But we woke up to find the tire flat."

Realizing that he had upset his customer, John held up his hands in a defensive gesture. "Look, I'm sorry, ma'am. I was just trying to make sure that Beth actually came out here last night, that's all. I didn't mean any harm."

"No, I'm sorry," Kay apologized. "I haven't had my coffee yet." She looked down at the cast. "And I'm still trying to get used to this darn thing, so I'm a bit touchy. Why don't you go ahead and take care of the tire, and I'll give you a cup of coffee to make up for it. I feel really—" She stopped in mid-sentence when she realized what he had said. "Did you say Beth? That wouldn't happen to be Beth Rogers, would it?"

"Yeah. She drives the night shift. Bitches about it most of the time, too," he added. "Didn't you see her last night?"

Kay shook her head. "No. My friend met her at the door. I never saw her." *That means Beth knew that Randi was here. Would she do something like this? She can be mean, and has a vindictive streak. But stooping to vandalism?*

Her mental musings were interrupted when John cleared his throat. "You okay, miss? Do you know Beth?"

"You could say that, John." Kay decided a tactical retreat was in order. "I think I'll go make that coffee. Just knock on the door when you're finished, all right?"

He nodded. "Sure thing." John watched as the door closed. "If I live to be a hundred, I don't think I'll ever understand women," he muttered, walking down the steps.

Feeling almost human after a shower and a change of clothes, Randi tossed her duffel bag into the back seat of the Impala. She had just finished assuring the manager of the motel that everything was fine, and that her not staying in her room the two previous days had nothing to do with the accommodations. As she tried to dial out on the cell phone, she realized that the battery was dead. "Is everything out to get me today, or what?" she complained to no one in particular. Realizing the auto charger was in the Corvette, and the one in her overnight bag required a house outlet, Randi tossed the cell phone into the back seat with her bag.

She drove through the quiet town, smiling when she came upon a large grocery store. "Think I'll pick up a few things for Kay. Might as well make her a good meal before I have to leave." Randi parked the car, then went inside to search the aisles of the store. She had placed several items in her basket when she heard a voice behind her.

"Randi? Is that you?"

With an aggrieved groan, Randi turned around. "Hello, Amy. What a surprise."

The platinum blonde smiled insincerely. "Isn't it, cousin? I thought that you'd be back in your big city by now, playing with the animals." Amy stepped forward and glanced in Randi's basket. "Shopping?" She let her eyes rake down her cousin's body. "Maybe you should concern yourself with more...low fat...items."

"And maybe you shouldn't concern yourself at all with what I do," Randi snapped. "And while you're at it," she barked, stepping away, "try going to a gym once in a while yourself." She was surprised that Amy hadn't commented on her absence at the cemetery, but figured that, as self-centered as her family was, no one had missed her. *Wouldn't be the first time.* Randi was used to being the "invisible" one in her family; as a general rule, she liked it that way. But realizing that her disappearance raised no questions still hurt.

Amy watched as the other woman quickly rounded the end of the aisle and disappeared. "Touchy, touchy." She smiled. "I bet Grandmama would *love* to know that Randi is still in town. I just can't wait to share the news with her."

Kay sat at the kitchen table, slowly sipping her third cup of coffee. Her right leg was propped up on another chair, and she had been mentally arguing with herself whether she should tell Randi about Beth or just let the matter drop. *After all, it's not like I have any proof that she had anything to do with Randi's flat tire.* The man from the Auto Club had told her that a large nail was embedded in the tire, and had offered to take the tire in and have it repaired. *I hope I did the right thing, letting him take the tire into town.*

He had promised that the tire would be ready by early afternoon, and he even offered to bring it back and put it on the car himself. Kay couldn't help but feel like he was trying to impress her, but she gratefully accepted his offer anyway. She heard a key turn in the front lock, and smiled as she heard Randi bustle into the house.

"Kay?"

"I'm in here," Kay called, her smile widening as her friend stepped into the kitchen. "Wow. You clean up nice."

Randi blushed. The faded jeans fit her well, and the dark green sweater brought out the different shades in her brown eyes. "Thanks, I think." She carried two paper bags in and set them down on the countertop. "I picked up a few things at the store. Thought I'd make you a good lunch."

"That sounds great. Oh, by the way, the tow truck driver said the tire had a nail in it. I hope you don't mind, but I told him he could take it into town and have it repaired."

Randi looked up from where she was pulling items out of the bags. "No, that's great, thanks." She noticed the worried look on Kay's face and stopped what she was doing. "Hey. What's up?" A few steps later and she was standing next to Kay's chair. "Are you all right?"

Kay nodded. "I'm fine. Just been thinking too much."

"Thinking? About what?" Randi placed one hand on Kay's shoulder and squeezed gently. "Anything I can help with?"

"No, it's silly." Kay linked her fingers with Randi's and held them tightly.

"C'mon, tell me. You know you want to," Randi said, then her wide smile faded. "I'd really like to help, if I could." She felt a sudden need to get closer and, not releasing her grip, knelt down next to Kay.

Kay studied their hands. "I was just wondering." She took a deep breath and looked into Randi's eyes. "How long can you stay?" *Lord. Can I sound any more pitiful?*

Brown eyes twinkled with amusement, and something else. "How long do you want me?"

Oh, God. Don't ask me that. The answer might scare you to death, Randi. "um." Seeing the glint in the other woman's eyes, Kay slowly leaned over until their faces were inches apart.

Randi echoed the movement, tilting her head up slowly. She saw Kay close her eyes as their lips edged closer. Her eyes closed as well, and she could feel the younger woman's breath lightly tickle her face.

Ring!

Both women jumped apart as the shrill ring of the telephone broke the moment. Kay almost slid out of her chair, and Randi ended up on her rear end on the floor. The blonde looked down at her friend and fought back a case of nervous giggles.

Ring!

"I'll get it," Randi grumbled, getting to her feet and going into the living room. She brought back the cordless phone and handed it to Kay. "I've got to go get my bag out of your car," she whispered, pointing over her shoulder to the living room.

Kay nodded and hit the "talk" button on the phone. "Hello?"

"Katherine! Why haven't you called me?" Louise Weatherby whined into the phone. "I've been worried sick. I just knew you'd call me last night, or at least first thing this morning."

Right. I wonder what she needs this time. "I'm sorry, Aunt Louise. What's wrong?"

"Wrong? Everything's wrong! Nancy's due to come in this afternoon, and she doesn't have a way home from the church. She's going to need her car back, you know."

"Please, calm down. Why don't you have her take a cab out here, and she can drive her car home." Kay suggested, automatically reaching up and rubbing her forehead with her free hand. Her aunt's hysterics always brought on a headache.

"A cab? Are you serious? My poor baby has been off in the wilds for months on retreat. You can't honestly think that she'd want to take another long drive so soon after coming home." Louise sniffled dramatically. "I suppose you don't care that Nancy is probably exhausted from her journey."

Kay rolled her eyes. "For God's sake, Aunt Louise, don't be so melodramatic. I don't live that far away." Her voice had gotten louder, and she looked up to see a concerned Randi standing in the doorway. She reached out with one hand and was relieved when the other woman crossed the room and sat in the chair next to her, taking her hand.

"That's the thanks I get, after all I've done for you. Why I should have never—"

Randi could see tears of frustration welling up in Kay's eyes. "Is there something I can do?" she whispered.

"Aunt Louise, hold on a minute." Kay held the phone to her chest and sighed. "My aunt is going ballistic because my cousin, Nancy, is due back in town this afternoon."

"And?"

"Well, that's Nancy's car out there in the driveway. Mine broke down right after she left, and my aunt loaned me hers so that I could drive her around town."

Randi nodded. "Okay. So your cousin needs her car back?"

Pinching the bridge of her nose, Kay expelled another heavy breath. "That, and Aunt Louise claims she also needs a ride home from the church. It's only about four blocks from their house," she grumbled.

"Where's your car now?"

"In a junkyard somewhere, I'm sure. The mechanic told me it would cost more to repair it than what it's worth. So, I've been saving up to buy another one." *Although, now that I think about it, maybe Beth just told me that so I'd be more dependent on her. This is such a mess.*

"Your nest egg?" Randi asked, wondering if perhaps Kay wasn't in as good a financial shape as she had been led to believe. *Poor thing. Finally gets enough money together to buy a car, and she's going to have to live off of it until her leg heals. Rotten timing.*

Kay nodded. "I'm afraid so." She heard a muffled sound coming from the phone and put it back up to her ear. "I'm sorry, Aunt Louise. What were you saying?"

"You never listen to me," the older woman complained loudly. "I don't know what I'm going to do. How will poor Nancy get home?"

Randi heard the woman's accusatory shrieks from where she was sitting. She pointed at her chest and pantomimed driving a car, causing a relieved smile to break across Kay's face.

"Thank you," Kay mouthed to Randi. "Aunt Louise? I have a friend here that will go with me to pick up Nancy. Then we'll take a cab home. Will that be all right?"

"A friend?" Louise warbled. "It's not that frightful roommate of yours, is it?"

Kay had to stifle a giggle. The last time that Aunt Louise had been to her house, she was still living with Beth. Her girlfriend had taken exception to the way the older woman was acting, and had told her in no uncertain terms that she was no longer welcome in their home. *Shame she only did that because Aunt Louise called her a dirty hooligan. Serves Beth right for not cleaning up before coming home from work.* "No, she doesn't live here anymore. This is someone you haven't met."

"Oh. Well, that's good. That woman scared me." Louise sniffled. "The bus that the church sent to the airport gets in at three. Can you be there?"

"We'll be there. Goodbye, Aunt Louise." Kay hit the "off" button before her aunt could say another word. She looked up into the amused eyes of her friend. "I'm sorry to get you mixed up in this mess."

Randi shook her head. "You have nothing to apologize for, Kay. Believe me, I understand how family can be." *After all, her cousin is probably a sweetheart compared to those two bitches I'm related to.* She stood up and stretched. "How about I fix up a couple of sandwiches for us, and then we'll head on into town."

"Sounds like a winner to me," Kay said. "I think I'll go wash up." She reached for her crutches, but Randi was quicker and handed them to her instead. "Thanks," Kay said, wishing that the phone call hadn't interrupted them earlier. She hobbled out of the kitchen, her mind drifting back to the kiss that almost was.

The parking lot at the Spring Street Church of Christ where they were to pick up Nancy was filled with people and cars. Several clusters of happy families were scattered around, relatives greeting those who had just returned from the long missionary expedition. Randi expertly guided the old Impala through the rows of parked vehicles, while Kay searched through the thinning crowd around the church itself for some sign of her cousin. She spotted a lone figure surrounded by luggage at the edge of the church steps. Squinting, she studied the person for a long moment before laughing out loud. "Oh, my God. Would you look at her?"

Randi directed her attention to where Kay was pointing. "What? Is that—" She fought back a snort of laughter herself. "*That's* your cousin? She looks like a skunk died on her head." Still chuckling, she pulled the car up close to the steps.

Nancy's hair had grown out at least four or five inches while she was on her trip. Her naturally mousy brown hair crept down past her ears, and only the bottom half of her hair retained the platinum blonde color that she so proudly wore. The large woman didn't look as if she'd lost any weight during her travels, but it was hard to tell with the oversized housedress she was wearing—bright blue with pink and yellow flowers, she would be easy to spot any-where. Nancy looked up as the Impala approached, her eyes nar-rowing. "It's about time," she huffed at Kay, who had her window down. "Who's driving my car?"

The vehicle stopped, and Randi climbed out and hurried around to the other side. "Hi, I'm Randi. Would you like me to help you with your bags?" She held out her hand in a polite ges-ture, but was almost knocked to the ground by Nancy as the heavier woman rushed by her to get to the driver's side.

"Just put them in the trunk, Sandy. I'll drive." She squeezed herself behind the wheel of the car. With a groan, Nancy pushed the seat back until she was no longer pinned by the steering wheel. "It feels so good to be home." As soon as she saw the other woman walking around the car, Nancy pulled the keys out of the ignition and held them out the window. "Hurry up, Sandy. I'm just dying to get home and have a nice hot bath."

"Watch how you speak to my friend," Kay warned. "And her name is *Randi*." She glared at her cousin. "Did you leave your manners in that foreign country, too?"

Nancy glanced down her nose at Kay, taking in the cast on her leg. "Good Lord, Katherine. What have you done to your-self?" She looked in the rearview mirror and watched as Randi struggled to get all of the luggage into the trunk. "Where did you find that one, cousin? And what happened to that truck driver that you had?"

Kay sighed. "Beth wasn't a truck driver. She worked in a mechanics shop." *And obviously has graduated to driving tow trucks.* She turned slightly so that she could see Randi, who was almost finished with the luggage. "We broke up months ago. I'd appreciate it if you wouldn't talk about her anymore."

"Fine, fine. What does this one do? She's a bit older than what you normally go for, isn't she?" Nancy loved to bait her cousin, knowing how private Kay was. "Kind of cute, though."

"We're just friends," Kay said defensively. "Randi found me after I fell and broke my ankle. She took me to the hospital and has been helping me out."

The rear door opened, and the object of their conversation sat down behind Kay. Randi reached over the seat and handed the keys to Nancy, who took them without comment.

The silence was stifling as the Impala pulled out of the church parking lot. Randi looked at the back of Nancy's head, then Kay's. Neither woman looked as if they were going to say a word, so she took it upon herself to try and break the ice. "So, Nancy, how was your trip?" *Nice safe subject, I think.* She couldn't have been more wrong, which she realized the moment Nancy opened her mouth to speak.

"Oh, it was just horrible," the heavyset woman whined. "Where we stayed, the apartments, if you could call them that, didn't even have hot water. There was a lavatory on each floor," her voice took on a quieter tone, as if she were telling a nasty secret, "and we actually had to *share* with the peasants who also stayed there." She looked over at Kay once the car was stopped at a red light. "I swear, had I known it was going to be that revolting, I'd never have gone to begin with."

Frowning, Kay turned in her seat so that she could face her cousin. "I never understood why you went in the first place, Nancy."

Nancy rolled her eyes. "Well, let me tell you, it's not something I'm bound to repeat any time soon." Her features softened. "Have you ever met someone, and no matter what your brain told you, your heart wouldn't listen?" She shook her head. "Bert told me it would be a glorious experience, and that we'd have so much fun together."

"What happened?" Kay asked sympathetically. Even though they didn't get along, she understood all too well what her cousin was talking about.

"The sorry son-of-a-bitch got appendicitis the second day we were there, and when he was able to fly, they sent him home," Nancy snapped. "The rest of us were stuck in that Godforsaken country because of some ridiculous agreement that we had signed before we left." When the light turned green, she punched the accelerator. "Stupid idea, trying to bring the gospel of Jesus Christ to a bunch of filthy, unappreciative heathens."

Minutes later, Nancy pulled into the driveway of the home she shared with her mother. The two-story structure had been built in the nineteen-twenties, and was finished in a dark-brown brick that was crumbling in several places. Large hedges engulfed the front of the house, and the front door could only be seen through the greenery once the car was parked in front of the one-car garage, the same garage that had been Kay's home when she'd lived there. Shrubbery grew wild over the front lawn, which was nothing more than dirt and weeds. The home that had once been a showplace had deteriorated after Harold Weatherby passed away.

Kay looked around in dismay, wondering once again how she could be related to people who would allow their home to exist in such a state of disrepair. She knew her aunt had been left a goodly sum of money after the death of her husband, and couldn't understand why Louise didn't spend a little of it on the house itself. She jumped when Nancy climbed out of the car and slammed the driver's door.

"Randa, be a dear and grab my things, will you? I must check on my poor mother." With that, Nancy hurried up the front steps as fast as her bulk would allow.

"I'm sorry, Randi. I never expected my cousin to act like that," Kay said, as Randi helped her from the car. She accepted the crutches gratefully. "Thanks."

Randi chuckled. "You're welcome." She looked up at the overgrown hedge. "Think it's safe to go in?"

"Only if you want to. If you think my cousin is unpleasant, wait until you meet my aunt." Kay watched as Randi walked back to the rear of the car. "Don't you dare get her luggage for her, *Randa-dear.* The lazy old cow can just get it herself."

Oooh. Someone's in a bit of a snit. Randi hurried back to where her friend was waiting. "Yes, ma'am." She studied the ground in front of them carefully, then turned back to Kay and winked. "Do you think you can navigate this, or would you like a ride?"

Although Kay would have liked nothing more than to be draped over Randi's back, she shook her head. "Uh, no. I don't want to give them any more ammunition than they probably already have. C'mon." She led the way, feeling thoughtful eyes on her back.

They entered the house and found the two women standing in the front room, wrapped around each other and crying. Randi guessed from the way the older of the two was carrying on, that she was Louise. Although about the same girth, she was an inch or two shorter than her daughter, and her hair was so blonde it was almost silver in the bright lights of the room. *I bet she never misses a beauty appointment,* Randi chuckled to herself.

"My baby, my baby," Louise blubbered, rocking the larger woman back and forth. "You've finally come home to me." Realizing that they were no longer alone in the room, she pulled back slightly to acknowledge the visitors who were standing in the open hallway. "Well, who do we have here? Katherine, step into the parlor so that I can see you better."

The "parlor" was actually Louise's affectation for the living room. The rectangular-shaped area was filled with uncomfortable furniture and tiny knickknacks adorning every available surface. Dark, heavy velour curtains covered the windows, and the entire house smelled of cheap perfume and mold.

Randi quietly stood in the hallway as Kay crutched forward to greet her aunt. The stale air in the house was almost oppressive, and she tried to imagine her friend living in such a state. *No wonder she lives where she does. I'd be a fresh-air freak myself if I had to spend any time in this mausoleum.*

"Hello, Aunt Louise." Kay leaned forward and accepted the dry air-kiss from the older woman.

"Goodness, girl. What have you done to yourself? You're almost skin and bones," Louise chided, stepping back and studying her niece. "You're not doing drugs, or anything like that, are you?" she whispered.

Kay felt like slapping her aunt. *Just because I'm not the size of a house, she thinks I'm doing drugs? Gee, thanks for the vote of confidence.* "No, I'm not doing drugs. It's called exercise, Aunt Louise. I take a lot of long walks out where I live, and enjoy the fresh air."

"Don't get smart with me, young lady." Louise looked down at Kay's cast. "And walking can't be that good for you—just look at yourself."

Having heard enough of the conversation, Randi hurried over to Kay's side. "Accidents can happen to anyone. I'd think that you'd be glad that Kay wasn't more seriously injured."

Louise's eyebrow rose as she stood face to face with Kay's protector. "And just who might *you* be? I don't recall seeing you around before."

"My name is Randi Meyers, and I'm a friend of Kay's." Although she was five feet and eight inches tall, Randi felt dwarfed by the shorter Louise. She held out her hand and was surprised when it was taken and squeezed—hard. Blood red nails dug into her flesh, and it took all that Randi had not to cry out.

"I see. And just how long *have* you known *our Katherine*?" Louise pulled Randi close to her and glared into her brown eyes.

Nancy stepped over and nudged her cousin. "I don't think Mama likes your friend, Katherine."

"That's enough!" Kay ordered, stepping in between Louise and Randi. "As soon as I call us a cab, we'll be leaving." As she backed away, her crutches almost caused her to fall.

Randi waited while Kay made her phone call, then followed her into the front hallway. She could feel her friend's upset, and was worried that she had done something wrong. It took all of her self-control to walk out the door when she heard Louise's voice echo through the house, "That's right. Run away like you always do, Katherine. You're weak, just like that miserable excuse for a father of yours!" Randi wanted to go back inside and slap some sense into the old woman.

Getting a little bit of satisfaction out of slamming the front door, Randi hurried to catch up with her friend, who appeared to be trying to set a land speed record on crutches. "Hey, wait up."

Kay stopped, but didn't turn around. She felt a gentle hand on her back and fought to hold back the tears that she knew she wouldn't be able to stop.

"Hey," Randi said, walking around until she was standing in front of the younger woman. She saw Kay's lower lip tremble and was just barely prepared for the armful of crying woman that lunged into her arms.

Unable to control herself, Kay let the tears flow. She felt strong arms wrap around her body, and gratefully accepted the physical support that Randi offered. "I can't believe I let them get to me like that," she said a few minutes later, as she sniffled and wiped away tears.

"Yeah, well, I can't believe I didn't sock one or both of them in the nose when I had the chance," Randi said ruefully. "Are you sure you're related to them?"

"She's my mother's sister. Mom was a lot like that, too. Always complaining, thinking that the world owed her more than she got," Kay said. "Dad was more of a dreamer, never really caring about money or social position. He finally got fed up with Mom's constant whining and moaning, and took off with a manicurist from the mall." She looked up into the concerned brown eyes above her. "I don't know if he's alive, or dead. We never heard another word from him after he left."

Randi reached down and wiped at the damp tracks on Kay's face. "Some guys just can't handle being a father," she said. The honk from the taxi that pulled into the driveway caused her to look up. "You ready to go?"

"Definitely," Kay said, slowly making her way to the waiting cab.

When the driver pulled the cab up next to her Corvette, Randi was happy to see that the repaired tire was in place. *Pretty quick service. I'll call and compliment them as soon as I get home.* She assisted Kay out of the car and up the stairs, then unlocked the door and stood back to allow the injured woman entry.

Kay had barely gotten into her living room when she heard a shrill ring, different from the sound of her own telephone.

"I hope you don't mind, but I plugged my cell phone into one of your wall outlets," Randi explained, closing the door and hurrying over to the device. "I must have accidentally turned it on after I plugged it in." She picked up the phone and pushed a button. "Hello?"

Sitting down and propping her injured leg up on the sofa, Kay couldn't help but listen in on her friend's conversation. *I hope that if she wants privacy, she'll leave the room. I hate to just sit here, but what else can I do?*

"I know. Well, I've been away from the phone for a couple of days." Randi paused to listen, then ran one hand through her hair. "Look. I'll be back on Monday, all right?" Another pause. "You tell Dr. Wilde that unless he wants to do everything himself from now on, he'll give me this weekend. Now, you— Oh, Dr. Wilde." She listened for a long moment. "Something very important has come up," Randi tried to explain. "No, *you* listen. As far as I'm concerned, you can shove Mrs. Thompson's cat right up your—" An incredulous look crossed her face. "That sorry son-of-a-bitch hung up on me!"

Kay scooted down until she was sitting on the middle cushion. She reached out, and her hand was immediately taken. "Come sit down and tell me all about it."

Still upset, Randi did as she was asked. "He hung up on me," she repeated.

"I know, honey. But can you really blame him? You did suggest a cat enema to the man," Kay said with a touch of wry amusement.

Randi looked into her friend's eyes and smiled. "Wasn't the most tactful thing I could have said, was it?"

"Not really." Kay looked down at their joined hands. "So, when are you going back?"

"Sunday." *No way I'm leaving tonight, just so I can "fix" a damned cat first thing Saturday morning. He can just neuter Ruffles his own self.* Randi squeezed the hand she was holding, waiting until Kay looked up at her. "I," Randi's voice cracked, "I don't want to leave you." Somehow, in just the past few days, she had come to care for the woman sitting next to her, more than she would have thought possible.

Kay bit her lip. "I don't want you to leave," she said. Her heart was heavy at the thought of not seeing Randi again. "But you have a job you have to get back to. Will you be coming back to town to spend Thanksgiving with your family?"

Randi nodded. "Yeah, I'm supposed to." She reached up and touched the younger woman's cheek with her fingertips. "But I'd rather spend it with you." *Good Lord, you've taken complete leave of your senses, Randi. You've only known this woman for a couple of days,* she berated herself. *But I'd like to get to know her better,* Randi said to the doubtful voice inside of her.

"I'd really like that, too," Kay whispered, as she leaned into the gentle touch. "I just wish we didn't have to wait three weeks."

"We don't," Randi blurted. "Come back with me." *Am I out of my mind?*

Is she out of her mind? She barely knows me. Kay studied the face across from her. "You're serious, aren't you?"

Randi nodded. "Hell, yeah, I'm serious." She blinked. "I mean, yes, I am. Look, you're stuck out here with no transportation, and I have a feeling that your family will be less than helpful while your ankle heals."

"True, but—"

"Wait! Hear me out." Randi took a deep breath before continuing. "You said yourself that you can't look for a job right away. I live alone in a two-bedroom apartment, so there's plenty of room." She took the plunge and said what was in her heart. "Kay, I really like you. And no matter how tough you talk," she smiled, "I know that it would be hard to take care of yourself all alone without any help." Randi looked down again, unable to meet Kay's eyes. "Before I met you, I was barely existing, Kay. And although I can think of better circumstances under which to meet, the two days we've spent together have been some of the best I can remember." To try and diffuse the seriousness of the conversation, she chuckled. "Hell, I ran out of cigarettes yesterday afternoon, and haven't even wanted one. Doesn't that tell you something?"

Kay laughed and shook her head. "That tells me that you're going to live a bit longer, if you keep it up," she said. "Randi, I really appreciate your offer, but it wouldn't be right for me to take advantage of your sweet nature by letting you take care of me for a few weeks."

"Sweet nature? Are you crazy? I'm one of the crankiest people around. Just ask Dr. Wilde."

"I can't believe you actually work with another vet named Wilde." Kay looked into sad brown eyes. "Oh, Randi, don't look at me like that."

Randi tilted her head slightly, never changing her expression.

"You're not playing fair," Kay complained. Less than half a minute later, she threw up her hands. "I give up! All right, Randi, you win. I'll go back with you." *Like it was that hard of a choice. There's no way I could let her leave without me. Something about those eyes.*

"All right!" Randi exclaimed, jumping up from the couch. "This is gonna be great, Kay. I think you'll really like Fort Worth."

Chapter
4

The early glare of the sun was bright but not completely uncomfortable, since they had waited until mid-morning to travel. They had stayed up well past midnight the evening before, while Kay tried to pack everything that she thought she might need for the three-week stay. *Glad I packed light for the trip down here, otherwise her stuff would have never fit in my car.* Randi adjusted her sunglasses, and even the glare off the truck bumper in front of them couldn't wipe the smile off her face. She glanced over at her friend, who had dozed off shortly after they left Woodbridge.

Kay was curled up in the bucket seat, facing Randi, using the other woman's jacket as a blanket. The car heater worked fine, but when Randi saw her snuggle up after dozing off, she couldn't help but cover Kay with whatever she had available.

She just looks so cute. Randi shook her head at the thought. *I've got it bad.* She thought back to the conversation of the evening before. Kay never even blinked at her outburst when she was on the cell phone with her associate. *She even made a joke about it,* Randi recalled fondly. *And then she... Wait! Did she call me honey?* The smile widened into a full-fledged grin. *She did!* "Yes!" Randi cheered, slapping the steering wheel in excitement.

"What?" Kay mumbled, waking up and looking around. "Did I miss something?"

Oops. Busted. "Uh, no. You didn't miss anything, really. Sorry I woke you." But the smile that had blossomed on her face didn't waver.

Kay was charmed by the undisguised joy on her friend's face. Although Randi was wearing sunglasses, she could easily imagine the sparkle in the brown eyes that usually accompanied the wide grin. *She's just so adorable.* Realizing that she was staring, Kay cleared her throat and looked ahead through the windshield. "So, how much further?" she asked, sitting up.

Randi knew the question was just to cover Kay's embarrass-

ment for staring, but decided to play along. "About twenty minutes, actually. Have you ever been to Fort Worth?"

"No. This is the first time I've ever been north of Woodbridge, to tell you the truth. I've been further southwest to visit
friends or family a few times, but that's about it. I haven't lived a
very exciting life." Kay looked around at the grass-covered hills.
She could barely make out a cluster of tall buildings off in the distance, and was awed by the amount of traffic they were already
encountering on the multi-lane road. "It's nice, seeing all this
open land before you get to the city," she remarked.

Unable to help herself, Randi laughed. "I'm sorry, I'm not
laughing at you. But the reason for all this open land is because it
can't be built on. The ground itself is too unstable."

Intrigued, Kay studied the passing scenery with interest.
"Really? It doesn't look unstable. They're grazing cattle on it."

"Oh, it's safe for cattle," Randi assured her. "But buildings
would probably sink. That's the old landfill."

Kay turned and looked at her friend. Her nose wrinkled.
"You mean, garbage? Eeew. That's gross."

Randi laughed. "True. But it's much nicer to look at than garbage, don't you agree?" She had to hold on to the steering wheel
with both hands as a large truck barreled by.

"I don't know how you drive in all this traffic," Kay said. "I
don't think I could handle it." Truthfully, she was somewhat
frightened by all the different lanes of traffic and the apparent
fearlessness of the other drivers.

"You get used to it," Randi said. "When I first moved here
years ago, I swore I'd never drive on the freeways. But now it's like
second nature to me."

Unconvinced, Kay turned her attention back to the scenery.
Buildings passed through her field of vision at a rapid pace—convenience markets, liquor stores, and old shopping centers dotted
the landscape. All the businesses had bars on the windows, and
there were tall fences that she assumed had houses hidden behind
them. "I don't think I could live like that," she said.

"Like what?"

"Hidden away behind barred windows," Kay sad sadly. "Are
you that afraid of crime here?"

Randi shook her head. "*I'm* not. But then again, my apartment complex is in the suburbs. Believe me, where I live is more
like Woodbridge than the 'hood."

I hope so. Kay realized that she had never asked what kind of
apartment Randi lived in. *Not too smart, considering I'm going to
be spending the next three weeks there. What if I hate it? What if*

there are all sorts of criminals lurking about? She looked at Randi and mentally shook her head. *She doesn't look like the type who would live in a bad neighborhood.*

Randi reached over and touched Kay's arm. "You all right?" Recognizing the other woman's reticence as nerves, she wracked her mind for something that would calm Kay's fears. "I'm really glad I live on the ground floor," she blurted out.

Kay turned around and smiled. "What?"

"um, well. I just realized that you'd have trouble navigating any stairs. So, I'm glad I live in a ground-floor apartment." She used to hate it. But it had belonged to her ex-girlfriend, Melissa, and she had gotten it by default when Melissa found someone else and moved out one day while Randi was at work.

"That *would* have been a problem," Kay said with amusement. She loved how Randi would stammer when she became nervous. *I have a feeling this is going to be an interesting three weeks.*

Exiting the freeway, Randi drove through more sedate city streets for several minutes. She pointed out different businesses to her friend, showing Kay where she bought groceries, picked up her dry cleaning, and even a couple of quaint restaurants she liked to frequent. Open strip shopping centers seemed to be on every corner, while offices were camouflaged as expensive brick houses. Driving the car through a wrought-iron gate, Randi cautiously guided the Corvette through the winding private drive of her apartment complex. Trees and well-manicured lawns gave the area a serene atmosphere, especially after driving on the local freeways.

Kay's eyes widened at the homes. They were more like condominiums than the typical box-like apartments she was used to seeing. "You live here?"

"Yep." Randi parked the car under an open carport and pointed to the building in front of them. "Mine's the one on the left." The building looked like a house, only it had four doors instead of the usual one. On the second floor, beautiful white stairs led up each side, and the light red brick was several different shades. Each half of the lower level was dressed up by neatly trimmed landscaping, and the white entry doors had polished brass knockers in their center.

"It's beautiful," Kay exclaimed, opening her door. The cool breeze that ruffled her hair was welcome after being cooped up inside the car for over two and a half hours. "It's so quiet here."

Randi stepped around the vehicle and pulled Kay's crutches from the trunk. Before they left Woodbridge, she had jammed them in last, barely able to close the hatch when she had finished packing the car. "Yeah. That's one of the reasons I've never moved. It's quiet, but close enough to things that I don't have to spend all day in the car." A quick study of the crutches revealed no damage, so she walked over to where Kay was sitting and held out her hand. "Need some help?"

"Thanks." Kay allowed herself to be pulled from the car. She took the crutches from Randi and grimaced when she placed them under her arms.

"What's wrong?"

"Either I'm going to have to get tougher, or these darn things are going to have to get a lot softer," she complained. "Six weeks of this may drive me crazy."

Randi nodded compassionately. "I know what you mean. I have to use them every time I have knee surgery, and I develop the most interesting calluses. Let me show you the apartment, then I'll come back for the bags." She swept one arm out in front of her. "After you, ma'am."

Kay rolled her eyes, but silently moved ahead of the other woman.

After she had unlocked the front door, Randi reached in and flipped a light switch. "Watch your step," she warned, holding the door open for Kay, who hobbled in and looked around.

The living area was cluttered with mismatched furniture, some obviously in need of repair. A beige sofa sat against the front wall to the left of the window, with several newspapers scattered across the cushions. They spilled onto the heavy oak coffee table that sat in front of the sofa. The forest green loveseat was at a right angle to the sofa and had been restitched in several places, while the dark blue recliner opposite it was covered by a well-used afghan. An empty glass sat on a rickety end table between the sofa and recliner, sharing space with a clear, glass-based lamp that was topped by a yellowed shade. The thirty-two inch television set housed in a tall, light oak entertainment center seemed out of place amidst the shabby furniture. More video and audio equipment covered the lower shelves, and there were fist-sized speakers hanging in the upper corners of the living room.

Kay tried to reconcile the furnishings with the exterior of the obviously expensive apartment. "This is, um—"

"A pigsty?" Randi said helpfully. She closed the door behind them and ushered Kay into the living room. "The furniture is just some odds and ends that I picked up at garage sales and used furniture stores when my...roommate," she bit off the word, "moved out and took all the furniture with her. I've been slowly buying new pieces, but just haven't gotten around to the living room yet."

She saw Kay's eyes track to the television. "Well, maybe a little bit."

Kay sat down on the sofa. It was surprisingly comfortable considering the condition it was in. She looked up at her friend, who was smiling. "I love it. It's really homey."

"That's a polite word for it." Randi laughed, scooping up the newspapers and folding them more neatly. "It's usually not quite so messy, but the cleaning lady hasn't been here yet."

"Really? You have a cleaning lady?" Kay asked, surprised. To her, the vet didn't seem like the type to pay someone to keep her house clean.

Randi laughed again. "Nah. Actually, I was running behind before I left, and just didn't pick up after myself. Didn't figure I'd have anyone coming by to see what a pig I am."

Kay laughed with her. "I see. Now I find out how you really are." She gasped in surprise when Randi gently lifted her cast and set it on the coffee table. "Oh, I can't do that, I'll scratch it." She studied the wood closely, noticing the heavy pockmarks and scars that covered the table. "Okay, so I'll scratch it even *more*. This table looks expensive, Randi."

"Oh, yeah. It cost me ten dollars almost a year ago," Randi assured her. "Don't worry about it. I want you to be comfortable. Besides," she sat down next to Kay and mimicked her posture, stretching her legs out and placing her scuffed leather sneakers next to the cast, "I'll feel really guilty if I'm the only one sitting like this."

"We wouldn't want that, would we?" Kay leaned back and sighed. She looked around the room and noticed an open doorway to the right, and a hallway to the left. "It's really sweet of you to put me up for a few weeks, Randi. I don't know how I'll be able to repay you."

Randi turned her head and smiled. "I'm sure we can come up with something." She blushed suddenly when she realized what she had said. "I mean, uh, we can work something out," she stammered, then groaned and covered her face with one hand. "Damn. I'm sorry, Kay. I think I'll shut up before I end up putting *both* feet in my mouth." A light touch on one arm caused her to peck out through her fingers.

"It's okay, Randi. Really." Kay found her friend's nervous chatter endearing. "I knew exactly what you meant."

"Thanks." Randi moved her hand down to her lap and looked up shyly when it was grasped. She watched, mesmerized, as Kay leaned over and her face edged closer and closer. Without realizing it, Randi leaned forward as well. Inches away, Randi could almost feel the softness of the other woman's lips.

Ring!

Startled, Randi's forehead bumped into Kay's nose. "Damn."

Ring!

With an audible growl, the angry woman jumped up from the sofa and walked down the hallway. "I'm getting to the point where I hate telephones," she muttered as she stomped out of sight.

Several minutes after her hasty departure, Randi walked back into the living room. "I'm sorry about the interruption. That was the pet boardinghouse where I left Spike. He's gone on a hunger strike since yesterday, and they've been trying to call me."

"Spike?" Kay asked, intrigued. *I should have known she'd have a pet. Although I'm a bit curious about one with a name like Spike.*

Randi nodded. "Yeah. You want to go with me to pick him up? It's only a few blocks from here."

"Sure. I'd love to see more of the neighborhood, anyway." Kay struggled to her feet and slipped the crutches under her arms. "Lead on."

The short drive was spent in companionable silence, except for the few instances when Randi pointed out areas she thought might be of interest to her friend. She pulled the Corvette into a strip shopping center and parked in front of a storefront that read, "Paws to Reflect—Pet Spa and Boarding House."

Kay giggled. "That's just too cute." She enjoyed the long-suffering look her companion gave her before Randi climbed out of the car. "Do you send Spike to the spa, too?" Kay asked as Randi helped her from the vehicle. "I've never seen an animal spa before. This could be fun."

With a shake of her head, Randi held the door open for the injured woman. They were barely in the door, when a teenaged girl appeared from the back room and rushed over to them.

"Oh, my ga-awd!" she practically sang, tossing her blonde hair over one shoulder. "I'm, like, so glad you're here, Ms. Meyers." She turned her head and yelled to the other room, "Mo-ther! Spike's mommy is here."

Unable to help herself, Kay giggled again. *Spike's mommy? Just how funny is that? Randi doesn't look too pleased with the label, if you ask me.* She watched in amusement as a very short, very rotund woman walked through the doorway in the back, holding a puppy-sized black creature to her chest.

"Ms. Meyers," she warbled, "I'm so glad you were able to come. Poor Spike has missed you terribly. I'm afraid he thought he had been abandoned." She held out the animal to Randi, who automatically accepted him.

The bundle came to life once he recognized the person holding him. Whining and wiggling, the little black and tan dog rose up and happily began to lick the dark-haired woman's face. "Calm down, Spike," Randi muttered, trying to avoid the pink tongue. "It's okay, boy. I'm not going to leave you again."

"*That's* Spike?" Kay spurted. She couldn't believe that such a small animal could have such a rough sounding name. "But he's a—"

"Miniature Doberman Pinscher," the shop owner supplied helpfully. "He's such a sweet boy, too." She leaned close to the excited animal and scratched his back. "Aren't you, honey-poo?"

Randi rolled her eyes. "Thanks for taking care of him, Mrs. Landers. If you'll just charge my card that's on file, I'll take Spike home and see if I can't get him to eat something."

The heavyset woman nodded. "That's just fine, dear. You give us a call if you need anything else, all right?"

"Will do, Mrs. Landers," Randi assured her. She turned around and met the amused glance of her friend. *I know I'm not going to hear the end of this,* she thought to herself. Much to her surprise, Kay didn't say a word until they were in the car and Spike was licking her hand.

"He's adorable, Randi," she said, giggling as the diminutive tongue continued to clean all of her fingers. "How long have you had him?"

Smiling, Randi backed the car out of the parking space and left the lot. "About a year. He originally belonged to my mother. But, ever since my dad retired, they've been going on a lot of trips, not leaving much time to take care of poor Spike, there." She drove for a moment before stopping at a red light. "And, since I'm the only one in my family who doesn't have children, Spike came to live with me."

"I would think he'd like children," Kay said. "He's so hyper and friendly," she added, chuckling when Spike decided to taste her earlobe.

Randi looked over at the pair. *Lucky dog.* The sound of a car horn caused her to shake her head and shift the car into first gear. "Well, I think at one time he did like children," she replied, trying to keep the conversation going.

Kay turned her head and looked at Randi. "What happened?"

"One of my nephews visited my parents at Christmas, and thought Spike was a chew toy. Poor dog is terrified of kids now." Thankfully, she turned the Corvette into the apartment complex. "Let's see if we can get Spike to nibble on something besides you,"

Randi teased, parking the car in its assigned space.

"Good idea," Kay said. "And I think I could use a good scrubbing, without a tongue."

Randi's eyes widened. *Oh, don't tempt me, Kay.* She quickly jumped out of the car before she said something that might embarrass them both.

With Spike resting peacefully in her lap, Kay sat on the sofa and surfed through the available television channels. She could hear Randi puttering around in the kitchen, but since there wasn't a table or chairs in there, Kay had been relegated to the living room. Tired of watching the programs flash by, she settled on the Discovery Channel and stroked the silky fur of her new friend. The little dog had practically inhaled his food once Randi set it down, and now was content to snuggle with Kay and look up at her every now and then with his dark brown eyes.

"You look just like Randi," Kay told him, smiling down as he licked her hand. "And you have me just about as wrapped around your paws as she does."

Randi poked her head out of the kitchen. "Did you say something?"

The younger woman blushed. "Um, no. I was just talking to Spike." She scratched the dog behind the ears. "How did such a sweet animal end up with a name like Spike?"

"My mother has a warped sense of humor," Randi explained. "He was the runt of the litter—wasn't even expected to survive. The bitch had too many puppies and had kicked him out."

"That's horrible!"

Randi shrugged. "Survival of the fittest, and all that." She wiped her hands on a dishtowel and sat down on the loveseat. Spike raised up and looked at her, then sighed and dropped his head back down onto Kay's lap. *Don't blame you, fella. I'd do the same thing if I were you.* She tried to wipe the goofy smile off her face, but knew by Kay's answering smile that she had been unsuccessful. "Anyway, the breeder was a good friend of Mom's and called her about the puppy. Naturally, Mom couldn't stand the thought of him dying without a chance, so she brought the little guy home and fed him with an eyedropper, then a baby bottle."

"Oh, how sweet. I bet I'd like your mom," Kay said, picking up Spike and giving him a kiss on top of his head. "How could your own mother kick you away? You're just so sweet." She pulled him up to her chest and held him close. "Okay, so he's a survivor. But, Spike?"

"He wasn't always so sweet. When he was a puppy, Spike thought that he was a full-sized Dobie. Kept attacking toes, ankles, that sort of thing. As a joke, my Dad bought him one of those spiky collars. His registered name is Lord Wyndam of Devonshire. But after the collar incident, he became Spike."

Kay laughed. "That *is* a big name for such a tiny dog. So, is he one of those expensive pedigreed stud dogs?"

The brunette shook her head. "No. He's too small. So Mom went ahead and had him neutered. No sense in having him chase all the girls." Randi stood up and stretched. "Dinner should be ready in about twenty minutes. I hope you don't mind eating in here—I haven't gotten around to buying a dining room table, yet."

"That's fine, Randi. It will probably be easier on my leg if I keep it propped up, anyway." Kay patted the empty cushion next to her. "C'mere. I'm sure it wouldn't hurt you to sit down for a little while. You've been on your feet constantly since we got here."

Doing as she was asked, Randi sat down. Her legs began to bounce nervously, and her fingers picked at an imaginary spot on the sofa. When Kay touched one leg, she almost jumped out of her skin. "What?"

"What's wrong?"

"um...nothing," Randi mumbled, feeling the warmth of Kay's hand through her jeans. Warm tingles tickled her leg and slowly worked up to her stomach. She turned and looked at her friend. "Kay, I..."

Kay leaned forward to hear the quiet words coming from Randi's lips. "Yes?"

"It's, well, you know," Randi stammered, looking deeply into the hazel eyes so close to hers. "I really would like to, um..."

"You would?" Kay whispered, leaning closer still. She was determined to taste Randi's lips, interruptions and nerves be damned. She gently shifted Spike so that he wouldn't be crushed, then reached up and tangled one hand in the brown, wavy hair. Tired of waiting, she pulled Randi closer and did what she'd been wanting to do since she woke up at the hospital and saw the older woman sitting in the chair next to her bed.

Soft lips touched hers hesitantly, and Randi was overwhelmed by the feelings coursing through her body. The sensation was so overpowering that her heart pounded, and she almost forgot to breathe. When Kay's tongue touched her upper lip, Randi moaned and granted her access. The kiss deepened, and suddenly the veterinarian identified the "something" that had been missing all her life. She reached up and cupped Kay's face tenderly, finally pulling back to allow them both to catch their breath. "That was—"

"Perfect," Kay sighed, pulling Randi back to her and capturing her lips again. She couldn't get enough of Randi's taste, feeling an almost insatiable need to connect with her. Her tongue traced the inside of the other woman's mouth, causing Kay to moan as she experienced the sweetness of the moment. When she could no longer go without air, she drew back slightly and watched as Randi's eyes slowly fluttered open. "You are so beautiful," Kay whispered reverently.

Unfocused brown eyes blinked, while Randi tried to gather her wits. "I, uh, you..." she babbled. She licked her lips and took a few shaky breaths. "I don't think I've ever been kissed quite like that before."

Kay grinned, running a fingertip down the other woman's soft cheek. "I hope that's a good thing," she teased.

"That's a *very* good thing," Randi assured her. She reached over and gently pushed Spike out of Kay's lap and onto the cushion on the other side. "C'mere," she said, partially pulling the younger woman onto her lap. Wrapping her arms around Kay, Randi held her close to prolong the moment and to enjoy the feeling of the body in her arms.

Although dinner was much later than they had planned, they enjoyed the spaghetti Randi had prepared. After the fulfilling meal, they sat side by side on the sofa, both trying to stay awake as full stomachs and exhaustion from the trip kept the two women quiet. Watching Kay yawn for the third time in less than half an hour, Randi stood up and held out her hand. "Come on, sleepyhead. I think it's time we got you into bed."

"W-w-what?" Kay had enjoyed the kisses they had exchanged earlier, but was nervous about going any further so soon.

Randi laughed. "Hey, it's all right. I meant I was going to show you to *your* bedroom. We never did get around to that tour of the apartment." She enjoyed the blush on the other woman's face and decided to have a little bit more fun. "But don't be surprised if you get a bed partner in the middle of the night."

Kay's eyes widened momentarily. "Do you walk in your sleep?"

"No, but Spike does," Randi explained, suddenly glad that Kay was hobbled by the cast on her right leg.

"Oh! You!" Kay lurched forward and reached for Randi, but came away empty-handed. She shook her finger at the laughing woman. "I'll get you back for that." She plucked her crutches from the floor and situated them under her arms. "When you least expect it."

Holding out her hand in front of her, palm down, Randi grinned. "See this? Controlled fear." She led the way down the hallway, Kay following slowly on her heels. "The door on the left is the master bedroom, which is what I've been using," Randi explained, opening the door and turning on the light. "Don't look at the mess."

A queen-sized bed sat against the far wall, the wicker headboard matched by the tables on either side of it. Twin five-drawer dressers were by the doorway, and a partially open door stood against the left wall. "That's the master bathroom," Randi explained. "And the bi-fold doors hide the disaster that's my closet," she said sheepishly.

Although sparsely decorated, Kay could tell that Randi was comfortable in this room. "It's really very nice. And it's not half as messy as my bedroom at home."

"Cool. I'm glad you're not a neat freak." Randi switched off the light and pointed a few feet down the hallway. "Your room is the door on the right, and that door at the end of the hall can be your bathroom." She escorted Kay to the nearby room and turned on the light. "I just finished furnishing it about a month ago—you'll be the first to use the bed."

"Really?" Kay edged past Randi and stepped into the room. Like the other bedroom, the furnishings were few, but in good taste. The wrought iron, full-sized bed was covered with a plaid comforter, and the red curtains on the lone window matched perfectly. The nightstand held a silver gooseneck reading lamp, and across from the bed was a plain wooden desk that boasted a computer. The nineteen-inch monitor was dark, and it looked as if the computer itself had rarely been used. "You into computers, too?" Kay asked her friend.

Randi shook her head. "Not that much, really. I only use it to email my niece and nephews." She sighed. "It's about the only contact I get with them, I'm afraid. My oldest niece, Samantha, was supposed to be spending some time with me during her holiday break. That's why I fixed this up as a second bedroom."

"And now she's not?"

"No. My brother, Augustus, decided to take his family on a ski vacation, instead." Randi tried to keep the sadness out of her voice. "Maybe I'll get her for a few weeks next sumer. That would probably be better, anyway."

Kay touched her friend's arm in sympathy. "I'm sorry, Randi."

A smile appeared on Randi's face. "Don't worry about it. At

least this way, I had someplace for you to sleep, right?" She pointed to the closed door on the other side of the room. "The closet is empty, and there's a short dresser inside where I set your bags. If you need any help unpacking, just let me know." When she turned to leave, the light touch on her back caused Randi to turn around. "Yes?"

"Thank you for doing all of this for me, Randi. I hope I won't be too much trouble." Kay edged closer and kissed the other woman gently on the lips. "Goodnight."

Randi smiled. "It's truly my pleasure, Kay. I hope you sleep well." She backed out into the hallway. "Your bathroom should have plenty of towels and such. Just let me know if you need any thing else, all right?" She bumped into the wall behind her and gave a half-hearted wave. "Good night, Kay."

"Good night." Kay returned the wave, and almost giggled when she heard Randi mumble to herself as she bumped into another wall.

Chapter
5

"Don't let her bully you like that," Kay said. "You deserve to be treated better."

With tears in her eyes, the distraught woman continued. "I can't seem to help it. I suppose I've always had a weakness for the bad ones." Unable to control herself, she fell against the woman sitting beside her and sobbed.

Kay shook her head in disgust. "I can't stand to hear any more," she moaned, hitting the off button on the television remote. One look down at her lap confirmed that her brown-eyed companion didn't care one way or another. "Don't you just hate how those talk shows glorify misery?"

Spike raised his head and yawned widely. He gave her hand a half-hearted lick, then dropped his head back into her lap.

"You too, huh?" Kay laughed at her one-sided conversation, and picked up the book she had borrowed from Randi. It had been over five hours since the vet had regretfully left for work. To keep from going stir crazy, Kay realized that she would either have to find something more interesting to do, or Spike's conversational skills would have to improve. "No offense, handsome," she said, scratching him behind the ears, "but if I don't get someone to talk to soon, I'm going to go nuts."

Ten minutes into her book, Kay nearly leapt from the sofa when the doorbell rang. Startled, Spike jumped to the floor and raced to the source of the sound, barking furiously. His yapping became fiercer when whoever was at the door began to knock.

"Hold on, I'm coming," Kay called, hurrying as fast as the crutches would allow. She peered through the peephole and saw a woman dressed in an expensive forest green business suit, standing on the front step. The two-piece outfit fit her slender form well, and the skirt barely came to her mid-thighs. Unlocking the door, Kay opened it just far enough to keep the still-snarling animal inside. "Yes? May I help you?"

The redhead reached up with one brightly painted fingernail and pulled her sunglasses down on her nose, inspecting Kay carefully. "Oh, I'm terribly sorry. I was looking for Randi Meyers." Her silky voice held a strong Southern drawl, and her painted red lips curled into a self-satisfied smile.

Kay smiled at the woman, believing her to be a friend of Randi's. "Oh, yes, she lives here, but she's at work right now." She looked down at the dog at her feet. "Hush, Spike," she commanded. He stopped barking, but stood between Kay and the stranger, growling. "I'm sorry, I don't know what's up with him. He's usually very friendly."

"That's quite all right. I'm a cat person myself. Maybe he already figured that out," the woman said. "Are you a relative of Randi's?"

"No, just a good friend. Is there something I can help you with?" Kay asked, still not opening the door any further.

"That's just a shame," the woman sighed, checking her watch. "I was so hoping to catch her at home." She looked into Kay's trusting face. "Randi and I go way back, you know. I've been gone for several months, and I just flew in today." Running her hands down the front of her form-fitting suit, the woman sighed again, this time dropping her shoulders in defeat. "I suppose I can just leave her a note and try to reach her later. Would you mind giving her the number where I'm staying?"

Kay shook her head. "No, not at all." She studied the woman carefully. *She looks harmless enough to me.* "Would you like to come in?"

The redhead nodded. "Oh, yes. I'd love that." She waited until Kay backed away from the door, then entered and closed the door behind her.

Kay motioned to the loveseat. "Please, sit down. Would you like something to drink while I find a paper and pen?"

"No, thank you." The woman remained standing, looking around the room with interest. "She's done a bit of redecorating since I was here last," she mused, inspecting the furniture with a superior air. "Or was this your doing, hon?"

Suddenly feeling very defensive and protective of her friend, Kay frowned. "Uh, no, I had nothing to do with her selections in furniture. Randi had to start from scratch when her monster of a roommate cleaned her out."

"Is that what she told you? Perhaps you should check the facts before you go spouting off to strangers, little girl." Taking several steps forward until she was standing directly in front of Kay, the woman glared over her sunglasses. "Let me give you a word of warning, sugar: get out of here while you still can. Randi is far more interested in four legs than two—she'll push you off to the side the first chance she gets." She reached over and patted Kay on the cheek. "You just tell her that Melissa is back in town. I'm sure she'll be thrilled to hear that."

Before Kay could say another word, Melissa stalked from the apartment, slamming the door behind her. Kay looked down at Spike, who stood by her feet, growling. "I know what you mean, honey. She made my hackles rise, too." Kay dropped to the sofa, exhausted by the confrontation and wondering if she should call Randi to let her know about the unexpected visitor.

The balding man stood in the doorway, holding a paper mask over his face. "Once you're finished with that procedure, Dr. Meyers, I'd like to see you in my office," he said to the woman bent over the operating table.

Randi continued her work for another minute, then glanced up. The beagle she was spaying held all of her attention. "Right. I should be done in another fifteen minutes or so, Dr. Wilde."

"Very good. See that you are, Doctor." He backed out of the room quietly.

The woman assisting Randi rolled her eyes. A few years older than the vet, her blonde hair was covered with a light blue surgical cap, and the matching mask was almost the same color as her eyes. "This may sound cliché, considering where we work, but I think you're in the doghouse, Randi."

The vet snickered. "That *was* bad, Joyce. But I do believe you're right." She watched as Joyce expertly swabbed the area she was working on. "And you want to know something?"

"What?"

"It was well worth it," Randi said, accepting the suturing needle. With skilled hands, she deftly closed up the patient. "And I'd do it again in a heartbeat."

Ten minutes later, Randi knocked on the closed door of Dr. Wilde's office.

"Come in," he ordered. "And close the door behind you, *Doctor* Meyers." The man who owned the clinic didn't stand as she walked into the room, but stayed behind his desk, adopting a superior air. Already in his late sixties, Dr. Benjamin Wilde had run the clinic since his father had given it to him over thirty years before. He brushed one hand over the bald spot on his head while he watched the younger woman drop into the visitor's chair. As punishment for not returning on Saturday as he had requested, he had scheduled her to handle every operation and see as many animals in between surgeries as possible. Benjamin could see the exhaustion on her face and in her posture, and was certain it was only a matter of time before she broke down and apologized for her insubordination.

"What is it, Dr. Wilde? Is there something else you want me to handle for you? Maybe clean out the cages?" Randi asked angrily. She had worked for the pompous man for four years, and her love for the animals in her care and her attention to detail had built up his dying practice. Since Randi had started at the Wilde Animal Clinic, two more veterinary assistants and another office clerk had been added to the payroll to distribute the workload. They were still shorthanded for office help, but the old veterinarian was too cheap to hire anyone else.

He leaned forward and folded his hands on his desk. "You've got a real attitude problem lately, Doctor. Perhaps you'd be more comfortable working somewhere else?"

Randi frowned. "Are you threatening me, Dr. Wilde? Because if you are, it's not much of a threat."

"What makes you say that, young lady? I can bring in some kid fresh out of school and pay them a quarter less than I pay you." He pointed to the diplomas on the wall. "This *is* still my practice, you know."

She jumped to her feet. "You self-centered ass! I could walk out that door right now and take most of your clients with me. Not to mention the women that work here."

Dr. Wilde gave her a knowing smile. "And just what would you do with them? Set up practice in an alley somewhere? From what I've heard around the office, you lost your savings about the same time you lost your *roommate*, didn't you?" He knew of her "persuasion," as he called it and, because of it, refused to cut her any slack.

"That was a cheap shot, even for you, Wilde." With a disgusted sigh, she dropped back gracelessly into the chair. "What is it that you want?"

"I want you to lose the attitude and become a little bit more professional around here. Quit treating the help like they're your friends, and stop taking so much time with each animal. We could bring in more money if you'd quit playing around with them and just do what needs to be done."

Randi stood up again and opened the door. "I will *not* change the way I treat my colleagues *or* the animals in my care, Dr. Wilde. If you don't like it, then fire me." Slamming the door behind her, she walked out to the receptionist's desk and peered down at the gray-haired woman, trying to calm down. "So, Christina, who's my next patient?" A warm hand on her shoulder caused Randi to turn around and glare at Dr. Wilde, who was now wearing his jacket. "Yes?"

"I'm taking the rest of the week off, Dr. Meyers. You'll have to cover for me." He patted her on the back and walked through the door, not seeing the murderous look in Randi's eyes.

Christina reached up and squeezed the clenched fist that shook at Randi's side. "I was afraid of that, dear. I think he's been planning this ever since you asked to go out of town for your uncle's funeral."

Taking a calming breath, the vet looked down into the concerned eyes of her secretary. "Why do you think that?"

"He had me double book the next several days—I didn't think he had suddenly developed a conscience and decided to help around here." She glanced down at the appointment book. "Do you want me to call and try to reschedule?"

Randi shook her head. "No. It's not our clients' fault that Dr. Wilde is an asshole. I'll just have to do the best I can." She smiled at the older woman. Barely five feet tall, Christina was a very slender woman and the resident mother figure. Some of the others on the staff had even taken to calling her Mom. She had been with the clinic for almost twenty years, and not even Dr. Wilde crossed her. It was because of her and some of the others that Randi wouldn't leave, because she knew that they depended on the money she helped bring in. Dr. Wilde knew it as well, and used that to his advantage.

The phone rang and Christina picked it up. "Hello, Wilde Animal Clinic. How may I help you?" She listened for a moment and nodded. "Certainly. She's standing right here, as a matter of fact." Holding out the receiver, she whispered, "It's a young woman named Kay. She—"

Worried, Randi grabbed the phone before Christina finished her sentence. "Kay? Is everything all right?"

"Everything's fine. I'm sorry to bother you at work, but I wasn't sure what to do."

"About what? Is there something you need?" Randi turned around to try and ignore the curious look she was getting from the receptionist.

"No, nothing like that. Oh, I feel so silly, interrupting your day like this. Maybe I should have just waited until you got home."

The agitated doctor paced around the desk, almost tangling Christina in the long cord. Out of habit, she stuck her free hand in her lab coat pocket and wished for the tenth time that day that she had bought cigarettes on the way to work. "You're not interrupting anything, Kay. Please, just tell me what's wrong."

There was a short pause, followed by a heavy sigh. "You had a visitor today." Kay's voice was still shaky from the confrontation.

A feeling of dread bloomed in Randi's chest and mushroomed into her belly. "Who?"

"Some woman named Melissa." ·

The color drained from the vet's face, and Randi grabbed at the desk to keep from crumpling to the floor. The phone dropped from her nerveless fingers as she fought the sudden onslaught of painful memories that name brought to mind. Her eyes closed, and she breathed heavily, on the verge of hyperventilating. The history she had with Melissa was one of the most painful times in her life.

The last couple of months that they were together, Randi had taken on a heavier workload, in hopes of saving up enough not only to start her own practice, but to make a down-payment on a house, as well. She was tired of hearing Melissa complain about the apartment being too small for two people, and was looking for some way to placate the whining woman. One evening, a week before Melissa left, they had argued worse than usual.

Propped in the middle of the king-sized bed, Melissa watched as Randi searched the closet for a clean shirt. She slid her bare foot across the black satin sheets and yawned. Dressed in a dark-green, baby-doll nightie, the redhead couldn't understand why Randi insisted on leaving the apartment. "Wouldn't you rather stay here with me than go mess with some stinky animal?" she whined as she stretched provocatively, trying to get the other woman's attention.

"You know I have to work, Melissa. How else are we ever going to be able to afford to move out of here?" Randi turned around and kicked at a pile of clothes near her feet. "I thought you were going to do laundry today?"

"I did." Melissa lived off an inheritance she had received when her husband died over ten years earlier. Before that, her family, which was also well off, had taken care of her. Unfortunately for her, the inheritance hadn't been able to support her expensive habits, and was running dangerously low. That's the only reason she continued to live in the apartment, while, unbeknownst to her lover, keeping an eye out for "better options."

Randi put her hands on her hips and glared at the woman

stretched out across the bed. The nightgown didn't cover much of Melissa's considerable "assets," and even where it did, the sheer material left very little to the imagination. But at the moment, Randi wasn't the least bit interested in her body; all she could see was a very selfish woman. "If you did, then why don't I have at least one clean shirt? I asked you last night to wash a couple, and then I'd do the rest this weekend."

"Last I heard," Melissa drawled, raising her hands over her head, "I wasn't your maid." She looked down at her body and smiled. "Why don't you call in sick today, and I'll make it up to you?"

Glaring at the redhead for a long moment, Randi shook her head. "Bitch," she mumbled, bending over and reaching for one of the less-dirty shirts on the floor. She didn't see the foot that hit her in the shoulder, knocking her against the wall.

"Don't you dare call me a bitch!" Melissa screamed, jumping to her feet beside the bed. She kicked a dirty shirt into Randi's face. "I took you in, gave you my heart, and this is the way you repay me?"

"Your heart?" Randi asked. She pulled the shirt away from her face and struggled to her feet. With only a foot or two between them, Randi pointed her finger in the other woman's face. "You don't have a heart, you bitch," she enunciated slowly. "I've been working to buy you a damned house, because that's all I hear about. But you don't seem to have it in you to wash one of my fucking shirts?" She lowered her hand and shook her head. "I don't know why I even bother."

Melissa smiled. "Because I'm so good in bed," she bragged. "You can't get it that good anywhere else."

"Not without paying for it," Randi said. The sudden slap jerked her head sideways. She clenched her hands at her sides, trying to keep from returning the blow. "Don't you ever do that again, Melissa, or I'll forget why I don't hit women."

"Fuck you!" Melissa yelled, pushing by the enraged vet. "Go play with your nasty little animals, Randi." She turned around and stood in the doorway, her mane of auburn hair flowing wildly around her face. "I'm going out tonight, so don't wait up." She stalked down the hallway and slammed the bathroom door, hard.

Randi watched her leave the room, silently holding her hand to her aching cheek. "I wouldn't have waited, anyway," she mumbled. "Not anymore."

The vet continued to lean against the desk, barely able to stand. The memory of that final confrontation still made her sick to her stomach. After that, they were little more than antagonistic strangers, until the evening that Randi returned home from work to find Melissa gone and the house empty, except for Randi's dirty clothes scattered about the bedroom.

Christina jumped to her feet and directed Randi into her chair. She picked up the phone from the floor. "Hello?"

"What happened?" Kay said into the phone. "Is she all right?"

"I think she's just in a bit of shock, hon. Hold on a minute, okay?" Christina put the receiver down on the desk and touched Randi's cheek. "Randi, sweetheart, listen to my voice. Everything is all right." She lightly patted the pale face until the brown eyes fluttered open. "That's it. Just relax."

Randi shook her head. "I'm sorry, Christina. I don't know what happened." She took a deep breath and released it slowly. "It's just when Kay told me... Damn! I forgot about Kay!" She picked the phone up. "Kay? You still there?"

"Are you all right?"

"Yeah, I'm fine. Just caught me off guard, that's all. I'm sorry about that."

Kay exhaled in relief. "Are you sure? I knew I shouldn't have called you at work. This could have waited until you got home tonight."

"No, I'm glad you called," Randi assured her. "But do me a favor, okay?"

"Sure. What?"

"If she comes back, don't answer the door. I don't want that bitch anywhere near you." The venomous tone was uncharacteristic for the generally easygoing woman.

The line was silent for a moment. "All right. But do you promise to tell me all about it when you get home?"

Damn. "Yeah, I promise. Although I'm afraid I'm going to have to work late tonight. Dr. Wilde suddenly decided to take the week off."

"That's all right. I'm not going anywhere," Kay said. "I left my jogging shoes back in Woodbridge."

"Cute, Kay. Real cute." Randi couldn't help but smile. "How about we order a pizza tonight?"

"Sounds like a great idea, Randi. Be careful coming home, okay?"

Randi felt her heart swell at the entreaty. "I will. Call if you need anything. Christina will know to put you right through."

"Okay, I will. Bye."

"Bye." Randi sighed at the look on the receptionist's face.

"Don't say it."

The older woman smiled widely. "Say what, dear?" She took the receiver back and hung up the phone. "She sounds like a sweet woman. Is she the reason you risked the Wrath of Wilde?"

"Yeah," Randi said, embarrassed.

"Is she worth it?"

"Definitely."

Kay was in the guest bedroom using the computer to surf the Internet when she heard the front door open. A glance at her watch surprised her. She had expected Randi home before now, not knowing what there could be to do in the veterinary office until almost nine o'clock in the evening. Randi's consideration at having pizza delivered had surprised her over two and a half hours earlier, but she had stubbornly refused to touch the food until her friend came home. Gathering up her crutches, Kay hurried out of the room and down the hall. The sight that greeted her in the living room tore at her heart.

The exhausted vet was sprawled on one end of the sofa, her head thrown back and her eyes closed. The navy blue, short-sleeved polo shirt that had been so neatly tucked in early that morning had worked loose from her khaki slacks, which bore several dark spots. Randi cracked open her eyes when she heard Kay enter the room. "Sorry I'm so late." She lifted her head and ran her fingers through her disordered hair. "Just as I was about to lock up, a man brought in a sick puppy." She smiled as Spike, sensing his friend's bad day, jumped up into her lap and began to thoroughly clean her face.

"You have nothing to apologize for," Kay assured her, sitting down next to Randi. "Is the puppy going to be okay?"

Randi closed her eyes and shook her head. "No. I lost him." She felt an irrational pang of upset at the admission. The young Rottweiler was in the final stages of canine parvovirus, and had become too dehydrated to save. The troubled vet kept going over in her mind every action she'd taken. *Was I too tired to think of everything quickly enough? Could I have done something, anything, to prevent his death?* Randi remembered the look on the older man's face when she told him that she couldn't save his dog. *I hate seeing grown men cry. Why do people think that just because they don't live around any other dogs, they don't have to vaccinate their pets? Such a senseless waste.*

"I'm so sorry, Randi." Kay reached over and touched her friend's arm. "Is there anything I can do?"

"No," Randi shook her head, "but I appreciate you asking." She opened her eyes and studied the woman sitting next to her. "Did the pizza come?"

Kay nodded. "It did. I put it in the refrigerator."

"I see. You saved some for me, huh?" Randi's face creased into a smile at the gentle bantering.

"Uh, well," Kay looked down at the sofa, "I thought I'd wait until you got home, so you wouldn't have to eat alone." She looked back up at the silent face across from her.

Randi's smile widened. "That was incredibly sweet of you, Kay. Unnecessary, but sweet." She leaned over and dropped a quick kiss on the younger woman's cheek. "You sit right there, and I'll bring the pizza in, okay?"

"Sure," Kay said, as she touched her cheek and watched Randi leave the room, Spike hot on her heels. "Actually, just bring mine cold. I like it better that way," she yelled across the room.

After washing her face and hands in the kitchen, Randi returned with the pizza box and two bottles of soda. "I knew I liked you for a reason," she teased, setting the box down on the coffee table and handing one of the bottles to Kay. "Thought a coke would be good with pizza."

Kay accepted the drink and took a sip. "Great idea. Although I figured you for the beer type," she said.

"I used to be, but I haven't drunk any alcohol for a couple of years now."

Oh. Kay blushed, worried that she had upset her friend. "I didn't mean anything by it, Randi. I just, well, sometimes put my foot in my mouth without thinking."

"No, no. You didn't upset me, Kay. Actually, I feel a lot better now than I did when I was drinking. It wasn't that I craved it, or anything. But beer was a lot like potato chips to me." She shrugged. "You know, can't have just one? And at my age, it's a bit easier to keep from gaining as much weight if I'm not drinking a six-pack a night."

"I see." Kay studied the woman sitting next to her. It was true that Randi was far from being slender, but her stockier build fit her personality. She couldn't imagine what her friend would look like otherwise. "Well, I think you look great."

Randi blushed. "Um, thanks." Deciding a change of subject was in order, she reached over and took a piece of pizza from the box. "How was your day today, other than the confrontation with my ex? You weren't too bored, were you?" She bit into the slice and chewed.

"No, not really. Spike was great company, although his conversational skills could use a little work." Kay bit into her pizza, as well. "Mmm." She chewed for a moment and then looked around. "Speaking of my boyfriend, where is he?"

"In the kitchen, having *his* dinner. He won't eat until I'm home and doing the same thing," Randi explained. "Crazy little dog." She finished off her first slice of pizza and wiped her hands with a paper napkin.

Kay laughed. "I think he's cute. He's a great companion."

Ring!

Randi grimaced and dropped the piece of pizza she had just picked up. She reached beside the sofa, where she had moved the phone last night. "Hello?"

"Hello yourself. Been a while, hasn't it, Randi?" Melissa's sultry tones oozed through the line. "I tried to come by and see you today, but you weren't home."

"What do you want, Melissa?" Randi exchanged looks with Kay, who was watching with interest.

"That's no way to talk to me, hon. I thought you'd be glad to hear from me, after all this time."

Frowning, Randi ran one hand through her hair. "Yeah, right. Cut the bullshit and give me one good reason I shouldn't hang up on you."

"Who's your little friend? She's a bit young for you, isn't she?" The sexy voice deepened. "I've missed you, sugar."

Randi closed her eyes and fought back the feelings that came rushing back to her. "You're the one that left with everything in the damned apartment, Melissa. Now, if you'll excuse me, I've got better things to do than listen to you." She hit the "off" button on the phone to disconnect the call. "I *so* did not need this tonight," Randi muttered, staring down at the dark phone. She jumped slightly when Kay touched her shoulder.

"Are you all right?" the blonde asked, concerned.

"Yeah," Randi muttered.

Kay wasn't convinced. Her friend's body language spoke of someone who was carrying the weight of the world on her shoulders. "That was Melissa, huh? She call just to drive you crazy, or something?"

"Maybe." Randi slumped against the back of the sofa. "Last I had heard, she had latched on to a rare gems dealer and moved to California." The look of gentle inquiry on Kay's face helped her reach a decision. If she wanted any kind of relationship with Kay, she wanted her to know everything about her. "I met her when I was going to vet school," she said quietly. "Her brother and I were in the same class together."

"You don't have to tell me any more, Randi. I know this has got to be hard for you."

"No, it's okay. If she's going to keep coming around here, I'd like for you to know." Randi reached out and took Kay's hand, holding on to it as if it was a lifeline. "Anyway, Terry, her brother, asked me over for a Saturday barbecue, and that's where I met Melissa. She was a really charming older woman, and kept saying just the right things. I fell head-over-heels in love." She laughed mirthlessly. "Or so I thought." Randi stopped and looked down at their entwined hands. "Not too long after we met, the apartment complex I was living in was gutted in a fire. Melissa was living here, and offered me the guestroom. It was a great opportunity for me to save money, because all I had to do was pay half the rent and utilities."

Kay nodded. "Sounds like she was very sweet."

"I suppose," Randi said. "The first month or so, she would parade around the apartment in these slinky little negligees, and she was always touching me. At first, I didn't know what to think, so I pretty much ignored her." She shook her head. "One night, I woke up and she was in bed with me—with nothing on."

Kay gasped, eyes wide. "That must have been a shock." *Melissa's a pushy thing, it seems. Better keep my eye on her.* She had a feeling they hadn't seen the last of the woman, and, she was feeling more than a little protective of Randi.

"To put it mildly!" Randi chuckled. "Especially since I still hadn't quite figured out that I was gay."

"You're kidding?" Kay exclaimed, then covered her mouth with one hand. "Oh, damn. I'm sorry, Randi. It's just that you seem so, well, comfortable with yourself."

Randi laughed. "That's a new way of putting it," she said. "Actually, most of my life, I felt like I didn't fit in anywhere. Guess it was my wonderful Texas upbringing that kept me so clueless about my sexuality." She grabbed another piece of pizza and started eating again.

"Upbringing?"

"Yeah, you know: I could never figure out why I didn't like boys, but I was too damned stubborn to admit to myself that I might like girls. Mostly because I was afraid of what my family would think. Queers, as my dad called them, were just one rung above criminals in his book. He isn't the most progressive guy around."

Kay nodded, taking another slice of pizza for herself. She took a large bite before continuing. "I know what you mean. I guess I was lucky in that regard. I didn't give a damn what my aunt thought." She shifted into a more comfortable position, propping her cast on the coffee table. "So, what happened when Melissa came into your room? Did you have an epiphany?"

"Not exactly. I screamed like a banshee," Randi said, slightly embarrassed. "She crawled into my bed and was snuggling up next to me, waking me from a sound sleep. How was I supposed to react?"

"I bet that went over well." *Serves that bitch right.* "What happened then?"

Randi blushed. "She um, apologized. Told me she thought I wanted her, and then cried." Randi shook her head. "I felt guilty, so when she kissed me, I didn't push her away." Finished with her pizza, Randi rubbed her face with her hands. "Over the next few weeks, we'd kiss on the sofa, hold hands, that sort of thing. I guess the natural progression was that I finally went to bed with her."

"Did—" Kay cleared her throat. "Did you love her?"

"I don't think so. It was more of a comfort thing. I mean, at the time, I thought I did. But as the years wore on, I never felt that deep emotional connection that I thought I was supposed to feel." *Like I do with you, Kay. I've felt more emotion in the past few days than I have my entire life. How do I say that to you?* "I don't know how to explain it. My relationship with Melissa is something I can't even figure out for myself. As many times as I thought about leaving her, there was a part of me that couldn't walk out, no matter how badly she treated me. And then finally, she left me."

Kay felt the knot in her stomach loosen. "Were you upset when she left?"

"Part of me was. But we'd already had this big blowout when I graduated from veterinary school. She wanted me to go into animal research, because she thought that's where the big money was. I couldn't see myself doing that. And then, later, every word out of her mouth was whining about wanting a house. She was never satisfied. So, I wasn't too terribly surprised when she left. Although coming home to a completely empty apartment threw me for a loop," Randi said. "I guess I should be thankful that I hadn't done my laundry yet. My dirty clothes were still here, scattered all over the bedroom. She even took the soap out of the shower, and my toothpaste."

"What a bitch," Kay grumbled. "I wish I had known that earlier today. I'd have slapped that smirk right off her face." Her appetite gone, Kay tossed the half-eaten piece of pizza back in the box.

Randi patted her arm with her spare hand. "Nah, she's not

worth the effort." Catching her friend's yawn, she stood up and pulled Kay up with her. "C'mon. I think we both could use a good night's sleep."

Accepting the crutches that Randi picked up and handed her, Kay nodded. "I think you're right." She almost laughed at the look on Spike's face when he came out of the kitchen. He appeared disappointed when he noticed the two women standing in the living room. "Looks like someone is upset with us."

"He'll get over it," Randi assured her. She picked up the pizza box and took it into the kitchen, tossing what was left in the garbage. Randi stepped back out of the kitchen and once again stood in front of Kay. "I'd better take him for a walk, though. You want to come outside with us?"

"No, I think I'll get ready for bed." Kay tilted her head up slightly and kissed Randi on the lips. She felt warm hands grab her hips for balance. After a moment, Kay shifted back and smiled. "See you in a minute?"

"Uh, yeah," Randi mumbled. "Let me just," she pointed to the door, "take walk for a Spike."

Kay giggled as the hyper little dog tried to jump up and down while Randi fastened the lead onto his collar. She could see the vet's hands were shaking, and felt a rush of satisfaction that she was the cause. *This is definitely going to be an interesting three weeks.*

Chapter
6

Wednesday morning, Randi was sitting on the sofa with Kay enjoying a cup of coffee before she left the apartment, when the phone rang. She looked at her watch and sighed. "Who on earth would be calling here at six o'clock in the damned morning?" She picked up the phone. "Hello," she snapped into the phone, upset at having her time with Kay interrupted.

"Randi Suzanne, don't you dare bark at me like that!" Her grandmother's tone wasn't much friendlier. "I've been waiting to hear from you for days, now. Why haven't you called?"

Shit. I completely forgot about leaving the funeral. "Hello, Grandma. I'm sorry, but we've been shorthanded at work, and I—"

"Nonsense! Amy tells me she saw you at the market last week, days *after* your uncle's funeral. Which I find rather odd, since you seemed to have disappeared during the graveside services."

"Grandma, I can explain," Randi rushed, trying to cut the older woman off before she got completely immersed in her complaining. *So much for not being missed.* "A friend of mine fell and broke her ankle, and I had to get her to the hospital."

Not listening, Edna Meyers continued. "And then to find out that you stayed in town longer, without even bothering to call or stop by. I would have expected it of your brother, John, but not from you. I thought that you loved me, Randi Sue. But I guess you don't have time for an old woman like me." She sighed dramatically.

Randi covered her face with her free hand, dropping her elbow to brace it against her thigh. "Of course I love you, Grandma. And I'll be back for Thanksgiving." She peeped through her fingers at Kay, who was watching the exchange in amusement. "Did I mention I'm bringing a friend?"

"Oh, really? Is it that roommate of yours?" Edna asked.

"Because if it is, I'm afraid that—"

"No, Grandma. Melissa doesn't live with me any longer. I told you that months ago."

"Good. I never liked that girl. She always wore her clothes too tight, and I think she flirted with your brother, Augustus, too much." Edna abandoned that train of thought and launched right into her next sermon, one that Randi had been subjected to for years. "And speaking of Augustus, when are *you* going to settle down and give me some great-grandchildren? You're not getting any younger, Randi Sue."

Jesus. The woman has a one-track mind. "Grandma, you've already got four grandchildren and seven great-grandchildren. Isn't that enough?"

Edna laughed. "There's no such thing as enough grandchildren, girl. It's a status symbol, don't you know?" She lowered her voice. "All I want is for you to be happy, dear."

"I am happy, Grandma. You don't have to worry about me." Randi looked at Kay and smiled. "I'm happier now than I've ever been, as a matter of fact."

"You could have fooled me, Randi Sue. You're smoking too much; and by the looks of you, you're not eating right. When are you going to settle down?"

Randi studied the young woman sitting next to her on the sofa. "Soon, I hope. But I don't think I'll be having any children. At least, not any that I know of." She winked at Kay, who covered her mouth to keep from laughing out loud.

The older woman sighed. "Oh, you! Well, that's something, I suppose. As long as you're happy."

"I am, Grandma, very much so," Randi assured her. "But, I've got to get to work. I'll call you this weekend, all right?"

"You'd better, young lady."

Randi smiled. "Love you, Grandma. You take care of yourself, okay?"

"Of course I will. Can't depend on your worthless cousins to do it, can I?" Edna laughed. "I love you, too, dear," and she ended the connection.

"That old woman never ceases to surprise me," Randi said, hanging up the phone. "She can be such a tough old bird, but then she acts as if she genuinely cares about me."

Kay smiled. "Of course she cares about you, Randi. She's your grandmother." She had vague recollections of her own grandmother, who had died when she was only ten years old. Not even as big as Kay was now, the tiny, gray-haired woman seemed to live in her kitchen. Kay's fondest memories were of sitting on a stool in the kitchen as her grandmother mixed and baked. *I can still taste her biscuits and smell that rose water she always wore.*

"Kay?"

"Hmm?"

"Are you all right?" Randi placed one hand on Kay's leg and squeezed gently. "You kind of faded out on me for a minute, there."

"Oh, sorry. Yeah, I'm fine. Just thinking." Kay's smile grew wistful. "My grandmother used to let me help her in the kitchen all the time. I learned more about baking while sitting in her kitchen when I was 10, than I did in a year of Home Economics in high school. The woman was amazing."

Randi smiled too. "Sounds like it." She glanced down at her watch and frowned. "Damn. I'm going to have to get to the office. We've got a couple of surgeries scheduled for this morning." She was about to stand up when Kay stopped her. "What?"

"Aren't you forgetting something?" the younger woman asked, leaning forward slightly.

She's too cute. "Well, I don't think so," Randi said, being purposely obtuse. "I fed Spike, took him for his morning walk, talked to my grandmother..." She ticked off the items on one hand. "There's plenty of stuff for you to have lunch, so I don't think—"

Kay grabbed the front of Randi's shirt, pulling her close. "You are such a brat," she scolded, leaning in and lightly tracing the older woman's lips with her tongue. She felt the body she was holding shiver, and Randi's mouth immediately opened to accept her kiss.

"Mmm," Randi moaned, scooting closer and tangling her hands in Kay's hair. She could feel her heart begin to pound as hands caressed her back and traced their way up. Nimble fingers raced through her hair as Kay's tongue delved deeper into her mouth, causing Randi to feel faint from the sensations.

Several minutes and a rumpled shirt later, Randi stood up shakily. "Damn, you're good at that," she mumbled, trying to fingercomb her hair back into some semblance of order. She was glad to see that Kay's eyes were as unfocused as hers felt.

"I..." Kay took a deep breath. "I could say the same thing for you, Randi. We need to try this when we either have more time, or are not so tired."

"I don't know, Kay. If it got any more intense, you'd probably kill me." She willed her hands to stop shaking long enough to tuck her polo shirt back in to her khaki slacks. "But it'll be fun to try."

Kay again inhaled deeply, trying to fight off the libido that kicked into high gear at her friend's smile. *Does she have any idea what that smile does to me?* "See you tonight, honey. Be careful." The innocent endearment slipped from her mouth without thought, but seeing the smile it produced on Randi's face made Kay decide to use it more often.

"I sure will, Kay." *She did it again. Yes!* Randi leaned down and kissed the top of Kay's head. "Call me if you need anything, all right?"

"I will," Kay said. She gave Randi a tiny wave as the vet left the apartment. Looking down at the floor, she almost laughed at the look on Spike's face. "Well? You going to jump up here, or what?"

The tiny stub of a tail quivered furiously as the Spike leapt up onto the sofa. He snuggled up in his favorite lap, content to spend the day with his new best friend.

Kay looked across the table shyly. Less than two hours ago she had been sitting on the sofa, arguing with a silent Spike over how much hairspray Vanna White obviously used.

Randi had called about that time, and was dismayed to hear what Kay was doing. She requested that the younger woman get dressed in something "nice but comfortable," and had hurried home from the clinic. After changing clothes, Randi drove the two of them to Dallas. Now here they were, enjoying a nice dinner out.

The restaurant was split into several dining rooms, each just the right size to feel intimate. Dark paneling on the walls was decorated with well-placed paintings in just about every style imaginable. Booths lined the outer walls, while tables with blue linen cloths were scattered about in the center. The waitstaff, all dressed in dark slacks and white shirts with navy blue half aprons tied around their waists, hustled around quietly. Light instrumental music blended the many voices into a low murmur, and the soft lighting added to the relaxed atmosphere.

Fascinated, Kay watched as another pair of women sat down in the booth next to them, both on the same side. Her eyes widened when she glanced around the room. Everywhere she looked sat same-sex couples—some holding hands, while one pair of men in the corner leaned close and kissed often. "Um, Randi?"

"Yes?" Randi had watched as her friend made the connection. *You can take the girl out of the country, but you can't take the country out of the girl. I remember feeling the same way the first time I came down here to eat.*

"Is this a, um, gay restaurant?" Kay whispered.

Laughing, the dark-haired woman shook her head. "Not exactly. It's a restaurant in a predominantly gay section of town," she explained. "Why? Does it bother you?"

For an answer, Kay reached across the table and grasped Randi's hand. "Not at all. Actually, I feel more comfortable here than I have anywhere else in a long time."

"I'm glad." Randi squeezed Kay's hand. "I know you're not quite up to dancing, but would you like to go have a drink after dinner? You've got a built-in designated driver."

Kay batted her eyes. "Are you asking me to go into a," she leaned across the table, "lesbian bar with you?" she finished in a stage whisper. "Are you trying to corrupt this small-town girl?"

"I dunno," Randi evaded. "Is it working?"

"It certainly is," Kay said happily.

Randi laughed. "Great! Then it's a date." She looked up as their server brought their food. "Eat up, Kay. You're going to need your strength."

Oh, how I wish that were true, Kay thought wistfully. By unspoken agreement, both women seemed content to have the relationship progress at a slow pace. While it was fun and interesting, it was also wreaking havoc on Kay's libido. *I want more,* she thought, as she looked across the table at her companion. *Maybe she does, too, but is afraid to ask.* She looked into Randi's eyes and smiled. *We'll just have to see about that.*

"What would you like to drink?" Randi yelled into Kay's ear. She had found an open table near the dance floor, making certain to keep her friend's casted leg out of the traffic area.

"How about a coke?" Kay returned. "I don't want to drink any alcohol, in case I need a painkiller later." Actually, after hearing Randi talk about her problems with alcohol, Kay had promised herself to stop drinking as well. Since she rarely drank more than a glass of wine every few months, she didn't see it as a hardship. *Although,* she thought, *even if I drank several glasses a day, I'd give them up to keep Randi from being uncomfortable.*

Randi nodded and waded through the throng of people to get to the bar. The crowd was boisterous, and more than once during her trek, the dark-haired woman wished for a little peace and quiet. She wasn't much for crowds, but felt guilty that Kay had to sit at home alone all day with only Spike for company. Once she made it to the bar, Randi waited patiently until the bartender stood in front of her.

"What'll it be, hon?" the heavyset woman asked. She grinned

at Randi, who was trying her best to not stare at the multiple piercings adorning her brow.

"A coke and a ginger ale, please." The vet spoke loudly over the pounding beat of the dance music. A sweaty arm reached across Randi's shoulders, and she turned to see a large woman in leather pants and a too-small leather vest leering down at her. "Excuse me, I think you've got me mixed up with someone else," Randi told her, trying to squirm away.

The woman pulled her closer and leaned down into her face. "No, I don't think so, babe. You into threesomes? I saw you and that pretty little thing come in a few minutes ago."

Randi grabbed the woman's damp hand and shoved it away. "No, thanks. But I appreciate the offer," she said, pushing by the woman and back through the crowd. She finally made it back to the table and sat down next to Kay, then realized that the drinks were still on the bar. "Damn. I forgot your coke."

"That's okay, don't worry about it," Kay responded, turning her head frequently to watch all the people. She frowned when she saw a large woman reach for Randi's shoulder.

"Hey, I don't appreciate being brushed off like that," the big woman shouted, grabbing Randi and twisting her around.

The vet stood up and glared up into drunken eyes. "Look, I'm really sorry." She leaned forward where the woman could hear what she was saying. "This is our first date, and I really don't want to share her, if you know what I mean."

Understanding dawned on the woman's features. "Ahh! You wanna test the pond before letting anyone else fish, huh?" She laughed and elbowed Randi hard in the stomach. "No problem, babe. If she's any good, bring her back next Saturday night, and we'll get together, all right?" Without waiting for a reply, she swaggered away, proud of herself.

Kay watched as the woman left, then looked at her friend. "Are you all right?"

"Yeah." Randi walked around to Kay's side of the table and leaned into her ear. "I'm sorry, but this place is driving me crazy. Do you mind if we go?"

"Mind? I was just about to ask you the same thing," Kay laughed, allowing Randi to help her up from her chair.

Monday morning arrived with a vengeance. Cold, windy, and rainy, it seemed as if it was trying to collect a toll for the beautiful weather that had been predominant the days before. After an entire weekend of sightseeing, trips to the movies, and quiet romantic meals out, Kay found herself wondering when the other shoe was going to drop. This was the most exciting time in a relationship to her—getting to know Randi and sharing tidbits of herself. She remembered all too well this phase with Beth, and was somewhat leery of giving her heart too completely. To the vet's credit, Randi didn't act as if she was trying to make a good impression or just get Kay between the sheets, and her actions appeared to come very naturally to her.

Kay leaned back against the sofa and sipped on her coffee. Absently stroking Spike's soft coat, she thought about her ex-girlfriend. Beth had been quite charming when they first met. Kay had brought her car to the shop where the muscular woman worked, and they immediately hit it off. Beth had a forceful personality, and it never occurred to Kay to tell her no when she asked her out.

They hadn't been dating long when Beth began to leave some of her things at Kay's home—an extra change of clothes, in case she got too dirty during their walks in the woods, or a favorite book to read while Kay cooked meals for her. Before Kay had realized it, the other woman had practically moved in with her, and she didn't have the heart to ask her to leave. The first time Beth stayed the night, Kay remembered feeling somewhat let down as the burly woman lay next to her sleeping. Her first sexual experience had left her wanting, and also wondering if this was what all the fuss was about. No sparks, no fireworks, and certainly no joyful screaming of Beth's name. Over time, she began to feel as if there might be something wrong with *her*, since she rarely found satisfaction in their lovemaking.

Looking back, she realized that she hadn't stayed with the mechanic out of love, but more out of convenience. Beth frequently told her that she would never find anyone else in Woodbridge, and that she should be thankful for what they had. The hurt she had felt at finding Beth in bed with what she thought was a close friend of theirs wasn't because she had loved her, but because her trust had been betrayed.

A sudden surge of emotion caused Kay to pick up the little dog and hold him close to her chest. "Oh, Spike, just how dense can one woman be?" she said, burying her face in his clean-smelling fur. The feelings that kissing Randi evoked in her were like nothing she'd ever felt before, and she now realized just what a difference there was between the two relationships. Even on their first few dates, Beth had never made her feel as special as Randi did with just one look or touch. The solicitous nature of her new friend made her feel loved and cherished, as well as excited, all of which had been sorely lacking in her life.

A soft pink tongue began to clean the few tears that had fallen. Kay chuckled and kissed the top of Spike's head. "Thanks, cutie. You sure know how to make a woman feel appreciated." She smiled and sighed. "Must get that from your mom."

Randi walked into the clinic with a large smile plastered on her face. She had tried to control it during the drive over, but had finally given up and allowed it to grace her features. "Good morning, Christina," she said to the receptionist. "Beautiful day we're having, isn't it?"

The older woman glanced out through the door. Heavy clouds hid the sun, and the cold rain that had begun falling earlier showed no signs of letting up. "I suppose, if you're a duck," she teased the veterinarian. "Dr. Wilde is in his office already," she warned.

"He is? Since he took most of last week off, I wasn't expecting him back today." Shaking her head to rid it of beads of rain, Randi unbuttoned her coat.

Christina shrugged. "Changed his mind, I suppose. Who knows with that man?"

"I know what you mean." Randi took off her raincoat and hung it on a peg next to the door. She grabbed her lab coat from another peg and pulled it on. "So, what's on the agenda for today?" she asked, walking around to stand behind Christina.

"Not much, at least not for this morning," the receptionist said. "I asked Dr. Wilde if I should call you and tell you to stay home until this afternoon, but he wouldn't hear of it." She was about to say more when the phone buzzed. "Wilde Animal Clinic, how may I help you?" Christina listened for a moment, then frowned. "No, we're not a *wild* animal clinic, ma'am. The clinic is owned by a *Doctor Wilde,* with an e."

Randi leaned down, trying to listen in on the conversation. She couldn't make out the words, but could tell that the woman on the other end of the line was upset.

"Well, yes, I can let you talk to him, but I don't see—" Christina sighed. "All right. Hold on, please." She hit the transfer button on the phone and buzzed the owner's office. "Dr. Wilde, I have a woman on line one who insists on speaking to you, personally. Yes, sir." She hung up the phone and turned to Randi. "That was an interesting call."

"What's going on?"

Before Christina could explain, Dr. Wilde stormed from his

office. "Dr. Meyers, I'll need you to come with me," he ordered, removing his suit jacket and slipping on a lab coat. "We've got a house call to make." He gathered up some supplies into a box and shoved them at Randi.

"House call?" Randi asked, taking the box in self-defense. "Since when do we make house calls?" She exchanged looks with Christina, who had stood up and placed Randi's raincoat over her shoulders. "Thanks." Not getting an answer from the other vet, Randi took a deep breath and followed him out to his car.

Dr. Wilde had never bothered to buy a company vehicle, and the man was too vain to be seen in anything but a new Cadillac every two years. He climbed in behind the wheel of the sedan and tapped his fingertips impatiently on the steering wheel, waiting for Randi to place the box of supplies in the back seat and join him up front. "Don't take all day, Dr. Meyers. I've got more important things to do than wait for you."

Randi slammed her door and reached for her seatbelt. "Whatever you say, Wilde," she grumbled, falling back against the seat as he backed out of the parking lot.

As the Cadillac pulled through the electric gates, Randi glanced around with curiosity. They had driven for almost an hour and she had no idea where they were, except that it was far outside of town. A twelve-foot fence surrounded the property, and several strands of barbed wire at the top made it clear that trespassers would not be tolerated. She looked through her window and thought for a moment that she had seen a large animal disappear into the trees. The graveled road was well kept and wound through the dense foliage until they could no longer see the main road.

Dr. Wilde drove his car up to the rear of a sprawling ranch-style house, apparently following instructions that he had been given over the phone. He parked next to a large pickup truck, which had a canopied top over the two rows of seating in its bed. "Let me do all the talking, Dr. Meyers," he ordered briskly, climbing out of the car. "Don't forget the supplies," her reminded before he closed his door.

"Right, Dr. Asshole," Randi grumbled. She grabbed the box from the back seat and rushed to follow him across the compound to a one-story building set away from the main house. Once inside, Randi shook her head to rid her hair of the rain, then looked around. They were in a massive infirmary, where different sized cages lined two of the walls.

A thin woman in front of one of the cages rushed over to greet them. She was dressed in dark green workpants and long-sleeved shirt, and had the name "Eunice" embroidered over her right breast pocket. "Dr. Wilde? Thank you for coming." Her light brown hair was falling out of its ponytail, but she pushed it out of her eyes and reached out to shake his hand. "I'm Eunice Grauwyler. We spoke on the phone."

"Ms. Grauwyler," Dr. Wilde acknowledged. He pointed to the woman behind him. "This is my assistant," he introduced brusquely. "Where's the animal in need?"

"Over here." Eunice led him to a cage at the back of the room. "Our private vet is on vacation and can't be reached. When I called Information, they gave me your number. I thought yours was a wild animal clinic, and you'd know what to do."

The three of them stood in front of the cage, peering inside. A large, pale-coated creature lay on its side and glared back at them through pained eyes.

Randi was the first to speak. "What are you doing with a white tiger? Shouldn't," she glanced at the animal carefully, "she be in a zoo?"

"My boss runs a private wildlife sanctuary," Eunice explained. "He rescues these poor animals from people who buy them illegally for pets, and then takes care of them. Kendi here has been with us for almost two years now."

Dr. Wilde glared at Randi and then turned his attention back to the slender woman standing next to him. "That's a very noble cause, Ms. Grauwyler. Do you have any idea what could be wrong with the animal?" His area of expertise certainly didn't cover tigers, and he had almost completely stopped practicing veterinary medicine altogether once he had hired Randi. Something told him that he was in way over his head, but he was determined not to reveal that to their client.

Eunice looked at the older vet in confusion. "Well, as you can plainly see, she's due to have cubs at any time. I've witnessed quite a few births in the time I've worked here, so I noticed immediately that something was wrong. She's in extreme pain, and I'm afraid that she's going to need some help."

Dr. Wilde nodded. "Very well." He swallowed hard and turned back to look at Randi. "After you, Dr. Meyers."

Spike's frenetic jumping almost caused Kay to fall as she struggled to unlock the apartment door. She had decided to take the Dobie out for a short walk, and trying to wrestle with his leash while using crutches wasn't as easy as she had originally thought it might be. Thankful for the twenty-six foot retractable lead, Kay had ended up sitting on the front steps while the excitable little dog raced around happily.

Once inside, she unclipped the lead from his collar and placed it back on the table next to the door. She had just settled down on the sofa when the phone rang. Kay glanced at her watch and saw that it was almost noon. "Hello?"

"Is this Kay?" an older woman's voice asked. "This is Christina, from the veterinary clinic."

Frowning, Kay nodded, then realized that she couldn't be seen. "Yes, I'm Kay. Is there a problem?"

"Well, it's not really a problem, dear. I mean, it is, but it isn't. But since you're staying with Randi, I thought you might want to know."

"Know what?" The tone in the other woman's voice was beginning to worry Kay. "Is everything all right?"

Christina sighed. "I think so. I didn't mean to call and upset you, but—"

"But what?" Kay asked. The feeling of dread that had started in her stomach was quickly enveloping her entire body. "Please, tell me." She was thankful for the support of Spike, who recognized her distress, jumped up into her lap, and began to whine.

"Oh, dear. Let me just start at the beginning, all right?" The receptionist took a deep breath before continuing. "Dr. Wilde received a very strange phone call this morning. He raced from the office, dragging poor Randi along with him. Anyway, they had been gone about three hours when he called and told me they were at the hospital."

"Hospital? What happened?" Kay asked fearfully. "Is Randi all right?"

"I believe so. Dr. Wilde didn't give me any details, I'm afraid. I'm sure if it had been serious, he would have said something. I didn't mean to alarm you, but since you're staying with Randi right now, I thought you might want to know. We're not sure how long they'll be, so I didn't want you to worry if she was late getting home."

"Which hospital?"

"He didn't say. But I'm sure that... Wait! His car just pulled up. If you can hold on for a moment, I'll try to find out what's going on."

A sudden click and the sound of cheesy instrumental music caught Kay off guard, and she brought a shaky hand to her forehead to pinch the bridge of her nose to forestall the headache that was beginning to emerge.

"Dr. Wilde, I'm so glad to see you." Christina placed the handset on the desk and stood up. "How is Randi, I mean, Dr. Meyers?" She knew that the senior veterinarian disliked the casual relationship between his associate and the rest of his employees. He would often call the younger vet into his office and give her a stern dressing down for becoming too familiar with the "help."

The glowering man stripped off his jacket angrily. "Dr. Meyers will not be at work for a few days, Christina. Try to limit the number of appointments, since I'll be busy in my office." He stomped off to his inner sanctum and slammed the door behind him.

Christina stared after him in confusion. She heard, rather than saw, the yellow Corvette squeal from the parking lot. "Oh, my. I wonder what that was all about." Seeing the flashing light on the phone, she quickly picked up the receiver and punched the button. "Kay? Are you still there, dear?"

"Yes, I'm here. Did you find out anything?" The young woman's voice sounded somewhat shaky, but clear.

"Not really. But I do believe that Randi is on her way home now. Her car just left the parking lot."

Kay exhaled a sigh of relief. "Thank goodness. I really appreciate you calling me, Christina. Thank you."

"No thanks necessary, dear. I'm just sorry that I got you all upset." Christina stared at the closed office door and lowered her voice. "I'm not sure what went on, but Dr. Wilde told me that Randi wouldn't be at work for a few days. Could you have her call me later on, to let me know how she's doing? I don't think I'll be getting any information out of him."

"I will, don't worry," Kay assured her.

"Thank you, dear. Goodbye." Christina hung up the phone and shook her head. "I can't wait to see what *this* was all about," she muttered to the empty room.

Kay dropped the phone back into its cradle and looked down at the dog in her lap. "Well, Spike, what do you think about that?" The little animal cocked his head at her in question. His ears suddenly shifted, and he turned around and stared at the door, his tiny stump of a tail wiggling furiously.

The door opened and a very rumpled Randi stepped into the apartment. Her dark hair was plastered to her head by the rain that had continued to fall during the day. She struggled for a moment with the jacket that was draped across her shoulders. With a heavy sigh, Randi hung up the damp coat with her right hand and turned to face the room. "Hi."

"Dear Lord, what happened to you?" Kay asked, seeing Randi's left arm held close to her body in a sling. She was about to get up, but was halted by the other woman's raised hand.

"Hold on." Randi walked slowly over to the sofa and gingerly sat down. "Tough day," she said, then leaned back against the sofa and closed her eyes for a moment. The gentle touch of a cool nose on her unencumbered hand caused her eyes to open. "Cut it out, Spike," she ordered softly, moving her hand out of his reach to lightly scratch the top of his head. She gave Kay a half shrug. "Ever have one of those days you wish you had just stayed in bed?"

Unable to help herself, Kay smiled. "Not recently, no. But then again, the last week or so has been pretty great, so I can't complain." She extended one hand and touched the top of the sling. "You going to tell me what happened?"

Randi looked down at the hand and smiled. "It looks a lot worse than it is," she assured her friend. "We got a call this morning from a wildlife sanctuary, and went out to try and help a white tiger deliver her cubs."

"A tiger? You were mauled by a tiger?" Kay asked frantically. "Shouldn't you be in the hospital? Why would they release you so soon? Isn't there—" Her tirade was cut short by a gentle hand covering her mouth.

"Calm down, Kay. The tiger didn't hurt me. Well, not intentionally, anyway." Randi removed her hand and leaned over to leave a soft kiss in its place. "Now, where was I? Oh, yeah. Dr. Wilde and I climbed into the cage to help the tiger, and we discovered that the first cub was not turned correctly. So, I reached inside to help him out." She raised the injured limb. "Anyway, Dr. Wilde was *supposed* to be holding the mother's head and keeping her calm. She yawned and scared him." Here Randi began to chuckle. If it hadn't been so frightening at the time, the entire incident would have been humorous. "He screamed and jumped away from her, causing Kendi, that's the tiger," she told Kay unnecessarily, "to jump up as well, with me still, um, attached to her. Thankfully, both cubs survived, and they and mom are doing okay."

Kay looked up into the brown eyes. "Is it broken?" she asked, her hand still resting on the sling.

"No, just sprained. But, I do get out of work for a couple of days." Randi smiled. "So, got anything you want to do?"

"Do? Good Lord, Randi. You could have been seriously injured. I don't see how you can be so damned lackadaisical about it." Kay pulled her hand away and shifted so that she was facing

Randi. "We've just started to get to know one another. It scares me to think that I could have lost this," she waved her hands between them, "us, before we have the chance to explore our relationship."

Randi reached across and took one of Kay's hands. "It scares me, too," she said quietly. "But you have to realize that my job is rarely dangerous, unless you count cat scratches or dog bites. This tiger thing was a one-in-a-million shot. And besides," she winked, "I wasn't at the dangerous end, Dr. Chickenshit was," Randi said. She saw the smile that began to form on Kay's lips. "You should have heard him," she continued, trying to get more than a smile from her friend. "I didn't know a man could scream that high without being kicked or something."

"Oh," Kay laughed, covering her mouth with her free hand. "That's mean." She couldn't control the giggles that spilled through her fingers. "But funny."

"You want to know what's really funny? We had to stop by his house on the way back to the clinic. Supposedly so he could change shirts. But when he came back out, he had changed his entire suit." She winked conspiratorially. "I think he did more than scream, if you want my opinion."

Kay fell forward, laughing helplessly. "That's so evil, Randi." She hadn't met Dr. Wilde, but the things that she had learned from her friend caused her to not feel any sympathy for the man. *Probably deserved to dirty his pants. Especially the way he treats Randi.* She tilted her head up when she realized she was snuggled against the older woman's chest. The gentle touch of Randi's free hand could be felt tangling in her hair as their eyes met. Soft lips covered hers, and for a long moment, everything else disappeared.

Brown eyes blinked open in confusion as a wet tongue traced a path along her jaw. Randi looked around the semi-dark room and noticed two things—Kay was snuggled up next to her on the sofa, snoring softly, and her dog was standing on her chest. With her uninjured hand, she gently pushed him away. "Cut it out, Spike," the groggy woman whispered.

"Huh?" Kay mumbled, sitting up also. "What's going on?"

Kay's hair stood in many different directions, and her clothing was rumpled and slightly askew. Randi thought she had never seen a more beautiful sight. She reached over and brushed a few stray strands away from Kay's eyes. "I'm sorry, sweetheart. Spike decided it was time for me to wake up, and I was trying to talk him out of cleaning my face."

Kay wrinkled her nose. "Eeew. That's not one of my favorite ways to wake up, either." *Good grief. I can't believe we fell asleep on the sofa.* She looked down at the little dog that was sitting in Randi's lap, unrepentant. "Are you jealous, cutie?"

For an answer, the excitable pooch jumped from his human perch, raced to the door, and barked. He looked up at the table where his leash sat, then looked at the door again, barking louder to make his point.

"Demanding little monster, isn't he?" Randi observed as she stood up and turned on the light. "Guess I'd better do as His Majesty requests."

"He's certainly got you trained," Kay teased.

Randi laughed while she tried to attach the leash to the bouncing canine's collar. "No kidding. Calm down, buddy," she ordered, unable to capture the tiny clip on his collar using just one hand. With a disgusted huff, she set the leash down on the floor and pulled at the Velcro strap on the sling. "Stupid thing," she muttered, as she pulled the material away from her splinted arm.

"Randi, don't. You're going to hurt yourself," Kay warned, reaching for her crutches.

"Nah, it's okay. Doesn't even hurt that much anymore." She was able to hold the excitable dog still with her good hand, while she worked the clip with the injured one. "See? Nothing to it." Her left arm was in a cushioned metal splint from her elbow to the knuckles on her hand, and the entire thing was wrapped with an elastic bandage.

Not entirely convinced, Kay stood up and hobbled over to where Randi stood. She looked up and carefully studied her friend. The light-brown eyes were no longer dulled by pain, although the vet still looked tired. "Are you sure you're up to taking him out?"

"Sure. He's not that much trouble," Randi said, laughing as the little dog began to jump straight up in the air to get her attention. "Okay, Spike. I hear you." She tucked the retractable leash under her arm and opened the door. "Be back in a minute."

Kay nodded. "Okay. Hurry back," she whispered, leaning forward and kissing Randi on the cheek. A quick glimpse of a vehicle passing by in the parking lot caused her to look past Randi and frown. *No, that's impossible.*

"What's the matter?" Randi turned around and looked behind her. "Did I miss something?"

"I think my imagination's playing tricks on me," Kay answered. She pasted a smile on her face and gently pushed Randi outside. "Go on. I'm going to go see what we can scrounge up for dinner."

Confused, Randi nodded. "All right. We'll be back in a few minutes." She allowed Spike to lead her down the sidewalk.

Closing the door, Kay leaned against it for a long moment before making her way into the kitchen. "I must be losing my mind."

Outside, Randi watched in amusement as Spike searched for just the right spot to relieve himself. He circled and paced, sniffing the ground. "C'mon, buddy, it can't be that complicated," Randi muttered, blissfully unaware of the angry eyes glaring at her from a distance.

The unseasonably warm day brought a lot of people to the park, Kay noticed. The long-sleeved blue sweatshirt felt warm, and she wished that she had worn something a bit lighter. She was seated on a metal bench, watching from a short distance as Randi allowed several children to pet Spike. The vet was wearing faded jeans and a black T-shirt that proclaimed, "The Truth is Out There," and she had knelt down among half a dozen kids while holding the thrilled dog. He scrambled from her good hand and onto the ground, bouncing and barking, much to the delight of the children. Another woman sat down next to Kay and watched the interaction between the dog and kids for several minutes.

"Looks like they're all having a good time," Melissa noted sourly, crossing her arms over her chest. She was dressed in peach-colored slacks with a matching top and jacket, and her strong perfume wafted into Kay's face.

Stifling a sneeze, Kay nodded. "They are." She turned and glared at the older woman. "What are you doing here? Are you following us?"

Melissa laughed and waved a perfectly manicured hand. "Get real, hon. When I found out that Randi wasn't at home or work, I figured she'd be here." She rolled her eyes as the woman they were talking about coaxed Spike into doing tricks, making the children laugh. "She's such a sucker for the little brats," Melissa grumbled. Her eyes cut to Kay. "She always wanted kids of her own, you know. That was one of the things we used to fight about."

Torn between wanting to know more and allowing Randi her privacy, Kay stayed silent. *This is really none of my business. If Randi wants me to know these things about her, I'm sure she'll tell me in her own time.* She decided to try and ignore the woman sitting next to her.

"A shame, really," Melissa continued. "She dotes on her

nieces and nephews, the little time she gets to see them." She leaned back and sighed. "After we had been together for a while, she told me that she couldn't have children, and asked me if I'd be interested." The redhead laughed. "Can you imagine? Me, pregnant? I mean, really."

Kay felt her heart break at the hateful woman's words. *Poor Randi.* She watched as Randi stood up and showed the children how to make Spike dance, laughing the entire time. Unable to help herself she asked, "You never answered me. What is it you want?"

"Are you afraid I'll steal her away from you?" Melissa purred, running a brightly-painted nail across Kay's thigh, leaving a thin furrow in the gray cotton sweatpants. "Or, maybe you're more afraid I'll steal *you* away from her."

"You're crazy."

"Am I?" Melissa scooted closer and caressed the younger woman's cheek. "You can't deny that you feel something for me." She leaned down and was about to kiss Kay when a strong hand clamped down on her shoulder.

"What the hell do you think you're doing?"

Melissa looked up into Randi's murderous glare. The usually cheerful woman fairly trembled with anger, and Melissa had to fight to keep a smug look from her face. "Chill out, sugar. I was just making conversation with your sweetie." She brushed the hand from her shoulder and stood up. A growl from Spike caused her to laugh. "He's getting more like you every day, Randi dear." She winked at Kay and walked away, still chuckling.

Kay rubbed her arms and fought off the urge to run take a shower. *That woman makes me feel dirty whenever I see her. I wonder if she affects Randi the same way?* She looked up at her friend, who was staring after Melissa. "Randi?"

"Huh?"

"Why don't you have a seat?" Kay asked, patting the empty space beside her.

Taking a deep breath, Randi sat next to her friend and pulled Spike up into her lap. The tiny dog curled up and closed his eyes, exhausted from his play. *Damn. I really want to wrap my hands around Melissa's scrawny throat.* "Are you all right?"

"I'm fine. She was just being annoying," Kay assured her. She slipped a bit closer, until her left leg was touching Randi's. "Did you two have a good time?"

Randi nodded. "Yeah. Those little guys can really tire a body out, though. Did she happen to say what she wanted?"

"No. Just mentioned that she checked your office and then the apartment, then came to the park. I take it you come here often?"

"We do. Spike likes to come here and play with the kids." Randi looked up from where she was watching the children crawl all over the wooden play equipment. "When things used to get to me at home, I'd come here and just try to relax. The sound of children's laughter always calms me."

Kay reached over and squeezed Randi's leg, then began to pet Spike. "Melissa told me that you wanted children," she said quietly.

Fighting the urge to jump up and run away from the painful conversation, Randi sighed. "Yeah, I did; but my body wouldn't cooperate." She looked back down at the tiny bundle in her lap. "So, poor Spike has to bear the brunt of my maternal instincts," she said in a weak tone. "It's probably for the best, anyway. I don't know the first thing about raising children."

"I think you'd be a wonderful mom," Kay argued. "You've certainly got the heart for it."

"Right," Randi said, disbelief in her voice. "I'd be real good at teaching kids how to threaten to beat the crap out of anyone who messed with them." She pulled the sleeping dog to her chest and stood up. "Come on. Let's go get some lunch. There's a drive-through burger joint not too far away that Spike loves."

Kay allowed the change of subject, gathering up her crutches. *This conversation's not over, my friend. Not by a long shot.* She headed for the car, feeling Randi's eyes on her back.

Chapter
7

Kay sat in the steamy bathroom, running a brush through her damp hair. She was wrapped in a dark green towel and her right leg was still encased in the large trash bag that Randi had fixed for her earlier. The vet had received a phone sumons right after Kay had gotten into the tub, but had waited until she had finished with her bath before leaving. With a turn of her head, Kay studied her profile and smiled. The gaunt look that had been such a part of her for the past few months had faded, and in its place was a healthy glow. *Guess falling in love has been good for me*, she thought, then her eyes widened. *Love? Who said anything about love? Friendship, maybe*, she decided nervously.

A loud bark at her feet caught Kay's attention. "What?"

Spike looked at her, then raced through the doorway and barked again. He ran back into the dressing area of the bathroom and circled around Kay. The rambunctious dog stopped and bowed in front of her, his stubby tail furiously wiggling while his rear stood high in the air. Another growl, a bark, and he rushed from the room again.

"Now what's that all about?" Kay mused, reaching for the crutches and standing up. She was halfway through Randi's bedroom when her towel slipped and fell from her body. "Damn." A gasp at the doorway caused her to look up before she could grab the towel from the floor.

"I, um..." Randi stood in the doorway, her face burning red. "I forgot my wallet, so I..." She covered her eyes with her hand and turned around, bumping into the door. "I'm sorry, it's just that, I, uh, I mean," she stammered. *Oh, Lord.* Her mind raced around the slender form that she had caught a quick glimpse of. The younger woman's body wasn't muscular like an athlete's, but she didn't carry much flab, either. *And she's definitely a natural blonde,* Randi's twisted mind teased her. "I'll just," she waved down the hall, "be in the living room, while you get dressed."

Watching the flustered woman walk away, Kay's emotions vacillated between embarrassment and amusement. Amusement won out as she struggled to contain her laughter. *For someone as old as she is, Randi certainly gets flustered easily.* She quickly dressed in the new dark green sweat pants and shirt they had bought after they left the park the day before, and hurried down the hall.

Randi sat in the recliner, her face buried in her hands. She heard Kay come into the room, but her embarrassment kept her from looking up.

"You okay?" Kay asked, sitting in her usual spot on the sofa. Even between the fingers covering Randi's face, she could tell her friend was still disconcerted.

A quiet grunt was Randi's only response.

Okay, how do I play this? Ignore it, tell her it's okay, or... Kay smiled. "Was I that scary?"

Brown eyes peeked from behind splayed fingers. "What?"

"Did you see something that you haven't seen before?" Kay teased. "Maybe I could give you a biology lesson," she suggested, as she started to raise her sweatshirt over her head. "Nothing's labeled, but if you point out what you don't understand—"

"Wait!" Randi cried, leaping up and pulling the shirt down with her uninjured hand. "Are you nuts?" Her rebellious heart began to pound at the thought of seeing Kay's body again. *Stop it! She's just trying to get you over your embarrassment, you idiot.* As she sat down next to Kay, she willed her shaky hand not to touch the soft skin that was so tantalizingly close.

Kay watched Randi's face as the other woman battled her conscience. She could tell by the look in her eyes that Randi wanted her. Without hesitation, Kay leaned forward and pulled Randi's face close. Their lips met hurriedly, and both women groaned at the contact.

Unable to control herself, Randi's hand snaked underneath Kay's loose shirt. Her fingers traced a heated path across the smooth skin, while she felt hands threading through her hair. Their lips continued to taste one another as their hands explored in earnest.

When an insistent hand caressed her breast, Randi pulled back. "Kay, wait," she panted, trying to catch her breath.

"More," Kay moaned, grabbing another handful of dark hair and pulling Randi close once again. "Please," she mumbled before their lips met.

The telephone rang, causing them to break apart slightly.

Randi moved to get the phone, but was quickly pulled back down again.

"Don't answer it," Kay begged, placing bites on the older woman's throat. "Let them call back." Her mind was telling her to slow down, but her libido refused to listen.

Tilting her head, Randi leaned against the back of the sofa while Kay continued the assault on her neck. The phone continued to ring; and for the first time in her life, the vet wished she had an answering machine. "I can't," she moaned, breaking away regretfully. She picked up the handset and took a deep breath. "Hello?" After listening for a moment, she frowned and handed the phone to Kay. "It's for you."

"Hello?"

"What are you doing there, Katie? Have you completely taken leave of your senses?" an angry voice rasped.

Beth? "How did you find me? What do you want?" Kay saw the concerned look on Randi's face and patted the other woman on the thigh to reassure her.

"I went by your house to see you, and you weren't there. Why did you leave?"

Kay shook her head to try and clear her thoughts. "It's really none of your business. How did you get this phone number?"

"None of my business?" Beth said. "You are my business, baby. We belong together. Silvia didn't mean a thing to me, and you know it." She lowered her voice. "Come back to me, Katie. I went to a lot of trouble to find you, darlin'. Doesn't that mean anything to you?"

"I'm sorry, but that part of my life is over. Please don't call here again." Kay disconnected the call and looked up at Randi. "That was my ex-girlfriend, Beth. She said she wanted us to get back together again."

"D..." Randi cleared her throat. "Do you want to get back together with her?" She steeled herself for the answer. *After all, they both live in the same town, know the same people, even lived together for quite a few years. A history like that is hard to compete with.*

Slowly, so as not to startle her, Kay reached up and placed her hand flat against Randi's cheek. "I have no desire to be anywhere near her, no." She caressed the soft skin and smiled. "But I have other desires, and I think you can help me with those."

"I'd like that, Kay," Randi whispered. Her mind kept trying to process what Kay had told her. *Wait a minute. Did she say Beth?* "Your ex's name is Beth?"

Kay nodded. "Yes. She was the tow truck driver that jump-started your car," Kay said. "Although I didn't find out about that until the other driver came to fix the flat."

"I guess that explains a few things," Randi noted.

"Like what?"

Randi pulled back, somewhat miffed that Kay had kept her lover's identity from her. "Like why she was so downright hostile toward me when she thought I was staying with you, and why she cheered up when she found out I lived in Fort Worth." She could feel the upset gnawing at her stomach. *Get a grip. You have no claim on Kay, and she certainly owes you no explanations.*

"Hostile?" Kay felt a sense of loss when Randi scooted away from her. She held out her hand and was relieved to have it grasped. "I'm sorry, Randi. I really wasn't trying to hide anything from you. I just didn't want you to get upset for no reason."

"No, I'm the one who should apologize." Randi pulled their linked hands to her lips and gently kissed Kay's knuckles. "I'm sorry. It was petty and unreasonable of me; I have no hold on you."

An impish smile formed on Kay's mouth. She looked at their joined hands and the smile widened. "Oh, I don't know. Looks like you have a pretty good hold on me right now," she teased, trying to lighten the moment.

"You think?" Randi quipped, grinning also. "Well, just for the record," she leaned forward and hovered inches away from Kay's lips, "you've got me pretty well wrapped, too."

The earlier urgency faded as they spent several leisurely moments trading gentle kisses. With a heavy sigh, Randi regretfully pulled away. "I've got to get to work." She looked down at the woman in her arms. "But I don't want to leave."

"I know what you mean," Kay said, reaching up and combing her fingers through the unruly dark hair. "But you're going to be late, as it is." She leaned forward and gave Randi a deep kiss. "One for the road."

"Whoo," Randi breathed, swallowing hard and getting shakily to her feet. "You're really good at that, you know." She straightened her shirt and tried to regain her composure. "Call me if you need anything, okay?" A few steps, and she grabbed her jacket hanging by the door.

Kay watched as her friend tried to wrestle a coat over the splint on her left arm. "Randi, there's something I think I ought to tell you."

"What's that?"

"Do you remember the other evening, when we fell asleep on the sofa?"

Randi grinned. "Oh, yeah. I sure do." She walked over and leaned against the arm of the recliner. "Why?"

"Well, when you took Spike out for his walk, I thought I saw something. Then, I thought it was just my imagination." Kay exhaled heavily. "But now, I'm not so sure."

"All right. What is it that you think you saw?"

Kay beckoned with an outstretched hand. Randi took the hand and sat down next to her on the sofa, a concerned look on her face. "Like I said, I thought it was just my eyes playing tricks on me, since I was still groggy from our little nap." She looked up into the brown eyes that were patiently waiting. "I thought I saw a tow truck from Beth's company drive by."

"Do you think she'd be crazy enough to drive all the way up here?" Randi asked. "It's not like you're still living together or anything."

"That's what I thought, too," Kay said. "But after getting a phone call from her, I'm not so sure."

Randi shook her head. "I think we're getting a bit ahead of ourselves here. All she did was call you." But she couldn't seem to shake the unsettling feeling that they were going to hear more from Beth.

"True. But she never did tell me how she got your number, only that she had gone to a lot of trouble to get it." Kay squeezed the hand she was still holding. "Do me a favor?"

"Sure. Name it."

"Just watch your back, will you? Beth always had a nasty temper, and I'd hate for her to take it out on you." The thought of something happening to Randi brought tears to Kay's eyes.

Alarmed, Randi released her hand and wiped the tears away with her fingertips. "Hey, it's all right. All she had to do was look up my contact information with the tow truck service. I filled out some paperwork and left my address and phone number. It's not like she followed us, or anything."

Kay sniffled. "Still, I want you to be extra careful." She forced a smile onto her face. "I saw her break the glass out of a door once, just because her key wouldn't work right. She's big, strong, and has a nasty mean streak."

"Nothing to worry about there," Randi said. "I'm a lover, not a fighter. And, although my knees complain about it, I can still run fairly fast." She kissed Kay on the lips. "Everything's going to be just fine," she assured Kay after they broke apart. *At least, I hope so.*

Several days went by with no contact from either Melissa or Beth. Although they continued to trade kisses, by mutual consent neither woman was quite ready to go any further. Feeling less paranoid after not hearing from either woman, Kay happily accepted her friend's offer of a shopping trip to a nearby mall. Due to her injury, Randi had worked shorter hours each day for the rest of the week, but by the time the weekend arrived, she was finally able to use her injured arm again without much pain. She huffed as she pushed a rented wheelchair up a particularly steep incline. "How about we stop for lunch?"

"That sounds like a great idea," Kay said. "I'm starving." *And I know that Randi could use a break from wheeling me all over the place.* When Randi had decided to rent the vehicle, Kay had tried to argue, telling her that she could walk on the crutches for a while before tiring too badly. But the vet wouldn't hear of it; so here they were, several hours later, with bags stuffed under the seat of the rental wheelchair.

Randi guided the chair into the food court, which was a large U-shaped area in the center of the mall. Tall, small-leafed, natural trees were strategically set up around the area, and colorful tables held a scattering of people. In the middle of the court, a wide stairway dropped down into a noisy game room; and the electric sounds of video games echoed against the piped in music that blared from speakers in the trees. Restaurants lined the outer walls, hawking everything from Mexican food to hot dogs. "So," Randi paused in full view of all the eateries, "what are you hungry for?"

"Mmm." Kay closed her eyes as the quietly asked question sent delicious shivers down her spine. *If I tell her, think I'll get it? Bad, Kay. Very bad.* The heavy petting sessions that filled their evenings were beginning to take a toll on her libido, and Kay feared she would spontaneously combust any day. "I'm pretty easy," she said, turning in the chair to smile at Randi. "What sounds good to you?"

Oh, hell. She would have to ask that. After spending the morning with Kay's perfume teasing her senses, Randi's self-control was quickly dissipating as well. She blinked several times to try and get her emotions back on track. "Uh, yeah. How about some barbecue? That's almost always good."

Kay nodded. "Yum. I haven't had barbecue in months—that sounds great." She allowed Randi to wheel her over to an empty table where she could watch most of the area, including people coming and going from the game room downstairs.

"Any particular barbecue you're hungry for?" Randi asked,

leaning over slightly so that she wouldn't have to yell over the noise around them.

"Just a sliced brisket plate, I think. Oh, and iced tea to drink." Kay patted the hand that Randi had rested on her arm. "And a salad."

Laughing, Randi straightened up and nodded. "Gotcha." She had walked several steps and was almost even with the game room. Turning around to face her friend, she held out her hands. "What kind of dressing for the salad?" she yelled, walking backwards.

"Ranch," Kay hollered after her. Seeing a teenaged boy running for the stairway, she raised her hand and tried to stand up from the chair. "Watch out!"

The boy's shoulder grazed Randi's outstretched arm, and in almost slow motion she found herself falling back, her body angled to tumble down the steps. In that instant, her eyes met Kay's; and she saw the fear for her reflected in the other woman's eyes. Heart pounding, the noises around Randi coalesced until all she heard was a steady roar in her ears as she toppled backwards.

Voices mingled outside as medical personnel scurried to and from the emergency room. A harried voice constantly paged doctors via the overhead speakers, and a child's cry could be heard over the din.

An impatient woman wearing an awkward cast reclined alone in a room, her attempts to obtain information fruitless. When an older woman dressed in scrubs came into the room and picked up a nearby chart, Kay could hold her tongue no longer. "Excuse me."

"Yes?"

"Please, is the doctor coming back in soon? I'd really like to know..."

The woman smiled gently. "She should be here in a few more minutes, dear. I believe she went to get the results of the x-rays."

Kay sighed. "Thank you." She looked up when the door opened again, and a familiar face came into view. "How did you get in here?"

"Told one of the nurses that I was your sister," Randi explained. "Have you found out anything yet?" She stepped into the room and stood at the foot of the bed where Kay's leg was stretched out.

"Not yet. But it doesn't even hurt anymore."

Randi shook her head. "I can't believe you ran across the

food court like that." She touched Kay's leg above the cast. The plaster had several chunks missing along the heel and was cracked along the bottom.

"I'll admit it wasn't the brightest thing I could have done," Kay said. "But when I saw you fall down the stairs, I freaked."

"That's an understatement," Randi said. She had only fallen back a couple of feet before she caught herself on the railing that ran along the side of the stairs. Bruised but not seriously injured, she had heard Kay screaming her name and was shocked to see her friend standing at the top of the stairs. When the adrenaline had worn off, the younger woman had collapsed in pain and was quickly transported to the emergency room to have her leg checked out.

The door opened once again, and a middle-aged woman with glasses rushed into the room. "Ms. Newcombe?" She accepted the chart from the nurse and quickly scribbled something on it before looking back up. "You're very lucky. There doesn't seem to be any new damage to your leg. As a matter of fact, it's healing quite nicely. That cast will have to be replaced, but I think we can make it one that you can walk on."

"Oh, I'd love that." Kay was more than tired of the crutches and couldn't wait for more freedom. "After I get the new cast, I can go home?"

Looking up from her notes, the doctor smiled. "Are you that anxious to leave us?" She turned her head to catch Randi's eye. "For the record, Dr. Meyers, no more acrobatics on stairways." At Kay's earlier request, she had thoroughly checked Randi for any injuries, finding only a few bruises. "I've prescribed some pain medication for you. You're going to be quite sore tomorrow, I'm afraid."

"Thank you, Doctor."

The doctor chuckled and handed Kay a clipboard and a pen. "If you'll just sign here, we'll get you taken care of, Ms. Newcombe; and then I'll have you on your way."

Spike's sharp bark caused Kay to open her eyes on Sunday morning. She reached for her watch on the nightstand and was surprised to see how late it was. *Eleven-thirty?* Normally on the weekends, Randi's attempts to sneak quietly through the house would have awakened her long before now. Another shrill bark forced Kay to climb out of bed.

Once she was out in the hallway, she realized that the barking was coming from Randi's room. Alarmed, Kay pushed open the partially closed door to peek inside. The tiny dog was standing atop the covers, barking loudly at the top of the bed.

"Go 'way," a weary voice grumbled from beneath the bed-clothes.

When Spike grabbed a mouthful of the comforter and pulled, a hand snaked slowly from its hiding place and gently pushed him away. "Stop it, you crazy dog," Randi growled. The giggle from the doorway made her pull the covers back just far enough to see. "Kay?"

"I'm sorry, Randi," Kay apologized, hobbling further into the room. "I heard Spike bark and was worried about you." She waited until she was beside the bed and could look down into the other woman's eyes. "Are you okay?"

Randi sighed. "Pretty much. I jus' can't seem to get out of bed," she said sheepishly.

Kay sat down on the bed next to her. "What do you mean, you *can't* get out of bed? Are you hurt?" She was afraid that Randi's fall had done more damage than the doctor had been able to ascertain. "Should I call an ambulance?"

"No." Randi closed her eyes. "That's jus' it," she slurred slightly. "I'm feelin' *no* pain. Took a pill in th' middle of th' night, and now I can't get up." Her eyes opened and she smiled. "I'm verrry relaxed, as a matter of fact."

Relieved, Kay smiled back at her and reached down to brush the hair out of Randi's eyes. "I'll just bet you are." She looked over at the dog, which was sitting on Randi's chest staring at her, his head cocked at a comical angle. "I can take a hint, Spike. Let me get dressed, and I'll get you outside, okay?" Two sets of brown eyes looked at her with the identical expression. "Don't tell me you need to go outside, too?" Kay jokingly asked her friend.

"Huh?" Randi blinked and frowned. "Why would I wan' to go outside? It's nice and warm in here."

"Never mind." Kay stood up and patted Randi's leg. "Why don't you get some rest, and we'll talk later, okay?" She looked down at Randi, who was already fast asleep. "Pleasant dreams, honey," she whispered, leaning down and placing a soft kiss on the resting woman's brow. Straightening up, Kay headed for the door. "Come on, dog. You can watch me get dressed. I know you like that," she said.

Spike barked in agreement as he pranced behind her.

"I can't believe it's time to go back," Kay lamented, watching the passing scenery. She took her attention away from the window and glanced down at the dozing bundle in her lap. Spike had fallen asleep not long after they had left Fort Worth, and hadn't moved in over an hour.

Randi sighed. "I know what you mean. This was the shortest three weeks in history, I think." The thought of leaving Kay in Woodbridge brought a lump to her throat. "I'm glad you agreed to join me and my family for Thanksgiving dinner, Kay."

"You've talked about your family so much, I feel as if I already know them," Kay responded. "Besides, I'm dying to meet your mom and see what kind of stories she has to tell about you."

"Great. That's just what I need, my mom telling tales." Randi forced a smile onto her face and sneaked a peek at her friend. *She looks so sad. And even though she denied it, I could tell that she had been crying this morning before we left. This is ridiculous. I don't want to leave her back in Woodbridge.* Several different times she had wanted to ask Kay to stay with her, but didn't know how her request would be received. *We've had a lot of fun getting to know one another, but it's unfair of me to ask her to uproot and move up here after three short weeks of being together.* Randi forced herself to study the road ahead. She mentally shook her head when she thought about all the old lesbian jokes that mentioned moving vans after first dates. *Just what she needs—someone who wants her to live a cliché.*

Kay could almost feel the upset roiling from the other woman. She had a pretty good idea what it was all about, but like Randi, was afraid to say anything. *These past few weeks have been some of the best I've ever known. I hate that they're over so soon.* "You will come back and visit, won't you?" she asked.

"Visit?"

"Yeah. Visit." Kay continued to stroke Spike's soft fur. "I know you're pretty busy with work and all, but I'd really like to see you again."

Idiot. Pay attention to the conversation, and quit feeling so sorry for yourself. "I'm sorry, Kay. Of course I'll visit—you'll probably get tired of seeing me."

"I doubt that."

"You say that now," Randi teased, trying to lighten the mood. "But wait until I show up on your doorstep every weekend. You'll probably want to move to get away from me."

Kay shook her head. "Not at all. The only place I'd move is—" Her words were cut off by Randi's curse as a tractor-trailer rig tried to suddenly swerve into their lane.

"Damn! Hold on," Randi said, hitting the brakes and turning the wheel sharply. The Corvette skidded to a stop on the graveled shoulder of the road, while the truck with its oblivious driver continued on its way. Taking a shaky breath, Randi looked at Kay. "Are you all right?"

"I think so." Shaken, Kay pulled Spike up to her chest and held him close. "That was a nice bit of driving. Our little friend here didn't even wake up."

Randi smiled and ducked her head, embarrassed. "Thanks. It happens more than I care to admit."

"Really?"

"Sure." Taking a deep breath, Randi checked the road and cautiously drove the car onto the highway once again. "I'm not certain if this car is an idiot magnet, or people are just getting less cautious when they drive. You'd think the bright yellow would be easy to spot."

Less than an hour later, the Corvette pulled into Kay's driveway. Randi turned off the ignition and looked over at her friend. "Doesn't look any different, does it?"

Looks...lonelier, Kay thought to herself. "Not really," she said aloud. "Do you have a place to stay for the holiday?"

"I thought I'd just grab a hotel room somewhere."

Kay reached across the car and touched the other woman on the arm. "No, don't. I know my sofa isn't that comfortable, but I'd love it if you'd stay here with me," she said awkwardly.

Charmed by the offer, Randi couldn't see how she could refuse. "I'd like that. Your sofa beats a hotel bed for comfort, believe me." Lost for a moment in the hazel eyes, she struggled to regain her composure. "How about we get everything into the house, and I'll take you out for lunch?"

"That sounds like a great idea," Kay said. She picked up the retractable lead from the floor of the car and clipped it to Spike's collar. "C'mon, cutie. Let's stretch those little legs a bit."

Randi held the restaurant door open so that Kay could exit without much trouble. They were almost to the car when they noticed a large, red tow truck parked directly behind the Corvette. "What the—"

"Hello, Katie." Beth stood at the front of the yellow vehicle, leaning back against the hood, her arms crossed over her chest. "I figured this was your ride—not too many of these babies around."

Stopping a few feet away from the burly woman, Kay was thankful for the comforting presence of Randi directly behind her. "What do you want, Beth? Haven't you bothered us enough?" When Beth stood up straight and took a step closer, she fought the impulse to recoil.

"I don't know what you're talking about, Katie. All I did was call to make sure you were okay." Beth glared at the woman standing behind Kay. "Especially since you took off with someone who's virtually a stranger. That's not very smart."

"You're wrong. The only 'not very smart' thing I've ever done was hooking up with you," Kay spat out. She felt a calming hand grip her shoulder from behind, and reached up to cover it with her own hand. "Please move your truck, Beth. I don't have anything more to say to you."

Beth took another step forward and grabbed Kay's arm. "Don't get so bitchy with me, Katie."

"Let go of her," Randi ordered, stepping around Kay to face the larger woman.

Laughing, Beth released her grip and poked Randi in the chest. "What are you going to do about it, old woman? I could kick your ass."

"Aren't you a little old to be playing schoolyard bully?" Randi asked, her own face breaking into a very unfriendly smile. "You lay another hand on Kay, or me, and I'll have *your ass* in jail faster than you can say redneck." She walked around and opened the passenger door of the car. "Now move your truck, before I call your boss and file a formal complaint."

Her face reddening, Beth stalked to the large rig. "Bitch," she yelled, climbing into the truck and backing it out of the parking lot.

Kay allowed Randi to help her into the Corvette. "That was good," she complimented. "I've never seen Beth back down from a fight before."

"Yeah, well, like I told you," Randi commented as she got in behind the steering wheel, "I'm a lover, not a fighter. And I wasn't about to get into a fistfight with a woman who is at least ten years younger than me."

"Not to mention, a whole lot uglier," Kay said as they drove out of the restaurant parking lot. "Thanks for standing up for me." She placed her hand over Randi's, which was resting on the stickshift. "No one's ever done that for me before."

Randi smiled at her friend. "You're welcome. You can always count on my support, Kay." She turned her right hand over and twined her fingers with Kay's.

After an enjoyable evening spent quietly at home with Randi, Kay decided to call and break the news to her aunt that she wouldn't be joining them for dinner the next day. She figured that it wouldn't be a pleasant experience, and Louise didn't disappoint.

"What do you mean, you won't be coming with us this year? Our family always has Thanksgiving dinner at Ray's Cafeteria," Louise complained. "He gave us free pie last year because you flirted with him."

Rolling her eyes, Kay gripped the phone tighter, trying her best to ignore the looks she was receiving from Randi, who sat on the other end of the sofa. "That's not true, Aunt Louise. He gave us free pie because you wouldn't shut up until he did."

The older woman huffed. "You always were a selfish one, Katherine. I really had something to talk to you about, but I guess it'll have to wait. Sometimes I wonder why I even bother with you." She began to cry, and then Kay heard a thumping and a rustle before another voice came on the line.

"Katherine? What did you say to mother? She's practically inconsolable."

Try tossing her a cookie, Kay thought bitterly. "I told her that I had other plans for Thanksgiving dinner tomorrow, so I won't be joining you two at Ray's for the all-you-can-eat turkey buffet."

Overhearing that part of the conversation, Randi almost rolled off the sofa while trying to control her laughter. Kay's warning finger only added to her mirth, and Randi finally gave up and walked into the kitchen, but her outburst could still be heard quite clearly.

"What was that?" Nancy asked, still upset that Kay had caused her mother distress.

"Nothing," Kay assured her. Spike jumped down from her lap where he had been perched, and followed the sound of laughter into the kitchen. He barked at Randi, which caused her to laugh even harder.

"Is that a barking dog I hear? When did you get a dog?"

Kay felt the beginnings of a headache coming on. She rubbed her forehead and closed her eyes. "It's not mine," she explained as calmly as she could. "He belongs to a friend who's staying with me for a few days."

"Oh? Is this that friend of yours, Mindy Something-or-other? The one you went to Fort Worth with?" Nancy sounded thrilled at the idea of gossip she could hold over her cousin's head.

"Her name is Randi," Kay corrected patiently. "And yes, he's her dog." She looked up as a repentant Randi came back into the living room, carrying cups of hot chocolate as a peace offering. Kay smiled and accepted one of the mugs. "If you don't have anything else, I've got to go."

Nancy sniffed. "Well, I suppose that if you're going to be that way—"

"Goodbye, Nancy. Happy Thanksgiving." Kay quickly disconnected the call before her cousin could say another word. She looked up at Randi and shook her head. "I don't know why I continue to put up with those two."

Randi sat down next to Kay and patted her leg. "Because you're a good person, and family is important to you."

"Maybe," Kay hedged. She frowned and stared at the phone. "Aunt Louise said she had something to tell me, but she started blubbering before she could tell me what it was."

"We could always stop by tomorrow on the way over to my grandmother's. Maybe take her some flowers, or something." Randi reached around Kay's shoulders and pulled the younger woman close. *And, maybe after you meet my family, I'll have the guts to ask you to move back to Fort Worth with me, permanently.*

Kay maneuvered her way up the pitted walkway, doing her best to dodge the weeds that had broken through the concrete walk. She reached the steps of the rundown house and turned to look at her friend, who was carrying a huge spray of flowers. "I can't believe you picked the most expensive bouquet," she chided. "These two are really not going to appreciate the gesture."

"I was hoping they'd be so overjoyed at the flowers, they wouldn't see us leave," Randi said as she tried to peer around the bundle in her hands. "Let's just drop these off, make our apologies, and run."

"Good idea," Kay said, climbing the steps slowly and ringing the doorbell. She had never felt comfortable in the old house, so even though she had spent several years living there, she still rang the bell like a stranger.

"Who is it?" Nancy's voice sing-songed on the other side of the heavy oak door. The sound of several locks being turned clicked loudly, and the big door opened wide. "Well, well. Look who decided to drop by." She turned and yelled behind her, "Mother! Katherine and her *friend* are here." She wrinkled her nose and stepped back. "Don't just stand there, come on inside. Don't want our neighbors to think we turned away family on a holiday, do we?"

Kay allowed her cousin to lead them into the living room area, where Louise was entertaining a middle-aged man with a silly story. Louise looked at Nancy, who shrugged and dropped down into a nearby chair, ignoring her guests. "Aunt Louise? I'm sorry to come by unannounced, but we thought we'd bring these flowers." She motioned to Randi, who took the not-so-subtle hint and handed the heavy vase to Louise.

"Mrs. Weatherby, I wanted to thank you for graciously allowing Kay to spend this holiday with me and my family. I hope you can forgive me for taking her away from you today." Randi gave the matron her most charming smile.

"Oh, you sweet girls," Louise gushed. She set the bouquet down on the end table next to the sofa and engulfed a shocked Kay in a firm hug. "That's so thoughtful of you, dear. Please, sit down for a moment. I'd like to introduce you to someone." She waited until the two women were seated, then held out her hand to the gentleman who had stood up when they entered the room earlier. "Mr. Richard Stone, I'd like to present to you my favorite niece, Katherine Newcombe."

The tall, slightly balding man reached down and shook Kay's hand. "It's a pleasure to meet you, Katherine. Your aunt has told me so much about you." He looked over at Randi, who held out her hand.

"Randi Meyers. I'm a friend of Kay's," she explained, taking her hand back and fighting the urge to wipe it on her slacks. The limp, sweaty grip of the older man gave her the creeps.

"Charmed," he said as he nodded.

Louise smiled as he took his place next to her on the sofa. "Richard is an accountant," she explained to the newcomers. "And he's graciously offered to let you come to work for him, beginning this Friday."

"What?" Kay sat up, alarmed. Although she knew her savings would have to be carefully managed in order to last until she was back on her feet, Kay didn't think she wanted to work for a man she had just met. Especially if that man was a friend of her aunt.

Richard smiled at the younger woman. "I wouldn't call it gracious, exactly. I need someone who is skilled at entering data into a computer, and your aunt told me you needed a job. It will be a permanent position, and I can guarantee top pay."

"Then it's settled," Louise stated. "Your cousin has already agreed that she'll drive you until your leg is healed."

"I don't know what to say," Kay stammered. She could feel her world spinning out of control, and couldn't find the words to stop it. *Maybe it's for the best. At least this way, I won't be a burden to anyone. And I can keep my savings intact to buy a car, whenever I can start driving again. Maybe even make a few trips to Fort Worth.*

Nancy watched the expressions cross Randi's face, and fought back a smile. *That ought to keep you away from my cousin for a while. Now she won't be so dependent on you, will she?* The thought of Kay being happy, while she herself was so miserable, was something that Nancy wanted to try and avoid. Looking over at Kay, her smile widened. "You don't have to say anything. I'll be more than happy to drive you until you can get around again on your own. It's the least I can do, since you took such good care of Mama while I was gone."

Her decision made for her, Kay literally shrugged her shoulders. *I don't have much of a choice, do I?* She forced what she hoped was a polite smile onto her face. "Mr. Stone, thank you for the opportunity. I'll do my best for you."

"I'm sure you will, Katherine. I hope you don't mind, and I know it's the day after a holiday, but we've got a lot of work to catch up on so I'll need you to come in tomorrow. You can fill out all the paperwork then." He shook her hand again, a wide smile on his face.

So much for asking Kay to come back with me. Randi struggled to keep a neutral look on her face, while Kay's aunt and cousin chattered on about how happy they were for her. *This day can't get any worse.*

Chapter
8

Mature trees lined the streets of the well-established neighborhood. Comfortable brick homes dating back to the late nineteen-sixties were set back from the road, and the yards and shrubbery around the houses were neatly kept. Kay looked around curiously when Randi parked the car on the street in front of such a home. "Your grandmother lives here?"

"Yep. She and Grandpa used to live in a tiny house in the western part of town, but by the time their kids grew up and left, the area had gotten a bit run down. So they decided to move into a nicer neighborhood." Still upset over the earlier events, Randi struggled to put on a happy countenance. She turned to face Kay after unclipping her seat belt. "I've got to warn you, it gets pretty hectic during one of these things. Kids are usually running around like crazy, and most of the family is either in the living room watching football, or in the kitchen talking about the ones in the living room."

Kay laughed. "Sounds like fun." She watched Randi step out of the car and walk around to open her door. Accepting the offered hand, Kay climbed out of the vehicle. The uncomfortable strain between them continued, and she couldn't help but wonder if it had been such a good idea to accept Mr. Stone's job offer so quickly. *Like I had much of a choice. I do believe I was railroaded, and surely Randi understands that? Besides, I've got to support myself somehow.*

The front door opened up before they reached it, and a shorter, older version of Randi rushed out. "Hello, sweetheart. I was hoping you'd be able to make it." The woman embraced Randi and rubbed her hands down her back. "It's so good to see you." Pulling away and noticing Kay for the first time, she smiled at her. "Oh, I'm sorry."

"No, I'm sorry. I don't know where my head is at," Randi apologized. "Kay Newcombe, this is my mother, Patricia Meyers." She then gestured to Kay. "Mom, Kay's a very good friend of mine."

Patricia held out her hand and studied the woman standing before her. She could tell by her daughter's body language that "good friend" didn't quite cover her feelings. But, she also sensed a sadness in Randi, and couldn't wait to get her alone to find out what was going on. "It's very nice to meet you, Kay."

"It's nice to meet you, too, Mrs. Meyers. Randi has told me so much about you."

"Please, call me Patricia." Randi's mother opened the door and waved the younger women inside. "Let's get you settled somewhere, Kay. You can't be too comfortable standing around on that cast." The young woman's injury had Patricia curious, but she decided to wait and ask her daughter what had happened, not wanting to seem too inquisitive.

Once inside, Kay realized that Randi's warning was true; a mingling of voices could be heard coming from different areas of the house, while mouthwatering smells tickled her nose. Somewhere a baby was crying, and the clattering of dishes came from down the hall to the left. A young boy, not older than four, peeked around a corner and promptly disappeared. Kay glanced at her friend, whose face was a closed mask. "Are you okay?"

Randi nodded. "Yeah, I'm fine," she said in a grim voice as she allowed her mother to lead them into the kitchen, then steeled herself for the inquisition that was about to take place.

Several women milled around the kitchen area; the smallest one turned at the sound of the door opening and headed for the newcomers. "Randi Sue! It's about time you got here," she scolded, barely looking at Patricia, who was helping Kay get seated at the nearby table. Edna Meyers stalked over to her youngest granddaughter and hugged her. She pulled back and glared up into the light brown eyes. "You gonna run off again today like you did at the funeral?"

"I didn't..." Randi stopped at the glare she received. "No, ma'am. I'm not." She led her grandmother over to where Patricia had seated Kay. "Grandma, I'd like to introduce you to a friend of mine, Kay Newcombe."

Kay met the steely gaze with one of her own, and held out her hand. "It's a pleasure to meet you, Mrs. Meyers. Randi's told me so much about you."

"She has, has she?" Edna asked. "And you're still pleased to meet me? Brave girl." She patted Kay's hand, studying the younger woman. "You must be the one I keep hearing about."

"If you mean the one that Randi rescued, then you're right." Kay took back her hand and smiled. "You should be very proud of her—she probably saved my life."

Embarrassed by the conversation, Randi met her mother's eyes. "She's exaggerating, really." She was saved from any further comments when the kitchen door swung open again, and a twelve-year-old girl came racing into the room.

"Aunt Randi! You're here," the girl squealed, taking a leap and jumping up into her aunt's arms. Her dark blonde hair was pulled back into a ponytail, and her slender body attested to her athleticism. She buried her face in Randi's neck and held on tight, only loosening her grip when Edna swatted her on the rear.

"Get down from there, girl. You're getting too big to be jumping all over your aunt like that," Edna scolded.

Randi didn't release her hold. "She's fine, Grandma." Looking into her niece's face, she could see herself reflected in the girl's dark brown eyes. "I've missed you too, squirt. How's school?"

Patricia sat down next to Kay in an effort to help sort out any confusion. "That's Samantha, or Sam, as we call her," she told the younger woman quietly. "She's the oldest of my oldest, Augustus."

"Randi's spoken of her," Kay told her. "She's very proud of her."

"She certainly is, and the feeling is mutual, I can tell you," Patricia explained with pride. "Sam has her aunt's athletic ability in softball. I just wish they didn't live so far away, so that Randi could see more of her." She sighed, then leaned closer and lowered her voice. "Those two bickering at the stove are Amy and Andi, Randi's cousins. Watch out for them."

Kay nodded. "I will. Thank you."

As she was led toward the kitchen door, Randi stopped at the table on her way by. "Will you be all right here for a minute? Sam wants to show me something."

"We'll be fine, dear. Go play," Patricia answered, waving her daughter off. "I'm sure I can keep Kay occupied with some stories."

"Stories? Maybe I should—"

Both women laughed. "Go on," Kay said. "We'll try not to trade too many secrets, I promise." She was really enjoying Patricia's company and hoped to get more insight into Randi by speaking with her mother.

"I'm doomed," Randi moaned as she allowed Sam to pull her

out of the kitchen.

A gentle touch on her back caused Randi to turn around and
look down into the worried face of her mother. "What's up?" It
had been well over an hour since they had cleared away the noon
dinner dishes, and most of the family members were either chatting in the kitchen, or sleeping in front of the TV. She was standing in the doorway of the large game room in the back of the
house, where Kay was enjoying playing a board game with several
of the children. Samantha sat to Kay's left, and it appeared as if
the injured woman had made a new friend.

"I was just going to ask you the same thing. You've been
unusually quiet today." Patricia thought at first her daughter
wasn't going to answer her, until Randi put a hand on her shoulder and led her away from the doorway back into the hall.

"What do you think of Kay?"

Confused, Patricia frowned. "I think she's a really sweet girl,
why? Are you two having problems?" Although they rarely talked
about it, she was quite aware of her daughter's sexual orientation.

Randi shook her head, then sighed and ran one hand through
her hair. "Not really. I mean, I don't think so. But she lives here,
and I live in Fort Worth—and we're only just getting to know each
other. Things are complicated. It's not like I've proclaimed my
undying love to her, or anything like that."

"How do you mean?" Of her three children, it was Randi that
Patricia worried about the most. She knew that her daughter took
relationships seriously. *Probably too seriously. Sometimes I
wished she'd just loosen up and have some fun, and quit over-ana-
lyzing everything.* "Do you love her?"

"I don't...it's just that..." Randi sighed again, fighting the
urge to bang her head against the wall. Her mother's insightful
questions always got to the heart of the matter. "I care for Kay a
lot. But we've only known each other for three weeks—that's not
enough time to know whether or not it would work out."

Patricia stepped closer and shook her head. She raised one
hand and touched her daughter's cheek. "I've seen the way you
look at her, and how she looks at you. That's a strong point in
your favor. Besides," she grinned, "I met your father at a party,
and we eloped a week later."

"But that's different," Randi protested.

"Not really." Patricia pulled her daughter back to the doorway and pointed at Kay. "Take a good, long look at her, Randi.
How do you feel?"

Watching Kay interact with her nieces, nephews, and cousins, Randi couldn't help herself as a smile slowly formed on her face. When the younger woman reached across the table and tweaked four-year-old Edward's nose, her heart swelled with affection. "I think I love her," she said. "God help me, but I really think I do."

A triumphant smile broke across Patricia's face. She squeezed her daughter's shoulder and pulled her back into the hallway. "That wasn't so hard, was it?"

"No," Randi said. She thought for a moment, then her face fell. "But it's still complicated."

"Aaargh!" Patricia stomped away, waving her hands in the air. "Stubborn kid."

The unseasonably warm weather had sent different members of the family outside into the late afternoon sun, and there was a group of men huddled nearby comparing notes on NFL teams. Randi's father, Samuel, sat down beside Kay on the porch swing. It was a good view of the backyard, where they could watch Randi, along with some of the children, playing a wild game of touch football. "How are you doing?" he asked. He didn't know why, but his wife had requested that he try and get to know the young woman. So, being the dutiful husband he liked to claim to be, here he was.

"I'm doing all right, thank you." Kay shifted slightly. Before Randi had chased off across the yard with the children, she had set up a padded lawn chair for Kay to use as a footstool. It was fairly comfortable, but the sudden interest in her from Randi's quiet father made her squirm. "um, great weather today, isn't it?" *Oh, that was original, you idiot. He probably thinks I'm some sort of moron now.*

Samuel chuckled and patted Kay on her uninjured leg. "That it is. Don't worry, I'm not going to give you the third degree, or anything. Just wanted to make sure that you're comfortable." He leaned back and watched the action on the lawn.

Relieved, Kay took a moment to study him more carefully. His once dark hair was losing a battle with the gray, and although cut short, looked to be thinning on top. Blue eyes sparkled, and Kay could tell where Randi got her adorable smile. "I'm very comfortable, actually. You've got a wonderful family. Thank you for letting me share the day with you."

"You're very welcome. As a matter of fact, you're the first girlfriend Randi has ever brought to one of the family dinners who seemed to fit in. We're glad that you could come." He grinned at her embarrassment.

"Girlfriend? But I'm not really—"

"Sure you are." Samuel leaned closer to her and lowered his voice. "I don't normally butt into my children's business, Kay, but it's plain to see how my daughter feels about you. Please don't break her heart."

Kay looked into his eyes, then down at her lap, where her hands were twisting nervously. "Mr. Meyers...Samuel," she corrected at a pointed look from him. "Randi is very dear to me. But honestly, we're just friends."

Not convinced, he leaned back again. "Uh-huh. Well, I still hope you don't hurt her. She's been hurt enough by so-called friends." Taking a deep breath, Samuel looked out onto the lawn and watched as his three grandchildren attacked Randi. "Hey, no triple-teaming," he yelled good-naturedly.

Loud giggles could be heard from the pile of people, as Randi fought back and began to tickle with a vengeance. "Thanks, Dad," she returned loudly. "Aaargh!" Young Sam came in from behind her and tackled Randi around the shoulders, dragging her back to the ground.

"Kids." Samuel looked over at Kay, who was watching the game with interest. "Do you like children, Kay?"

"I do." She grimaced when she saw Randi's face being driven into the thick grass. "I hope they don't hurt her."

Samuel shook his head. "If they do, we'll never know it. But she really enjoys playing with them. It's a shame she'll never have any of her own. I think my daughter would be a good mother."

"I think she would, too," Kay said quietly. "Maybe she will be, someday."

Blue eyes twinkled as a smile worked its way onto Samuel's face. "Maybe so."

"Your poor face," Kay said, touching the bruise gently with one fingertip. Close to the end of the football game, Randi was accidentally kicked in the face by her ten-year-old nephew, Todd. Now she sported a purplish knot underneath her right eye.

"It really doesn't hurt much," she assured her friend. They were in one of the spare bedrooms of the house, after Randi had been ordered by her mother to lie down and keep an icepack on the injury for a while.

A quiet knock on the door caused Kay to turn around from where she was sitting on the far side of the bed. "Come in."

Todd shuffled into the room, a paper in one hand. "Aunt

Randi? Mama said I could bring this to you, if I was quiet." He was thin and had dark blonde hair like his older sister, Sam; but where she was athletic, he was more studious. "I'm really sorry I hurt you."

"Come here," Randi requested, removing the ice pack and holding out one arm. She waited until Todd was sitting beside her on the bed before looking at the paper he handed her. The colorful beams of a rainbow covered the page, and the words "I'm sorry" were neatly penned at the bottom. "Thank you, Todd. This is very sweet." She pulled him close and kissed the top of his head. "Don't worry—you know I've got a really hard head. Your grandma says so, doesn't she?"

He nodded, and a smile slowly took over his face. "That's right. That's exactly what Grandma says." Todd kissed the uninjured side of Randi's face and jumped off the bed. "Glad you're okay," he told her. "Grandma says that it's almost time for cake and ice cream. I was supposed to tell you." With a bashful smile for Kay, he raced from the room.

"He's a cutie." Kay flinched as Todd accidentally slammed the door on his way out. She reached over and grabbed the ice pack, gently placing it back on Randi's face. "Better leave this on for a few more minutes. You don't want the swelling to get out of hand, do you?"

Randi sighed, but accepted the ice pack. "No, I guess not." She looked at her friend with her good eye. "You haven't been too bored here today, have you? I'm sorry we haven't gotten to spend much time together."

"I've had a wonderful time, Randi. I love your family," Kay assured her. "And while I'd love to have more alone time with you, I'd have to say this is one of the best Thanksgiving days I've ever had." She took one of Randi's hands in hers and squeezed it gently. "Thank you for sharing all of them with me."

"You're welcome, Kay. I'm glad you could be here." *That's a pleasant change from when I'd bring Melissa. All she did was complain because I wasn't paying enough attention to her.* The redhead couldn't stand children. When Randi tried to play with her niece and nephews, Melissa always complained and tried to get back at her by flirting with whomever was available at the time. *I'm so glad I'm rid of that bitch.*

Kay watched as different expressions played across Randi's face. She brushed a bit of hair out of the brown eyes and smiled. "You look tired. Why don't you try to take a quick nap?"

Only if you'll join me, Randi's rebellious mind bartered. *Stop it. She's already made a decision about her future, and it doesn't include you. Get over it.* "Nah, I'm fine. Besides, I'll need to take you home soon. You've got a busy day ahead of you tomorrow, beginning a new job and all."

"Oh, that's right." *I was having such a wonderful time here, I almost forgot about tomorrow.* Kay fought to keep the quiver out of her voice. "Well, any time you're ready to go, just let me know."

Randi sat up and removed the ice pack. "Sure." She swung her legs off the bed. "Why don't we go get some ice cream? Don't want the kids to have all the fun, do we?"

"No, of course not," Kay said, following her friend out of the room. *I don't want this day to end. It's too soon.* She forced a smile onto her face when she heard the squeals of happiness coming from the kitchen.

They were all standing on the front lawn while Randi and Kay said their goodbyes. "Thank you again for having me over," Kay said to Edna, as she accepted a hug from the older woman. "I had a wonderful time today."

Edna patted her cheek before stepping back. "It was nice having you, dear. I know you live around here. Don't be a stranger." She wasn't going to hold her breath, but she hoped that the feelings her granddaughter had for this young woman would bring Randi back to Woodbridge. *Maybe even permanently.*

"How long will you be staying?" Randi asked her mother, who kept a companionable arm around her waist. "And do you fly out of Dallas?"

Patricia squeezed her daughter closer to her. "We're driving up to Dallas on Saturday, since we have an early flight out on Sunday. Are you..."

"I'm going back to Fort Worth in the morning," Randi explained quietly. "Kay is starting a new job here tomorrow, and I really need to get back to work."

"So that's it? You're just going to leave?" Patricia couldn't believe her daughter could be so hardheaded.

Randi pulled her mother away from the crowd and turned to face her. "What am I supposed to do, Mom?" she whispered. "Get down on my knees and beg the woman to come back with me? She's got a life here, and I have one in Fort Worth." She wiped away an errant tear that squeezed out without permission. "I'll just have to come back and visit on weekends, that's all."

"Honey, please." Patricia pulled her daughter close to her so that they wouldn't be overheard. "Talk to her. Don't just assume things without talking them out first." She felt a hand on her back and turned to smile up into Samuel's eyes. "Hi, handsome."

"You two okay?" he asked, looking at his daughter.

"Yeah, we're fine," Randi assured him. "I was just telling Mom that you two should stay with me on Saturday. I have plenty of room."

Not convinced that had been the topic, he nevertheless accepted Randi's offer. "Sure, sweetheart. We'd love that. Gives us a chance to visit more." Samuel took his daughter into his arms and held her close for a long moment. "We love you, Randi. You be careful going home, and we'll see you on Saturday, all right?"

"Sounds good, Dad. I love you, too." Randi walked away to finish her goodbyes to the rest of the family.

"What are we going to do with that girl?" Samuel asked his wife.

Patricia looked on as Randi knelt down to tell the children goodbye. "Well, since talking didn't work, we could always give her a good paddling," she said.

"If I thought it would work, I'd surely do just that," he said.

As she spoke to Randi, Samantha fought to keep the tears from falling. "Daddy says that I can come visit next sumer," she sniffled. "But that's a long way off." She loved spending time with her aunt Randi, because she treated her like an adult, not a kid. "I'm going to miss you."

"I'll miss you, too, sweetheart," Randi choked out, fighting back tears of her own. "Maybe I can try and come visit you first."

"That would be great!" Sam brightened. "Will you bring Kay?"

I wish. "I don't know, Sam. It just depends. But I will try to see you, maybe on one of your school breaks, okay?"

"Cool." The young girl wrapped her arms around Randi's neck and hugged her tight. "You're the best."

"So are you," Randi whispered, her composure close to shattering. "I love you, Samantha. You take care of your brothers and sister for me, okay?"

Sam pulled back and nodded seriously. "I will. I love you, too." She finally allowed Randi to stand up. "Mama says that I'm a good sister for baby Sophia," she shared proudly.

"I'm sure you are." Randi touched the top of the girl's head and walked over to the car. She looked over at Kay, who had just gotten hugs from Todd and Edward. "You ready?"

Kay nodded. "As ready as I'll ever be, I suppose." She waved to the family, and then turned to walk back to the Corvette that was parked on the street. "You have a wonderful family, Randi.

Thank you again for today."

"My pleasure, Kay." Randi helped her friend into the car. "I think they were pretty fond of you, too." With a final wave to the group on the front lawn, Randi climbed into the car and drove off into the approaching night.

The ride back to Kay's was quiet, each woman caught up in her own thoughts and feelings. Randi stared directly ahead, concentrating on the road. Her still face belied the inner turmoil she felt over the impending separation from Kay. *Maybe Mom was right. It couldn't hurt to talk to Kay about our relationship.* She spared a glance over at her friend as the car pulled into the familiar driveway. "We're here."

Kay jumped slightly at the sound of Randi's voice. "Oh." She unbuckled her seatbelt and allowed Randi to open her door for her. "Thank you."

"You're welcome." Randi followed Kay up to the house, almost laughing at the excited barking that came from inside. "Sounds like someone missed us."

Laughing as she hobbled up the steps, Kay had to agree. "It sure does. But after being over at your grandmother's, I can see why you left him here."

Randi opened the door and reached down to grab Spike before he could race from the house. "All those kids would have driven him nuts, that's for sure." She pushed the door open further so that Kay could get inside. "Guess I'd better take him for his walk, or he'll never forgive me."

"All right." Kay grabbed the lead from the coffee table and tossed it to Randi. "Mind if I stand on the porch and keep you company?"

"Not at all." After several tries, Randi finally succeeded in clipping the lead to the bouncing animal's collar. "Come on, psycho-dog." She put him on the ground and almost got the leash jerked out of her hands. "Slow down, Spike."

Kay laughed as she watched the little dog take Randi for a walk. She didn't know who she was going to miss more: Randi, or the animal that had quickly stolen her heart. *Don't kid yourself. Randi took your heart before Spike had the chance, and you know it.* Kay looked at the woods that surrounded her house. *Would I be so unhappy living in Fort Worth? It's not like I have that much to keep me here, other than a new job that I didn't even ask for.*

Randi caught sight of the still figure on the porch out of the corner of one eye. *She loves it out here. How can I be so selfish as to ask her to leave her home and her family?* She shook her head and sighed heavily. "C'mon, Spike. Let's go try to enjoy our last night here. No sense in making Kay miserable too, is there?" She bent down and picked him up, and they all went back into the house.

The younger woman sat down on the sofa and propped her cast on the coffee table. Unhooking the lead from Spike's collar, Randi put him down, and shook her head when he immediately jumped up into Kay's lap. "Do you want something to drink?" Randi asked.

"No, thank you." Kay picked Spike up and pulled him close to her face. His soft fur smelled like the outdoors, and he licked her ear with excitement. "Oh, honey. I love you, too," she said quietly, feeling ridiculous about the tears that threatened to fall. Kay waited until Randi sat down next to her before she asked, "Will you bring him with you when you come back to visit?"

Randi nodded. "Sure. He'd probably never forgive me if I didn't." When she reached over to pet Spike, her hand touched Kay's and she swallowed hard to keep from crying. "I'm going to miss you, Kay," she whispered, trying to keep her voice from breaking.

"I'll miss you, too," Kay said. She slid Spike gently to the other side of her lap and pulled Randi closer to her. "These past few weeks have been wonderful."

"Yeah, they have," Randi said. Her free hand reached over and caressed the younger woman's face. "But, I guess it's back to reality, huh?"

Kay blinked several times to fight off the tears that threatened to fall. "I guess so. Especially since I've got a new job. At least I don't have to worry about money, and I can still save up for a car." She leaned into the touch and closed her eyes. "You mentioned something earlier today about coming back on the weekends?"

"If you want me to, I can." *I guess that settles it. I know she's an independent sort, so this job offer came at the perfect time for her—even if not for me.* Randi leaned forward and placed a tender kiss on Kay's lips. "No more talk about leaving, okay? Let's just enjoy tonight."

"That's a great idea." Kay tangled her free hand in Randi's hair and returned her kiss. She felt a gentle tongue tracing the contours of her lips, and quickly opened her mouth to capture it. A warm hand reached underneath Kay's shirt and traced the smooth skin on her back, causing her to moan.

Randi's heart started to pound when Kay touched her breast, caressing softly. Her own hand was still tracing a pattern down the younger woman's spine, until she was pushed onto her back by Kay. Breaking lip contact for an instant, she gasped in surprise

when both of Kay's hands found their way under her shirt, pushing the material up. "Wha—"

"Sssh," Kay commanded, laying light kisses on Randi's bare
stomach. "I just need to feel your skin," she said. She leaned her
face against the soft skin and took a deep breath. Gentle fingers
combed through blonde hair, and Kay raised her head enough to
look up into Randi's eyes. "Please, hold me?" she whispered, her
voice breaking on the last word.

Nodding, Randi helped Kay get comfortable beside her, both
of them lying on their sides on the couch. She wrapped both arms
around the other woman and buried her face in the blonde hair,
tears falling silently down her face.

Morning arrived with little fanfare, and much too soon. Kay
had fallen asleep scrunched up next to Randi on the sofa, and now
she woke up to Spike pulling on her hair. She raised her head from
the sleeping woman's chest and looked down at Randi's peaceful
face. They hadn't made love last night, but they had come pretty
close. Part of her wished that they had, while another part of her
was glad that she hadn't resorted to sex to try and keep the vet
with her. *Life sucks, sometimes.* A glance at the clock on the wall
showed it was almost six-thirty. Nancy would arrive in about an
hour to take her to work, so she knew she had to get up and get
moving. She traced a light fingertip over the sleeping woman's
face. "Randi?"

"Mmm."

"Come on, honey. It's morning." Kay's light tracing turned
into a gentle caress, which finally caused the brown eyes to slowly
open.

"Morning?" Randi rasped, blinking several times. "What time
is it?"

Kay smiled. *She's so cute. I could really get used to... Cut it
out, Kay. You're only making it harder on yourself.* "Almost six-
thirty. My cousin will be here in an hour to take me to work."

Harsh reality slapped Randi in the face and tore away all ves-
tiges of her wonderful dream. "Oh, yeah." She watched as Kay sat
up and rearranged her shirt, which had somehow come unbuttoned the night before. *Maybe if we had gone a bit further last
night, today would be different. Or it would make leaving even
harder.*

"Would you like some breakfast before you go?" Kay asked,
awkwardly rolling off the sofa and climbing to her feet. Her hair
was in complete disarray, and she had missed a button when clos-

ing her shirt.

Randi thought Kay had never looked more beautiful. "No, that's okay. I know you've got a lot to do before you leave this morning; I'd hate to mess that up for you." She sat up and combed her fingers through her hair, hoping that it looked a bit more presentable. "But thanks for the offer."

"You're welcome." Loathe to see Randi leave before it was absolutely necessary, Kay tried another tactic. "Would you mind waiting until I get out of the bath? I'd like to make sure I can do it alone, but without being alone, if you know what I mean."

"Sure, no problem." Randi stood up. "Let me go get cleaned up a bit first."

Kay watched Randi leave the room, then looked down at Spike. "What do you think, handsome?"

The miniature Dobie looked up into her eyes and cocked his head to one side. His tail quivered, almost as if he was trying to cheer Kay up. They both stood there for several minutes, neither one moving.

Randi hustled back into the kitchen, her face still slightly damp from where she had washed it. "I'm back." She bent down and picked up Spike in one fluid motion. "Let me just take care of His Majesty, and I'll be right here if you need me, all right?"

Kay smiled. "That would be great, thank you." She headed into the bedroom, but stopped and turned around when she got inside the doorway. "I..." *Go ahead, say it, you idiot.* "I really appreciate everything you've done for me, Randi." *Chicken.* Tired of arguing with herself, she pushed the bedroom door closed and undressed. *Maybe some time away from each other will be a good thing—might be easier to see if our feelings are real, or just the by-product of what we've been through.* Turning on the water in the tub, she shook her head. *Or maybe I'm just trying to find some way of convincing myself that her leaving and my new job are for the best, when all I really want to do is grab hold of her and never let her go.* She watched as her tears fell and mixed with the bath water.

Bringing Spike back inside the house, Randi went into the kitchen to give him a bit of food before the long drive. She stood with her back against the kitchen counter, watching the tiny dog inhale his ration. Looking around the neat room, she realized again how comfortable Kay was in her home. Prints took up spaces on the walls and homey knickknacks adorned shelves and counter space. While not overly fancy, the kitchen had a relaxed atmosphere that her own apartment was missing. *And I was going to take her away from this?* "Don't have much in my head for brains, do I, Spike?" A quick look at her watch told Randi it was almost time to leave. "I'm not sure if I can do this," she lamented to no one in particular. *Quit being so selfish, and get yourself together. You can come back to visit next weekend.* "This sucks."

"What's that?" Kay asked from the doorway. She was dressed in a sweater and colorful skirt, and her hair was pulled back away from her face with decorative combs just above her ears. "Is everything all right?"

Randi took a deep breath and nodded. "Yeah, everything's fine." *Tell her, while you have the chance.* "I lo...like that outfit," she finished. *I am such a chickenshit.* "You look really nice."

Blushing, Kay ducked her head. "Thanks. I thought I'd try to make a decent impression on my first day of work." *Be honest with yourself. You wanted to look nice for Randi, too.*

"Well..."

"Yes, well..." Neither woman moved. Kay finally swallowed and held out her arms. "Give me a hug?"

Definitely. Randi crossed the room in a heartbeat, pulling Kay into her arms and holding her close. She felt Kay's face snuggle into her chest, while she buried her own face against a fragrant neck. *Get a grip. It's only for a week.* "I'm really gonna miss you," she rasped, trying to soak up as much of Kay's scent as she possibly could.

"Me, too," Kay sniffled, unable to keep the tears from staining Randi's shirt. She took several deep breaths before looking up into the anguished face of her friend. "But you'll be back next weekend, right?" *God. Could I sound any more pitiful?*

"You betcha," Randi said. She bent her head and covered Kay's lips with her own.

The honking of a car horn outside caused the women to break apart after several minutes. Kay dropped her head to Randi's chest once again. "That must be Nancy."

"Yeah." She stepped back and looked at Kay for a long moment. "Guess I'd better go, so that you can leave, too, huh?"

Kay nodded. "I guess." She watched as Randi gathered up Spike's bowls, rinsed them out, and placed them in the sink. "Just leave those. I'll take care of them tonight."

"Are you sure?" Randi turned from the sink. "It won't take me but a minute."

"I'm sure. Walk me out?"

Randi blinked several times, then bent down to pick up Spike. "Sure." She quietly followed Kay, grabbing her overnight bag and Spike's lead on the way out of the house. While Kay walked to Nancy's car, Randi quickly tossed her bag in the Corvette, then jogged over to hold the door for her friend. "If you need anything, call me. No matter what time it is, all right?"

"I will." Kay reached over and scratched Spike on top of the head. "You take care of your mommy for me, okay?" she told the dog. His pink tongue reached out and licked her fingertips. Fighting back her tears, Kay looked up into Randi's watery eyes. "That goes for you, too," she whispered.

Unable to speak for a moment, Randi nodded. "I'll call you tonight," she promised.

"You'd better." Kay tried to make her voice teasing. She quickly kissed Randi on the cheek, and got into her cousin's car.

Randi closed the door and pulled Spike up to her chest. As Nancy backed out of the driveway, Randi waved until she could no longer see the car. With a heavy heart, she walked over to the Corvette and opened the door. She sat down behind the wheel and buried her face in Spike's coat, finally letting the tears flow freely.

"You sure made a spectacle of yourself," Nancy chided, driving down the deserted road. She couldn't understand what all the fuss was about, anyway. *It's not like she can feel anything* real *for another woman. I just don't understand my cousin at all.*

Kay continued to look out her window, wiping the tears from her face. She could hear Nancy speaking, but didn't feel like trying to understand what the other woman was saying. All she could think about was the look on Randi's face as they drove away. *She looked so lost and alone—just how I feel.* The closer she got to work, the more she felt like she had been wrong not to ask to go with Randi.

"Hey, get yourself together, Katherine. Mama went to a lot of trouble to get you this job, the least you could do is show a little gratitude." She reached over and pinched Kay on the arm.

"Ow!" Kay turned away from the window and glared at Nancy. "What did you do that for?"

Nancy sniffed righteously. "Just trying to help you pull it together, cousin. You act as if you just lost the love of your life, or something."

"Maybe I did." Kay sighed. She was tired of always defending herself to her family. "What are you? Jealous?"

"Of you and that...that woman? Dear Lord, just listen to yourself." Nancy stopped at a red light and turned to look at Kay. "You've always been unnatural, cavorting around with other girls like that."

Something in Kay snapped at that last remark. "You *are* jealous! Well, I have news for you, dear cousin—when women chose other women, they're *very* picky. You'd never stand a chance." She crossed her arms over her chest and stared out through the window again.

"Like I'd even want another woman to think of me like that. It's sick. Maybe that's the real reason your daddy ran off when you were a kid—he knew what a sick pervert you'd grow up to be."

"You bitch."

"Truth hurts, doesn't it, Katherine?" Nancy parked her old car in front of a brick building with several plate glass windows across its front. Green awning stretched out over the windows and the glass door, which had *Stone Accounting* stenciled across it in white block lettering. "Just because we're family, doesn't mean I have to like you. I don't know why Mama puts up with your attitude." She watched in satisfaction as Kay struggled to get out of the car. "I might be late picking you up," Nancy snapped, before her cousin closed the car door.

Kay hobbled to the front door of the building, relieved when Richard Stone appeared and opened the door for her. "Thank you."

"No problem, Katherine. I'm glad to see you," he assured her. "Come on in, and I'll show you where your desk is." He led her to the rear of the large room that was filled with individual cubicles. Pointing to the last desk before the back door, he smiled. "I hope this will be all right. This door leads to the restrooms and the break room, and I thought with your injury, the closer the better."

"It's just fine, Mr. Stone. Thank you so much." Kay smiled as he assisted her into the large padded chair. "This is very nice."

"We're a privately-owned business, but fairly prosperous. Most of our employees have been here for many years, and we like to take good care of them." He pointed to the computer on one side of the desk. "That's brand new, so if there are any problems with it, just let me know. I'll go ahead and bring the paperwork you need to fill out, and you can be taking care of that until Lucy gets here."

"Lucy?"

He had the good grace to be embarrassed. "Yes, I'm sorry. Lucy Whitington. She'll be showing you the ropes, so to speak. And please, call me Richard. We're very informal around here."

Kay nodded. "Oh. All right, Richard. My friends call me Kay." She smiled at him. "Thank you again for this job opportunity."

"No need to thank me. When your aunt told me about you, I

thought this would be a perfect solution for both our problems."
He brushed off the front of his slacks in a nervous gesture and ran
one hand across his balding head. "Do you drink coffee? I'll be
glad to bring you a cup back when I bring your paperwork."

"Why yes, thank you. I'd love some—but only if it wouldn't
be too much trouble." Kay placed her purse in an empty desk
drawer.

Richard tapped the side of the cubicle. "No trouble at all.
How do you take it?"

"Light cream and sugar, please."

"Fine. I'll be right back," he said, ducking through the door.

Kay leaned back in her chair and looked at her desk. The
office was more compact and neater than the law office she had
worked in previously; and although she didn't know Richard very
well, she had a really good feeling about her boss. *Richard really
is a nice man. I wonder what he's doing with my aunt.* She chuckled at the uncharitable thought and checked her watch. *I hope
Randi's doing okay. I miss her already.*

The miles blurred together as Randi sped along the interstate.
Spike had given up trying to get her attention, and was happily
curled up in the passenger's seat, fast asleep. When the familiar
skyline of Fort Worth welcomed her home, she angrily wiped the
tears from her face. She had cried most of the drive back, and the
memory of Kay's excitement over seeing Fort Worth for the first
time hit her hard.

Another car cut into her lane, causing Randi to honk the
horn. "Watch what you're doing, asshole," she yelled at the driver.
A whine beside her made Randi turn to glance down at Spike.
"What?"

He cocked his dark head to one side and tentatively wiggled
his stumpy tail.

"Don't look at me like that," she warned, turning her attention back to the traffic. "Aren't I allowed to be upset?" Spike
didn't answer her, but she continued anyway. "Why didn't I tell
her I loved her? Do you think that would have made a difference?"

After a quick glance over her shoulder, Randi changed lanes.
"She told me that she had stayed with Beth because she didn't
have anything better. Do you think that she would do the same
with me?"

Spike whined and continued to wag his tail.

"You could be right, boy. I feel like what we have is something special, too. Maybe I'll know more by next weekend." She

took her exit and continued along the quiet city streets. "I'm going to just have to wait and see, Spike. I don't want to force Kay into anything she doesn't really want." Randi parked the car in her assigned spot and turned off the engine. She picked up the dog and pulled him close. His soft fur had a lingering scent of the perfume that Kay wore, which caused her to break into tears again. "I miss her already," she whispered, crying into his coat.

Chapter
9

"Hold on, I'm coming," Randi yelled at the door. She had spent over two hours on the phone with Kay the night before, and her eyes still hurt from crying for a long time after hanging up. *I really need to get a grip on myself,* she thought, rubbing her face and opening the door. "Oh. Hi."

Patricia and Samuel Meyers stood in the doorway, their happy smiles fading when they looked at their daughter. Randi was dressed in faded, baggy jeans and a very wrinkled T-shirt. Her feet were bare, and her clothes appeared to have been slept in. "Are you feeling ill, Randi?" Patricia asked, easing her way inside the apartment. She reached up to touch her daughter's forehead, but her hand was batted away.

"I'm fine, Mom." Once her father was inside, Randi closed the door and looked at them both. "You're a bit early, aren't you? It's barely past noon."

"We decided to get an early start. And by the looks of you, it was a good idea." Patricia bent down to pick up a jumping Spike. "Hello there, handsome. Is she treating you all right?" She snuggled the excited animal close to her chest and looked at her daughter. "I'm so glad you agreed to keep Spike, Randi. With all the traveling we do now, I'd hate to leave him boarded for such long periods of time."

"I'm glad he's here," Randi said. "He's been really good company these last few months. I don't know what I'd do without him."

Patricia studied her daughter carefully. *She looks terrible.* Randi's movements were stiff, and her normally sparkling eyes were dull and sad. *Pining away for Kay, if I'm not mistaken. I'm glad we decided to stop here before leaving tomorrow. She needs a bit of parental "tough love."*

Randi took one of the suitcases that her father had carried

inside. "Here, let me help you with those. I thought I'd put you in the master bedroom, and I'll take the guestroom for tonight. All I need to do is put clean sheets on your bed." She led him down the hallway, while her mother stayed behind and fussed over Spike.

"I hate to think we're taking your bed," Samuel argued.

"No, that's okay, Dad. Really." Randi didn't want to admit that she hadn't slept in her own bed the night before. She could still detect Kay's scent on the guest room sheets, and couldn't bring herself to change that bed for her parents to sleep in.

Samuel glanced into the second bedroom and noticed the unmade bed. *I wonder what's up with that?*

"I'll get the sheets taken care of in a little while," Randi said. She placed the suitcase on the foot of the bed and turned around to look at her father, who had set his down just inside the doorway. "I'm really glad you're here, Dad."

He crossed the room and took her into his arms. "I'm glad we are too, sweetheart." Samuel's heart broke at the sobs that wracked his daughter's body. He continued to stand and hold her until she got herself back under control.

"I'm sorry. It's just been a really rotten couple of days," Randi said. She wiped her face with the heel of one hand and took a deep breath.

"Did you ever talk to Kay?" He was afraid that the younger woman had dumped his daughter and broken her heart. *No, I don't think she would have done that. I could have sworn she felt something for Randi, too.*

Randi shook her head. "I've talked to her, but not about how I feel. I didn't deal with that yet."

Patricia stood in the doorway holding Spike in her arms. "Well, why on earth not? That poor girl is probably just as miserable as you are."

"You don't understand, Mom. Things are—"

"Complicated. Yes, you've told me that several times already." Patricia walked into the room and handed Spike to Samuel, who took the dog and the hint, and left. "Sit down, Randi."

Uh-oh. Why do I feel like I'm about to get into trouble? "But—"

"Don't 'but' me, young lady. Now sit down, be quiet, and listen."

"Yes, ma'am." Randi dropped down onto the bed. *Might as well let her get it over with. Lord knows I won't have any peace until she speaks her mind.*

Patricia sat down next to her daughter and grasped one of Randi's hands. "Now you know we don't like to interfere in our children's lives," she started, but stopped when an unbelieving snort came from Randi. She used her spare hand to lightly slap a denim-covered thigh. "Hush. Now, where was I?"

"Not interfering," Randi mumbled sarcastically.

"Right. I know we don't talk about your, um, lifestyle much," Patricia said, "but just because I don't exactly understand it, doesn't mean I don't love you."

An embarrassed smile broke out on Randi's face. "I know, Mom. You and Dad were both a lot better about it than I thought you'd be, to tell you the truth."

"Really? How so, honey?"

Why are we getting into this discussion now? I've been out to my parents for years, and they've never asked. Oh, well. In for a penny... "Well, considering Dad always referred to homosexuals as 'queers' or 'fags,' I was really scared that when you found out I was gay, you'd disown me."

"Disown you? Why would we do such a thing?" Patricia asked, outraged. "I'll admit it took a while for us to come to terms with it and to stop questioning ourselves, but we love you. How could you even think that we'd do something like disown you?"

"It's happened in families closer than ours," Randi said patiently. "I've heard all sorts of horror stories about how kids were getting disowned, or beaten by their 'loving' families after telling them they were gay." She looked up into her mother's upset face. "And, as much as I love Dad, sometimes his Texas 'good-old-boy' attitude scared me to death."

Patricia hugged her daughter. "He's not the most modern man around, but he loves you, dear. All we both want is for our children to be happy, no matter what brings that happiness about."

"I realize that now," Randi sniffled, fighting back more tears. *When am I going to stop crying like a damned baby? This is getting ridiculous.*

"Now, back to what I started to say earlier," her mother said gently. "Why won't you tell that sweet girl how you feel about her? Do you *like* being so miserable?"

Releasing her hold on her mother, Randi dropped back onto the bed and covered her eyes with her arm. "Kay's a very independent woman, Mom. She has a life in Woodbridge, and just started a new job yesterday. I have a job here, with several people depending on me for their livelihood. Neither one of us can just pick up and move on a whim."

"Is that what this is all about? Some warped sense of duty?" The older woman reached over and pushed Randi's arm away

from her face. "Do you think that either one of you can be satisfied with a long-distance relationship? If you truly care for Kay,
then you're going to have to make some big decisions, Randi."

"I know that, Mom. But it's—"

"If you say 'complicated' one more time, I'm going to paddle
your behind," Patricia warned. "Do me a favor, please?"

Randi sat up and wiped at her face. "What?"

Taking both of Randi's hands in hers, Patricia waited until
she had her daughter's undivided attention. "Stop and think about
how you feel about her, and what she means to you. You might
also want to consider how you'd feel if she found someone else
because you were too damned busy being noble."

"I'm not—"

"Hush. Just take a while and think about what makes you
happy, Randi. That's all I ask of you."

She's right. I've got some serious thinking to do. "Thanks,
Mom. I will." Randi pulled her mother to her and hugged the
older woman. "I love you."

"I love you too, stubborn kid of mine," Patricia said. "Now,
let's go see how much trouble your dad and Spike got into while
we were in here."

The channels on the television set were flashing by too
quickly to discern content, but the woman sitting alone on the
sofa didn't seem to mind. Kay's foot was comfortably propped on
the coffee table in front of her, and a forgotten cup of coffee sat
perilously close to the edge. She looked up at the clock on the wall
and saw it was a little after three o'clock in the afternoon. *I wonder if Randi's parents are there yet?* The vet had confided to Kay
on the phone the night before that if she hadn't already offered her
parents a place to stay, she'd have come back to Woodbridge for
the weekend.

"Not like I would have minded," Kay mumbled out loud. She
continued to track through the television stations without caring
what she was doing. "I'm so pathetic. It's only been one day since
I last saw her, and here I am talking to myself." She dropped the
remote into her lap and closed her eyes. "Is it Friday, yet?" Lonely
and depressed, Kay fell into a restless sleep.

A short time later, the ringing of her telephone awakened her.
She limped to the bedroom to answer the call. With her heart
pounding anxiously, Kay picked up the phone. "Hello?"

"Katherine? You sound all out of breath. Is everything all
right?"

Damn. "Aunt Louise? Yes, I'm fine. Why are you calling?"

"Do I need a reason to call? Maybe I was just concerned about you," Louise whined.

Disappointed that it wasn't Randi on the phone, Kay flopped onto the mattress. "I'm sorry. I was in the living room and had to rush into the bedroom to answer the phone. It's really very sweet of you to call and check on me, Aunt Louise. Thank you."

"No thanks are necessary, Katherine. We are family, after all." Louise paused for a moment. "But, I did have something I wanted to ask you."

Of course you do. I've never known you to actually give a damn about anyone else but yourself, Kay thought bitterly. "I don't know what I can do for you, since I'm stuck here at home."

"Actually, it's something we can do for you, dear," Louise said. "I've asked Richard to come over for lunch after church tomorrow, and he asked if you'd be here. I believe that family is extremely important to him, so I thought it would be nice to have Nancy pick you up and bring you here. He seems to really like you, Katherine."

"Lunch? Tomorrow? I don't know—"

Louise jumped in, anxious. "Of course, you'll be here. I'm going to need some help with the menu, too. Richard is on a special diet, and I don't have the foggiest idea what to fix."

I should have known she'd have an ulterior motive. She's never been nice except when she wants something. "I'm sorry, Aunt Louise. I just don't feel like socializing right now. Maybe another time."

"Of course. Don't help your poor aunt out. After all I've done for you, this is how you repay me," Louise moaned. "I ask one little favor, and you can't take time out of your busy life to—"

"All right!" Kay snapped, tired of hearing her aunt's complaining. "I'll help you with lunch tomorrow, but I want to come home directly afterwards, okay?"

Knowing she had won, Louise sniffed. "Fine. You don't have to be so testy, Katherine. It's only lunch." The smile in her voice was evident. "If you'll make up a menu and call Nancy about the ingredients, she'll pick them up this afternoon when she goes to the market. See you tomorrow." She hung up the phone before her niece could argue with her.

"Wonderful." Kay sighed, hung up the phone, and fell back on the bed. "A crappy ending to a crappy weekend. Perfect."

"That's not good for you," Patricia admonished as she

stepped out onto the front porch next to her daughter. She placed her hand on Randi's shoulder and squeezed. "Do you want to talk about it?"

Randi took another drag from the cigarette. They had just returned from dinner, and she had gone outside to have a smoke. She had never smoked inside the apartment, at first because Melissa hated it, and then after she left, out of habit. Now that her parents were here, she didn't want to expose them to the smoke, either. "Talk about what, Mom?" She continued to look out into the darkness, fighting a chill that had nothing to do with the cool temperature. City lights dimmed the stars, but she could still make out a few of them in the evening haze.

"About what's bothering you, honey. You barely touched your dinner tonight."

"I just wasn't that hungry," Randi said, tossing the cigarette to the ground and stepping on it. She bent down to pick up the crushed butt. "What time do you and Dad have to leave tomorrow?"

Changing the subject won't help, stubborn girl of mine. "Our flight is at one, but we'll need to turn in the rental car first." Patricia used the grip she had on Randi's shoulder to gently turn the younger woman around. The unshed tears in her daughter's eyes tore at her heart. "Oh, baby."

Struggling to keep her composure, Randi cleared her throat. "Mom, please. I'm fine, really."

"That's a load of bunk, and you know it, Randi Suzanne. Why won't you talk to me?" Patricia longed to pull her daughter into her arms and comfort her, but was afraid of being rebuffed. "I'd like to help, if I can."

"There's nothing you can do, Mom. It's just something I need to work out on my own." Randi pulled out another cigarette and lit it, careful to blow the smoke well away from her mother. "Why don't you go back inside, and I'll join you in a minute?" Part of her wanted to fall into her mother's arms and cry, while the mature, more stubborn side refused to allow such a display of weakness.

Patricia looked into the haunted eyes of her youngest child and bit back the sharp retort that sat on her tongue. *She's hurting, and the last thing she needs is to be harped at. I can at least respect her wishes.* "Okay, sweetheart. But don't stay out too long in this night air, or you'll make yourself sick." She touched her daughter's cheek and went back into the apartment.

I'm already sick, Mom. And the only cure is over two hundred miles away. Randi swallowed the bitter ache of loneliness and took another drag, looking to the western sky. *I don't know if I'm going to survive an entire week of this.*

Morning came, and Samuel noticed his daughter looked even worse than she had the day before. He had gotten up in the middle of the night for some water, and could hear the keys of the computer clicking away in the guest room. *I wonder if she got any sleep at all*, he mused, sitting on the sofa next to his wife. The three of them were having coffee after Randi had made them all breakfast, and it wasn't much longer before he and his wife would have to leave. "Thank you again for breakfast, sweetheart. That was one of the best omelets I've ever had."

"You're welcome, Dad." Randi looked down into her coffee mug then smiled back up at him. "Maybe next time you're here, I'll have an actual table for you to sit at."

"Not a problem. When we're at home, we usually eat in the living room, too. Your mother won't let me put a television in the dining room," Samuel said, putting his arm around his wife. "Rather narrow-minded of her, don't you think?"

Patricia feigned outrage at her husband's comments. "Narrow-minded, am I?" She poked him in the ribs, causing him to jump and chuckle. "Teach you to mess with me, mister."

Randi smiled at her parents' antics. *They're so happy, even after all these years. I hope that Kay and I can...* She paused as a sad pang of loss hit her in the chest. *What am I thinking? I've probably blown any chance of having something like what they have.* Her smile faltered, and she fought the lump in her throat.

"Are you all right, Randi?" Patricia asked, seeing the change in her daughter's demeanor.

"I'm fine, Mom. Just a little tired," she fibbed. She was tired, but it had nothing to do with how she felt. The emptiness in her heart kept her from sleeping. After tossing and turning for over an hour the night before, she got up and turned on the computer to check her email. Bored and restless, she stayed up and surfed the Internet until she heard her parents stirring across the hall. Randi shut down the machine and went to the bathroom to splash some water on her face, hoping that they couldn't tell that she had been up all night. *I should have known better. They don't miss a damned thing.*

Not convinced, Patricia nodded. "Uh-huh. Right." She exchanged looks with her husband, who shrugged. Standing up, the older woman set her mug down on the coffee table and put her hands on her hips. "Whenever you get ready to talk, I'll be more than ready to listen." Patricia looked back at Samuel. "We'd better get going, if we're going to get the car turned in and our bags checked."

"All right," he said, standing as well. "I'll go get our things."

She waited until he was out of earshot before giving her daughter another look. "I don't know what you think you're accomplishing with this martyr act, Randi; but you need to pull yourself together and think about what you're doing, to yourself *and* that sweet girl. Do something before it's too late." She looked up as Samuel walked back into the room, carrying their luggage. "Thank you, honey."

"You're welcome." Samuel knew that his wife was thanking him for giving her a moment alone with their daughter, not for gathering up the bags. By the look on Randi's face, he could tell that his wife had given her something to think about. *I just hope it did some good. That girl is as mule-headed as her mother is.*

Randi stood up and walked Patricia to the door. She hugged her father and kissed him on the cheek. "You two need to come back again soon," she told him. "Don't wait for a holiday, next time."

"That goes both ways, you know. Just because we're living in Santa Fe now, doesn't mean we wouldn't be glad to see you. You could probably use the vacation."

"I might just do that," Randi said, stepping out of his arms and giving her mother a strong embrace. "You two have a good flight and give me a call when you get home, okay?"

Patricia nodded. "We will." She cupped Randi's face in her hands and stared intently into her brown eyes. "Think about what I said, honey. Don't let your pride ruin your life."

Swallowing hard, Randi nodded. "Okay. I'm not promising anything, but I'll think about it." She leaned forward and kissed her mother on the cheek. "I love you, Mom."

"I love you too, baby." Patricia knelt to pick up Spike, who had been standing quietly, watching the activity. "You take good care of her for me, handsome." She kissed the top of his head, set him down, and then followed her husband out into the parking lot. "Don't forget," she yelled, waving at her daughter before climbing into their car.

Randi stood on the front porch, Spike sitting at her feet. She waved at the car until it drove out of sight, then looked down at her dog. "What do you think, boy? Am I being stubborn?"

He stood up and wagged his stump of a tail. Sensing her distress, Spike jumped up onto her leg and whined.

"You're probably right," she told the dog, picking him up and cuddling him close. "We'll just have to wait until next weekend and see how it goes." With a final look over her shoulder, Randi walked back into the apartment and closed the door behind her.

Kay sat in the office break room and sipped her coffee. Richard had offered to bring it to her, but she'd wanted to get away from her desk for a few minutes. She had chosen the table closest to the coffee machine because, although she was no longer on crutches, walking still tired her.

Another woman rushed in and poured herself a cup of coffee, barely glancing at the young woman nearby. She added sugar and creamer, then hurried back out of the room without so much as a word.

"Nice talking to you," Kay mumbled. The only person who had spoken to her on Friday, besides Richard, was her supervisor. All the other women in the office were closemouthed, almost to the point of rudeness. Now on her second day of work, she noticed them gathering together in exclusive groups, but was rebuffed whenever she attempted conversation. *I don't know why they're being so standoffish, but I hope they get over it soon. I don't know how long I can work like this.*

Her break finished, Kay stood up and placed her mug on the counter, then stood at the sink and rinsed it out. Two more women came into the quiet room, chatting.

"...and Irma said that he's at her desk more than his own," one of them tittered. A nudge from her companion caused her to quiet. "Oh."

"Don't worry, I was just leaving," Kay told them. Her patience exhausted, she pushed by the two women in silence.

Back at her desk, Kay dropped gracelessly into her leather chair and fought back tears of frustration. She had been up late the night before, talking with Randi on the phone, and knew that part of her being sensitive stemmed from lack of sleep. *But she sounded so sad. I didn't have the heart to hang up the phone.*

Although it was only Monday, each day of their separation was harder than the last, and Kay was beginning to wonder if she hadn't made a big mistake by allowing Randi to leave. It was obvious to her that the vet was having just as rough a time as she was, and she was worried if they'd both last the entire week.

"That's twice today," Joyce said, bending down to pick up the fallen instrument. She was assisting Randi with stitching up a

Siamese cat, and the veterinarian had already dropped or knocked two items from the nearby tray. The dark circles underneath Randi's eyes were prominent, and Joyce was concerned for her friend. "If you keep this up, we won't have any sterile instruments left to do procedures with."

Randi blinked several times to clear her vision. She tied off the sutures and stepped back, glad that the operation was complete. "Sorry about that, Joyce. I don't know what's come over me today." With a snap, she jerked off the latex gloves and tossed them in the trash. "Would you mind finishing this up?" Not waiting for a response, Randi hurried from the room and out the rear door of the clinic.

Reaching into the pocket of her lab coat, she pulled out a nearly empty package of cigarettes and took one out with her teeth, while her other hand fished in her pants pocket for the silver lighter that she carried. A flick of her thumb and she waved the flame under the cigarette, and the end glowed as Randi sucked in a deep breath. She felt the burn as the smoke hit her lungs, and the too-deep drag caused her to cough heavily.

"That's the slow way, you know." Christina's wise voice spoke from behind her.

Randi turned around and glared. "What are you talking about?" she said, wiping away the tears that the coughing spell had caused.

Christina closed the door behind her and leaned back against it. She crossed her arms over her chest and peered over her glasses at the younger woman. "There are quicker ways to kill yourself than to go without sleep for days and smoke like a chimney." Her voice was gentle, but her concern was evident.

"I don't know what you're talking about," Randi said, intentionally taking a long pull from the cigarette. Her stomach took advantage of the silence between the two women, and issued a loud growl.

"When was the last time you ate something, Randi?" Christina asked, stepping forward and placing her hand on the vet's arm. She could see the cigarette shake as Randi raised it to her lips.

Biting back a nasty retort, Randi pulled away and leaned against the side of the building. "Breakfast," she muttered. *Yesterday,* her rebellious mind supplied helpfully. Food didn't appeal to her, and she felt as if she were losing control. "I'm fine, Christina. Just let me finish my break, and I'll be back inside in a minute." *Please go back inside before I say something I'll regret. I don't want to hurt you, too.* When Kay had asked her last night how she was, Randi had snapped back her answer. She knew that her short remark had hurt Kay and had apologized immediately, but realized that the damage had already been done.

The receptionist sighed. She had a pretty good idea what was going on with Randi, and hated to see her hurting. "All right." Christina started back into the clinic, but turned around and stood in the doorway. "But if you need someone to talk to, I'm here," she said, smiling gently and closing the door behind her.

"This just sucks," Randi complained to no one in particular, taking another long drag from her cigarette.

Chapter
10

Tuesday went by much like Monday, with Randi working all day at the clinic on only a couple of hours of sleep. She was thankful that Dr. Wilde had decided to take the day off, because she wasn't in the mood to argue with him.

Joyce stood at the front desk beside Christina, and they both watched as Randi walked down the hallway and out the back door. Joyce turned and shared a look with the receptionist. "Do you have any idea what bug bit her on the butt? I think she's grumpier today than she was yesterday, if that's at all possible."

"I think she's hurting," Christina answered quietly. "I wish she'd let us help her."

"If you ask me, she needs a good meal and a decent night's sleep. Doesn't look like she's had either lately."

Christina nodded. "You could be right, Joyce. Let me see what I can do."

Some time later, Randi stopped by the reception desk and peered over Christina's shoulder. The waiting room was empty, although she could have sworn they had several appointments booked for the afternoon. "What do we have next, Christina? I don't see anyone here."

"Well, that's just the thing," the receptionist said. "All three afternoon appointments canceled, so we're done for the day. I was just on my way to tell you." She busied herself by writing something on the appointment book, afraid that if she looked up, Randi would see right through her.

"That's strange," Randi said. She leaned against the desk and yawned widely. "Sorry about that."

Christina brought her pen up to her mouth in an attempt to hide her grin. "That's quite all right, dear. Why don't you go home and try to get some rest, and I'll give you a call if something comes up?"

Randi shook her head. "I couldn't do that. You might need me." But the thought of lying down for a few minutes was beginning to sound good.

"Believe me, if we need you, I'll call. I want to clean out some files today, and you'd just get underfoot, like last time." Months earlier, in her attempt to help box up the old files, Randi had accidentally knocked a two-foot stack onto the floor, causing the other woman hours of work trying to put them back in order again.

"That was an accident," Randi said. "But if you're sure you don't need me, I think I will go home for a little while."

Thankfully! Christina pursed her lips to keep from laughing. "And while you're at it, get something to eat, too. It'll help you rest."

Hanging up her lab coat, Randi pulled on her black leather jacket and zipped up the front. "Yes, Mom," she teased. Her stomach rumbled, causing her to blush. "Remember to call me if anything comes up," she said, as she walked out the door into the cold November air.

Kay watched with regret as several of the office women stepped out for lunch. She had brought her own, but she would have gladly put it in the break room refrigerator had she been asked to go with them. Chiding herself for her thoughts, she went to the office kitchen for another lonely meal.

Although she wasn't the most outgoing person, Kay was hurt by the attitude of her fellow workers. She thought that the coolness they had displayed for the past couple of days would have thawed by now. Fighting back irrational tears, she took the paper bag that held her lunch and sat down in the empty break room.

Her thoughts went back to the phone call the evening before. Randi had sounded exhausted, but after the harsh words on Sunday night, she was afraid to broach the subject again. *We can't keep going on like this. Something has got to give.* Taking a bite of her sandwich, Kay looked up as the door opened and Richard walked into the room.

"Kay, hello. What are you doing in here all by yourself?" he asked, opening the freezer door and pulling out a frozen dinner.

"Having lunch. Why aren't you out with the rest of them?" She took a sip of her water and watched in amusement as he struggled with the cellophane wrapping covering his meal.

Richard put the tray into the microwave and hit several buttons, then walked over to Kay's table. "Do you mind if I join you? I normally don't socialize with anyone in the office. That's why I stay here at lunch."

She gestured to the chair across the table from her. "Please, sit down." Kay smiled at her boss. *He really is a nice guy, although I don't know what he sees in Aunt Louise.*

"Thanks." Richard took a chair and smiled. "I enjoyed lunch Sunday. Something tells me that you cooked it, though."

"What makes you say that?"

"I didn't need half a bottle of antacids afterwards," he said. "Your aunt is a nice woman, but I'm afraid she's not too skilled in the kitchen."

Kay laughed. "Uh, no, she never has been. When I lived with them, I did most of the cooking, out of self defense."

He nodded, then stood up and waited the extra few seconds for the microwave to finish heating his meal. "I always thought I had a strong constitution," Richard said, pulling the dinner from the microwave and carrying it back to the table. He pointed at the tray. "After all, I live off these things."

"No contest," Kay told him. "I once saw her 'gravy' eat the finish off a fork."

"I can believe that. Although, I can't complain, since she's been kind enough to ask me over for meals several times." He looked down at the enchilada dinner. "And it was a bit better than this." Taking a bite, he chewed and swallowed. "I hear that you've got to leave early today."

"Yes, I have a doctor's appointment," Kay said. "I hope that's okay."

His mouth full, Richard nodded, then swallowed again. "Of course. Do you need a ride?"

Kay shook her head. "No. Nancy will pick me up." Her cousin had complained loudly when she was asked if she could make the extra stop, until Kay reminded her that the sooner she was rid of the cast, the sooner she could get a car and drive herself around. *Hopefully the doctor will tell me when I'll be rid of this stupid thing. I'm sick of putting up with my cousin's carping about everything.*

"Okay. But remember, if for some reason she can't help you, just let me know," he said. The door opened and one of the office women came in and walked over to the coffee machine. Richard didn't pay any attention to her, but he reached across the table and patted Kay on the arm. "It's the least I can do."

The woman glanced casually over her shoulder at the table. The smile on her face didn't quite reach her eyes, as she hurriedly poured her coffee and left the room.

Randi opened the apartment door and stepped around Spike, who greeted her excitedly. "I'm glad to see you too, buddy," she told him, pushing the door closed with her shoulder.

He looked at the paper bag in her left hand and whined.

"No, this isn't for you," she scolded. After the reprimand from Christina, Randi had decided to stop at a fast-food restaurant and pick up something quick to eat. She still didn't feel much like eating, but on the way home, she realized that Spike was following her example and hadn't touched his food for almost two days.

Walking into the kitchen, she noticed that the contents of his food dish still sat untouched. "What am I going to do with you, Spike?" Randi asked him. He stood by the dish and cocked his head, but made no move to eat. "You're worse than Christina," she said, bending down to pick up the bowl. "C'mon. I'm too damned tired to eat standing in the kitchen."

Spike happily followed Randi into the living room, where she placed his bowl of dry food next to the sofa. His stub of a tail wriggled as he watched her sit down.

"Well, go on. Eat." Randi opened the bag and dug out the greasy hamburger and took a small bite. The action spurred Spike on, and he quickly stuffed his nose into his bowl, happily munching away. *Spoiled mutt.* The taste of one bite of food was all it took before she followed Spike's lead and hurriedly devoured the burger.

Her hunger sated a few minutes later, Randi's last conscious thought was of how she wasn't sleepy, before she leaned back on the sofa and fell fast asleep.

It took longer at the doctor's office than Kay had anticipated, because he insisted on all new x-rays after hearing of her escapade at the mall. Luckily, there was no new damage, and he assured her that if the bone continued to heal like it was, she'd be out of the walking cast in a couple more weeks.

A plastic bag of groceries around each wrist, Kay struggled with the lock on her front door as Nancy spun out of her driveway. Even without the crutches, it took her twice as long to get inside.

Closing the door behind her, Kay struggled to get the bags into the kitchen, thankfully setting them onto the counter with a heavy sigh. She checked her watch and was relieved that she hadn't missed Randi's evening call. *Only six-thirty. I've still got half an hour to go.*

A quick glance in her refrigerator yielded a bowl of leftover pasta, which she placed in the microwave. While it was heating, she put away the groceries she'd bought, and thought of Randi. "Three more days," she moaned. "I don't think I can make it." Though, from what Kay could tell from their conversations, she was doing much better than her friend.

After her meal was finished and all the dishes washed and put away, Kay checked her watch for the tenth time. *Six fifty-five. Only five more minutes!* She wiped her hands on a dishtowel and hurried to her bedroom, wanting to be comfortable when Randi called.

Fifteen minutes later, Kay was worried. It was ten minutes after seven, and she hadn't heard from Randi. *I hope she's all right.* Her imagination was getting the better of her, and all sorts of scenarios passed through her mind. *What if she's had a wreck and is hurt somewhere? Or maybe she fell in the shower and is lying on the floor, unconscious.* Kay's logical mind broke into her musings. *She might have had an emergency and is just working late. Or she could have forgotten. I'm sure there's a perfectly good explanation for why she hasn't called yet.*

The far off ringing of the telephone caused Randi to slowly return to wakefulness. She looked around the darkened room and tried to figure out where she was and what was going on. Her foggy brain finally realized that she was at home, but she couldn't remember why she was asleep on the sofa.

Spike had been curled up in her lap asleep, but he jumped down when she woke up. The phone continued to ring in the bedroom, where Randi had returned it after she took Kay home at Thanksgiving. She stood up and rubbed her face with one hand, then stumbled down the hallway to silence the offensive device. Jerking the handset off the base, she pulled it up to her ear. "What?" she snapped.

"Randi? Are you all right?" Kay's worried voice asked.

"Huh?" She sat down on her bed and rubbed at her eyes. "Kay?"

"Are you all right?" Kay repeated, still concerned. "It's after eight o'clock. I've been trying to reach you for almost half an hour."

"What?" Randi blinked a couple of times before realizing what Kay was saying. "Oh, shit!"

"Randi, what's the matter? Are you okay?"

"I'm so sorry, Kay," Randi apologized. "I came home this afternoon and fell asleep." *Eight o'clock? I've been asleep on the sofa for six hours?* "I'm really sorry I worried you, sweetheart." As tired as she still was, Randi didn't realize what she had said.

But Kay understood, and a wave of relief passed over her. "That's all right. I was just concerned when you didn't call, and then again when I couldn't get you to answer the phone." She laughed self-consciously. "I'm afraid I conjured up all sorts of reasons why you didn't answer."

Randi felt horrible. She knew that if she were in Kay's shoes, she might not be quite so forgiving. "I can't believe I did that. I don't even remember falling asleep."

"Honey, it's okay. Really." Kay quieted for a moment while the conversation played back in her mind. "Did you say you came home this afternoon? What happened?"

"Nothing serious," Randi assured her. "We didn't have any appointments this afternoon, and since I haven't been sleeping all that well, Christina thought it would be a good idea if I went home for a while." The silence on the other end of the phone worried her. "Kay? Are you still there?"

"Yes, I'm sorry. I was just thinking."

Lying back on the bed to get more comfortable, Randi fluffed her pillow. "What were you thinking about?"

"I just thought it was interesting that you haven't been sleeping. I'm having a bit of a problem with that myself," Kay said. Her sleep had been restless, and punctuated by waking up almost every hour all night long. She'd thought it was crazy, until she heard that Randi was having the same problem.

"You are?"

"Uh-huh."

"Oh." Randi took a moment to think about the implications of Kay's confession. *That must mean that she misses me as much as I miss her. Or, she's worried about her job.* "How's work?"

"Work?"

"Yeah. You like it there okay?"

"It's all right," Kay said. "Boring, but all right. Oh, I went to the doctor today. He told me that I should be out of my cast in the next couple of weeks."

Randi smiled at the excited tone in her friend's voice. "That's great news, Kay." She snuggled down on the bed. "Tell me all about it." They talked long into the night, each longing to tell the other something she was too afraid to voice.

Chapter
11

Another pile of papers was dropped onto her desk, and Kay looked up to see an apologetic Richard. "Gee, thanks."

"I'm sorry, Kay. I'll find some way of making it up to you," he promised.

She laughed. "No, that's all right. I just was hoping to get done fairly early tonight."

"Hot date?" Richard queried. He'd noticed that she kept no personal pictures on her desk, and according to the office grapevine, she never spoke of anyone special.

"Not exactly. I'm just expecting a long-distance call tonight, and wanted to get home and get a few things done first." She hated to think what Randi's phone bill was going to look like. The veterinarian had called her every evening, and they always spent several hours talking on the phone.

Richard nodding understandingly. "I see. Well, I won't keep you, then." He waved and wandered off, huming to himself.

A dark head poked over Kay's cubicle wall. "Oh, good. You've got the next batch already." Lucy Whitington was Kay immediate supervisor, and she couldn't believe how quickly Kay had caught on to their system. Married with four children, the forty-two-year-old woman always looked harried and rarely stopped for more than a moment. "Wednesday night is Ladies Night at Larson's, and a bunch of us are going to stop by for a quick drink tonight. Do you want to join us?"

Kay shook her head. "No, thank you. I can't."

Skirting the wall, Lucy pushed some papers out of the way and perched on the edge of Kay's desk. "Can I tell you something, Kay?"

"Sure. What's the problem?"

"Look. Some of the women in the office have been talking. They say you think you're better than everyone else, and that you're Richard's little pet. I was hoping you'd come with us and show them what I already know—that you're a good person." Lucy's dark eyes softened. She really liked Kay and wanted her to succeed. "Just come with us for one drink, then I'll take you home. Please?"

What could it hurt? I should still get back in plenty of time to talk to Randi. "All right. That sounds like fun," Kay said. "But I do have to be home pretty early tonight, if that's okay."

Lucy smiled widely. "Not a problem at all. I have to get home to the brood. But we like to go out as a group every now and then to keep things loose here at work." She tapped the desk and stood up. "You're going to have a great time, Kay. I guarantee it."

"I'm looking forward to it," Kay told the retreating woman. *Maybe I've passed their test, or something. It's about time.* She picked up the phone and dialed a number from memory.

"Hello?"

"Hi, Nancy."

A heavy sigh from the other end of the line expressed Nancy's feelings. "What is it, Katherine? *Judge Judy* comes on in five minutes, and I haven't seen this episode before."

What a lazy cow. "I just wanted to let you know that I won't need a ride home from work tonight, that's all. So you can go back to your stupid television show," Kay snapped, practically slamming down the receiver. "I hope it gets preempted," she grumbled.

"Randi? There's a call for you on line two," Christina announced as the vet walked by her desk. Before she could tell Randi who it was, the younger woman grabbed the phone.

"Hello?"

"Dr. Meyers? This is Anne Crawford. I called yesterday about my St. Bernard, Clarice?"

Shaking off her pang of disappointment that the caller wasn't Kay, Randi leaned against Christina's desk. "Yes, Ms. Crawford, I remember you. Didn't Dr. Wilde take care of Clarice last week?" She gratefully accepted the file from the secretary, quickly glancing through it. "It was just a routine spaying, wasn't it?"

"Yes, it was. But poor Clarice has been getting more and more listless, and just a few moments ago she started throwing up blood. I'm terribly worried about her." The woman's voice was steady, but she did sound upset. "And frankly, I didn't want to talk to that other doctor. He has ignored my calls the last couple of days."

Shit. "Okay. Can you get Clarice up here right away?" Randi exchanged worried glances with the receptionist.

"No, I can't. All I have is a sports car, and I don't know any-one that has a vehicle big enough to transport her. What am I going to do?"

Randi bit her lip in concentration. *Think.* She looked over at Dr. Wilde's closed door, and grinned. "Do we have your correct address?"

The woman paused for a moment. "I believe so. 1736 Sycamore. Why?"

"Because I'm on my way over with a nice big car," Randi assured her. "It should only take me about ten minutes to get there."

"Bless you, Dr. Meyers. We'll be waiting for you." The min-gled relief and concern were evident in her voice, and Randi quickly terminated the call, anxious to be on her way.

Christina shook her head. "You're not going to do what I think you are, are you?" She watched as Randi walked over to the coat rack and searched Dr. Wilde's coat pockets. "What if he finds out?"

"I don't have time to mess with him, Christina. It may already be too late for that poor dog." Randi pulled out the keys and waved them around. "I'll handle Dr. Asshole when I return." She rushed from the clinic without looking back.

Pulling up in front of a large, expensive home, Randi shook her head. *What in the hell was I thinking? I must be losing my mind.* "Maybe the lack of sleep these past few days is starting to wear on me," she mumbled as she walked up the steps. Before she reached the door, it opened, and a concerned dark-haired woman greeted her.

"Dr. Meyers?" she asked, looking at Randi. Her blue eyes were red-rimmed, and her shoulder-length brown hair was in dis-array. "Thank you so much for coming." She held the door open and ushered the vet into the home.

Randi glanced around as she followed Ms. Crawford through the house. Clarice's owner looked to be in her late twenties, and the jeans and sweatshirt she wore had several dark stains on them. *Probably the dog's blood. I hope we can save her.* She was led into a kitchen, where the St. Bernard lay panting in one corner on top of a soiled blanket.

"Here she is, Doctor," Ms. Crawford announced unnecessar-ily. "Clarice, sweetie, this nice lady is going to help you," she told the dog in a soft voice.

As Randi edged closer, baleful brown eyes tracked to her and the dog whined. "I know, girl. Just hang on." She reached down and placed her hand gently near the sutures, feeling the heat emanating from the spot. The hair was already starting to grow back where the incision had been made, and the stitches looked fine. *Has to be some sort of internal bleeding.* She turned to look at the woman. "We're going to have to take her in."

"How are we going to do that? She was able to climb into the car herself the last time. I don't think I'm strong enough to slide her across the floor, much less pick her up."

The vet eyed the other woman. *She's smaller than Kay, and would probably have trouble picking up Spike. How do I get myself into these things?* "Okay, what we're going to have to do is use the blanket as a type of stretcher. Do you think you can manage?"

"I'll manage," Ms. Crawford said grimly.

Kay looked around as she followed Lucy and some of the other women into the bar. Round tables surrounded by soft leather chairs filled the main room, and a tiny dance floor took up a few square feet of one corner. A long bar with mirrors behind it ran along the opposite wall, and there were only two or three tables being used. *Nice. Not at all like I expected.* She followed the women to the area away from the dance floor, where they pushed several of the tables together.

"So," one of the women across from Kay addressed her, "what happened to your leg?"

Nosy. Now, what was her name again? Oh, yeah. "I took a tumble down a hill and broke it. Irma, isn't it?" Kay responded sweetly.

The woman nodded. "Yeah. That's a shame. It must be tough to get around with that cast. Do you have anyone to help you, a boyfriend, maybe?" She looked around the table, as if to get up the nerve to ask something else, but stayed silent.

Before Kay could answer, Lucy walked up to the table with a tray of drinks. "Irma, why don't you get a life of your own, so you can quit worrying about everyone else's?" She handed Kay a glass of white wine.

"Thanks." Kay took the drink and placed it on the table, then looked across at Irma. "To answer your question, no, I don't have a boyfriend."

"Figures," Irma grumbled. She was about to make another snide comment, when a large group of people came in from outside and took up a couple of tables near the bar. One of them said something that caused several others to laugh out loud, and another woman at Kay's table shook her head.

"That's the only bad thing about coming in here," she complained. "We have to put up with the likes of them." An older woman, she touched one side of her industrial-strength sprayed hair as she glanced around the table. "It's getting so's a decent woman can't go out and have a little fun without being harassed."

Irma laughed. "You've got to be kidding, Judy. None of those grease-monkeys would have a thing to do with your withered old ass, anyway." She tilted up her drink and drained the glass.

Looking over at the group that had come in, Kay's eyes widened when she recognized one of the "grease monkeys." *Just great. Why is it my luck never seems to change?* She felt eyes on her and looked at Irma. "What?"

"Nothing. I was just wondering, since you don't have a boyfriend, do you have your sights set on Richard? After all, he does *own* the company. Be a nice way to get out of working, don't you think, ladies?" She looked around to see if the other women agreed, but no one else said a word. Glaring back at Kay, she snarled, "Well?"

"Shut up, Irma," Lucy snapped. "Leave the woman alone." She patted Kay on the hand. "Don't listen to her, honey. She's always bitchy."

Mary, the quietest of the group, looked up at Lucy through her wire-framed glasses. Her dark curly hair framed her face, and she kept playing with the napkin on which her glass was sitting. "He does seem to dote on her, Lucy. We've all seen it." She gave Kay an apologetic shrug. "No offense."

Unable to help herself, Kay laughed. "You think I'm after Richard?"

"Well, what do you expect us to think?" Judy asked. "We've seen how he acts around you. And we've never seen you with a boyfriend, or heard you speak of anyone else. You've got to admit, it does sound fishy."

Kay rubbed her forehead, feeling a familiar ache. *These women are just like my aunt: always seeing what they want to, and never listening to reason.* "You've never heard me speak of a boyfriend because I don't have one," she tried to explain. "That doesn't mean that I'm looking for one." She looked over at Lucy. "I'm really going to have to get home, if that's okay with you."

"Sure," Lucy said. "Let's go." She looked at the other women around the tables. "You should all make it a short night, ladies. Tomorrow's a work day."

"Yes, Mother," Irma grumbled. She waved the waitress over and ordered another round of drinks.

As they worked their way through the maze of chairs, Kay tried to keep Lucy between her and the boisterous table, hoping that she wouldn't be spotted.

The two women were almost to Lucy's car when her cell phone rang. "Hold on." She dug it out of her purse and flipped it open. "Hello?" Listening for a moment, she shook her head. "No, you listen to me. You tell Cindy that if the dishes aren't done by the time I get home, her butt will be grounded for a week!"

Kay was waiting impatiently, trying to keep from listening to Lucy's conversation, when a tap on her shoulder caused her to turn around. "Oh. Hi."

"Hi there yourself, Katie. Didn't think I'd be seeing you so soon," Beth said. She looked over at Lucy, who was still arguing on the phone, and frowned. "Got you another one, already? What ever happened to that obnoxious bitch with the Corvette?"

"Like it's any of your business, but Randi is back in Fort Worth," Kay said. "And Lucy is just a co-worker. Several of us went out for a drink tonight, that's all."

Beth grabbed Kay by the arm and pulled her closer. "Quit being so snotty, Katie. I care about you, and I don't want to see you hurt."

The smell of beer on her breath almost caused Kay to gag. "Let go of me, Beth." She was trying to twist away when Lucy turned around and saw the angry woman holding Kay by the arm.

"What the hell is going on here?"

"None of your damned business, lady. Katie and I are old friends." Beth squeezed Kay's arm until she cried out.

Lucy shook her head and waved her cell phone in the air. "I don't think so. Let her go, before I call the police."

"Tell her to get lost, or you'll both get hurt," Beth whispered angrily to Kay. She released the younger woman's arm and stepped back. "See? Just a misunderstanding, that's all."

Not convinced, Lucy flipped her phone open. "Get out of here."

The muscular woman glared at Lucy, but started to walk away. "I'll talk to you later, Katie," she called, before she stepped back into the bar.

"What was that all about?" Lucy asked, as she waited for Kay to get seated in her car. "How well did you know that drunken woman?"

Kay rubbed her arm where it had been grabbed. *Going to have a bruise there, I bet.* She sighed. "Too well, I'm afraid," she said. "Turn left at this light. I live a couple of miles past the cemetery."

"Okay." They drove along in silence for several minutes before Lucy's curiosity got the better of her. "Just how well is that?"

"What? Oh," Kay watched the passing scenery for a moment, then looked back over at the woman driving. "We lived together for several years. She's my ex-girlfriend."

Lucy was quiet for several minutes. When she was stopped by a red light, she turned in her seat to look at Kay. "Girlfriend? As in—"

"Lesbian," Kay supplied. "I'm gay."

"Oh." The light changed, and the car hurried down the road. "So, I guess that's why you're not interested in Richard, huh?"

Kay nodded. "Pretty much. Does it bother you?"

Thinking for a moment, Lucy frowned. "I'm not sure," she answered honestly. "I've never known a lesbian before."

"You probably have, but they just didn't tell you," Kay said.

"Gee, that's a nice thing to know," the dark-haired woman said sarcastically. "Were you ever going to tell us? Or were you just going to keep it a secret?"

"What does it matter? Why should I have told you?"

Lucy cut her eyes over at her passenger. "You just should have, that's all."

"Do you go around telling everyone that you meet that you're heterosexual?" Kay asked.

"Of course not!"

"Why not?"

"Because I don't have to," Lucy retorted.

Kay wasn't going to give up. "Why don't you?"

"Because they already know it, that's why." She turned the car onto the cemetery road and slowed down.

"Do they? Are you absolutely sure?" Kay pressed. "Or do you just assume that because you're heterosexual, everyone you know, and all of your friends, have to be too? Isn't that a little narrow-minded?" She looked up and pointed down the road. "My driveway is up there next to that mailbox."

Wordlessly, Lucy pulled her car into the graveled driveway. She stopped and put the vehicle in park, but wouldn't look at Kay.

"Thank you for the ride." Kay got out of the car, then turned back before closing the door. "I'm still the same person, Lucy. Just think about that, all right?" Not getting an answer, she closed the car door and started for the porch. The vehicle didn't leave until she was inside the house, but Kay realized with a sad heart that she had just lost another friend.

Exhausted, Randi walked out of the operating room and smiled at Ms. Crawford. Before she could speak to the woman, the door to Dr. Wilde's office opened and the furious man stepped in front of her.

"In my office at once, *Doctor* Meyers," he commanded in a cold tone.

Randi glared at him. "In a minute, Dr.—"

"*Now!*" he snapped, then turned and stalked back to his office, slamming the door behind him.

Ignoring the man completely, Randi turned her attention back to Ms. Crawford. "Clarice came through just fine," she assured the woman, who hugged the vet in exuberance.

"Thank you so much, Dr. Meyers," she gushed. "I don't know what to say."

"It's all right," Randi said, pulling back from the embrace. "I'm afraid it's going to take her a little longer to heal. I'd like to keep her here for a few days to keep a close eye on her."

Ms. Crawford nodded. "Yes, please. Whatever it takes." She touched the vet's arm. "I know you'll probably think I've lost my mind, acting like this over a silly animal. But she was the last gift my father gave me before he passed away, and she means everything to me."

Randi nodded. "I understand completely." She gently disengaged the woman's hand from her arm, uncomfortable at the attention. "There's going to be a significant scar, but barring any unforeseen complications, she should be as good as new in a few weeks."

"Thank you again." The petite woman looked at the closed office door. "You're in a lot of trouble for what you did today, aren't you?"

"I could be," the vet said. "But don't worry about it."

A wicked smile covered Ms. Crawford's face. "I'm not, and neither should you."

"What do you mean?"

"This clinic is owned by that other doctor, isn't it? The name outside is the same as his," Ms. Crawford asked. At Randi's nod, she continued. "You just tell him my name, and what you did for me." She hugged the vet again, and turned to walk out the door. "I'm going to go make a few phone calls, Dr. Meyers. By the time I get through with him, he's going to wish he never heard of me. Oh, and I'll be back a bit later to see Clarice, if it's okay."

"Uh, sure." Randi waved at the woman and looked over at Christina, who had a huge smile on her face. "What was that all about?"

The older woman shrugged her shoulders. "I'm sure I don't know, dear. Are you going home, now?"

"Not yet. I still have to listen to Dr. Asshole whine about something." Randi waved a hand and stepped into Dr. Wilde's office.

"Close the door," he ordered, leaning back in his chair.

Randi did as she was told, and leaned against the wood. "What is it that you want, Wilde? I was just on my way out."

"Truer words were never spoken, Dr. Meyers."

"What's that supposed to mean?" she asked, stepping further into the room until she was standing directly in front of the desk.

The smile that crossed his face was anything but friendly. "It means, that once and for all you've given me the perfect opportunity to get rid of you, and there's not a damned thing you can do about it." Dr. Wilde placed his elbows on the desk and rested his chin on his steepled fingers. "You're fired."

"Fired?" Randi laughed. "I pulled your sorry ass out of trouble, possibly saving you from an expensive lawsuit, and you're firing me? On what grounds?"

"Grand theft auto, for one. I'm still trying to decide whether or not to call the police and press charges. I have several witnesses."

Randi placed her hands on the desk and leaned forward. "I don't think anyone will testify to that, you pathetic asshole. As a matter of fact, *my* witnesses will testify that you offered me the use of your car."

He frowned. "So what? I still want you out of this clinic, Meyers. When I get through with you, there won't be a place that you'll be able to work in this entire state. Now get out of my sight!"

"Fine! But when you're up to your ears in patients, don't come crying to me to bail your worthless ass out again!" Randi turned from the room and slammed the door behind her. She yanked her jacket off the coat rack and slipped it on over her scrubs. "Goodbye, Christina. I'll be back later for my things." With another wave to Joyce, who had just stepped into the waiting room, Randi stalked out into the cool night air.

Kay hung up the phone, upset. It was just after eight o'clock in the evening, and Randi wasn't answering her phone. The confrontation with Lucy had upset her more than she cared to admit. The most upsetting part of all was that she hadn't gotten home in time for the phone call from Randi, which she desperately needed. Not knowing if Randi had called earlier or not, she vowed to buy a much-needed answering machine.

Depressed, Kay got undressed and climbed into bed, hoping that Randi would call her soon. "Where are you?" she asked the empty room, tears slowly tracking down her face. When the phone rang, she almost broke her other leg scrambling to pick it up. "Hello?"

"Katie? It's me."

Slamming the phone down in disgust, she fell back against the bed. "What part of no doesn't she understand?" The shrill ring drowned out her thoughts. "Hello?"

"Please, don't hang up," Beth pleaded. "I just want to talk to you."

"I think we said all we needed to say to each other earlier, thank you very much." Kay was about to slam the phone down again when she heard sniffling on the other end of the line. "Beth?"

"I'm sorry, baby. I didn't mean to act like such a pain in the ass tonight. Are you all right?"

Kay frowned at the phone. *This doesn't sound like Beth. I wonder what she's up to?* "I'm fine, Beth. But I really don't have anything else to say to you." She heard what sounded suspiciously like crying. "Are you okay?"

"No, I'm not," Beth said. "I need you, Katie. You don't know what I've been going through these past seven months; it's been hell without you."

"You should have thought of that before you started screwing around, Beth." Kay closed her eyes at the open weeping the other woman was doing. "Beth, stop it. Crying isn't going to help."

The older woman continued to cry. "I can't help it, Katie. You mean everything to me. I can't stand the thought of you with anyone else. Please, please, give me another chance."

"I can't, Beth. I don't love you," Kay said gently. "You don't want someone who doesn't love you, do you?"

"Just give me a chance, baby. I can make you love me again, I know I can."

Ouch. How do I tell her the truth? Just spit it out, I guess. "Beth, I cared for you, really. But I was never *in love* with you. I'm sorry."

The crying stopped. "What do you mean, you were never in love with me? Of course you were—we were together for so many years."

"No, I wasn't. I cared for you, but it wasn't love." Kay looked at the clock. *I need to try and call Randi again. She's probably worried sick.* "Beth, hang up the phone. We can talk again when you're not drunk."

"I'm not drunk," Beth argued, then belched. "I've had a couple of beers, but I'm not drunk. Not completely." She started to cry again. "And I'm not hanging up the phone until you tell me you love me, and that we'll get back together."

Oh, for God's sake. I don't need this tonight. "Beth, I'm never going to tell you either one of those things. Now hang up the phone, and get some rest. You'll feel better tomorrow."

"No."

"Please? I can't have my phone tied up all night." Kay could feel tears of frustration welling up in her eyes. *First that fight with Lucy, and now this. I can't take much more.* She held back a sob. *I need Randi.*

"Tell me you lo-ove me," Beth sang.

"I'm not going to do that, Beth. Please hang up the phone." Kay continued to fight her tears. "Please."

Beth belched again. "I'll be back in a minute," she said, then set down her phone. The sound of a car door opening could be heard.

Damn. She's on her stupid cell phone. She could be anywhere. "Beth? Are you there?" But all Kay could hear were cars driving by and drunken giggling.

Randi paced the floor of the apartment, checking her watch. "I don't like this," she told Spike, who was sitting on the sofa watching her with thoughtful eyes. "What's going on? I always call at seven, and now it's after ten. She can't have been on the phone all this time." She had rushed home from her office after the vicious argument with Dr. Wilde, and still wore her surgical scrubs as she stomped around the living room, dialing and re-dialing. Her nerves already shot from her earlier confrontation, Randi continued to try to call Kay all evening, with no success.

She considered calling the police, but didn't think they'd agree that it was an emergency. Exhausted, she sat down on the sofa and pulled Spike into her lap. "Do you think I'm losing it, boy? I'm sure there's a reasonable explanation why her phone has been busy all night." She leaned back and closed her eyes, the stress of the day beginning to catch up to her.

Hours later, the feeling of being watched caused Randi to open her eyes. A familiar figure stood next to the sofa, his sad eyes focused intently on her. Randi wracked her brain to remember his name. "Jared? What are you doing here?"

"Kiki's so sad," he said, tears in his eyes. "She needs you."

"What do you mean?" Randi sat up and reached for him, but he backed away. "No, wait!" She fell back against the sofa. "Please, tell me, Jared. Is something wrong with Kay?"

"She needs you," he repeated.

Shit. Playing Twenty Questions with a boy who's been dead for five years isn't my idea of fun. "Okay, Jared, we've established that she needs me. But is she hurt? Is someone threatening her? What?"

He shook his head. "Kiki needs you. Her heart hurts."

"Her heart? Is she having heart problems, Jared?" When the boy started to fade away, she reached out for him again. "No, wait! Tell me, please! What's wrong with Kay?"

She needs you...

Waking up with a start, Randi blinked several times and looked around the dark living room. "Shit."

Spike woke up from his warm nest in her lap and looked up at her. He yawned and then dropped his head back down onto her legs.

"That was creepy," Randi told the dog, who continued to ignore her. "Was it a dream? It sure seemed real enough," she mumbled, placing Spike gently on the floor and then standing up.

After splashing water on her face, Randi glanced at the clock in the bedroom and saw that it was almost one o'clock in the morning. Concerned, she picked up the phone and hit the speed dial for Kay's again. The obnoxious beeping tones made Randi slam it down again in disgust. "Still busy? What the hell is going on?"

Spike jumped up on the bed and barked.

"You think so too, huh?" Randi picked up the dog and carried him out of the room. "That's it, buddy. We're taking a road trip."

Pulling into the outskirts of Woodbridge, Randi rubbed her tired eyes. "What the hell was I thinking? Driving halfway across Texas in the middle of the night, just because a phone was busy?" *And all because I may or may not have been visited by the ghost of Kay's dead brother. Was it a dream? Or...* Randi shook her head. *I don't think I want to know the answer to that.* She looked down at

Spike, who stretched and yawned. "Don't look at me like that. It was just as much your idea as it was mine." She drove the loop around the sleepy city and took the exit for the cemetery.

"I've spent the last two hours talking to a dog. I must be losing my mind." Since the interstate was practically deserted, Randi had enjoyed using the powerful engine to cut some time off her trip. She was quite thankful that the Highway Patrol had better things to do than run speed traps on the roadways, although that wouldn't have stopped her from trying to get to Woodbridge as soon as she possibly could.

The deserted road that led to Kay's house was so dark that she had to slow down in order to see, and she almost missed the familiar tow truck that was parked just before the entrance to Kay's driveway. Randi reached across the seat and held Spike, while she slammed on the brakes. "Hold on, buddy. I need to check something out." She turned off the engine but left the lights on. "I'll be right back."

Walking up to the darkened cab, Randi pounded on the door. "Beth? Are you in there?" She continued to beat her hand against the metal.

"Stop it," a pitiful moan begged from inside.

"Dammit, Beth! Open this goddamned door!" Randi used her fist and kept slamming it into the door.

"Nooo."

The angry and exhausted vet jerked on the handle of the door and was startled when Beth came tumbling out on top of her. Randi lay on the blacktopped road, squirming to shove the dead weight off. The heavy smell of stale beer almost made her sick. "Jesus! What the hell are you doing out here?"

Beth belched and swallowed the bile that rose in her throat. "You're in Worth Fort," she groaned. "How'd I get there?"

"That's Fort Worth, dumb ass. Now get off me, you drunken idiot," Randi complained, finally worming her way out from underneath the inebriated woman. She grabbed Beth by the front of her shirt and pulled her into a sitting position. "What the hell are you doing out here? Is Kay all right?"

"I just want her to love me," Beth whined. "That's all." She struggled to stand up, glaring at Randi. "But no, she wouldn't. It's all your fault, you bitch!" she screamed, running at Randi and swinging her arms.

Although she was tired, Randi had no problem avoiding Beth's pitiful attempts at a fight. When the drunken woman charged her again, Randi used her hands to push her into the side of the truck, causing Beth to fall to the ground and start crying.

"You're a mean bitch," she moaned, holding her head in her hands. "Kay deserves better than you." Beth continued to cry as Randi helped her back into the truck. "I love her."

"So do I," Randi said to her quietly. "Now just lie down and sleep. You'll feel better when you wake up." She knew it was a lie and actually, she found herself wishing the worst hangover of all time on Beth. Waiting until the drunk did as she was asked, Randi reached into the ignition and removed the keys. She placed them on the back bumper of the truck. *I'll call her office and tell the dispatcher where the keys are, after she's had time to sober up. No sense in taking any chances.*

She got back in the Corvette and looked over at Spike, who stood with his front paws on the windowsill of his side of the car, his tail wriggling furiously. "You know where we are, don't you, Spike?" His whine caused Randi to smile for the first time that evening. "Come on, let's go check on Kay."

Pulling up to the dark house, Randi debated whether to knock on the door, or wait until daylight. "What do you think, buddy? Now, or wait?"

Spike looked at the house and barked. His tail continued to quiver, and he kept jumping from one foot to the other.

"I guess that's one vote for 'now,'" she laughed. "Come on."

Randi stood at the front door with Spike squirming in her arms. She raised one shaky hand and firmly knocked on the door. *Come on, Kay. Be home. Be okay. Please.* She was about to knock again when the porch light lit up and almost blinded her. The front door swung open, causing the animal in her arms to bark again.

"Randi?" Kay gasped, bringing one hand to her mouth in shock. "Is it really you?" Clad only in a long T-shirt, she looked like she had just awakened, which, considering the time, was highly likely.

"Uh, yeah. Are you all right? I got home a little late tonight and didn't call when I was supposed to. Then, when I finally got home, I kept trying to call, and—"

Kay grabbed the babbling woman and pulled her inside. "Get in here, you nut!" After slamming the door closed, she wrapped her arms around Randi. "Oh, God, I'm so damned glad to see you," she said, almost crushing Spike in the process. Both women laughed as the miniature Dobie barked his protest.

After closing the door, Randi put Spike on the floor and followed Kay over to the sofa. "I'm sorry to be barging in like this in the middle of the night, but I was worried."

"Is that dried blood?" Kay asked, touching the scrubs that

Randi still wore. She shook her head at the sheepish expression. "It's not yours, is it?"

"Uh, no. I had an emergency surgery this afternoon. That's why I was late calling." Randi pulled Kay close to her and buried her face in the blonde hair. "I really missed you."

"I missed you, too. This day has been awful." Kay wrapped her arms around the other woman and enjoyed the feeling of being in Randi's arms. "How did you know I needed you?"

Randi opened her eyes and frowned. "I'm not sure. It could have been a dream, or maybe a premonition." *Or a little help from a friend.* "Can we talk about it more tomorrow? I'm really beat." After the adrenaline had worn off, Randi felt as if she had run a marathon—in mud. Her exhaustion was so complete, she felt as if she could fall asleep sitting up.

"That's a good idea. Tomorrow is soon enough," Kay said. She stood, then reached out and smiled when Randi took her hand. "Come on. No more couch for you."

Suddenly awake, Randi blinked. "What? But—"

Kay laughed. "Don't look so scared, Doc. Just come to bed with me. I'm not going to ravish you." She winked. "At least, not until we can both enjoy it."

"Oh boy," Randi muttered, a stupid smile on her face. She dutifully followed Kay into the bedroom and stood while the younger woman climbed into the bed and got comfortable.

"Well?" Kay patted the space beside her. "Take off those nasty clothes and climb in. We'll worry about getting you something else to wear tomorrow."

Randi quickly shed her shoes and sat on the edge of the bed. "Kay, I—"

"Shhh. We'll talk tomorrow, okay?" Kay waited until Randi had stripped off the bloody scrubs and crawled under the covers then patted herself on the chest. "Nice soft pillow," she said, wanting the chance to hold the vet in her arms all night. "I promise I don't snore."

"Oh boy," Randi repeated, snuggling up beside her. She dropped her head onto Kay's chest and rested her arm across the flat stomach. "Just let me know if I squash you."

Kay started playing with Randi's hair. "No chance of that, honey. Now get some sleep." The soft snores that answered her caused a tender smile to etch itself on Kay's face. "Goodnight, my hero." With a quick glance at the foot of the bed where Spike had curled up, Kay kissed the top of the unruly locks and closed her eyes as well.

Chapter
12

Caught between wakefulness and sleep, Randi tried to snuggle deeper into her pillow, then realized it was warm, and...moving? She slowly opened her eyes and saw lacy white underwear. Somehow during the night, Kay's sleepshirt had ridden up, and Randi had made herself at home on her bare stomach. *Oh boy.* A quick glance up at Kay's sleeping face assured her that she hadn't been noticed, so Randi closed her eyes and relaxed.

Waking up lying next to Kay was one of the best feelings she had ever experienced, but Randi was still a bit uncertain about where their relationship was heading. *Although, I guess I don't have a job to worry about right now,* she thought ruefully. Now that she was able to think more clearly, the vet realized that she wasn't ready to give up everything she'd worked so hard for so easily. *I'll worry about it later. Right now, I've got some serious snuggling to catch up on.*

It seemed as if she had just fallen back asleep when the blare of the alarm clock caused Randi's eyes to pop open again. Her head was still resting comfortably on Kay's stomach, and part of her wanted to stay in that position all day. Before she could sit up, she felt the gentle touch of fingers combing through her thick hair. Unable to stop a smile from spreading across her face, Randi felt her "pillow" move as Kay chuckled softly.

"Good morning," Kay whispered. She continued her light ministrations until Randi turned her head.

"Morning," Randi drawled, the soft tickle of her breath causing goose bumps to rise on Kay's stomach.

Kay brushed the hair out of Randi's eyes and then continued to caress her face. "You still look worn out," she observed. There were dark circles underneath the bloodshot brown eyes, and a resigned weariness that she hadn't seen before.

"I am," Randi sighed. "But I guess I'd better let you up, huh?" She started to sit up, but was held down by Kay's hand.

"No, don't."

"But you need to get ready for work," Randi argued. "I don't want to be the cause of you getting into any trouble your first week on the job." To her dismay, tears began to slide down Kay's cheeks. "Hey, what's wrong?" She quickly scrambled into a sitting position and pulled Kay into her arms.

"It's stupid," Kay sniffled. The harder she tried to get her emotions under control, the further away she felt them slipping. "Damn."

Randi held the crying woman close to her chest, murmuring words of encouragement and softly rubbing Kay's back. She looked down at Spike, who had wandered up from his sleeping place at the foot of the bed and now looked at Kay. Randi made a slight shooing motion with one hand, and the little dog yawned and went back to his previous spot.

After several minutes, Kay finally calmed down enough to talk. "Ever since I started this job, the other women in the office have been pretty distant. I thought they were just giving me time to get settled in my job before they started to try and get to know me, but then I found out last night that wasn't the case."

"What do you mean?" Randi asked, getting angry. "What happened last night?"

"My supervisor, Lucy, asked me to join some of them after work. They like to go to a bar for Ladies Night, have a couple of drinks, and socialize for a bit outside of the office."

No wonder she wasn't home when I called last night. "That's great, sweetheart. So you went out with the ladies for a bit of fun?"

Kay nodded. "I didn't want to, but Lucy told me that the other women thought I was being stuck up." She looked up into Randi's eyes and frowned. "Me, of all people." With a heavy sigh, she once again leaned against her friend. "So, Lucy promised me that we'd only stay for a few minutes, then she'd take me home." Here, Kay started crying again.

"What happened?"

"It would probably be easier to tell you what *didn't* happen. The entire night was a disaster from the beginning."

Randi held Kay a little tighter. "Go ahead, Kay. Let it all out."

"One of the women, Irma, started in on me almost before we sat down. She kept asking me all of these personal questions, which I wasn't comfortable answering."

"None of her damned business anyway," Randi grumbled. She looked down into Kay's amused eyes. "I'm sorry. Go ahead."

I may have to have a little talk with this Irma.

Patting her protector on the stomach, Kay continued. "Well, she and a couple of the other women got it into their heads that I was interested in Mr. Stone, just because he's been so nice to me. Then they started asking if I had a boyfriend, and—"

"What did you tell them?"

"That no, I didn't, and it wasn't any of their business, anyway."

Randi snickered. "Good for you. Bunch of dried up old prudes."

Another heavy sigh. "You can say that again. But then, I saw Beth come into the bar with a bunch of the guys she works with—didn't take them long to get pretty wasted."

"Yeah, I know."

"What?" Kay looked back up at Randi.

"Nothing," the vet evaded. When Kay continued to look at her, Randi sighed. "I'll tell you when you're finished with your story, all right?"

Kay frowned, but nodded. "Okay." She thought for a moment. "Anyway, I was tired of the Inquisition, and asked Lucy if she'd mind taking me home. We'd almost made it to her car when Beth came up behind me and stopped us."

"Uh-oh."

"Yeah, uh-oh is right. She was on her way to being real drunk, and was pretty obnoxious. Grabbed my arm and threatened to hurt me and Lucy if I didn't do what she wanted."

"That bitch," Randi shouted, sitting up straighter. "Did she hurt you?"

Shaking her head, Kay showed her arm. There was a light discoloration, but it didn't look serious. "She didn't get a chance. Lucy waved her cell phone in Beth's face and threatened to call the police. She took off after that."

"Lucy sounds like a smart lady."

"I thought so, too, until the ride home," Kay said quietly.

"Why? What happened then?"

The wounds from last night reopened, and Kay felt her emotions crumble again. "I thought she was my friend, but she's just as narrow-minded as the rest of them."

I'm definitely going to have to make a trip up to that damned office. Bunch of old harpies have nothing better to do than hurt innocent people. "What did she say?"

"After we left Beth, Lucy asked me how I knew her. So, I told her the truth."

" I bet that went over well," Randi said. "Did she freak out?"

Kay sighed. "No. Well, maybe. Actually, she got all pissed off because I didn't tell her I was gay sooner."

"What the hell does that have to do with anything?" Randi asked, outraged. "You've only worked there for a few days. Does she think we make it a habit of going around and telling complete strangers our life histories? What kind of fucked up standards are those?"

"Exactly. I told her I didn't think it was anyone's business but my own, and then I asked her if she went around telling people she was straight."

Randi laughed. "Serves her right."

"Yeah," Kay said sadly. She brushed the tears from her face and released a heavy breath. "It really hurt, though. She was one of the only people in the office, besides Richard, who treated me nicely."

Okay, chickenshit, here's your opening. Try not to blow it this time. Randi kissed the top of Kay's head and squeezed her close again. "Do you like the job?"

"It's okay. Not really what I'd want to do with my life, but I guess it'll do until I find something else." Kay looked up into Randi's face. "What?"

Taking a deep breath to bolster her courage, Randi smiled at her friend. "Kay, these past few days have made me stop and think about what's important in my life. Up until a few weeks ago, I would have told you that my work was the only thing I truly cared about." Seeing the acceptance on Kay's face, she continued. "Meeting you has changed all of that."

"It's done the same for me," Kay said quietly.

"I'm glad." Randi bent her head and kissed Kay softly on the lips. "I love you, Kay. I have for a while, but I was too chicken to admit it."

Kay's smile grew. "I love you, too, Randi." She laughed at the look on the older woman's face. "Guess we've both been pretty chicken, haven't we?" She was answered by another kiss, this one much longer.

Glancing in the bathroom mirror at the image behind her, Kay smiled. "Are you sure you don't mind? I'd be glad to stay home with you today."

Randi shook her head. "No, you were right. If you decide to quit, do it on your own terms, not on the basis of how ignorant your coworkers are." She pushed off from the door frame that she had been leaning against and walked up behind Kay to put her hands on her shoulders. "Besides, if they get too obnoxious, I can just kiss you goodbye at the front door of Stone's Accounting and give them something to talk about."

"That could be fun," Kay said. She turned around and studied Randi's attire. "You want to just strip and wash those while I'm gone?" Embarrassed by being only in her undergarments, Randi had pulled on her dirty scrubs when she got out of bed.

A smirk answered her. "You trying to get me out of my clothes?"

Kay reached up and laced her fingers behind Randi's head. "If I was trying to do that, do you think I'd be getting ready for work?" She pulled Randi closer and kissed her thoroughly. When she pulled away, Kay was quite proud of the dazed look on her friend's face. "So, what are you going to do while I'm trying to work?"

"Huh?" Randi blinked several times and licked her lips, but couldn't seem to lose the silly grin that covered her face.

"I asked," Kay started for the bedroom, poking Randi in the stomach on her way by, "what are you going to do while I am at work?"

"Oh." Randi watched as Kay sat on the edge of the bed and put her one shoe on. "I thought I'd go pick up a few things, then come back here and change."

Shoe tied, Kay stood up and ran her hands down the navy blue, knee-length skirt she wore that complemented her ivory silk blouse. "That sounds like a good idea." She paused for a moment, then asked in a quiet voice, "How long will you be staying?"

Randi pulled on her old leather sneakers without untying them. "Actually, if you don't mind, I'd kind of like to take you out to dinner tonight to talk about that. What do you say?"

"Works for me."

"Cool." Randi followed Kay into the living room and bent to pick up Spike, who had jumped down from his perch on the bed and followed them. "I'd better grab some chow for this guy, too. He gets grumpy if he misses a meal." She scratched the wriggling animal behind the ears. "Right, buddy?" Spike licked her hand and looked up at Randi with complete hero worship in his eyes.

Kay laughed and grabbed her purse, slipping the strap over one shoulder. "If you two can be separated long enough, you want to drive me to work?" she teased.

"I don't know," Randi deadpanned. "We're pretty close." She walked over and held the animal up to Kay's face. "Think you can compete?"

Kay took Spike and kissed the top of his head. "Can you?"

"Brat."

A few minutes later, Randi pulled the Corvette onto the main road and it wasn't until then that Kay noticed Beth's tow truck. Frowning, she stared at it as they drove by. "I can't believe she parked that close to my house last night."

"You knew she was out there?" the vet asked, continuing down the road without another glance back.

"Not exactly. I knew she was out in her truck somewhere, because she called me last night from her cell phone. She refused to hang up unless I told her I loved her and that we'd get back together."

Randi nodded, but didn't say anything. She continued to keep her eyes on the road, but listened carefully to every word.

Kay looked at her for a moment, then sighed. "She must have followed me home last night. She kept crying and begging me to take her back. I kept telling her I didn't love her, but she wouldn't listen." The stony silence from Randi was beginning to worry her. "I'm sorry, Randi. If I would have just lied to her, she would have probably gotten off the phone, and you wouldn't have had to drive down here in the middle of the night."

"Don't apologize." Randi looked over at Kay and smiled. "The trip was well worth it."

"But what about your job?"

"It's not that important," Randi assured her, turning her attention back to the road. "Besides, I may have to find another job."

"What happened?"

Her eyes still on the road, Randi shrugged. "Got into another argument with Dr. Ass...I mean, Dr. Wilde. I 'borrowed' his car to pick up a patient, and he got all bent out of shape."

"You what? Why would you do that?"

"Because," Randi snapped, "if I hadn't, that dog would have died. And it was his fault."

Kay looked down at her lap. "Oh. I'm sorry, Randi, I—"

"No," Randi pulled the car over and reached for Kay's hand. "I'm sorry. I guess I'm just tired and cranky. Forgive me?"

Smiling, Kay raised their joined hands to her lips and kissed Randi's knuckles. "Of course. But why did you borrow his car?"

"Because it was a St. Bernard. There was no way I could have gotten her into my car."

"Ahh. So, is the dog okay?"

Another reason I love her. She cares about animals, too. How did I ever get so lucky? "Yeah. She'll be just fine, as long as Dr. Wilde doesn't try to treat her in the future," Randi finished bitterly. She was remembering how much grief Melissa would give her whenever she'd have to work late. *"They're just stupid animals. I should be more important to you than playing with smelly animals all day,"* her ex used to say. She looked over at Kay and nodded her head slowly. *Yup, I'm sure lucky. Very lucky.* Becoming conscious of the time, Randi edged back onto the road.

They drove in silence for several minutes, Randi thinking about the argument with Dr. Wilde, and Kay worried about going back in to work. "Which way?" Randi asked, once they got to a light.

"Turn left, then go about six blocks to Holiday, then turn right. It's the first building on the right after that."

"All right." Randi followed the directions until they were parked in front of Stone's Accounting. "Do you want me to go in with you?" she asked.

Kay shook her head. "No, I'll be all right. But thanks." She'd started to get out of the car when Randi's voice stopped her.

"I'm going to Price Mart to grab a few things, then I'll be back at your house." Randi held up the key chain that Kay had given her earlier. "Shouldn't take more than an hour, okay? So just call me if you need me."

Leaning back into the car, Kay smiled. "I'll always need you," she whispered. "But I think things will be all right." She winked and straightened up, closing the door behind her.

"They will be now," Randi said, watching the younger woman make her way into the building. "I'll see to it."

Although she had only been there for an hour, Kay felt as if every eye in the room was focused on her. *I wonder if Lucy told everyone my "dirty little secret." Or maybe they all still think I'm interested in Richard.* She shook her head. *He's old enough to be my father. Even if he were my type, he's way too old.*

"Ahem."

Kay looked up and saw Lucy standing by her desk. Still hurt from the previous day's events, she decided to keep a professional distance. "Yes?"

"Look, I think we need to clear the air," the older woman stated quietly.

"You think?" Kay muttered, grabbing a stack of papers and shuffling them. "Or did you just come over here to enlighten me on the sins of my lifestyle?"

Lucy had the good grace to be embarrassed. "I guess I deserved that." She looked around the room. "Can we go outside to talk? Too many nosy people in here."

"Sure." Kay put down her pen and followed Lucy out to the front of the building. She leaned back against the brick with her arms crossed over her chest and stared at the other woman until Lucy looked away. "Well?"

With a heavy sigh, Lucy looked around until her eyes finally rested on Kay's features. "I don't know where to begin. This is hard for me," she started, but was interrupted.

All the hurt and anger that was welling up inside Kay demanded to be released. "Hard for *you*? Lady, you have no idea what hard is," Kay said. "Hard is growing up feeling responsible for your mother's death, or getting a call at work and being told your little brother was killed by a drunk driver." She pointed an angry finger in Lucy's face. "Hard is coming to terms with your own sexuality and having it thrown in your face at every opportunity—even by people you thought were your friends." Kay took a deep breath to calm down. "Hard is finally finding the one person in the world who makes you feel whole, and living two hundred miles apart. Don't try and tell me what's hard." Emotionally spent, she fell back against the wall and closed her eyes, until a light touch on her arm caused them to open again.

Lucy looked at her with tears in her eyes. "You don't have to get all bent out of shape. I just wanted to apologize for yesterday. I'm sorry for the way I acted."

Kay frowned. "For the way you acted? Like I was some sort of leper, or something?"

"Kay, listen. You caught me off guard yesterday with that little bombshell. How was I supposed to act?"

"Like a friend?" came the soft response.

Lucy lowered her head. "I don't understand you, Kay. I thought you were like me."

"And how's that?" Years of being labeled "different" finally put Kay at the breaking point. "Did you think I was narrow-minded and hypocritical? Or maybe self-centered and judgmental?"

"Hold on! You've got this chip on your shoulder, and when someone finally sees it, you get all militant and hateful. You're no better than I am, Kay."

Kay raised sad eyes and shook her head. "But I'm no worse, either." She lifted one hand and wiped at her face. "No one's the same. We just have to be able to accept each other's differences and learn to get along."

"I don't know if I can," Lucy said honestly. "I really liked you."

"Past tense? Liked? What's changed about me? Is it because of who I decide to sleep with?"

Lucy frowned and backed away. "Please, I don't want to hear about that."

Kay stalked forward. "Do you think it's any easier for me to listen to all of you compare notes on your husbands' lovemaking skills? Why is there such a double standard?"

"I don't know!" Lucy said, covering her face with her hands. "I don't know," she repeated, more quietly.

Feeling sorry for the other woman, Kay reached out for her, but drew her hand back before she made contact. "All I want is to be treated with a little decency and respect. Is that too much to ask?" She waited until Lucy looked at her and held up a hand. "Just forget it." Kay started to walk back into the building.

"I'll try," Lucy's anguished voice followed.

Kay turned around at the door and looked back. "So will I," she said, limping back inside the office. She had just passed Irma's desk when she heard a quiet voice.

"Dyke."

Turning around, Kay glanced back behind her. All heads were faced away, although she had a pretty good idea who had said it. Disgusted, she ignored the dig and continued on to her desk.

Richard stood up from where he was squatting to look through the bottom drawer of a filing cabinet. His eyes searched around the room, watching Kay's progress. Looking around again, he followed her. "Kay?"

She stopped just as she reached her desk and glanced over her shoulder. "Yes, Richard?"

"Can I see you in my office?"

Great. Just what I need. "Sure." Kay sighed and followed him, unsure of what was going to happen next.

Chapter
13

Richard held his office door open for the fuming woman. "Sit down, Kay." He waited until she was seated, then walked around his desk and dropped gracelessly into his chair.

Tired and on edge, Kay decided the best defense was a good offense. "So, are you going to start on me, too?" she asked.

"Start on you?" Richard leaned forward and frowned. "What do you mean by that?"

"I'm sure you heard what Irma said about me," Kay said. "This meeting is just a little too coincidental."

He pulled on one earlobe and looked at the woman sitting across the desk from him. "All right, Kay. Yes, I heard someone use a derogatory term. But the main reason I wanted to talk to you was that you seem to be upset today. What's going on?"

Kay leaned forward, angry. "You want to know what's going on? I'm gay, Richard. You might as well know, because obviously the entire company has made it their business to know. There's a dyke, a faggot, a queer, a...lesbian, in your midst."

"So?" Richard leaned back and sighed. "Does it affect how you do your job?"

Caught off guard by the question, Kay fell back in her seat as she felt her anger dissipate. "Uh, no."

"Are you going to be lusting after the other women in the office?" he asked, with a smile on his face.

Unable to help herself, Kay chuckled. "Definitely not."

Richard leaned across the desk. "Me, either," he whispered loudly. After they shared a laugh, he stood up. "Kay, I don't care if you're a cross-dressing atheist who likes to bicycle nude on weekends; as long as you do your job, I'll be happy."

Kay sat very quietly for a moment. *Even though Richard seems supportive, do I really want to work in a hostile setting? Will I be happy with these bitchy women on my case, day in and day out? There's really nothing keeping me here.* "No," she answered aloud.

"What?" He looked confused as he stepped around the desk.

"I'm sorry, Richard." Kay stood. "I respect you, and I think you're a fine person. But I just can't work in this environment." She held out her hand and smiled when it was accepted. "Thank you for everything."

He walked over and held open the door for her. "I hate to see you go, Kay. What will you do?"

Blue eyes looked up and sparkled. "I have some pretty good options, I think." She winked. "Thanks again. I'll just go clean out my desk and then call my ride."

"Good luck, Kay." Richard called after her. He looked at the women sitting in the front of the office. "Time for some house-cleaning, I think."

When she pulled up to Kay's house, the body language of the woman on the front porch should have warned Randi to stay in the car. The hung over mechanic was seated on the second step from the top, leaning back on her arms. Her eyes snapped open when she heard tires crunching gravel.

Randi had spent over an hour buying clothes, toiletries, dog food, and the like; and all she wanted to do was get inside and feed Spike. She stepped out of the bright yellow vehicle, then reached back in and retrieved several plastic bags. "Excuse me," she muttered, trying to step around the reclining body. Fumbling the front door open, she didn't see her unwelcome guest climb to her feet to follow her inside. Spike's excited bark welcomed the vet, who struggled with the bags in her hands.

"Where the fuck's my truck keys?" Beth yelled, shoving Randi in the back and causing her to fall into the lamp, knocking it to the floor.

That's it. I've about had it with Miss Manners. Randi slowly got to her feet and looked down at the broken lamp. "You're going to have to pay for that, Beth."

The muscular woman stood a few feet away, her arms crossed over her chest. "Oh yeah? You gonna make me?"

"I'm not getting into a pissing contest with you." The smell of stale beer turned Randi's stomach. "Why don't you go home and get cleaned up?"

"I would, if I knew where my goddamned truck keys were!" She started toward Randi, but was stopped by the small canine growling at her feet. "You've got to be fucking kidding me," she laughed, kicking out at Spike.

The dog barely escaped the heavy boot, but continued to bark.

Randi rushed over and picked up Spike. "Don't you *dare* touch my dog," she shouted, holding him close to her body.

"That little thing is a dog?" Beth laughed. "I've stepped on bigger cockroaches."

"Then you need to clean house more often," Randi retorted, backing away.

"Bitch! I'm going to take care of you once and for all." Beth rushed forward and shoved Randi again, smirking as the older woman twisted at the last minute as she tried to break her fall and protect the dog in her arms. She got a sense of smug satisfaction out of the pained grunt that escaped Randi's lips.

Fighting the nausea caused by the throbbing pain in her knees, Randi grimaced and shakily released Spike, who stood in front of her protectively, still barking at Beth. "Spike, hush."

Spike turned and looked at her, then whined. He dropped down on his rear, but continued to growl at the tow truck driver.

"Who's gonna protect you now, old woman?" Beth laughed, as Randi slowly climbed to her feet.

"I'm not going to fight with you, Beth," Randi said, backing up painfully. "I'm sorry about your keys. I left them on the back bumper of your truck because you were too drunk to drive last night, and I didn't want you out on the roads."

Beth frowned. "Yeah, right. You expect me to believe that you give a damn what happens to me? I'm the competition."

"There is no competition. I know we're never going to be friends; but there's no reason you have to keep trying to rip me apart, either. Like you said, I'm an old woman." *I'm too old to be brawling like a teenager. This is ridiculous.* As the other woman started forward again, she held out a hand. "You say you want Kay back?"

"Hell, yeah." Beth started forward again. "And the sooner I get you out of the picture, the sooner she'll come back to me."

Randi limped away from her. "Do you really think that beating the hell out of me is going to accomplish that?" She stood behind the recliner, trying to keep a barrier between her and the unreasoning woman.

Confused, Beth stopped. "Why wouldn't it?"

Maybe I can get her to listen to reason. "What's one of the things you love about Kay?"

Beth smiled lasciviously. "She's got a great ass."

It took all her self-control for Randi not to roll her eyes at that answer. "Okay. What else?"

Beth thought for a moment. "She's really sweet. I don't think I've ever met anyone as nice as Katie."

"That's right. She's kind and gentle. Do you think violence would appeal to her?" *Dear God, please let her be able to put more than one thought together at a time. I'm running out of ideas, here.*

"She doesn't have to know." Beth edged around the coffee table on her way to the recliner.

Randi shook her head, her heart pounding in fear at what Beth could do to her. "She'll know. And then you'll never have a chance of getting her back."

The ringing of the phone caused both women to jump. "I'd better get that," Randi said. "It's probably Kay."

Beth frowned. She didn't want to completely ruin her chances with the woman she loved. She backed up until she was at the front door. Pointing a warning finger at Randi, she threatened, "I'll be back for you later." She rushed through the door and down the driveway, deciding she needed a new plan to reclaim the woman she loved.

Randi limped over to grab the ringing phone. "I take back every nasty thought I've ever had about phones," she muttered.

The bright yellow Corvette screeched to a stop in front of the accounting office. Kay couldn't help but smile at her friend's protective streak as Randi jumped out of the car almost before the engine died.

"Are you all right?" Randi asked breathlessly. "Sorry it took me so long to get here."

Kay glanced at her watch as Randi picked up the paper bag that contained the few belongings she'd had at the office. "Honey, any faster and you would have been here before I called. I'm fine." Her smile didn't waver as Randi held open the car door for her. "I didn't realize you'd be bringing my favorite guy along, too," she teased, scooping up Spike before he could escape.

"I didn't feel comfortable leaving him at the house," Randi said before she closed the door. She circled around the car and got in behind the wheel. "I hope you don't mind."

"Not at all." Kay held the excited animal close, trying to calm him down. "Did he have an accident this morning?" She couldn't think of any other reason that Randi might not want him to stay behind.

Randi shook her head. "No." Not wanting to talk about the trouble she'd had with Beth, she nodded toward the building.

"What happened in there?" Although Kay had sounded perfectly calm when she called to be picked up, she had explained that she had quit.

"Let's just say I didn't want to be a part of a hostile work environment, and leave it at that, okay?"

"Hostile? Were they giving you a hard time because they found out you were gay?" Randi slapped the steering wheel. "Maybe I should go in there and show them 'hostile.'"

Kay reached over and grabbed Randi by the arm. "No, wait. Please." She waited until the stormy brown eyes calmed slightly. "Richard was very sweet and tried to talk me into staying, but I just didn't feel like this was the right place for me." Kay squeezed the arm she was still holding. "Let's get out of here, all right?"

"Okay, but only if you're sure." After the confrontation with Beth earlier, Randi still felt like she needed to release some excess energy. Backing the car out of the parking space, she asked, "Do you know of any little parks around here? I think Spike could use some fresh air." *Not to mention that I think I could, too.*

Not fooled, Kay nodded. "Sure. There's one on the way to the mall. Just turn left at the light."

"Cool."

Following Kay's directions, they were able to pull into a parking lot next to a quiet park a few minutes later. Only a couple of cars were in evidence, giving Randi her choice of spaces. Mostly grass and trees, the area was practically deserted except for a few joggers passing by periodically on a paved path. Randi glanced around and noticed a picnic table nearby. "How about we sit over there, and I'll just let the lead out on Spike's leash?"

"Sounds good to me," Kay said.

They sat silently for several minutes, watching the dog run out as far as the lead would allow. Spike would stand fearlessly and bark at the passing runners, some of whom glanced down and smiled as they jogged by.

"He's a protective little thing, isn't he?" Kay marveled, amazed at the courage the diminutive animal possessed.

"Too much, sometimes," Randi said. "I'm afraid his heart is bigger than his brain, and that could get him seriously hurt someday."

The sad tone in Randi's voice concerned Kay. "What do you mean?"

Turning her head, Randi looked into Kay's eyes for a long moment before she spoke. "We had a little visit from Beth this morning."

"Beth? What on earth did she want?"

Smiling slightly, Randi ducked her head. "Her truck keys." She looked up and saw the unspoken question on Kay's face. "Before I came to your house last night, I saw her truck parked close to your driveway, and I stopped. I thought maybe she had something to do with me not being able to get in touch with you."

Kay sighed. "Well, in a roundabout way, she did."

"Yeah, I know. But at the time, I guess I wasn't thinking too clearly. I rousted her out of the truck and yelled at her. When I realized that she was drunk, I convinced her to sleep it off, hid her keys on the back bumper, and then left."

"I'm sure she was thankful for that," Kay said sarcastically. "So she remembered seeing you and came to the house, thinking you had her keys?"

"That was part of it," Randi answered cryptically. "She also decided that she wanted to fight me for you."

Kay sat up, alarmed. "Fight? She picked a fight with you?" She looked Randi over carefully. "You look okay."

"I'm fine," Randi assured her. "We never actually fought, although the lamp in your living room got broken." She smiled to try to ease Kay's fears. "Like I told you, I'm a lover, not a fighter. But, Mr. Macho over there," she pointed to Spike, who was still "protecting" them from passersby, "almost got kicked for his bravery."

"She kicked at Spike? That crazy bitch has gone too far now." Trembling with anger, Kay felt like hunting Beth down and cracking one of her discarded crutches over her head.

Randi reached over and took Kay's hands in hers. She rubbed the fists until they loosened and Kay's fingers linked with hers. "Everything turned out okay, but I was really thankful that you called when you did," she said.

"I'm sorry, Randi. I knew Beth was set on getting back together with me, but I never thought she'd try something as stupid as that."

Tired of barking at joggers, Spike came back and sat at Randi's feet, cocking his head at a comical angle. She bent over and picked him up, unclipping the lead and holding him in her lap. "No real harm done. We just have to get you another lamp."

"I don't care about the stupid lamp," Kay snapped, then softened her tone. "I care about you, and what could have happened." With a heavy sigh, she leaned back against the concrete tabletop that was behind them. "Maybe it's just all starting to get to me."

"Kay," Randi turned to face the younger woman, "I love you."

That caused a smile to start on Kay's face. She looked into

Randi's eyes. "I love you, too."

Randi smiled as well. "I've been pretty miserable this past week," she stated.

"Me, too."

"You were? Oh." Randi took a deep breath to muster her courage. "I'm sorry about your job, Kay. I know that you value your independence, and all."

Where is she going with this? "That's all right, Randi. Independence is nice, but I really never felt very comfortable there. I'm sure something will turn up."

"That's what I want to talk to you about, actually." *Just spit it out, chickenshit. All she can do is say no.* "I've got that nice extra bedroom, and I can help you out until your cast comes off," she blurted. "Job opportunities are better in a bigger city; and we can just be roommates, if you want."

Biting her lip to keep from laughing, Kay fixed a serious look on her face. "Roommates? Are you asking me to move in with you?"

Randi nodded. "Uh, yes. Yes, I am. But there's no pressure or anything, Kay. I just—" Her mouth was covered by a hand, and she looked questioningly at Kay.

"There's really nothing for me here, Randi. But, if I were to say yes and move to Fort Worth with you, we'd have to set some ground rules." She removed her hand when it appeared that the other woman wanted to talk.

"Okay."

"You don't know what they are yet," Kay warned her.

"I don't care. Whatever you want, as long as we're together," Randi said. "So, what are the ground rules?"

Kay smiled. "Let's go back to the house and talk about them there, all right? There's something that I want to show you."

Randi stood up, holding Spike with one arm while helping Kay to her feet with the other. *That sounds interesting. I wonder what she's up to.*

Once they returned to Kay's house, Kay excused herself to the bedroom and Randi set about cleaning up the broken lamp and putting away the groceries that weren't spoiled by sitting out. With the mess taken care of, Randi sat down on the sofa and gave Spike the lap he needed. "Well, she didn't come right out and say no," she told him, rubbing the back of his neck. "I guess that's something."

The little dog began to lick her free hand, then looked up with dark brown eyes. He jumped down and trotted to the kitchen doorway, where he stopped and looked at her again.

"Guess you're ready for lunch, huh?" With a heavy sigh, she slowly got to her feet and followed him. After pouring some dried dog food in a bowl, Randi washed her hands and watched him eat. "You act as if I've starved you to death," she teased, then sobered. "I guess I pretty much did, didn't I?" She had brought the food back after her shopping trip, but between the confrontation with Beth and then hurrying off to pick up Kay, she had forgotten all about feeding the dog. "I'm sorry, Spike." His stump wriggled while he continued to eat, so she guessed that she was forgiven for the oversight.

"Randi, could you come here for a moment?" Kay called from the other part of the house.

Pushing off from the cabinet, Randi walked through the living room and stopped in the doorway of the bedroom. "What do you—" She stopped in mid-sentence at the sight that greeted her. "Whoa!"

The room was dark, except for the glow of several strategically placed candles. Kay lay in the middle of the bed, a sexy smile on her face. She wore a silky, pale-blue gown that was partially untied in the front, and was leaning back against a pile of pillows. "Come in and close the door, Randi." She held out one hand, beckoning her into the room.

"Wha—" Randi swallowed as she closed the door, and then tried to speak again. "What's all this?" She sat down on the bed and took Kay's hand.

"The ground rules." Kay was enjoying catching Randi off guard. "I don't want to move into the guest room."

"You don't?"

Kay shook her head slowly. "No, I don't." She released Randi's hand and reached up to stroke the surprised woman's cheek. "I'm not sure how you feel about this, but I for one am tired of the miscommunication around here."

"Miscommunication?" Randi repeated. She was doing well to get any words out of her mouth, since her brain seemed to be locked up for the time being.

"Mmm-hmm." Kay ran one fingertip down the side of Randi's jaw, then continued to trace a path to the top button of the cotton, long-sleeved shirt that the vet had bought earlier. She unfastened the material and was rewarded with a glimpse of Randi's bra. "I wanted to tell you that I loved you on Thanksgiving, before you left for Fort Worth, but I didn't, mostly because I was afraid it was too soon."

Randi's breath quickened and her heart started to pound. She tried to think of something to say, but her mouth was too dry to form words. All she could do was sit there and enjoy where Kay was taking her.

"Every night that we spoke on the phone..." Kay continued her story, while her hand was busy slowly opening the button-down shirt, "I ached to tell you that I needed you, and that I wanted you to come back. But," three more buttons gone, and the navy blue shirt stood open, "I didn't want to pressure you, and was worried that if I did say something, you might only recipro-cate out of some sense of pity." She slid the garment from Randi's shoulders and smiled.

"I wanted to say the same thing," Randi was finally able to say. "But I didn't want to force you into another relationship that you might regret." She trembled and closed her eyes as Kay traced a gentle outline across the fabric covering her breasts, the short fingernail raking her skin through the soft cotton material of her bra.

Enjoying the power she wielded, Kay continued to smile. Her hand brushed down the front of Randi's abdomen until she found the fastener on the new jeans. "I've decided to quit over-thinking," she said, working the clasp free. "When I move back with you, it won't be as your roommate."

"O...okay," Randi stammered, opening her eyes and looking into the passionate gaze. Unable to take the teasing anymore, she leaned down and covered Kay's mouth with hers. Kay's hands moved up Randi's arms and threaded through her hair, causing Randi to moan. As their tongues danced back and forth inside one mouth and then the other, Randi slid her hand along the silky material barely covering Kay's body.

Kay took her hands from the dark, unruly hair and tried to remove Randi's bra. After several failed attempts, she pulled back slightly. "Off," she ordered gruffly.

Randi smiled and sat up, reaching behind and unclasping the bra. Slightly self-conscious, she let it fall to the floor. All of her doubts were washed away by the smoldering look of appreciation in Kay's eyes. Hands struggled to lower the zipper on her jeans, so Randi stood up and assisted, pushing the denim down her legs and stepping out of them. "Better?" she rasped, her hands shaking.

"Much." She pulled at the waistband of Randi's underwear. "Next, please."

Fighting the blush that started on her face and was quickly working its way down her body, Randi slid the cotton fabric off. She reached for the one tie that held Kay's nightgown closed.

"You, too."

Yes! Kay studied Randi while she felt the material slip away from her skin. Wide shouldered, Randi's body was soft in all the right places. Her well-endowed breasts were too close not to take advantage of, so Kay leaned forward slightly and took the nearest bit of flesh into her mouth.

"Oh, God," Randi moaned, feeling her legs almost give way beneath her. She glanced down and enjoyed the view of Kay's body. "Beautiful," she murmured, running her hands along the satin expanse of skin. Randi leaned back down and kissed the younger woman tenderly. "I do so love you," she whispered reverently. "And I can't wait to show you how much."

Kay blinked back tears. "I love you, too." She pulled Randi down on top of her, as the candles burned down to the sounds of their lovemaking.

Chapter
14

The next morning, Randi was awakened by subtle sunlight drifting across her face and gentle kisses along her chin. They had spent the entire afternoon and evening making love, and she couldn't remember the last time she had slept so well through an entire night. She opened her eyes and smiled sleepily down at Kay. "Good morning."

"It certainly is," Kay said, propping her chin on Randi's chest. A loud rumble from below caused Kay to giggle. "I guess I'm going to have to feed you," she teased.

"Probably wouldn't hurt," Randi said. She motioned to an empty box sitting on the computer desk a few feet away. "Although Pop Tarts at midnight quell the hungries pretty good, too."

Kay laughed, then bent down to leave a kiss on Randi's mouth. "I think," she left another quick peck, "that after yesterday's activities, we're going to need more than junk food. Especially since I plan on repeating them, often." She ran one hand across Randi's chest, taking in a handful of soft flesh and kneading gently.

"God, Kay," Randi moaned happily, "you're going to kill me." She raised into a sitting position and stretched. "Although I can think of worse ways to go." Randi groaned as her vertebrae snapped back into place, then stood up and circled the bed to get to the bathroom. "Be back in a flash," she promised with a wink.

Watching the door close behind Randi's nude form, Kay fell back to the bed. She felt happy, relaxed, sated, and...*complete. Last night was probably the most incredible experience of my life.* She closed her eyes in remembrance. *Not just because of the sex, although that was fantastic.* A warmth settled in her belly at the thought. *No, I think it's because of the closeness we shared.* Kay had never felt so loved or needed before. Their lovemaking brought a whole new dimension to the relationship. *But it wasn't the best part. The best is...becoming a part of someone and having that feeling reciprocated.* The bathroom door opened, and Kay rolled over onto her right side and propped her head up with her hand. "Hey there, cutie."

Randi stood in the doorway, slightly embarrassed by her nudity. She knew that she didn't have the body of a twenty-five-year-old, but the appreciative glances she was receiving from her lover caused her uncertainty to melt away. "Hey there yourself, beautiful." The answering gasp from Kay caused her to stop in the middle of the bedroom. "What's wrong?"

"What happened to your knees?" Two livid bruises covered Randi's kneecaps, making Kay ache just looking at them.

"What?" Randi looked down at her body, holding one leg out to inspect it more carefully. *Ouch. Those do look nasty. What did I... Oh, yeah.* "I fell yesterday," she advised. "They really don't hurt."

Kay sat up and held out her arms. "Come here."

Doing as she was asked, Randi walked over and sat down on the edge of the bed. She pulled Kay into her arms and held her close. "I could get used to this," she said.

"Good. Because I plan on this lasting for a very long time." Kay pulled back and patted the empty space beside her. "Come back to bed?"

Not needing to be asked twice, Randi quickly crawled under the covers and waited for Kay to snuggle up next to her. Her arms automatically went around her lover, and Randi realized with sudden clarity that this was what she had been missing all of her life. The sudden onslaught of emotions brought tears to her eyes, and she buried her face in Kay's hair. "I love you so much, Kay," she said.

"I love you, too." She allowed a few quiet minutes to pass while the awareness of how things had changed overnight soaked in.

"When do you want—"

"When should I—"

Both laughed as they spoke at the same time. "You go first," Randi said.

Kay giggled. "Okay." She traced a lazy line over Randi's stomach. "I was just going to ask when I should start packing for the move."

"Ahh. Well, I was going to ask when you wanted to move," Randi said sheepishly. "Guess we're on the same wavelength, huh?"

"Sure seems like it," Kay said.

Although her professional future looked uncertain, Randi knew for a fact that she couldn't leave again unless Kay was with her. *I'll get a job washing cars or flipping hamburgers, if I have to. Nothing else matters more than being with Kay.*

Kay's forehead furrowed as she looked around the room. "Most of the furniture here isn't mine. It came with the house. So basically, all I have to take with me are some knick knacks and my clothes." She pointed over to the desk. "And, of course, the experiment in progress. I've been 'upgrading' my computer for a couple of months now. But I think the damned thing is a hopeless cause."

Randi laughed. "Don't tell me I've gone and fallen for a geek." The hand that had been caressing her skin slapped her lightly. "Ow."

"Brat." Kay went back to stroking the soft skin. "I'm afraid I'm not smart enough to be a geek," she said. "More like a geek-wannabe."

"You still probably know more than I do. Thank God for simple instructions, or the one I have would probably still be in the box. My twelve-year-old niece knows more than I do," Randi lamented. Getting back to the matter at hand, she asked, "How much notice do you have to give your landlord?"

"Not much, I don't think. Mr. Rayfield, the owner, would probably be happy to get someone else in here, so he could raise the rent. He's always treated me more like a granddaughter than a tenant; and no matter how hard I tried to pay him more, he'd never take it." Another thought caused Kay to groan.

"What's the matter?"

Kay sighed. "I just realized that I'm going to have to tell my family. Aunt Louise is going to throw a fit."

No kidding. Who'll she have to complain to if Kay moves away? "Will you miss them?"

"You've met my family, Randi. Would you?"

Randi laughed. *Good point.* "Well, Louise isn't *that* bad, but that cousin of yours..." She waved a threatening fist in the air. "I'd just as soon slap her as look at her." Another loud grumble from her stomach caused Kay to break into giggles again, and Randi addressed the complaining organ. "All right. I can take a hint." She tickled Kay's ribs. "Come on. Let's get cleaned up, and I'll make us some breakfast."

After taking a very disgruntled Spike for a walk, Randi stood at the counter and watched him eat, while Kay washed up the breakfast dishes. As soon as breakfast was finished, Randi had cleaned off the table and loaded the sink with soapy water. Before she could do anything more, Kay had bumped her out of the way and taken over, citing the house rule that since Randi had cooked, the least she could do was the dishes. *Another argument lost. When did I become such a softy? I'm already so whipped.* Randi smiled at the thought. *Yeah.*

Looking at Spike reminded Randi of Clarice. *I wonder how she's doing?* She patted Kay on the rear. "I'll be right back. Just want to get my cell phone to make a call."

"Okay." Kay smiled at her lover, and watched as she left the kitchen. "You can just use my phone, if you want," she called after Randi.

"That's all right," Randi said, walking back into the kitchen. "On the cell, it's a local call to Fort Worth, and I don't want to run up your long distance." She kissed Kay on the cheek before sitting down at the table. "Thanks, anyway." She hit a button for speed dial and waited patiently.

"Wilde Animal Clinic. How may I help you?"

"Christina, hi. I just wanted to—"

"Randi? Where have you been? We've been looking for you!"

Frowning, Randi looked down at the phone in her hand, then put it back up to her ear. "What's wrong?"

"All hell's broken loose, that's what's wrong." Christina paused for a moment to catch her breath. "That Ms. Crawford came by yesterday morning, and she and Dr. Wilde were in his office for well over an hour. After she left, he started yelling about closing down and firing everyone. Then he told me to get in touch with you."

Oh, shit. "Is he there now?"

"No, he hasn't come in yet. Which is fine with me, although I've had to reschedule several appointments already, and send a couple of others to another clinic. Where have you been, anyway? We were all very concerned about you."

"I'm sorry, Christina. I went out of town for an emergency. I should have at least left word with you as to where I was going." Randi stood up and began pacing the kitchen. "You said that Ms. Crawford met with Dr. Wilde? How is her dog, Clarice?"

"She's just fine, dear. Up and frisky—I was going to ask you when she could go home. I think Ms. Crawford misses her."

Randi thought for a long moment. "Have Joyce look over her stitches and check for any signs of infection. If she says the stitches look all right, then call Ms. Crawford and tell her it's okay to take Clarice home."

"I certainly will." The receptionist muted the phone, then

returned. "All taken care of. Now, about that emergency, is everything okay?"

"Everything's fine," Randi assured her, looking over at Kay and smiling. "Very fine, in fact."

"Do I detect a hint of happiness in that voice?" Christina teased. She had a pretty good idea where the vet was. "I'm very glad for you, Randi." She lowered her voice. "I didn't want this to get out, but Ms. Crawford asked me to give you her phone number. She said that she had something that she wanted to talk to you about."

Uh-oh. I hope it isn't what I think. She was almost a little too grateful for my tending to her dog. Randi watched as Kay turned away from the sink and winked at her. *Too bad. I'm already taken.* "Did she give you any hint as to what it was about, Christina? I don't even work at the clinic any more."

Hearing Randi's words, Kay dried off her hands and hobbled over to sit at the table. *She doesn't work there anymore? But I thought she said that it was just an argument with Dr. Wilde. Did she quit?*

"No, dear, I'm sorry. All she did was ask me to have you call her as soon as you could. She said it was pretty important."

"Well, all right." Randi grabbed a notepad that was on a nearby counter. "Give me the number, and I'll call her later." She took the information from Christina, tore off the top sheet of paper, and slipped it into her shirt pocket. "Thanks. I'll leave my cell phone on so that you can get in touch with me, okay?"

"Thank you, Randi. I'm sorry to have bothered you with all of this, but I thought you should know."

"No problem. I'll talk to you later, Christina. Goodbye." Randi disconnected the call and looked over at Kay. She could tell by her lover's body language that she was upset. "What's wrong?"

"I'm sorry. I didn't mean to eavesdrop," Kay said, "but I couldn't help but overhear that you don't work at the clinic anymore."

Oops. Guess I didn't really go into much detail about that, did I? "Uh, yeah." Randi walked over and sat down next to Kay. "Remember when I told you yesterday that I had gotten into a big argument with Dr. Asshole?"

Kay nodded. "Yes. Something about borrowing his car?"

"Uh-huh. Well, after we yelled at each other a bit, he fired me."

"What?" Kay frowned. "Isn't that cutting off his nose to spite his face? From what you've told me, he's not going to do much work."

Randi shrugged. "You're probably right. The woman whose dog I treated came in yesterday, and when she left he was really upset. According to Christina, he threatened to just close down the office and fire everyone."

"You're not going to let that happen, are you?" Kay asked.

"I don't know if there's much I can do about it, to tell you the truth. He's already fired me." Randi placed the cell phone on the table and rubbed her face with both hands. "And, to top it all off, Ms. Crawford, the dog's owner, left word that she wants me to call her."

Concerned, Kay reached over and rubbed one of Randi's arms. "Did she say why?"

"No. But she was very grateful for what I did for her dog." Randi raised her eyebrows and nodded. "*Very* grateful, if you catch my drift. She kept hugging on me and stuff."

"Oh? Do you think she's interested in you?"

Shrugging again, Randi sighed. "I don't know what to think." She took a deep breath and released it slowly. "How about we go see about renting a truck and getting some boxes, and on the way back we can drop by your aunt's house to tell her the good news?" She grinned mischievously.

Kay accepted the change of subject amicably. "Sure. Might as well get the not-so-fun stuff out of the way first." She looked down at the floor by her chair, where Spike sat patiently. "What about him?"

"Let's take him with us. I doubt if Beth would come back out here, but I really don't want to take any chances."

"Good idea. But if I ever see her again, I'm going to give her a swift kick in the ass with my cast," Kay said as she lifted up the animal. "Picking on my sweet little guy here."

Randi rolled her eyes. *She's going to spoil him so bad, I won't be able to stand him. Oh well.* She stood up, leaning over and taking Spike from Kay so that she could get out of her chair. "You're loving every minute of this, aren't ya, boy?" she asked the dog, who licked her chin.

"Those guys were nice," Kay said, holding on to Spike while Randi got into the car. The manager of the truck rental place had offered to give them boxes for free, as long as they didn't mind used ones. He had a large pile that he was going to have to break down and throw away, all because the previous movers had already written all over them. His assistant helped Randi load them into a truck; and they had also given her a good price on a trailer to haul the Corvette.

Buckling her seat belt, Randi nodded. "They sure were. We'll swing back by here after seeing your family, if that's okay. The sooner we can get your stuff boxed up and loaded, the better off we'll be, I think."

"Sounds good to me." Kay looked over at Randi. "I can't wait to get out of here."

"Really? I thought that you liked it here." Piloting the car out of the parking lot, Randi took a quick glance at her friend. "That's one of the reasons I was so worried about asking you to move to Fort Worth with me."

Kay reached out and covered Randi's hand where it rested on the stick shift. "Promise me you won't hold anything back from me again? Because the only reason I've stayed in this boring little town for as long as I have is because I didn't have anywhere else to go."

Turning her hand over, Randi interlaced fingers with Kay. "I can certainly understand that. I took off as soon as I graduated from high school."

" So, you grew up around here? I didn't realize that." Kay knew that Randi's grandmother and cousins lived in Woodbridge, but as far as she knew, they were the only ones. "But you're always asking me for directions."

The dark-haired woman blushed. "In case you hadn't noticed, I can get lost in a parking lot. Why do you think it took me so long to get back to you that first night at your house? I can't navigate my way out of a paper bag," she lamented. "Before I graduated from high school, I told my parents that I wanted to go to college and become a veterinarian. My dad, being the supportive parent he was," here she grinned, "made me a very detailed map from here, to College Station, and back. Even marked the exit numbers for where I could get gasoline, food, or emergency auto repair."

"That sounds very sweet," Kay told her. "So—"

"He also gave me a compass." Randi laughed. "And believe me, he got really aggravated the first time I drove down to Texas A & M and got lost anyway."

Kay laughed so loudly that Spike barked.

"It's not *that* funny," Randi grumbled.

"I'm sorry," Kay said, snuggling the dog close to her chest. "We didn't mean anything by it, did we, sweetie?" But the twinkle in her eyes belied the truth of her comment.

Spike appeared unrepentant, as well. He stared at Randi and wagged his stubby tail.

"Is this what I have to look forward to?" Randi asked.

Another giggle and more wagging answered her.

Randi held Spike in her arms as Kay led them up the over-grown path to her aunt's house. She thought she had seen one of the curtains in the front window move, but couldn't be sure. *It's like walking up to a haunted house in a horror movie. I half expect Vincent Price to open the door.*

The front door opened at that moment, and an even more hideous sight greeted them. Nancy was wearing a green facial mask, and her recently dyed hair was bound in multi-colored rollers. The orange and yellow housecoat and matching fuzzy slippers added to her comical appearance, and Randi was hard-pressed to keep from laughing out loud. "I thought I heard car doors slam," Nancy grumbled. "What are you doing here so early, Katherine?"

"I've come to talk to you and Aunt Louise," Kay said patiently. "May we come in?"

Nancy stepped back to let them enter, but frowned when she saw the dog in Randi's arms. "You're not bringing that little beast into our house, are you? What if he bites?"

"Don't worry, Nancy. He's had his shots, so biting you shouldn't make him sick," Kay retorted, pushing by her cousin. "C'mon, Randi. Let's get this over with."

A smirk and a raised eyebrow from Randi as she passed by caused Nancy to frown and slam the door. She started through the entrance hall, looking down at her fuzzy slippers. "Rude little bitch," she mumbled, bumping into Randi, who stopped when she heard Nancy's comment.

"Actually," the taller woman deadpanned, "he's a male. And he's not really rude, just shy." Randi turned away from Nancy and followed Kay into the living room. She didn't see the murderous glare aimed at her back.

Louise stood up from where she had been sitting in front of the television and placed her hands on Kay's shoulders, giving the younger woman "air kisses" on both cheeks. She motioned to the sofa. "Sit down, Katherine." Doing a double take at Randi and Spike, she didn't extend them the same courtesy. "What brings you here this time of day? I thought you'd be at work."

Taking a place at one end of the sofa, Kay sat back and looked at her aunt. "I had a few problems at work, Aunt Louise. I thought it best if I just quit." Kay mentally braced herself for the outburst that was sure to come, and she wasn't disappointed.

"You quit? What is the matter with you, Katherine Renee? I go to all that trouble to see you're taken care of, and this is how you repay me?" Louise sat in the chair opposite Kay and glared at Randi. "I suppose you're the cause of all this, aren't you? Katherine rarely acted this way until you came along."

"Now just a damned minute," Kay said, leaning forward. "Don't you *dare* take that tone with her. She had nothing to do with me quitting."

Nancy pushed by Randi, who moved to stand next to Kay. "Oh, really?" Nancy asked, sitting down in another chair, this one closer to the television set. "She shows up again, and you quit that very same day? Pretty convenient coincidence, if you ask me." Nancy had been surprised when Kay called to tell her that she didn't need a ride to work. She looked at Randi, who continued to keep quiet. "What did you offer her to quit?"

My heart, you nasty bitch. But you wouldn't know anything about that, would you? Randi decided to maintain a discreet silence, hoping that Kay would hurry up and get to the reason they were there.

"Would you just shut up, Nancy?" Kay asked. She turned back to her aunt. "I quit for several reasons, Aunt Louise. It just wasn't right for me."

"Not right? But all you had to do was sit and type things into a computer, Katherine. How hard is that?" Louise waved her hands in front of her. "Never mind. I don't want to hear any more. As it is, I probably won't be able to show my face in church. Richard is probably devastated by your disloyalty. He may never come over for dinner again."

Only because your cooking should be registered as a lethal weapon. Kay sighed. "Please. Richard was fine with it. He even wished me luck with whatever I choose to do next."

Shifting in her chair, Nancy sniffed and aimed an unconvincing smile at Randi. "I'll just bet."

Kay stood up. "That's it. I should have known you two couldn't be civil for even five minutes. Let's go, Randi."

"Katherine! Calm yourself and sit back down," Louise ordered. "You never drop by just to visit, so how are we supposed to act?" She realized that she'd never find out what Kay wanted, unless she played along. "Why don't you sit down, too?" she said to Randi, flicking one hand at the furniture. "We can all have a nice cozy visit."

Cozy, my ass. The Spanish Inquisition was friendlier. Randi looked at Kay, who shrugged and returned to her seat. "Thanks," the vet said politely as she lowered herself next to Kay.

Louise sat back in her chair and smiled. "Now, isn't this nice?" She finally acknowledged Spike, who kept trying to wriggle out of Randi's arms. "What a cute dog. Do you take him with you everywhere?"

"Not usually," Randi answered. She shared a look with Kay, who took the squirming dog and placed him on her lap. Spike curled up and closed his eyes almost immediately.

Traitor. Randi felt eyes on her and glanced up to see Nancy glaring her way. She returned the glare, and the other woman quickly turned away. *Heh. I've had steaks tougher than you.*

"So, are we going to find out why you've graced us with your presence, or do we have to guess?" Nancy asked her cousin. "You need to borrow money?"

Kay shook her head. "No, nothing like that. I just have some news to share, and I thought you'd like to hear it in person."

Her cousin laughed. "Well, I can bet you're not pregnant, are you?"

"Nancy Michelle! That's enough," Louise scolded. She looked back at Kay. "That's not it, is it, dear? You know you can tell me anything."

"No, Aunt Louise, I'm not pregnant. That's not even a concern for me," Kay assured her. "I just wanted to tell you that I'm moving."

Louise's eyes widened. "You are? Back into town?" she asked hopefully.

Kay shook her head again. "No." She reached over and grasped Randi's hand, needing the support. "I'm moving to Fort Worth," she announced proudly.

"What in the Sam Hill is in Fort—" Louise stopped in midsentence. "You?" She pointed an accusing finger at Randi. "You're luring her away with fancy promises, aren't you? What are you holding over Katherine's head to make her leave her only family?"

Randi had heard enough. She only hoped that what she was about to say wouldn't upset Kay too much. "I love your niece, Mrs. Weatherby. And the only promises that I've made her are that I'll love her and respect her." She stood up, scooping Spike from Kay's lap and helping the injured woman to her feet. "And you may be related to Kay by blood, but as far as I'm concerned, you don't *deserve* to be called her family. Come on, Kay. Let's get out of here."

Wow, Kay marveled. *They're right. It's always the quiet ones you have to watch out for.* She followed her lover, but turned around at the living room doorway. "Goodbye, Aunt Louise, Nancy. I'll call you once I'm settled in." She walked out the door that Randi held open for her, storing the stunned look on her

aunt's face in her memory and closing a sad chapter in her life forever.

Several minutes passed. As they drove through town, Randi
kept sneaking looks at Kay, trying to figure out her mood. Tired of
guessing, she cleared her throat. "Um, are you going to be okay?"

"For the first time in my life, I know I will," Kay tells her. "It
feels like a huge weight has been lifted from my shoulders, and I
have you to thank for that." She laid her hand on Randi's, twining
their fingers together, grateful for her new love's support.

"You're welcome." Randi smiled. "You know, you can come
back to visit any time you want."

Kay looked at her. "I can't think of one good reason I'd want
to come back to this town, unless it was to visit *your* family." She
squeezed her lover's hand. "You were right, you know."

"About what?"

"Those two bitter and hateful women have never been family
to me. It's taken me this long to realize that no matter what I do,
it won't be good enough for them. I'm going to live my life for me,
and they can just go to hell," Kay stated bitterly.

Randi pulled Kay's hand up to her lips and kissed the knuckles. "That's a good attitude to have, sweetheart. They're certainly
not worthy of you."

That soft kiss melted away all of Kay's animosity and left a
warmth in its place. "I love you," Kay said gently.

"I love you, too. Want to go load a moving truck?"

"Most definitely."

Chapter
15

Randi was halfway to the moving truck with a heavy box in her hands when she heard the familiar tones of her cell phone ringing in the house. She debated whether to put the box down and run for it, or let it ring.

"I've got it," Kay hollered from inside. Moments later, she was standing at the front door waving the device in the air. "It's Christina."

"Thanks." Randi climbed out of the back of the truck and trotted up the stairs. She dropped a quick kiss on Kay's cheek and took the phone. "Hello?"

"I'm sorry to bother you, but Ms. Crawford has called twice for you again today. I think she's just a bit anxious to talk to you," Christina said.

Stretching to work the kinks out of her back from carrying boxes to the truck, Randi sighed. "Twice? Did she happen to mention what it was about? I'm a little busy here."

"No, I'm afraid not." Christina lowered her voice, as if afraid to be overheard. "This morning, Dr. Wilde told Joyce that she'd better start looking for another job."

"He what?" Randi yelled. She started pacing the floor in the living room, running one hand through her hair in a nervous gesture.

"Please, Randi, calm down. I think he was actually being nice, for a change."

Randi closed her eyes and mentally counted to ten before continuing. "Being nice? How is firing someone being nice?" She felt a reassuring touch on her arm, and opened her eyes to look down into the concerned face of her lover.

"He didn't fire her, at least not yet," Christina corrected. "But he's been telling us that there's no way he can continue to run the clinic, and he's seriously considering closing down. So, I think he just told Joyce in order to give her time to find something else."

Oh. But what would he have to gain by being nice? He's certainly never done that before. I don't know what the old bastard is up to, but I'd better get back up there and find out. "All right, Christina. I'll go ahead and give Ms. Crawford a call, so she'll leave you alone."

"Thank you, dear. I know you've probably got more pressing matters to attend to, but I'd appreciate it. The woman is relentless." She paused for a moment. "Good afternoon, Dr. Wilde. No, she hasn't called today. Yes, I will." Waiting until the door slammed behind the vet, Christina spoke quietly into the phone. "Dr. Wilde finally showed up, and he's asking about you."

Realizing the older woman had basically lied to her ex-colleague, Randi shook her head. "Christina, what am I going to do with you?"

"Now, now...I didn't say anything that wasn't the truth," Christina said. "He asked if you had called, and you haven't, at least not today. I called you, remember?"

Another heavy sigh escaped from Randi. "Christina," she warned. Taking a moment to look around the house, she realized that they didn't have much more to take to the moving truck. "I'll make you a deal," she told the woman on the other end of the phone. "If you can keep from antagonizing Dr. Wilde for one more day, I should be home tomorrow, and then I'll give you a call. We'll see what we can do about the clinic then, okay?"

"Tomorrow? But what about—"

"I'll explain everything when I get back to town, I promise." Randi met Kay's eyes and smiled. "Just try to keep from getting fired between now and then."

Christina laughed. "Honey, I've been doing that for close to twenty years. Another day or two won't change a thing. You be careful coming home, Randi. It sounds like you have lots of explaining to do, and you know what a nosy old woman I can be." She hung up the phone before the younger woman could say a word.

Randi pulled the phone away from her ear and looked at it. "I can't believe she got the final word in—again." She clipped the device onto her belt and pulled Kay into her arms. "What say we take a break?"

Looking up into the mischievous brown eyes a few inches away, Kay couldn't help but smile as well. "That sounds like a wonderful idea to me. I talked to Mr. Rayfield and he wished me luck, so that's handled. The bedroom is finished, and there are only a couple of boxes left in the kitchen, so we're almost done."

"Great!" Randi leaned down and placed a tender kiss on

Kay's lips. When she pulled away, she marveled at the dreamy look that appeared on Kay's face. "You hungry?"

Kay slowly opened her eyes and licked her lips. "Mmm-hmm," she agreed. "But not for food." Both hands reached up and linked behind Randi's neck, and she pulled the dark head closer and captured the soft lips one more time.

"We might want to close the front door the next time," Randi mumbled, twisting to get comfortable on the sofa. Her clothes were in a pile on the floor, and the nude form of her lover was nestled between her and the back of the couch.

Kay smiled and continued to trace a lazy pattern across Randi's chest, which was still slightly damp with perspiration. "I rarely have any visitors. Besides," her smile turned into a smirk, "you're the one who started undressing me in the living room."

Randi blushed. "I couldn't help it. When you kissed me like that, I lost all semblance of control." She picked up Kay's hand and brought it to her lips. "Sweetheart, if you keep that up, we'll never finish packing."

"I'm trying to figure out why that's a bad thing," Kay teased. The sound of tires rolling over the gravel in the front drive caused her to frown. "Did you hear..."

"Shit!" Randi extricated herself and tossed Kay's clothes to her. Grabbing hers also, she rushed over and closed the front door. "Never have any visitors, huh?" Foregoing her underwear, she hurriedly pulled on her jeans and polo shirt. She turned to ask Kay a question, and saw her limping for the bedroom. With an appreciative glance at Kay's bare backside as it disappeared into the other room, she smiled. *I hate to agree with Beth, but she's right: Kay has a really nice—*

Hard pounding on the front door broke into Randi's thoughts. Angry at having her enjoyment of the exquisite view interrupted, she jerked the door open.

"'Bout time you answered," Beth growled, pushing her way past Randi and stepping into the house. "What the hell is going on here?"

Spike raced from the partially open bedroom door and stopped, bracing himself in a defensive posture and growling at the bulky woman. He didn't even flinch as she took a step closer. Beth stopped when Randi placed a warning hand on her arm.

"That's far enough." Randi used her grip on the heavier woman's arm to pull her around. "I won't be quite so forgiving, this time," she warned, moving to stand in the middle of the living room with her arms crossed over her chest.

Beth glared at her. "Don't you fucking tell me what to do, you bitch. Maybe this time I'll do more than knock your ass to the floor." She started to close the distance between her and Randi.

"What?" Kay stepped out of the room, dressed and upset. "Beth, what are you doing here?" She stopped once she was beside Randi, a few feet away from the tow truck driver.

Beth halted in mid-stride, wiping her hands on the front of her jeans. "I just came by to see you, baby. What's with the truck out front?" When Kay did not reply, she added, "I was here before, but you were at work."

Kay leaned closer to Randi, who unconsciously placed her hand on the small of Kay's back. "So I heard. What was that you were saying about throwing Randi to the floor?"

Beth frowned. "That was just a little misunderstanding, Katie. Her damned dog tried to attack me, and I was just defending myself."

"From Spike?" Kay asked, incredulous. She shook her head. "I don't think so, Beth. You need to leave, now."

"I'm not going anywhere until you tell me what the fuck's going on!" Beth scowled, taking another step. She pointed a finger in Randi's face. "This is all your fault. I ought to...*urk!*" Her progress was stopped by Kay's outstretched hand, which hit her in the middle of her chest.

"Back off, *Bethany*," Kay threatened, pushing hard. She fought to keep the satisfied smile off her face when Beth almost fell backwards. "I asked you nicely once. Leave."

Beth rubbed the spot on her chest where she had been shoved. "Now, wait just a damned minute. I'm—"

"Not welcome here," Kay finished for her. "After today, I won't be here, anyway. I'm leaving."

"With her?" Beth said, glaring at Randi. "What's she got that I don't?"

Do you want a list? Kay's mind supplied helpfully. *Stop it, Kay. That's not going to help matters any.* "My love," she answered, turning to look into Randi's eyes. "My heart," she finished quietly, smiling at the love that radiated her way.

"This is complete bullshit." Beth looked from one woman to the other, realizing that they were completely focused on each other, and had forgotten that she was even in the room. "Fuck." She walked to the door and turned around, pointing at Kay. "You don't know what you're missing, Katie. You'll be begging for me to take you back in no time." She slammed the door behind her as she left the house.

Randi, having been quiet up to that point, put her hands on Kay's hips and leaned forward to plant a soft kiss on her lips. She pulled back and smiled. "You're pretty tough," she said. "Remind me to watch my step."

"You don't have a thing to worry about," Kay assured her. "Now," she locked eyes with Randi, "are you going to explain what she meant by attacking you?"

"um..." Taking a step back, Randi held out her hands defensively. "I didn't want to upset you, especially after the tough day you had been having."

Kay closed the distance between them again. "Didn't you think I'd be upset if I found out that you'd kept something like that from me?"

Nodding, Randi tried to back up another step, but was stopped by the wall. "Uh, yeah. I guess I should have thought of that. But honestly, Kay, I was so worried about you when you called, the incident with Beth went completely out of my mind." Not realizing when to leave well enough alone, she continued. "She'd never have pushed me down the second time, if I hadn't been holding Spike. The bruises on my knees hardly hurt at all."

"The *second* time?" Kay grabbed one of Randi's hands. "C'mon. We're sitting down." She waited until her lover was seated on the sofa then dropped down next to her, their thighs touching. "Now," she took Randi's hand in hers again, "you're going to tell me the whole story."

Shit. Randi looked down at their hands and was reassured by a strong squeeze. "There's not much to tell, really. When I got back from the store, she was on the porch waiting for me. When I opened the door and started inside, she pushed me, and that's when the lamp next to the sofa got broken." Embarrassed by her unwillingness to defend herself against Beth's attack, Randi fell silent.

"It's okay, honey," Kay prodded gently. "Go on."

"Right." Randi took a deep breath. "She was upset because I had hidden her truck keys... But I told you all about that, didn't I?"

Kay nodded.

"When she kicked at Spike, I picked him up and backed away. That's when she shoved me again. I was so worried about Spike, I forgot about myself; and I fell right on my knees." Randi closed her eyes and leaned back against the sofa. "I know I should have probably just whacked her one after the first shove, but I've never been very good at that sort of thing." She opened her eyes and cut them over to Kay. "I think I've been in four fights my entire life—

and I got my ass kicked in every one of them."

Shaking her head, Kay reached up and touched Randi's cheek. "I think you were incredibly brave."

"Brave? For letting someone like her push me around?" Randi sighed. "Here I am, older and bigger, and you're the one who ends up scaring Beth off. Some protection I am," she lamented.

"You protect me in the most important way," Kay whispered, taking Randi's other hand and pulling them both into her lap. "With your heart."

"I don't know if that's such a good thing, Kay."

Kay closed her eyes for a moment, swallowed, and opened them again. She locked eyes with Randi to make certain her words would be understood. "When my family treated me badly, you were there to hold me and make me feel loved. Did you know that for these past few weeks, you've brought more love into my life than I've known since my brother died?"

"Oh, sweetheart." Randi pulled her hands free and raised them to cup the sweet face before her. "I'll do my best to always make you feel loved."

"Don't discount the importance of what you are to me, Randi. I don't think there are words enough to explain to you just how incredibly lucky I feel to have you in my life." Kay closed her eyes as Randi placed a tender kiss on her forehead, then slowly kissed her way down to cover her lips.

Hours later, Randi stood beside Kay next to the front of the moving truck. "Sure you've got everything?" she asked, placing one arm around Kay's shoulders in support.

"Yeah." Kay looked around at the familiar landscape and exhaled. "You'd think that as long as I've lived here, I'd feel a bit sadder at leaving." The only feelings she was experiencing at the moment were excitement and elation at the thought of spending the rest of her life with the woman standing beside her.

"Not necessarily," Randi assured her. "When I left my parents' house to go off to college, I didn't feel much, either. And I had lived in that house for eighteen years."

Kay looked up at her lover. "Really? Why do you think that is?"

Opening the passenger door on the truck, Randi helped Kay climb up into the cab. Once she was inside, as well, she shrugged her shoulders. "Even though I had lived there my entire life, it really never felt like home. I mean, my parents loved me, and I loved them, but I never really felt like I fit in there, you know?"

"I know what you mean," Kay said, sparing one quick glance over her shoulder at the house she was leaving behind. "I lived in that house, but it never felt like home either, no matter what I did."

"Exactly." Randi maneuvered the mid-sized moving truck onto the main road. "Even surrounded by family, I felt alone. I think a lot of gays and lesbians do. Especially when they're trying to figure themselves out, like I was."

Kay pointed down the road. "Can we stop there, first? I'd like to say goodbye."

"Sure." Glad that the two-lane blacktop was deserted, Randi made a wide turn and drove into the cemetery. "Where exactly—"

"At the end of this row and on the left," Kay directed, taking a deep breath to calm her nerves. *I didn't realize it would be this hard.* She waited patiently until Randi got out of the truck and hurried around to open her door to help her down from the high vehicle. "Thanks."

Randi nodded. "No problem. Do you want—"

"Come with me, please?"

"Sure." Following Kay silently, Randi glanced around until she spotted the grave of her uncle, several rows away from them. *Sorry I skipped out on you, Uncle Randolph.* She offered up a quick prayer for the deceased man.

Kay stopped in front of a pink marble slab with black block lettering. She reached out and brushed her hand over the top, fighting back the tears that always threatened whenever she was here.

Jared Charles Newcombe
05-09-1986 to 10-31-1996
Beloved brother, taken too soon

"Hi there, handsome," Kay said. "Sorry it's been so long since I've been by, but you can see that it's a little hard for me to get around." She blinked several times before continuing. "I think you'd be happy for me, Jay Jay. I've finally found someone to love, who loves me."

Randi stood a few feet away, trying to retain her composure. She wanted to give Kay some privacy, but was afraid to leave her alone. So, she stood quietly and averted her eyes.

"I think you'd really like her, Jared. She's kind, considerate, and has the most beautiful brown eyes," Kay said. "And she treats me like I'm someone special."

You are special, Kay. And I plan on treating you like that for the rest of our lives. Randi slipped her hands into her jeans pockets and continued to look around the cemetery. She caught a quick movement out of one eye and jerked her head around, her heart pounding. *Jared?*

"I just wanted to drop by and tell you that I'm leaving with her, and I won't be by as often to visit. But, I promise to stop in when I'm in town, all right?" Kay kissed her fingertips and laid them on the top of the marble. "Rest well, little brother. I love you." She turned around and caught Randi looking back behind them. "Randi? Is everything okay?"

The rabbit hopped out of the shadow of the tombstone, causing Randi to shake her head at herself. *I think I'm losing my mind. Now I'm seeing ghosts everywhere.* She looked up at Kay and walked over to where she stood. "Are you all right?"

Kay nodded. "I'm fine." She patted Randi on the side. "You ready to go?"

"Sure. Lead on." As Kay hobbled away, Randi turned back to the grave marker and looked at it one more time. "Thank you," she whispered. A sudden cold chill chased down her back, and for just the briefest of moments, she was sure she heard a child's laughter on the wind. With a final nod at the marker, Randi turned around and walked back to the truck, and her future.

Chapter
16

The faded blue T-shirt flew from the closet and landed at the foot of the bed. Kay, comfortably propped at the head of the queen-sized bed, struggled to control her giggles. "Honey, really. I can just put my clothes in the closet in the guest room. You don't have to do everything in one day, you know." She absently stroked the dog resting comfortably in her lap.

Another shirt, a bright yellow polo that looked as though it had never been worn, landed atop the growing pile. "There's no way you can even get into the guest room," Randi said, her voice muffled by the closet, "much less maneuver to the closet in there. Too many boxes."

Kay leaned forward, careful to not crush the dozing Spike. She snatched the yellow shirt and checked it for tears or stains. "What's wrong with this one?" she asked, holding up the newest victim of Randi's re-organizing frenzy.

Randi stopped what she was doing and backed out of the shallow, three-foot wide closet. Wordlessly, she walked over and sat down next to Kay on the bed. She took the garment out of Kay's hands and held it up to her own body, making a face. "In case you haven't noticed, this is fluorescent yellow. I *don't wear* fluorescent yellow." Randi leaned back against the headboard and sighed. "Damn, it feels good to lie down."

"I feel really badly that you had to unload the moving truck all by yourself," Kay murmured, the bright shirt temporarily forgotten. She gestured down at her right foot, which was still covered in plaster from just below her knee to her ankle. "I can't wait until I get this stupid cast off."

Randi turned her head and smiled at her lover. "Well, at least you can unpack the things you want, and your cast should be ready to come off in another week or so, right?" Having been injured many times during her life, she could sympathize with the helplessness Kay was feeling. "I've got a pretty good orthopedic surgeon, if you want to use him."

"Thanks, I think I will. No sense in driving all the way to Woodbridge, since I wasn't that fond of my doctor, anyway." Kay took Randi's hand and squeezed it gently. "You've been at it since six o'clock this morning. How about a little break?"

After they had arrived with the moving truck late the afternoon before, Randi had insisted on unloading it immediately. She'd finally brought the last box into the apartment well after midnight, and had gotten out of bed a few hours later to begin making room for Kay's things. "That's not a bad idea. I need to get the truck turned in, anyway." Randi started to climb off the bed, but her progress was stopped by the strong grip Kay had on her hand. "What?"

Kay used her free hand to take the yellow shirt. "It's almost lunch time. How about we return the truck, then I'll buy lunch?" She tossed the shirt at the pile, then gently moved Spike off her lap.

"You don't have to—" The look on Kay's face stopped Randi in mid-sentence. *She's independent and not helpless. I've got to remember that.* "That sounds like a great idea. What are you hungry for?" When a hand darted underneath her shirt, Randi squirmed and fought back a laugh. "Besides that."

Rolling over onto her right side, Kay lifted Randi's gray T-shirt. "Why not? It's Saturday, and we're already in bed." Her smiled widened as she heard a gasp from Randi when she hit a particularly sensitive spot. "Oooh...like that, do you?" She leaned down and nibbled on the exposed flesh.

"I'd really like to get the truck... Oh, Lord," Randi gasped, at the feel of Kay's tongue. She blinked several times as she tried to remember what they'd been talking about.

"What about the truck?" Kay asked wickedly. Looking up, she watched as Randi's eyes closed. With a flick of her fingers, the brass button that held Randi's jeans closed popped loose, and Kay was able to slide the zipper down with little trouble.

The same warm hands that had pushed her shirt up were now sliding Randi's jeans down her legs. Soft breath on her bare thigh caused her to finally open her eyes. "Truck?" Her eyes closed again when Kay directed her attention to more important matters. "What truck?" Randi quickly lost herself to the feelings that her lover's skillful ministrations evoked.

A short time later, after a quick shower, Randi stood beside the bed pulling up her jeans. Still topless except for a white bra, she reached across the bed for her discarded T-shirt, but was stopped when Kay waved the bright yellow polo shirt under her nose.

"Why not wear this?" Kay was sitting on the bed, wearing nothing but her cast and a smile.

Randi shook her head. "No, I don't think so."

Not to be deterred, Kay held it out persistently. "Why not? With your tan and those gorgeous brown eyes of yours, you'd look great in it."

"Melissa gave it to me," Randi explained quietly. "She was forever trying to change the way I dressed."

Damn. Open mouth and insert foot, Kay. "I'm sorry, honey. I didn't—"

"Don't worry about it. I threw most of them out months ago. Must have just missed this one." Randi pulled her T-shirt over her head.

Kay looked at the shirt, noticing the tag still hanging from the sleeve. *One hundred and forty-eight dollars, for a shirt?* She looked up and saw Randi staring pensively at her. "What do you want to do with it?"

An evil smirk appeared on Randi's face. "The same thing that I did with the other seven or eight that she bought, in different, blinding colors."

"What was that?" Kay struggled into her undergarments and reached for the jogging suit that her lover had picked up for her on their last mall trip. Navy blue with white stripes down the sides, the nylon material snapped from the cuffs all the way up to her hips on both legs and was the most comfortable thing she had to wear. Gentle hands snapped the garment closed over her right thigh, leaving the portion along the cast open. Kay looked up into Randi's smiling face. "Thanks."

"You're welcome." Finished with her work, Randi leaned over and stole a kiss. A moment later, she pulled back and looked around the bed. "Where's your shirt?"

Kay pointed to the dresser on the other side of the room. Her light cotton top was draped over the bottles of cologne and other items that covered the five-drawer chest. "Where you threw it."

"Oops." Randi grinned and took the few steps to gather it up and return it to her lover. "Sorry about that."

"Thanks." Kay slipped the pale pink top over her head. "You never did tell me what you're going to do with the yellow shirt."

"Donate it to one of the homeless shelters downtown. I'd love to see the look on Melissa's face if she ever saw where her expensive shirts ended up." Randi brought Kay her lone sneaker. She sat on the bed next to her friend and watched as Kay easily pulled her foot up, her knee almost touching her chin. "Damn, I wish I could still do that," Randi muttered.

Concentrating on tying the shoe, Kay almost missed what Randi said. "Do what? Tie your shoe?" A gentle shoulder nudge from the other woman caused her to nudge back.

Randi chuckled as the nudging match continued, both women now rocking wildly back and forth. "No, silly. I'm not quite that old and feeble, just yet. I just haven't been able to pull my legs up like that in several years." The tiny grumble at her feet made them both look down.

Spike stood "guard" over one of Randi's sneakers, which had somehow landed on the opposite side of the bed from its mate. He couldn't figure out why his two humans were bouncing into each other, so he sat back on his haunches on the piece of footwear and let out a confused growl.

"Isn't that cute?" Kay reached down and picked up Spike. She cuddled him close to her chest and looked back over at Randi. "Do your knees give you that much trouble?" She hated to think of her lover in any pain, no matter what the reason.

"Not really, no." Randi looked at Spike. *I swear he's smiling.* The dog leaned happily into Kay's touch. "Think you can tear yourself away from him long enough to turn in the truck and grab a bite to eat?"

Kay kissed the top of Spike's head. "I suppose so," she teased. One last snuggle, and she gently transferred him to the bed. "Just give me a few minutes to freshen up, and I'll be ready to go."

"Works for me."

Kay reached up and grabbed a handful of Randi's shirt. "C'mere." She pulled her lover's head down until she had access to Randi's lips. "One for the road." Kay fell back onto the bed and brought Randi with her, their errand temporarily forgotten.

"Damn, it feels good to be driving my car again." Randi leaned back against the comfortable leather seat and almost closed her eyes in ecstasy. It had only taken a few minutes to return the moving truck and trailer, and now they were on their way to a local Mexican restaurant for a late lunch. When the light turned green, she moved the car slowly, savoring the familiar feel of the steering wheel.

Kay looked on in amusement. She'd never seen anyone so attached to a car before. *That's one of the many things I love about her. The way Randi can get enjoyment out of the most mun-*

dane things always brings a smile to my face. She was so engrossed in her observation of the woman beside her, that the ringing of the cell phone caused her to jump. "Do you want me to get that for you?"

"Sure." Randi pulled the device from her belt and handed it to Kay. "Saves me from having to pull over." She had seen too many wrecks involving idiots with cell phones and was not about to play any part in the growing statistics.

"Hello?" Kay frowned. "Um, hold on." She put one hand over the phone and looked at Randi. "It's that Crawford woman," Kay whispered. She remembered how Randi had tried to contact Ms. Crawford the evening before, but had had to settle for leaving a message on her machine. "Do you want me to take a message, or..."

Randi shook her head. "No, I'm tired of playing phone tag with her. Give me a second to park, and I'll talk to her."

"Okay." Kay put the phone back up to her ear. "Ms. Crawford? Randi will be with you in just a moment." She listened to something the other woman said and smiled. "Yes, I agree. She's very talented."

Afraid to ask what the conversation was about, Randi concentrated on wheeling the Corvette into a nearby parking lot. Once she'd turned off the engine, she accepted the phone from Kay, with a quiet, "Thanks," and using her left hand, placed it up to her ear. "Hello, Ms. Crawford? I'm sorry it's taken me so long to get back with you, but I had a family emergency out of town." She looked over at Kay and winked, tickled by the blush that covered her features at her attention. Listening for a moment, she nodded. "I suppose so. Let me check with my partner first."

Partner? Cool. I think I like the sound of that more than just "girlfriend." Of course, Beth usually just called me her "old lady," which always pissed me off. Kay smiled at Randi, who held the phone against her chest.

"Ms. Crawford wants me to stop by her house today. Want to do that after we have lunch?"

"You want me to go, too?" Kay asked, surprised.

"Of course. Unless you don't want to, that is. It's up to you."

The expectant look on Randi's face left no question in her heart about the answer. Not needing any time to think, Kay smiled again. "Sure. I'll be glad to go with you."

Good. This way, there'll be no question as to my unavailability. If that's what she's up to. Randi was beginning to believe there was more to the Crawford woman's persistence than just someone who was looking for a date. *But it never hurts to be careful,* she decided. " Ms. Crawford? Since it's a little after two now, we can be there around," she looked at her watch, "four, if that's all right with you." Nodding her head, Randi looked over at Kay. "Uh-huh. I remember. Sure. See you then." She hit the off button and looked down at the phone for a short time. "That's so weird. She seemed even more excited when I told her that you'd be with me."

"Maybe it's not what you think then," Kay offered, touching Randi's arm lightly.

"Mysteriouser and mysteriouser, that's for sure." Randi shrugged and clipped the phone back to her belt. "You ready for some lunch?"

Kay nodded. "Definitely." Her stomach had long ago started rumbling for something more substantial than the bowl of cereal she'd had for breakfast.

"Great. It's not that much further, I promise." Randi started up the car and pulled it out into traffic.

True to her word, they were in the parking lot of the family-owned restaurant in a matter of minutes. Although she trusted her partner's instincts when it came to things of importance, Kay was a bit leery of the food that might be found in such a building. The outside was done in bright pink stucco with teal trim, appearing as if someone had leftover paint from a child's playhouse and tried to keep from wasting it. Although it was after two in the afternoon, there were still quite a few cars in the parking lot. Kay was so busy looking at the building, she didn't notice that Randi getting out of the car and opening her door. "Oh!" Holding one hand against her chest, she shook a finger at Randi. "You scared me."

Randi laughed as she helped Kay out of the car. "That's what you get for daydreaming," she teased. "C'mon. I think you'll really like the food here."

Lunch was an enjoyable affair. Filled by chicken fajitas for two, the good food and wonderful service had Kay vowing to return to the restaurant soon. She looked over at Randi, who was once again skillfully maneuvering the Corvette through the city streets. The last couple of days had seen the weary look slowly fade, and the dark circles that had been so evident beneath her lover's eyes were almost gone as well. A sudden surge of emotion overtook Kay, and she reached out and covered Randi's hand where it rested on the gearshift between them.

Randi felt Kay's hand squeeze hers. She glanced across the car and smiled. "Hey there. Everything all right?"

"Yep. Just happy."

The smile on Randi's face grew wider. "Yeah, I know what you mean. It's almost overwhelming at times, isn't it?" She turned the car onto a quiet residential street. "For the record, I couldn't be any happier if I'd won the lottery."

"Me, either." Kay looked at the houses they were passing. Most were large two-story brick, with immaculate landscaping and expensive cars parked in the driveways. When Randi pulled the Corvette into one of the circular drives, Kay's eyes widened. "This is where you made a house call?"

"Yeah. Huge, isn't it?" Randi hurried around the car to help Kay. She walked beside her friend with one hand on her back as Kay slowly ascended the steps to the front door. "Just take your time, Kay. I won't let you fall."

Even through the exertion, Kay couldn't help but smile. "I know you won't." The gentle touch was more than comforting, making her feel very loved and protected.

Once they were both standing in front of the door, Randi rang the bell. Before her hand could pull away, the door opened and a tall, slender, blonde woman addressed them.

"Dr. Meyers?" Unfamiliar to Randi and dressed in faded jeans and a navy blue sweatshirt, the barefoot woman stepped back and gestured inside. "Please, won't you both come in?"

"Thank you." Kay followed the woman through a tiled entry-way, Randi close behind her. They were led into a large living room, where a more petite, dark-haired woman stood up to greet them.

Anne Crawford brushed her hands down her worn jeans. "Thank you so much for coming, Dr. Meyers." She looked at Kay with concern and said apologetically, "I hope our front walkway wasn't too difficult for you. Please, sit down and make yourself comfortable." Anne guided Kay to a comfortable-looking, taupe, leather loveseat. Once Kay was seated, her hostess gently pushed a matching ottoman in front of her.

While Anne was fussing over Kay, the woman who had led them into the living room turned to Randi. "Hi, I'm Laurie Griffin." She held out her hand and smiled as Randi shook it in a firm grip. "Thanks for coming over on a Saturday like this."

"No problem. It's nice to meet you, Ms. Griffin." Randi looked up into the other woman's eyes thoughtfully. Laurie was a couple of inches taller than she, with blue eyes. Her blonde hair was cut short and elegantly styled.

Randi took her place next to Kay and waited patiently until the other women sat down across from them. "How's Clarice?"

"She's doing great, thank you," Anne responded happily.

"She's probably asleep in the kitchen right now. We just got back from our walk. I'm so glad you were able to come over today."

"So am I. Since I was out of town on business when Clarice took ill, I wanted a chance to thank you in person for what you did." Laurie grasped Anne's hand and squeezed it. "We really appreciate you coming over on such short notice. I'm afraid my partner can be quite relentless at times, Dr. Meyers. Once she gets an idea into her head, there's not much chance of stopping her."

"Please, call me Randi." She placed her hand on Kay's leg. "And this is my partner, Kay Newcombe."

"All right...Randi," Laurie nodded. "It's nice to meet you, Kay. Since we're on a first-name basis, just call me Laurie." She looked over at Anne, who tilted her head slightly. Standing up, she asked, "Would you like something to drink? Coffee, iced tea, something stronger?"

Kay exchanged looks with her lover. "Tea would be nice, thank you."

"Anything in it? Sugar, artificial sweetener, lemon?"

"No, really, plain is just fine. Thank you."

Anne watched as her partner walked gracefully from the room. "I'm sure you're both wondering why I asked you here," she started, curling one foot underneath her in a more comfortable position.

"Well, yes. We are." Randi leaned forward and braced her elbows on her knees. "You've left cryptic messages at the clinic for a couple of days now. Although you probably know by now that I don't work there anymore."

"The receptionist mentioned something about it, yes. But I was under the impression that you enjoyed your work, Doctor. Excuse me, Randi." She looked up as Laurie came back into the room with a tray laden with clear glasses of iced tea. "Thanks, hon."

"Anytime," Laurie acknowledged, passing out the drinks. Setting the tray down on a nearby table, she resumed her seat by her partner.

Anne placed a hand on Laurie's knee and repeated the statement she had made while Laurie was out of the room. "I was just commenting to Doct...Randi, that she seemed to like her work." She turned to Randi expectantly, quite confident of the answer.

Randi took a sip from her glass. "You're right, Anne. I enjoy what I do. But there's not much I can do about it right now. Dr. Wilde can be pretty adamant once he makes up his mind; and he's made it quite clear that I'm not welcome at the clinic."

"Have you ever considered opening your own office?" Anne

asked.

"Yes, I have. But it's not something I can really afford to do at this time. I'll just do some checking around on Monday, and see if I can get in with someone else. Why do you ask?"

"Undoubtedly, you'd have no way of knowing this, but I'm one of the officers at Southwest Mutual in Dallas," Anne explained. At the confused look on Randi's face, she tried to be more specific. "Our bank specializes in small business loans."

With a heavy sigh, Randi shook her head, understanding where the conversation was going. "I don't have the collateral to put up for a business loan, Anne. Believe me, I've tried in the past." She stood up. "I'm sorry, but this was all a waste of your time."

"Please, sit down, Randi," Anne requested gently. She waited until Randi had complied before continuing. "You're a very caring, conscientious veterinarian, Dr. Meyers. Those are traits that are hard to come by these days, especially in this day and age. The people you work with hold very high opinions of you, you know."

"Uh, well—"

"No, really. I've had some very enlightening visits with them this past week." Seeing that her guest was embarrassed, Anne tried another tack. "Have you spoken with Dr. Wilde since he fired you?"

Randi shook her head. "No, I haven't. But I hear he's been looking for me." *Probably wants me to pay him for using his damned car, the rotten son-of-a-bitch.*

"I think he's planning on selling the clinic," Laurie chimed in, a smug look on her face. "Seems he's worried about the IRS checking into some of his more, shall we say, unconventional bookkeeping practices if he continues to do business."

"How would you know about that?" Kay asked, speaking for the first time. She had been rubbing gentle circles on Randi's back, trying to keep her calm, while taking in every word.

Anne and Laurie looked at each other and laughed. "It's really quite funny," Anne admitted. "After the trouble I had with Dr. Wilde over Clarice's surgery, I was angry, to say the least."

"I can understand that," Randi admitted. "But what does this have to do with him selling the clinic?"

"You took such good care of Clarice, and were so nice, I started wondering why you didn't have your own practice. So, I asked around at the clinic and found out how badly he had been treating you and the rest of the staff." Anne smiled. "So, I did a little research on the good doctor. I wanted to see how on earth he could keep that place open, being the inept, insensitive jerk that he is."

Randi raised her eyebrows. "Research?"

Anne nodded. "Yes. In my business, we run hundreds of credit reports a day. It was pretty easy to get enough information to run a check on Dr. Wilde. But I found a lot more than I bargained for."

"Like what?"

"Like the fact that he's been under investigation by the IRS. It's only a matter of time before his assets are frozen, and the clinic is shut down. But if he sold it, then he could avoid the public humiliation and fight the government privately." Anne leaned back and smiled at Randi, quite proud of herself.

Randi frowned. "Are you telling me that, under a veiled threat of blackmail, Wilde wants to sell me the clinic?" No matter how much she wanted her own clinic, and how much she despised her associate, Randi didn't feel right about this entire situation.

Laurie shook her head. "It's not blackmail, Randi. Dr. Wilde has been under investigation for almost two years. It was just pure coincidence that he found out about it when he did," she assured the vet. "I'm affiliated with a rather large law office, and when Annie told me about him, I had one of our investigators do a little bit of searching." She put her arm around her lover and pulled her close.

"That's about the gist of it," Anne agreed. "All it took was a few well-placed phone calls to find out all about the good doctor. So," she looked at Randi, "if you could get the funding, would you be interested in opening your own clinic?"

Randi was shocked into silence. *After all these years, making a damned house call could help make my dreams come true?* She turned her head to look into Kay's eyes. *I wonder what she thinks about all of this? Having my own clinic would require me to work more hours, and we wouldn't see much of each other. I think we need to talk, first.* "It's an intriguing offer, that's for sure," she told Anne. "But I think I'm going to need some time to mull all of this over."

Anne smiled to herself. *I thought I was right about her. Not one to jump right into something; that's good. I think she'll be a good loan risk.* She stood up and picked up a card from the side table. "Take all the time you need, Randi. Here's my card, and you already have our home number. Give me a call, day or night, when you've made your decision."

"Thanks." Randi accepted the card and studied it. *Senior Vice President? Damn. Nothing like going to the top.* She stood up and helped Kay get to her feet. "I'll get back to you soon, I promise."

Laurie and Anne walked them to the front door. "I have an idea," Laurie offered, after a slight nod from her partner. "What are you two doing next Saturday afternoon?"

"Nothing that I know of," Kay answered, seeing the shrug of Randi's shoulders. "Why?"

"Why don't you both come back over, and I'll cook up some steaks? I've been dying for an excuse to fire up my grill," Laurie admitted, opening the door. "No business talk, just socializing."

Randi smiled, relieved that her earlier fears were completely unfounded. The couple before her looked very happy. "I think I'd like that. What do you think, Kay?"

"Sounds like a great idea." Kay shook hands with Anne and Laurie. "Thank you both. I look forward to seeing you again." She had a pretty good idea why Randi hadn't accepted the offer outright, and was charmed by her lover's thoughtfulness. "I'm sure we'll have an answer for you by Saturday," she whispered into Anne's ear.

They finished their goodbyes and started down the steps, Randi walking beside Kay and holding her arm solicitously. "That was quite an interesting chat," Randi commented.

"It certainly was," Kay agreed, climbing into the Corvette. She waited until Randi was in the car and buckled up. "So, what do you think?"

"I think we have a few things to talk about." Randi turned the key in the ignition and drove off.

Chapter
17

"It's not that simple," Randi argued, as she held the apartment door open for Kay to enter. Once her lover was well into the
living room, Randi closed the door, fighting the temptation to
slam it.

Kay rolled her eyes. "You said yourself that you've always
wanted your own clinic. I just don't see what the problem is."
They had been going 'round and 'round on the subject ever since
they'd left Anne and Laurie's. For every reason Kay would give as
to why the banker's offer was a good idea, Randi seemed to find
an argument against it. *I just don't understand what her problem
is. Unless...* "You're scared."

"That's ridiculous," Randi scoffed, almost too quickly. She
waited until Kay was comfortably seated on the sofa and then
headed for the kitchen. "Do you want something to drink?"

*She is scared, but of what? All right, then. At least now I
know what I'm up against.* Kay smiled to herself. *She doesn't
stand a chance.* Noticing her lover still standing in the kitchen
doorway, she gave Randi what she hoped was a reassuring smile.
"I'll have whatever you're having."

"All right." Randi disappeared into the kitchen without
another word.

A tiny whine at her feet caused Kay to look down. Spike sat
almost on top of her sneaker, his fretful dark eyes melting her
heart. "Well, what are you waiting for? Come on." Kay patted her
lap. Seconds later, she was fending off dog kisses. "Spike, stop it."

Randi stood just inside the kitchen and watched the scene in
the living room. *Could she be right? Am I afraid?* She closed her
eyes and looked deep inside herself for the answer. She knew she
could handle running the clinic, and she knew that she wanted
Kay in her life; but she was afraid that she might not be able to
successfully balance the two. And she would not risk their relationship for anything, not even the possibility of seeing her dream

come true.

What weighed heavily on her mind were the months of Melissa's constant complaining and hateful remarks after she'd started working longer hours in order to make more money. The same thing could happen with Kay. Of course she was scared. Although she was almost forty years old, this was the first time in her life that she was *in* love, and Randi wasn't at all certain how to proceed from this point. As much as she loved Kay, getting used to their new relationship was difficult for Randi; and she wanted to avoid doing anything that might make it harder for either one of them. Randi sighed. *I think I need to call my mother. Maybe she'll know what to do.* Her mind made up, she squared her shoulders and continued on into the living room. "I hope cranapple juice is okay with you."

"That sounds great, thank you." Kay accepted the glass and was relieved when Randi sat down next to her. Randi's mood worried Kay, and she was afraid that the previous discussion was going to blow up into a full-scale argument. She placed her glass on the side table and turned to give Randi her full attention. "Randi, I'm so—"

"I'm sorr—"

This made them both laugh, disintegrating the tension between them. They looked at each other for several beats until Randi decided to break the silence. She took Kay's hands in hers and looked into her lover's eyes. "I've been acting like a complete jackass this evening, and I'm sorry." The understanding look from Kay gave her the fortitude to go on. "I know it's no excuse, but this is the first time that I've been in love, and I'm a nervous wreck. I guess it's getting in the way of me thinking clearly about much of anything." Now that she knew what the real thing felt like, Randi realized that her relationship with Melissa had been more of a sense of duty than actual love, so she didn't have anything tangible to base her emotional interactions with Kay on.

"Nervous? Oh, Randi." Kay pulled their hands up to her lips and kissed Randi's knuckles. "You have nothing to be nervous about. We wouldn't have much of a relationship if we never disagreed on anything." *Did she say "the first time"? I think we have a lot more in common than we realized.* She had cared for Beth, but it was a relationship borne of convenience, not love. "This is a first for me too, you know. I think the best thing we can do is keep the lines of communication open and be as honest as we can with each other."

"You're right." Randi leaned over and left a soft kiss on Kay's lips. "Thanks. Honesty, huh?"

Kay nodded. Although she was tempted to grab Randi and kiss her until they were both breathless, she knew that it was even more important that they talk things out first. "Do you want to tell me why you're thinking of turning down Anne's offer?"

"I'm not sure." Randi looked down at the dog in Kay's lap and couldn't help but smile. *He's pretty well stuck on her.* The thought caused her smile to widen. *Like owner, like dog.* Kay's subtle clearing of her throat brought Randi back to the conversation at hand. "So much could go wrong," Randi mumbled, still not looking up.

"That's true. But a lot more could go right, don't you think?" Kay pulled one of her hands free and stroked Randi's cheek. "Think about all the good you could do, if you were operating your own clinic."

Randi's eyes closed, and she leaned into the gentle touch. "Maybe."

"And what about the women that work there now? If Dr. Wilde follows through with his threat, they'll all be looking for jobs. If you bought the place, you could keep all of them on." Kay knew that she wasn't playing fair by bringing the welfare of the other employees into the conversation, but she wanted what was best for Randi; and following her dreams and having her own clinic was just what the vet needed, at least in Kay's opinion. "You practically run the place now, Randi. What's the harm in making it legal?"

Randi's eyes opened slowly, and she looked up into Kay's face. "I'd end up working a lot more hours, plus having to supervise all the paperwork and books."

"So? I know you can handle it, love." Kay found herself getting lost in Randi's light brown eyes. *I love her eyes. They're so...expressive. It's like looking into her soul.*

"Sure, I can handle it," Randi allowed. "But can *we* handle it?"

Kay frowned. "What do you mean? It's an incredible opportunity, something that you've always dreamed of."

"That dream means nothing to me, if it could even remotely jeopardize what we have." Randi's voice broke on the final words, and she could feel tears welling in her eyes. "I can't lose this." She reached up and held Kay's hand to her face. "I can't lose us."

"What makes you think that we'd lose what we have?" Kay's heart was breaking at the anguish on her lover's face. "Don't you have more faith in us than that?"

Randi fought the urge to jump from the sofa and run. The conversation was going in a direction she wasn't certain how to handle. "Of course I do! But the long hours would eventually come between us. You might start to regret talking me into doing this, and then we'd drift apart." Thoughts of Melissa's discontent sprang into her head. Her long work hours had become such a bone of contention, that it had been the beginning of the end. "We'd fight all the time, and then you'd finally get fed up enough to leave," Randi finished in barely a whisper, her eyes going distant.

Kay's narrowed her eyes and frowned. *What makes her think that...Melissa. That bitch keeps popping up. I should have whacked her when I had the chance.* Kay realized that their argument stemmed more from the past than the present or future. *The scars run deep.*

"Randi." Kay's voice was strong and no-nonsense. "Look at me." She waited until Randi's eyes were focused on her. Framing her lover's face with her hands, she leaned in close until they were inches apart. "I'm not going to leave you. I love you, Randi Suzanne Meyers." Using her thumbs to brush away the few tears that drifted down Randi's cheeks, she continued. "We're going to have disagreements. That's part of what makes a relationship work. But," here she smiled, "there's nothing that you can do or say that will cause me to stop loving you."

"I wish I could believe that," Randi rasped. "I want to believe it." Her heart and her mind were at odds. "I don't think I could survive going through that again." Even though the relationship with the redhead had been stormy and painful, the shock of coming home from work and finding the apartment empty nearly broke Randi's spirit for good.

"I'm not Melissa."

Worried, Randi tried to explain. "I know you're not." Unable to handle sitting still any longer, she stood up and began to pace the living room. "I can be pretty single-minded when it comes to my work. I always have been." She stopped and glanced out the window, avoiding Kay's gaze. "I've screwed up one relationship because of that. I can't take the chance that it would happen again." *Losing Kay would kill me. I've never felt like this for someone before, and it scares the hell out of me.*

Kay watched as Randi continued to beat herself up. *I'm going to wring that redheaded bitch's neck the next time I see her.* "Don't I have any say in the matter?"

Jarred from her musings, Randi turned away from the window. "What?"

"It takes two people to make a relationship succeed or fail. And I don't know about you, but I'm sure as hell going to do everything I can to make sure we succeed." Kay held out her hands. "Come here, please."

Randi hesitated. *Can I do this?* Her past failure with Melissa haunted her. *Maybe if I had done things differently... But if I had, then I wouldn't be with Kay now.* The look on Kay's face was one of pure love and trust. *Can I keep from hurting her? God, I don't want to hurt her.* Kay's words echoed in her head. *"I'm not Melissa"..."There's nothing you can do or say that will cause me to stop loving you"..."I'm sure as hell going to do everything I can to make sure we succeed." She's right. There's no comparison between her and that hateful bitch.* Her resolve strengthened, Randi stepped away from the window and returned to her place on the sofa. She took a deep breath and took Kay's hands in hers. "I love you so much, Kay. And I'm going to do everything that I can to make us work."

"*We,*" Kay emphasized, "*we* are going to make us work. Together." Her smile widened at Randi's answering nod. Wrapping her arms around Randi's neck, Kay pulled her close. "I love you, too," she murmured, feeling the answering hug from Randi. "We'll get through this, Randi. You'll see."

With the cordless phone wedged between her ear and her shoulder, Randi waited patiently while she scooped the ground coffee into the basket of the machine. The ringing stopped, and a woman's voice came onto the line.

"Hello?"

"Mom?" Now that she had her mother on the phone, Randi panicked. *What the hell am I doing? She's going to—*

"Randi, sweetheart, it's so good to hear from you." Patricia sounded thrilled to hear from her daughter. "To what do I owe this pleasure?"

Trying to think quickly, Randi poured water into the top of the coffee maker and turned it on. "I just thought I'd call and see how you're doing, that's all. Is everything okay there?"

"Everything's just fine, dear. But you're up awfully early, aren't you? By my watch, it's only eight o'clock there, and on a Sunday, to boot." Now living in Santa Fe, New Mexico, Patricia loved the city that she had spent her childhood in, but at times she missed having her children nearby. "Is something wrong?"

"I couldn't sleep," Randi admitted quietly.

"Does this have anything to do with Kay? You know you'd feel better if you talked to her."

Randi smiled. "I did talk to her, Mom. She's here now." Tiny clicks behind her alerted Randi that she had company in the kitchen. Spike's nails made his steps seem loud on the tile floor, and he walked to stand by his bowl with a perturbed look on his features. "That's what I want to talk to you about, actually," she finished, pouring a cup of dog food into the dish. *He's certainly got me trained.* Her mother's voice brought her attention back to the phone call. "I'm sorry, what did you say?"

"I asked if you were having problems. How long has Kay been there?"

"We got here on Friday evening. Kay's job wasn't going well, and I—"

"You'd better start at the beginning, Randi. Did you go back to get her, or did she find a way up to Fort Worth?"

With a heavy sigh, Randi poured herself a cup of coffee and slid down the wall to sit on the floor next to Spike. "Mom, wait. It's a long story, and it's—"

"If you say complicated, I'm going to be on the next flight out and tan your backside," Patricia threatened. Hearing her daughter laugh, she joined in. "All right, enough of that. Let's hear it."

Damn, she's persistent. Why the hell did I call her, anyway? Randi spent the next thirty minutes relating the events leading up to Kay's move. She conveniently left out Beth's part, thinking that it would do no good to get her mother upset. "So, anyway, now that she's here, I'm afraid I'm going to screw this up, Mom. And with the chance to run my own clinic, how can I balance work and home?"

"Sweetheart, listen to me. You're a fine person, and Kay obviously realizes that. I honestly don't think you're going to have any problems that the two of you can't work out. Your father and I balanced two careers, and still made time for each other and you kids. It can be done." Patricia was a retired nurse, and her husband had been a business analyst for a large firm. Family was important to both of them, and they'd been happily married for forty years. "What kind of work does Kay do, anyway?"

"She was a file clerk at a law office at one time, and the last job had to do with entering data into computers." Soon after he finished his meal, Spike had crawled up into Randi's lap and proceeded to gently chew on her fingers. "Why do you ask?"

"If you do buy the clinic, you might consider getting an office manager to handle most of the paperwork for you. That would leave you free to do what you like to do best: take care of the animals. Do you know anyone who might be interested in the job?" Patricia asked in a teasing tone.

"I haven't even decided if I'm going to take Anne Crawford

up on her offer, Mom. Not to mention that I'll still need to talk to Dr. Wilde and see if he would consider selling to me. I can't go around hiring people for positions that I don't have to offer yet." She rubbed her eyes with one hand, the long conversation beginning to wear on her.

Patricia sighed. Her daughter was highly intelligent, but could be quite dense at times. "Why don't you talk to Kay? Ask *her* about the office manager's job."

Randi couldn't figure out why her mother sounded so exasperated. "What would she know... Oh! You mean ask Kay if she'd like the job, right?" Randi felt like smacking herself on the forehead. "I'm sorry, Mom. I must be tired."

"That's quite all right, Randi. But at least it's something to think about, don't you agree? Kay seems like a very smart young woman. I'm sure she'd be good at anything she did." Patricia heard her daughter sputter on the other end of the line. "Are you okay?"

"Fine," Randi gasped. She was embarrassed to tell her mother what she had been thinking when Patricia mentioned how good Kay would be. *She's more than good, she's incredible.* Randi wiped at the coffee that now stained her T-shirt. Spike stood a few feet away, glaring at the woman who had spewed coffee all over him. "Sorry, buddy."

"What was that?"

"Nothing, Mom. I was just talking to Spike." Randi slowly climbed to her feet, wincing at the stiffness in her limbs. *I'm getting too damned old to be sitting on the floor. Maybe I can talk Kay into going furniture shopping. We really need to pick out a kitchen table and chairs.*

"You must be tired, if you're talking to the dog. Especially since you've got such fine company on the phone."

"Mom, I'm sorry. It's just that—"

Patricia laughed. "Hush. I was just teasing you, Randi Suzanne. Why don't you go back to bed? There's nothing you need to do today, is there?"

Randi thought for a long moment. "No, not really." She braced the phone between her ear and shoulder and used a dishtowel to wipe Spike dry, much to his displeasure. Thinking of the young woman still asleep, she grinned. "That's a good idea, Mom. I think I'll do that."

"Good for you. We love you, sweetheart; now go get some rest."

"I love you, too, Mom. Give Dad a hug from me, okay?" After her mother's acknowledgement, she hung up the phone and looked down at the upset dog. "How about a quick dash outside, then we go back and snuggle with Kay?"

Spike's ears perked up at the word "outside," and he beat a hasty path to the front door. Randi rinsed out her coffee mug and left it in the sink, following in her canine companion's footsteps.

Kay awakened to thoughtful brown eyes staring down at her. "Hi."

"Hi." Randi stroked her fingertips lightly across the tanned cheek. "How'd you sleep?"

"Mmm." Kay moaned, stretching slightly. "Really good. How about you?" She studied her lover's face and frowned. "You look tired."

Randi glanced down at the sheets. "Yeah, I am, a little bit. Been thinking."

"About?" Struggling to a sitting position, Kay unconsciously held the sheet up to her chest. Her heart started to pound, and she swallowed hard to try and dislodge the lump that appeared in her throat. *Is she having second thoughts? Maybe all of this is too much for her.*

Seeing the alarm on Kay's face and having a pretty good idea of the cause, Randi quickly brought her hands up and rubbed Kay's upper arms. "No, it's not that, sweetheart. Please don't look so scared." She scooted closer, never relinquishing her hold. "I've got a proposition for you. But, before you say anything, I want you to know that whatever your decision is, I'll understand."

"Proposition? Just what kind of proposition are we talking about here?"

"I talked to my mother this morning, while you were asleep. Since she practically read me the riot act before they left for home last week, I thought I'd better let her know that everything worked out for us." She smiled and ran her hands down her lover's arms, until she was holding Kay's hands. "She and Dad both gave me hell for not telling you how I really felt about you," Randi admitted sheepishly.

Kay grinned. "I like your parents." She loved the blush that covered Randi's face. "So, what's the proposition?"

"If, and it's a big if right now, I agree to try and buy the clinic, I'm going to need some help. Mom helped me realize that in order to keep it running well and still be able to handle patients like I want, I'm going to have to hire an office manager." Randi's smile turned bashful. "You wouldn't happen to know anyone who might be interested, would you?"

"Me? You're asking me to be an office manager?" Kay asked, incredulous. "But I don't know a thing about running an office."

"That's not true, Kay. With all the different skills you have, you'd be perfect for the job. And, I'm sure Christina would be more than willing to help you with anything that you might not be sure about."

"You're serious, aren't you?"

"Yep." Randi bounced on the bed excitedly. "Think about it. We'd be working together, so I wouldn't feel as bad about staying late at the office. And, to tell you the truth, you're about the only person I know I can trust to keep an eye on things for me. You're intelligent, kind—"

"And sleeping with the boss," Kay finished. "How well would that go over? I don't want to cause you any problems, Randi. You're going to have a hard enough time without having to worry about me, too."

"What makes you think that? Everyone in the office knows that I'm gay. It's never been a problem before."

Kay gave a sad little smile. "But I live with you, Randi. It would be bad enough that you'd be bringing in a stranger to run things, but how do you think they're going to feel when they find out I'm your girlfriend, too?" She shook her head. "I'd love to work with you, but not at the expense of ruining the relationships that you have there already."

Realizing that they were getting nowhere, Randi got off the bed. "I think we're getting ahead of ourselves here. I don't even know for sure that Wilde will want to sell, least of all to me." She walked around the bed and sat next to Kay. "Do me a favor?"

Oh, no. She's going to give me that look. "All right. What?"

Randi cocked her head slightly to one side and gave a tiny grin. "Just think about what I asked you? Maybe you can go up to the office with me on Monday and meet everyone, see what you think."

Damn. She doesn't play fair. I can't tell her no when she looks at me that way. "Okay. I'll think about it. But I'm not promising anything." Kay pointed her finger at Randi and shook it. "Now stop looking at me like that."

The smile widened, and Randi's head ducked lower. "What?"

"Oh, c'mon. I said I'd think about it," Kay begged, then grinned. "I bet I can change that look."

"Really? And how do you think you're going to—" Randi was silenced by Kay's lips covering hers. *That'll work.* She happily fell back to the bed to pursue the change in subject.

A couple of hours later, the ringing of the telephone woke the two women, both of whom were lethargic from lovemaking. Randi raised her head from where it was cushioned on Kay's stomach and frowned. "That damned thing is really beginning to get on my nerves." She rolled over onto her right side and grabbed the offending device. "What?"

"My, my, sugar, you're sure cranky. Don't tell me you were still asleep," Melissa's syrupy voice drawled. "It's after eleven o'clock in the morning. You were always an early riser before I left."

"It's none of your damned business what I was doing. What the hell do you want?" Randi sat up and swung her legs off the side of the bed. She could feel Kay's hand lightly rubbing her back, and was grateful for the calming touch.

"Temper, temper. I think I know what your problem is, Randi. You need to get laid."

Unable to control herself, Randi laughed. "Believe me, Melissa, that's not my problem." She turned to look over her shoulder at Kay, whose face had grown stormy. "Is that the only reason you called?" Randi shifted so that she could sit next to her angry lover, reaching up and gently smoothing away the crease in Kay's forehead that the frown created. "*I love you,*" she mouthed silently.

"I love you, too," Kay whispered, a smile replacing the frown and causing her eyes to soften with emotion.

"What did you say, Melissa? I wasn't listening." Randi heard the other woman's voice, but was too intent on looking into Kay's eyes to realize what she had said.

"That's the trouble with you, Randi. You never did pay attention to me. But I'm willing to overlook that one little detail and take you back."

"You'll what?" Randi yelled, spinning around and jumping off the bed. "What the hell makes you think I'd be interested in you?" Her outburst frightened Spike, who was sleeping on the pile of clothes that were to be donated. He jumped up onto the bed and stood between Randi and Kay, barking at Randi as if she had lost her mind.

Kay laughed at the small animal's antics and scooped him up to snuggle him close to her chest. "Shhh, tough guy. She's on the phone with Super Bitch." Her heart swelled with love over Spike's protective streak toward her.

"I've checked around, hon. From what I've heard, your little girlfriend went back to the boonies where she belongs, and you're all alone."

Wiping her hand down her face in exasperation, Randi sat on

the edge of the bed. *How would she know... Oh, yeah. Her "friend" that lives in one of the apartments in the next building. I didn't think they were speaking to each other anymore.* One of the last arguments they'd had when they were together was about the man who Melissa insisted was "just a friend." She'd come back from doing the laundry with her lipstick smeared and her clothes rumpled, and Randi knew in her heart that Ricky had been at the laundry cabana as well. He was more upset than Randi when Melissa moved away without so much as a goodbye. "Even if that were true, and I'm not saying it is, you'd be the last person on the face of the earth that I'd even remotely consider being with."

"You don't have to get nasty, baby. I know you don't do well alone, and I worry about you."

"Bullshit. You've never cared before now. Why the sudden change?" The pressure from fighting all the old emotions that Melissa evoked was wearing Randi down. She closed her eyes and bent her head, exhausted.

"Of course I care, darlin'. I know we had our little problems before, but I really want to try again." Melissa's tone sounded almost desperate.

Kay awkwardly scooted down the bed until she was sitting directly behind her lover. Placing her hands on Randi's shoulders, she attempted to relax her with a slow, deep massaging of the tight muscles there.

"What part of 'no' can you not get through your head? I told you I'm not interested, and I meant it." The warm hands on her bare skin soothed her frazzled nerves, and she was able to distance herself from the conversation. When Kay reached for the phone, Randi was more than happy to relinquish control and released her grip.

"Of course you are, baby. We're so good together, you and me. Just let me come on over there and—"

"Listen, you deep-fried, Southern belle wannabe," Kay spat out venomously. "We don't want, or need you in our lives, so just butt out."

A moment of shocked silence was followed by a giggle. "Oh, sugar. You really have no idea what you're in for, do you? You're a sweet young thing, but she's way out of your league."

"I know exactly what I'm in for," Kay retorted. "And it's precisely what I want."

Randi turned around and faced Kay. Her light brown eyes were weary, but she wore a tender smile on her face.

Kay reached across with her free hand and stroked Randi's cheek. "Do yourself a favor, Melissa. Find a nice rock and crawl under it." Before the other woman could say another word, she disconnected the call and tossed the handset back up near the top of the bed.

Randi chuckled. "Thanks. I don't think I would have been able to take much more from her right now." Randi thought back to part of Kay's brief conversation with Melissa. "Deep-fried Southern wannabe?"

Having the good grace to blush, Kay ducked her head and grinned. "Deep-fried Southern *belle* wannabe," she corrected. The comment got the desired effect, as Randi's face split into a wide smile. "Well, she is. The only other place I've heard an accent that pronounced is on television."

Randi wrapped her arms around Kay and squeezed. "You're something, you know that?"

"Yeah, well, figuring out what that 'something' is will probably be a full-time job. You up for it?"

"Most definitely," Randi assured her, kissing the top of Kay's head. Her stomach took that moment to announce its presence, causing Kay to giggle. "I can't help it. Someone kept me from having breakfast."

Kay ran her fingers down Randi's bare sides, causing the brunette to squirm. "If we work it just right, you can miss lunch, too." She nibbled on the nearest bit of flesh.

"I, um...ooh," Randi moaned, falling back on the bed with Kay in her arms. "Lunch is highly overrated, in my opinion." She started her own counter-attack, eliciting groans of pleasure from her companion.

Lunch was soon forgotten.

Chapter
18

"Tell me again what we're here for?" Randi asked, as she followed a determined Kay into the electronics department of the discount store. Kay had been quite vague about her reason for wanting to stop, but Randi soon found out that she couldn't say no to Kay. *I am so whipped.* She smiled. *Yeah.*

Kay either didn't hear her or ignored the question, but either way, she didn't stop until she was in the aisle with all the telephones and accessories. She studied the merchandise on both sides carefully, and then walked over and picked up a display to get a closer look. "What do you think of this?" she asked, holding up the phone for Randi to see.

"It's nice?" Randi queried, confused. "But why—"

"No more incidents like the one yesterday morning." Kay picked up the handset and held it to her ear. "It's not too heavy, and it fits my hand pretty well." She handed it to Randi. "You try it."

Randi looked at the phone. "Caller ID and an answering machine? Going high tech, huh?"

Laughing, Kay nodded. "Yep. Welcome to the Twenty-first Century, my friend. I can't believe you didn't already have one."

"You didn't have one," Randi pointed out. "What makes you think that I would?"

"Because of your line of work. What if you weren't home and they needed to reach you?" Kay took the handset back and placed it on the shelf.

"It hasn't really been necessary. I'm usually either at work or home, and I always carry my cell phone." Randi's voiced quieted. "Melissa had an answering machine, but she took it with her when she left, and I just never got around to getting another one."

Kay nodded in understanding. She was happy to see that Randi could talk about her ex-girlfriend with a lot less difficulty than before. *Maybe that phone call yesterday was a good thing, after all.* "Well, if you don't mind, I'd like to get this phone for the living room. That way we can see if we have messages as soon as we get in, but won't have to answer the phone if we don't want to."

"You don't have to ask my permission, Kay. It's your apartment, too." Randi grabbed a box that held the same style phone and tucked it under her arm. "Anything else you have your eye on?"

"Oh, yeah. But I think they might frown if I tossed you to the floor to have my way with you," Kay teased, enjoying the blush that her comments elicited.

Randi looked around to see if anyone had overheard Kay's aside. Relieved to see that they were alone, she shook her head. "You're insatiable."

"Only when it comes to you." Kay thought about Randi's remark. *I am, aren't I?* The emotions that their relationship evoked were like none that Kay had ever felt before. Her need to connect with Randi in every way imaginable was constant, and she didn't know if she could go an entire workday without some sort of contact. *That's one thing in favor of working in the same office. But I think I'd still like to wait and meet the rest of the staff before making any decision.*

They had been on their way to the veterinary clinic when Kay had seen the discount store and asked to stop. Since they weren't on any real schedule, Randi had agreed, and so here they were. Randi looked around again. "Is there anything else you want to get while we're here?" She wasn't even about to argue over who should buy the phone. *Learned my lesson on that one.* If Randi tried to keep Kay from spending her money on something that Randi was fully prepared to pay for, Kay's independent streak would come out full force.

"No, I think this will do for now," Kay answered. She started down the aisle, but stopped and turned to look over her shoulder at Randi. "And don't think that just because I'm letting you carry it, I'll let you pay for it."

"Never crossed my mind," Randi retorted. She smiled widely as Kay started back to the front of the store. *Definitely whipped. And loving every minute of it.*

The veterinary clinic was in a strip shopping center only a few minutes away from the apartments where they lived. The office was sandwiched between a dry cleaners and a health food store, and among the empty shops was an open pizzeria that offered delivery.

Kay peered pensively through the windshield and then looked up at her friend, who was standing beside the car holding the passenger's door open. Randi was wearing black slacks and a gray button-down dress shirt, and looked very nervous. Kay wasn't sure if her presence would be a help or a hindrance. "Are you sure you don't want me to just wait in the car?" she asked. "I don't want to be in the way, or anything."

"Actually, I'd like you to do me a favor, if you don't mind," Randi said, holding out her hand to help Kay from the vehicle. She smiled when her lover took her hand.

"Sure. What is it?" Kay would be thankful when she was finally out of the cast, and was glad that Randi had called her orthopedic surgeon and gotten her an appointment for later on in the week. *It'll be so nice, being able to wear regular clothes again.* Tired of the sweatpants, skirts, and knit pants she was forced to wear to accommodate the cast, Kay silently promised herself she'd stay away from those particular clothing items for as long as possible once her leg was healed.

Randi closed the car door and brushed the front of her slacks. "I'd kinda like to know how everyone else is doing. Do you think you could talk to them while I'm in with Dr. Asshole?"

"I'll be glad to try." Kay paused outside the door to the clinic and looked up at her lover. "But they don't even know me. What makes you think they'll talk to me?"

Opening the door, Randi smiled. "I'll introduce you, then they'll know you." She leaned down to whisper in Kay's ear. "Besides, you're sweet and kind. They'll open up to you immediately." She kissed the ear she had spoken into, then held the door fully open to allow Kay access.

"I'll get you back for that, later," Kay mumbled, hoping her face wasn't as red as it felt.

Randi winked. "I'm counting on it." She turned back to the reception room they had just entered and was greeted by a petite, gray-haired woman who quickly wrapped her arms around the stunned vet.

"Randi, it's so good to see you, dear," the older woman exclaimed. "We've missed you terribly, you know."

Embarrassed, Randi returned the hug and stepped back. "I've missed you, too, Christina. I'd like to introduce you to—"

"I'll just bet you're Kay, aren't you?" Christina moved to stand in front of Kay to give her a gentle hug.

"Yes, I am." Kay looked over at Randi, who shrugged. "You wouldn't happen to have some place I can sit while Randi talks to Dr. Wilde, would you? I'd really like to get off my leg for a few minutes."

Christina nodded. "Of course, dear. You follow me, and I'll introduce you around." She winked at Randi. "Go on, get your business done. We'll be back in the kitchen." She linked her arm with Kay's and started for the back of the clinic. "No sense in my waiting for the phone to ring. We haven't had any business in the last couple of days. Besides, there's an extension in the kitchen."

Randi waited until the two women left the foyer before taking a deep breath and knocking on the closed office door. *Here goes nothing.*

"What is it?" Dr. Wilde shouted, his voice scarcely muffled by the door. "I'm busy."

Randi slowly opened the door and stepped inside the office, closing the door behind her. "Dr. Wilde."

The balding man looked up from his desk. His face was sallow, and his hand shook as it reached for a coffee cup on the corner nearest him. "Dr. Meyers," he grumbled. "Never thought I'd see you back here."

"Yeah, well, I think we have a few things to discuss." Randi moved further into the room and stood behind one of the visitor's chairs. She placed both hands on the back of the leather seat and studied the older man for a long moment. He looked as if he had aged years since the last time she had seen him, and his usual arrogant demeanor was nowhere in evidence.

"Don't just stand there. Sit down, so I don't have to keep looking up at you." The old veterinarian pulled off his glasses and rubbed at them with a facial tissue, his hands trembling so badly that he almost dropped them several times before he put the frames back on his face. "What is it that you think we have to say to each other? I thought I fired you."

She took a deep breath and lowered herself into the visitor's chair on the opposite side of the desk from where he sat. "You did. But I've got a proposition that would be beneficial to both of us." Randi crossed her left leg over her right one, her ankle resting comfortably on her knee in a casual manner. The last thing she wanted to do was appear nervous, when in fact she was worried about her breakfast rebelling and embarrassing her. "That is, if you've got the time to listen."

"Go on." Dr. Wilde opened a desk drawer and pulled out a package of cigarettes, holding it halfway across the desk. "Smoke?"

God, yes! Whenever she was nervous or upset, the first thing Randi wanted was a cigarette. Knowing that Kay didn't smoke, Randi hadn't smoked since she'd brought Kay back with her, but every nerve in her body begged her to reconsider. "No, thank you," her rebellious mouth answered, much to her dismay. She fought the urge to jiggle her foot, wishing she had thought to bring breath mints or gum. *If he lights one up, I'll end up wrestling him for it.*

Dr. Wilde shrugged and tossed the pack back into the desk without removing a cigarette. "Suit yourself." He picked up a pen and began to tap it against the top of the desk. "Go ahead, I'm listening."

Tap. Tap. Tap. Randi watched the writing implement rap out a beat on the wooden surface, her nerves almost begging her to jump across the desk and cram it down the older man's throat. "Dr. Wilde," *Tap. Tap. Tap.* "it's come to my attention that you're considering closing down the clinic," she started, taking another deep breath to calm herself. *Tap. Tap. Tap.* "And I was wondering if you had thought about selling it, instead."

Tap. Tap. Tap. Tap. Tap. "Where did you hear that the clinic might be closing?" he asked. *Tap. Tap. Tap.*

"I have my sources," Randi told him. *Tap. Tap. Tap. Tap.*

"You do, do you?" *Tap. Tap. Tap. Tap. Tap.* "So what if I am?" *Tap. Tap. Tap. Tap.*

Dammit. I'm going to kill him if he doesn't stop that infernal noise. "If you are going to close down the clinic, I'd like to make you an offer for it."

Tap. Tap. Tap. Tap. Tap. The pen stopped momentarily as Dr. Wilde tilted his chin down and looked at her over his glasses. "You?" He started to laugh. "Don't be ridiculous." *Tap. Tap. Tap. Tap.* "You can't even afford a decent car, much less to buy this place from me." *Tap. Tap. Tap. Tap. Tap.*

Randi jumped to her feet, reached across the desk, grabbed the pen and threw it across the room. "For God's sake, will you stop that?" She remained standing, looking down at Dr. Wilde. "Look. You don't want this place anymore. Hell, you probably never did." She walked around the room and stopped to look at a diploma that was displayed on one wall. Turning around, Randi shoved her hands into the front pockets of her slacks. "Let me buy it from you, Dr. Wilde. At least that way, you'll get something out of it. What do you have to lose?"

Still miffed over the loss of his pen, Benjamin Wilde stood up slowly, bracing one hand on the desk for balance. "It might be worth it, just to see you fall flat on your arrogant face," he admitted gruffly. "You write up an offer, and I'll look it over." The old vet dropped back into his chair. "I might as well make some money off you."

"All right." Randi pulled her hands out of her pockets and held one across the desk. "Thank you, Dr. Wilde."

"Don't thank me, Meyers. Just leave me alone." He ignored her hand and turned the chair away from her. "I'm an old man. Don't make me wait too long."

Randi sighed. "Right." She walked over and opened the door. "I'll get back to you in a couple of days."

He waved one hand over his shoulder, still not looking at her. "Fine."

Asshole. Randi stepped through the door, fighting the urge to slam it closed. *I'm going to enjoy proving you wrong.* She shook off her anger and went in search of her partner. Stopping just outside the kitchen door, Randi could hear her lover's voice.

"...and she carried me up the hill and back to my house, with me unconscious," Kay related to the spellbound room, "then stayed all night with me at the hospital, not even knowing anything about me."

Three of the four women in the room were sitting around a formica-topped table, while the fourth was preparing coffee. A woman a few years younger than Kay propped her chin on her hand and sighed. "That's just so, oh, I don't know, gallant." She was sitting next to Joyce, across the table from Kay. "Like a knight in shining armor, or something."

"It was certainly heroic," Joyce agreed. "Not many people would do that for a total stranger." She looked over at the woman who was pouring water into the coffee machine. "Hurry up, Elaine. We could die of thirst before you get that made." She patted Kay on the arm. "Go on, we're listening."

Kay laughed. "There's really not that much left to tell. She stayed around for a couple of days; I think it was to make sure I wouldn't hurt myself again. Randi was worried that I couldn't take care of myself out where I lived, so she asked me to come back with her until she went back to her grandmother's for Thanksgiving." Afraid she was giving the other women the wrong idea, she waved her hands in front of her. "Her apartment has a really nice guest room," she rushed out.

The entire room broke out into laughter. "Oh, honey, you're priceless," Christina chuckled. "I knew she was stuck on you the moment I called her on the phone, and she told Dr. Wilde what he could do with a cat." She leaned over and whispered into Kay's ear, "To tell you the truth, she was completely miserable when she returned without you."

"I know," Kay murmured. "So was I." She looked up as the kitchen door opened and the topic of conversation stepped into the room. "Oh, hi."

"Why do I get the idea that you were talking about me?" Randi asked, grabbing a chair and sitting near Kay. She was too embarrassed to tell them that she had heard a large portion of the conversation.

Kay giggled. "Are you that full of yourself, Dr. Meyers?" She met the eyes of the other women around the table, who were all trying to keep from laughing out loud.

Randi shook her head. "Not quite. But I figured you must be gossiping about me, since you all got quiet when I walked in." She reached out and nonchalantly placed her arm around the back of Kay's chair.

"Kay was just telling us how you two met," Joyce explained. "If I had known you were strong enough to carry a woman around, I'd have invited you over when I moved furniture."

"Please. It was more of a piggy-back ride than carrying her." Randi tried to downplay her role in Kay's rescue. "And look at her. My niece could probably pick Kay up."

The young woman who sat next to Joyce had been quietly watching Randi since she'd come into the room, and she sighed again. *She's just so wonderful. Why can't I find someone like Dr. Meyers?* An elbow to her ribs jerked her out of her reverie.

"Stop that, Ramona," Elaine hissed under her breath as she sat down next to the starry-eyed girl. "Why don't you go out front and keep an eye out for clients? We'll be done here in a few minutes."

"I might as well," Ramona grumbled, pushing her chair back and standing up. "If you'll excuse me, I've got some things to do," she told the room's occupants, taking one last glance at Randi before stepping through the kitchen door.

Kay watched Ramona leave. She hadn't missed the looks the young woman had given her lover. *Someone's got a crush. I think Randi and I need to have a little talk when we get home. She probably doesn't even realize it.* The arm across the back of her chair snaked over her shoulders and squeezed. *Not that I have anything to worry about.* Kay turned her head slightly and looked into her lover's eyes. "Everything all right?" she whispered.

"I think so." Randi looked at the women around the table. "Ladies, if you'll forgive us, we've got an appointment in Dallas."

"Does this mean you're coming back to work soon?" Joyce asked. She was worried that the lack of patients over the last few days would become the norm, and the last thing she wanted to do was go looking for another job.

Randi stood up. "I can't really say. Not yet, anyway. But

hopefully I'll have something more concrete to tell you in a few days, all right?"

"Just don't keep us in the dark too long," Christina warned. "I'm an old woman, and I'd like to know something before my social security kicks in." She stood up and met Randi halfway, giving the younger woman another firm hug. "I'm glad you're so happy," she whispered in Randi's ear. "You take good care of each other, you hear?"

"Yes, ma'am," the vet agreed, just as quietly. "You can count on it." She escorted Kay to the kitchen door. "Let's see if Anne's going to be busy for lunch, shall we?"

Knowing what Randi meant, Kay just smiled. *Things are definitely looking up.*

The banker had been more than happy to meet Kay and Randi for lunch, and she suggested a Chinese restaurant not too far from her office. When she saw the two women enter, Anne stood up at her table and waved until Kay saw her.

"Have you been waiting long?" Kay asked, allowing a silent Randi to assist her in sitting down.

Anne shook her head. "I just got here. Did you have any trouble finding the place?" She looked at the sullen vet, who took a seat next to Kay without a word.

"No, not really," Kay fibbed. Her geographically challenged partner had taken several wrong turns, including going the wrong direction on a one-way street. *Thank God the traffic was light, and we were able to turn the car around so quickly. For someone who has lived here as long as she has, Randi sure gets lost easily.* "No problem at all."

Randi looked at Kay, but remained quiet. She was still upset with herself for the one-way street debacle. Kay hadn't said anything, but she knew that it had frightened her more than she'd let on. The incident shook Randi up as well. She felt responsible for her lover's well-being, and the fact that she could have gotten them both injured or killed weighed heavily on her mind.

Anne looked from one woman to the other, worry clearly evident on her face. "Uh-huh. Right. Why don't I believe you?"

"We would have been here a lot sooner if I didn't get lost every time I leave my own driveway." Randi picked up the glass of water that was sitting in front of her and took a long sip. "Not to mention the fact that I took a wrong turn a couple of blocks from here and had us going east on a westbound street."

"Oooh, that's tough on a person's ego," Anne said. "No wonder you're both looking pale and out of sorts! Let me lighten things up and tell you not too feel too badly, Randi. That happens a lot more often than you might think down here. As a matter of fact, a few weeks ago one of the city buses did that exact same thing. Only the results were not quite as lucky. I think the driver hit two cars and ended up getting fired."

"Really?" Kay turned to her partner and placed one hand on Randi's arm. "See, honey, I told you it was no big deal." Kay was still shaking inside from the entire episode, but she'd be damned if she'd let Randi know. "I personally don't know how anyone actually works here. I'd be scared to death to drive in this traffic every day."

"Well, if they're like me, they don't have to." Anne waved her hand discreetly at the waitress to get the woman's attention. "I drive to the train station that's closest to my house, and take the train in every day. It not only saves on gasoline, but my nerves stay intact. Then I usually just walk the couple of blocks from the end station to my office. No muss, no fuss."

The server chose that moment to come over and take their orders. Once everyone had selected their lunch entree, the server thanked them and hurried off to get their drink orders.

Randi sighed. "I don't know why I didn't think of that." She looked over at Kay. "Next time, we take the train. Deal?"

"Works for me." Kay was happy to see her friend coming out of her funk. "I don't know if I'll ever be ready to drive in this traffic."

"It's not too bad, once you get used to it." Randi shook her head ruefully. "Unless you're like me, and get lost in the parking lot at the mall."

Anne choked on the water she had just taken a sip from. "You're kidding, right?"

"Nope. You can ask anyone in my family. I'm famous for my sense of direction, or lack thereof."

"Have you considered getting a car with the interactive map features?" Anne asked. "My sister has trouble finding her way around, too. But she hasn't had any problems since she bought her last car."

"I don't know if I could give up my Corvette," Randi admitted. "That car is as much a part of me as what I do."

Kay saw the indecision on her lover's face. The last thing she wanted was for Randi to consider giving up something that was so obviously important to her. "Well, once this stupid cast comes off, I'll be in the market for a car," she announced. "Maybe I'll get one like that, and then when we have to go anywhere that we're not used to, we can take my car."

God, I love this woman. Who else would make that kind of an offer, just because she knows how much my car means to me? Randi gave Kay an appreciative smile. *Although, if the choice came down to keeping Kay safe or keeping the Corvette, I'd put an ad in the paper tomorrow.*

"That's a good idea." Anne was forestalled from making any other comments by the arrival of their food, which the server quickly distributed. After the woman left, Anne took a bite of her food and moaned. "I just love this place. They are incredibly fast, and the food is great."

They ate in silence for several minutes before the banker decided to ask the question that had been on her mind since Randi had phoned earlier. "So, I take it that you've made a decision about the loan?"

Randi chewed several times before swallowing. "Yes. I went to the clinic this morning and talked to Dr. Wilde. He was his usual obnoxious self, but told me to write up an offer and he'd take a look at it. I think he's about had it, to tell you the truth."

"Oh? What makes you say that?" Anne set her fork down on the edge of her plate. "Did he say something?"

"It wasn't so much what he said, as how he appeared. I think he's aged ten years in the past week." Although there was no love lost between the two, Randi was concerned that Wilde's business problems could be affecting his health. "I think I'll call his daughter in St. Louis, and see if she can come down and talk him into taking better care of himself."

Anne frowned. "That obnoxious old goat has a daughter? You mean that someone actually," she couldn't say the word, "had a child with him?" Her body shook in a fake shiver. "That's a scary thought."

This time it was Kay's turn to almost choke on her drink. She used her napkin to wipe her mouth before speaking. "Eeew. I haven't even met the man, and the thought scares me. What do you think, Randi? Could it have been one of those in-vitro things?"

"No." Randi snickered at the thought. "He was married at one time." She turned serious. "His wife passed away not long after I started working for him. She was a really sweet lady, and after she was gone, he changed." Randi thought back on how things used to be at the clinic before Mrs. Wilde had died. Benjamin Wilde was a caring, almost nurturing teacher, and had invited her over several times to have dinner with him and his wife. The love between the older couple was something that Randi never thought she'd see for herself, and she was thankful for Emma Wilde's acceptance of her in their home. The old veterinarian obviously adored his wife and had been devastated by her death.

"That's terrible," Kay murmured. She had always wondered why Randi would have agreed to work with someone as obnoxious as Dr. Wilde, and why she continually put up with his nasty temperament. She also knew that her partner had a very deep sense of loyalty and integrity, and now realized that's what had kept Randi at the clinic for so many years.

Randi said, "Yeah. It's a shame, really. It was like he turned into a different person, almost overnight. The man I started working for was a far cry from the guy who fired me last week." Randi studied her plate, trying to figure out if there was something that she could have done differently to keep things from progressing as they had. With a shake of her head, she realized that it was up to Dr. Wilde how he acted, and nothing that she did or said made much of a difference. "Maybe somewhere, deep down inside, the man I used to know is trying to get out. Perhaps that's why he so quickly agreed to sell the clinic to me." The comforting touch of Kay's hand on her arm warmed her heart. "Or, maybe he was just tired of messing with the whole thing and saw a way to get out from under it. We'll probably never really know."

"Well, whatever the reason," Anne waved her fork in the air, "let's just be thankful that he has come to his senses. I was hoping that you'd make up your mind to ask, and that he'd agree to sell. So, I've already got some people going through the paperwork."

Randi looked up. "You don't waste any time, do you? What made you so certain that I'd say yes?"

Anne's eyes took on a business-like glint. "Because, above all else, you want to do the right thing—both for you, and for the people you care about. I knew that after you thought about it, there'd be no doubt in your mind that owning the clinic would not only help you, but would also allow everyone else to keep their jobs." She took a sip of her drink before continuing. "I make it a point to study people, Randi. That's why I'm so successful at what I do." Anne smiled to soften her words. "So, tell me, was I wrong?"

Caught flatfooted, Randi blinked. *Was she?* "No, you're right. I guess I'm just a little surprised that you were able to figure me out so easily after knowing me for such a short period of time."

"Believe me, I have very good intuition. And after you risked your job to help someone that you didn't even know, I had a pretty good idea what kind of person you were."

Kay had been watching the exchange quietly while she

enjoyed her meal, her respect for the banker growing with every minute she listened. Anne seemed to have a keen insight into people and things that neither she nor Randi had yet developed, and it obviously made Anne successful in her career. Looking over at Randi, Kay smiled. It hadn't taken her any time at all to realize what a true treasure the vet was. Almost at first sight, Kay knew that she was a kind and sensitive person, and was thankful that Randi was the one that had found her in the woods that day.

"Thank you, Anne," Randi said. "I just hope I don't disappoint you." Not really full, but too keyed up to eat, Randi pushed her plate away, most of the food untouched. Just thinking about what she was about to embark on was enough to make her lose her appetite. "What do you need from me to get everything started legally?"

Anne wiped her mouth with her napkin. "If you don't mind, I would like to help you determine a fair offer. You shouldn't have to pay that old codger one cent more than the business is worth. Why don't you come back to my office, and you can fill out an authorization and sign a few papers. That way we can get the ball rolling and, hopefully, have the preliminaries done pretty quickly. I know you're probably itching to get back to work, but before you can take ownership and get him out of there, we have a lot of work to do."

"Well, I would like to have all of this done and behind me as soon as possible. It feels weird not going in to work every day." Randi looked at Kay and smiled. "Although, having a little time off right now is good, too."

Kay reached under the table and squeezed Randi's thigh. "I'm not going to disagree with you on that one. But I can tell you're beginning to get a little stir crazy."

Randi thought of refuting the gentle accusation, but knew that it was true. As much as she enjoyed spending so much time with Kay, a large part of her wanted to be back in the clinic, taking care of animals. It had been the one constant in her life, up until she met Kay, and she felt a little incomplete when she wasn't doing it. Her mind teemed with all of the opportunities that running her own clinic would provide, both for the staff and the clients.

Finished with her meal as well, Anne pushed her plate away and exchanged looks with Kay. They both smiled at the faraway look on the vet's face. "Well, ladies," Anne reached for the check that the server had left on the table, "let's go back to my office and get things underway, shall we?"

"You don't have to do that," Randi argued, pointing at the

bill. "We invited you."

Anne laughed. "Are you kidding? This was a business lunch. I have a generous expense account that rarely gets used. Don't worry about it." She left not only enough to cover the check, but a very large tip as well. "Ready?"

"As I'll ever be." Randi stood up and helped Kay from her chair. "Let's do this thing."

Chapter
19

Two days after the meeting with Anne Crawford, Kay watched Randi pace. They were at Randi's orthopedic surgeon's office for a consultation, and she had never seen her partner so nervous. She traded amused looks with another woman who sat across from her. "Randi, why don't you come over here and sit down?" Not receiving an answer, she gave the woman across from her an embarrassed grin and tried again. "Honey, please?"

"What?" The vet turned from where she had been studying a bookshelf holding medical journals. "Did you say something, Kay?"

Nodding, Kay looked back at the woman, who suddenly wouldn't meet her eyes. *'Phobe.* Biting off a sharp comment that would do no good, Kay patted the sofa cushion next to her. "Could you come here, please?"

"Sure." Randi crossed the room and dropped into the indicated seat. The doctor's office was filled with comfortable sofas and overstuffed chairs, giving the room a homey feel. Still antsy, she sat on the edge of the couch and bounced one knee. "What's up?"

"I was just going to ask you the same thing," Kay murmured, keeping her voice low so as not to disturb anyone else. "Did you have too much coffee, or something?"

Randi shook her head. "No, just the one cup of coffee this morning. Why?" She followed Kay's eyes to her leg, which still bounced nervously. "Oh. Sorry." The bouncing stopped, but Randi appeared to be ready to jump out of her chair at the slightest provocation.

Kay glanced at the woman across from them, who was studiously ignoring their conversation. The woman's demeanor had turned icy the moment she realized Kay and Randi were a couple. *To hell with her. She can just get over herself.* Placing one hand on her lover's thigh, Kay whispered, "What's wrong with you? I don't think I've ever seen you quite like this before."

"Nothing," Randi started, until she saw the look on Kay's face. *Damn. I can't get away with anything, can I?* She sighed. "I don't like doctors' offices."

"Not many people do, Randi."

Embarrassed, Randi suddenly found a spot on the carpet at her feet fascinating. "I don't know if it's the smell, or what, but it always freaks me out." *Pretty stupid, considering what I do for a living.* She was spared from making any further revelations when a side door opened and an older woman wearing bright-colored scrubs called Kay's name.

"Here." Kay handed Randi her purse and stood up. "Come with me?"

"Always." Randi followed the two women past the door and through a maze of counters and open doorways, until they were ushered into a tiny examination room. Not wanting to drive Kay crazy by pacing, Randi took a seat in the corner out of the way.

The nurse helped Kay sit on the padded table, then efficiently took her blood pressure and checked her pulse. Her duties completed, she scribbled a few notes on Kay's chart and patted the young woman on the leg. "Dr. Ramirez will be with you in a few minutes." With a polite nod to Randi, she left the room.

"Wow. They don't waste any time, do they?" Kay asked. The doctor she had been seeing in Woodbridge made his patients wait at least an hour in the waiting room, then another fifteen or twenty minutes once they were in the examination room.

Randi shook her head. "Nope. That's one of the reasons I come here, as a matter of fact. I don't have time to get too nervous." She was about to say something else when the door opened, and a middle-aged Latino man stepped into the room.

The bespectacled physician was an inch or two shorter than Randi, with a stockier build. His short hair was completely silver, and the friendly smile he wore was infectious. Holding out his hand to Kay, he introduced himself. "Hello, there. I'm Dr. Oscar Ramirez. You must be Katherine."

"Hi, Dr. Ramirez, I've heard a lot about you. You can call me Kay," she told him, shaking his hand. Kay was relieved at the cool, dry handshake, and glad to see that the doctor looked her directly in the eyes. *Points in his favor.* The doctor she had been forced to see in Woodbridge not only had clammy hands, but he'd had trouble meeting her gaze.

"All good, I hope." A quick glance at the quiet woman in the corner caused his smile to grow. "Randi! It's good to see you again."

"Hi, Dr. Ramirez. I thought that since I haven't been in for a while, I'd bring you another customer."

"That's great." He looked at Kay. "I don't mean that it's great *you* have to be here, just that I'm glad Randi thinks enough of me to give a referral." Dr. Ramirez studied Kay's chart for a moment. When he got to the area that told how the injury had happened, he cringed. "Ouch." Setting the paperwork back on the counter, he headed for the door. "All right, Kay. Let me get someone to wheel you to x-ray, and we'll go from there." He waved at Randi and hurried from the room.

Moments later, the nurse who had taken Kay's vitals brought in a wheelchair. "Miss Newcombe, let's get some pictures of that leg, shall we?" With some help from Randi, she assisted Kay from the table to the chair. "You can just wait here, if you want," she offered to Randi. "It shouldn't take too long."

Randi let out a heavy breath as she watched them leave. She sat back in the chair and scrubbed her face with her hands. As much as she usually disliked doctors' offices, she was glad that Dr. Ramirez was seeing Kay. He was one of the few physicians she trusted, since he was the one responsible for the fact that she was still walking after so many leg surgeries. Crossing her arms over her chest, she closed her eyes and tilted her head back until it rested against the wall.

"I can't wait to get home and do something about this." Kay limped to the car as fast as she could, causing Randi to practically jog to keep up with her.

Randi, struggling to catch her breath, finally caught up with her distraught lover at the Corvette, and unlocked the passenger door. "It's only temporary." Sliding into the driver's seat, she tried to ignore the glare Kay aimed her way.

Dr. Ramirez had declared Kay's injured limb healed and removed the cast, but he warned her that it would take some time for it to look "normal" again. Kay didn't know what mortified her more – the slight limp that she still had, or seeing the condition her leg was in once the cast was cut away. She had almost cried at the sight of all the dead skin, complaining that it looked as if she had turned into an alligator. Randi hadn't been much help, joking that she could always get a job on the television program which starred the Australian who wrestled with crocs.

Remembering that conversation, Kay glared at the woman driving. "I can't believe you said that," she grumbled.

Not realizing what Kay had been thinking, Randi assumed

she meant her comment about it being temporary. "Why not? It's true."

"Argh!" Kay threw up her hands in disgust. She looked down at her right leg, which was not only covered with dead skin, but with extremely long hair as well. "You don't have to be so damned smug about it." She knew that she wasn't being fair to Randi, but seeing the condition her leg was in after coming out of the cast put her in a foul mood. Dr. Ramirez had assured her that the skin would look better in no time, but the way her leg look embarrassed her just the same.

Uh-oh. Randi cringed at the tone in Kay's voice. *Somebody is cranky, and it looks like I'm in the doghouse.* She kept her eyes on the road, wracking her brain for something clever to say. Coming up empty, she tried another tack. "I'm sorry for whatever I might have said that upset you, Kay."

Kay scowled at her lover. "A job with that crocodile guy? How could you?" She crossed her arms over her chest and stared out the passenger window.

She's still mad about that? But I already apologized for that one. "Would ice cream help?"

"Maybe."

Randi frowned, but didn't look at Kay. "Ice cream served in bed, with hot fudge and whipped cream?"

Struggling to keep the smile off her face, Kay bit her lip. "With a cherry on top?"

"I'll give you all the cherries you want," Randi agreed, stopping at the red light.

Kay turned and looked at Randi. "You will, huh? I didn't think you had one, anymore," she teased.

Relieved that she was no longer in trouble, the vet grinned and wriggled her eyebrows. "I might not have the cherry, but I've got the box it came in."

"I can't believe you said that." Kay laughed and reached for Randi's arm to give it a gentle squeeze. "Forgive me for being such a whiny baby?"

"You have nothing to apologize for, Kay. I can understand why you're so upset." When the light turned green, Randi put the car in gear and took off. "I should never have made that crack about the crocodile guy."

Kay shook her head, then realized that Randi couldn't see her. "I shouldn't have been so sensitive. You were just trying to inject a little humor."

The next few minutes went by quietly, as each woman was relieved that the argument had ended so quickly. Randi hated fighting with Kay, no matter what the reason, and she felt horrible that she might have somehow hurt her partner's feelings. When she noticed a supermarket up ahead, she resolved to buy a few extra things and try to make it up to Kay. Dr. Ramirez had given them instructions on how to recondition the skin that had been under the cast, and she wanted to pick up the supplies that they would need. *Not to mention the ice cream, hot fudge, whipped cream, and cherries. I know that'll make her feel better.* She grinned. *Especially if I serve it up just right.*

Kay looked down at her lover, who was deeply engrossed in her task. Randi's head was bent forward in quiet concentration, and her hands moved gently and methodically. "Really, Randi. You don't have to—"

"Does it feel any better?" Without glancing up, Randi continued to lightly work the baby oil into the skin. She was determined to do the best job possible, no matter what Kay said.

"That's not the point."

Brown eyes peered up. "That's exactly the point, Kay. The doctor told us that this would help, and would also alleviate the itching. I know it's about to drive you crazy." Randi continued to work the oil into the skin on Kay's leg. When she had coated the limb to her satisfaction, she carefully wrapped a soft towel around the area and eased it from her lap onto the bed. "Now all we have to do is wait, then go from there."

"Thank you," Kay murmured. She was still upset over the day's events, and was secretly embarrassed that Randi not only saw the condition of her leg, but also didn't seem to have any qualms about touching it. *I don't think I could put my hands on that scaly, hairy mess. I can't wait until I can shave my leg again.* The doctor had explained to her that the skin would be extremely sensitive for several days, and that trying to scrub or shave the leg too soon would result in a lot of unnecessary discomfort. She had to admit that Randi's touch was more gentle than her own would have been. *No wonder she's such a good vet. With those hands, she could have been a surgeon.*

"Are you all right? I didn't hurt you, did I?" Randi sported a worried frown on her face.

Kay shook her head. "No, not at all. I was just thinking."

"About?"

"How gentle your hands are." Kay enjoyed the blush that covered Randi's features. "Did you ever think about becoming a people doctor?"

Randi cocked her head slightly, reminiscent of Spike, and chuckled. "Uh, no. For most of my life, I haven't even liked people, much less wanted to listen to their gripes and groans about how bad they feel. Animals are much easier, and usually a lot more appreciative."

Kay looked over at Spike, who had been chased off the bed and now sat near the bedroom door, his back to the bed. Randi had forced him down after he kept trying to lick the baby oil off Kay's leg. "I don't know, hon. He doesn't look too appreciative right now."

"He doesn't, does he?" Randi patted the bed next to her. "Hey, Spike. C'mere, fella." The little dog's ears twitched, but he gave no other indication that he had heard her. *Spoiled mutt.* With a heavy sigh, Randi stood up and walked over to the door. "Come on, buddy. It was for your own good, you know." Stooping to pick him up, she snuggled the animal to her chest. "I swear, you're worse than a kid sometimes."

"Why don't you bring him over here, and I'll try to appease him." Kay held out her hands. She looked down at the towel-wrapped limb and wriggled her toes. Relieved to not feel any pain, she slowly moved her foot from side to side. *Not too bad. I guess the doctor was right when he said that my youth worked in my favor.* She looked up as Randi handed Spike to her. "You poor baby. She was mean to you, wasn't she?"

Spike stretched his neck so that he could lick Kay's chin. Randi looked at the mutual love-fest and shook her head. "You have gotten him so spoiled," she accused good-naturedly. Once again, she considered herself lucky to have Kay with her. A lover who liked animals and who was also her best friend, Kay embodied just about everything Randi could want in the person who shared her life.

Seeing the faraway look on Randi's face caused Kay to smile. *I don't know what she's thinking, but it must be good.* She watched as Randi shook herself out of her reverie and sat on the end of the bed. "What's next on today's agenda?"

"Hmm?" Randi blinked and took a deep breath. "Sorry about that. Um, how about we see how your leg is doing, then think about lunch?"

"Sounds good to me." Kay didn't even grimace as Randi gently unwrapped her leg. "How does it look?"

Randi's eyes twinkled. "Do you really want me to say? I've gotten into enough trouble today, don't you think?" Not waiting for an answer, she set the leg down on the open towel and stood up. "Let me go get some warm water and a washcloth."

Kay gazed after her lover as Randi left the room. "She's pretty special, don't you think?" she asked Spike. Not getting an answer from the little dog, Kay leaned back against the headboard of the bed and sighed in contentment.

Randi lifted the cover off the skillet and peered inside. The fragrant steam wafted up and tickled her senses, causing her mouth to almost water in anticipation.

"Smells good."

Dropping the lid, Randi whirled around in surprise. "Jeez! You scared the crap out of me," she chastised Kay, who was grinning widely.

Kay stepped closer and then wrapped her arms around her lover. "God, I've been wanting to do this for forever."

Randi felt the strong arms around her squeeze tighter as she buried her face in Kay's hair. Overcome by emotion, she closed her eyes and swallowed hard. Knowing that the woman she loved was healthy, safe, and no longer hampered with the uncomfortable cast, Randi sent up a silent prayer of gratitude. "Me, too," she rasped, struggling with her feelings.

Pulling back slightly, Kay forced her lover to look her in the eye. "Hey, are you all right?"

"Yeah," Randi exhaled. "Just really glad you're doing better." The clatter of the lid covering the skillet brought her mind back to the matters at hand. "Damn." She spun around and turned the heat off, sliding the pan to a cool burner. "Dinner's ready."

"So I can see," Kay giggled. "What is it?" She tried to sneak a peek, but was gently bumped away. "I'm going to find out sooner or later, you know."

Randi shook her head. "You're almost as bad as Spike." A sharp bark at her feet told Randi that she had been heard. "Oh, so now you'll bark. Where were you when I was being sneaked up on?"

"Grr." Spike crouched down with his rear end up in the air, the tiny stub of a tail wriggling furiously. He jumped sideways and took up the same stance a few steps away. "Yark!"

"Good grief." Randi looked over to Kay, who covered her mouth with one hand to keep from laughing. "I can't believe he's on your side." She was secretly amused by Spike's devotion to her lover, but was not about to tell either one of them what she thought.

Kay reached up and scratched Randi underneath the chin and cooed. "Does this help?"

"Do you want dinner, or not?"

"Depends. What's for dinner?"

Knowing when she had been beaten, Randi lifted the lid to the skillet. "Sloppy Joes," she said proudly. "My own recipe."

"Mmm." Kay stepped gingerly over to the cabinet and brought down two plates, while Randi opened the package of hamburger buns. "This is so cool."

"What's that?"

Kay turned around with her hands full. "I get to help now." She brought the plates over to Randi, not even trying to keep the silly grin off her face. "I never thought I'd want to do household chores again, but you really do miss doing the simplest things when you can't do them anymore."

"I know what you mean," Randi said, heaping large mounds of the hamburger mixture on top of the buns. "I've always hated that helpless feeling." Randi gathered up the plates. "If you'll grab a couple glasses of tea, I'll bring the food."

"You've got it," Kay said, happily pulling two glasses from another cabinet.

Some time later, they were sprawled on the sofa together, watching a mindless situation comedy. Kay snuggled up close to Randi and leaned back into her lover's body. "This is nice."

"Sure is." Seeing an opening, Randi bent forward and nibbled on Kay's throat. "Really nice."

"Oooh." Twisting slightly, Kay was able to capture Randi's lips. She tangled her fingers in short, dark hair and pulled her lover closer. Insistent hands lifted the hem of her T-shirt, and Kay gasped at the sensations when one of those hands stroked her stomach. Pulling away so that she could see Randi's face, she choked out, "Bedroom. Now."

A wicked grin covered the vet's face as she assisted Kay to her feet. "What's the matter? Aren't you in the mood to make out on the couch?" Her hand was yanked hard as Kay started for the back of the apartment.

"Not when we have a perfectly good bed a few steps away." Kay led them into the master bedroom and pushed Randi onto the mattress. She grabbed the bottom of the navy-blue polo shirt Randi wore and quickly pulled it over the dark head, her eyes sparking with desire. When Randi reached behind herself to unclasp her bra, Kay shook her head. "No. Let me." She quickly stripped off her own shirt and leaned forward.

Randi noticed fuzzily that Kay had forgone her bra the

moment two breasts brushed up against her face, as Kay reached behind her to unhook the undergarment. Unable to control herself, Randi placed her hands on Kay's hips for balance and leaned over to nibble on the offering, huming happily.

"Oh, God," Kay moaned, her hands finally finding purchase on Randi's bare shoulders. She tried to remember what she had been doing, but gave up and leaned into the contact instead. The sweat pants and panties that she had slipped on earlier were quickly whisked down her legs, and Kay automatically stepped out of them. She closed her eyes when two strong hands squeezed her bare bottom and pulled her closer.

A quick spin and Randi was able to lay her lover on the bed, so that she could lean over the moaning woman. She finally released the hold her mouth had on Kay's breast, deciding instead to kiss and nibble a path down her stomach. When she felt fingers tangle in her hair, Randi smiled to herself at Kay's enthusiasm. Those same hands began to rub up and down her back, stopping when they felt the waistband of Randi's jeans.

"Off," Kay ordered, fighting with the brass button that held the denim closed. "I need to feel you," she begged, wanting the touch of bare skin. Her hands shook as they struggled with the button. "Please."

Randi took pity on Kay and helped her unsnap the jeans. She felt the insistent hands pulling them down while she tried to stand up long enough to remove the pants. As her foot hit the floor, her leg twisted and caused a searing pain in her knee. "Damn!" Randi turned and fell onto the bed on one hip, tears in her eyes as she wrapped both hands around the aching joint.

"Oh, God. Randi?" Kay sat up, alarmed. All amorous thoughts receded as she scooted around and leaned over the other woman. Randi's eyes were closed, and she silently rocked back and forth. Kay touched her shoulder gently, clearly at a loss. "What can I do?"

"Just give me a minute," Randi gasped, her eyes still tightly closed.

Kay looked on helplessly while her lover continued to rock slowly. She kept one hand on Randi's shoulder, trying to will the pain away. "I'm so sorry."

At the tone of Kay's voice, Randi forced her eyes open and looked up into the concerned face. The pain was finally beginning to ease enough that she could concentrate on something else. "No, Kay. You didn't do anything. I just stepped wrong and turned it, that's all." She sat up and looked at the jeans that were still around her ankles. "Um, could you..."

"Oh! Of course." Kay slid to the end of the bed and carefully eased the jeans from Randi's legs.

Once the pants were removed, Randi used her arms to drag herself up to the top of the bed, where she leaned back against the headboard with a pained release of breath. "Sorry about killing the mood."

"Don't you dare apologize," Kay ordered, then softened her tone. "Do I need to take you to the doctor?" She looked down at the offending knee, noting the swelling. "Or maybe get you an ice-pack?"

"An icepack would be great, thanks." Randi leaned forward and tried to put a pillow beneath her leg. The pillow was quickly taken away from her and Kay solicitously lifted the limb, tucking the pillow under it.

Kay crawled off the bed and started for the door. "I'll bring you some ice, and maybe some aspirin, too?"

Randi nodded. Although the leg still pained her considerably, she couldn't help but admire her lover's nude body. "Uh, sure. Aspirin's good." *And lots of ice,* she added to herself. *It's going to be a long night.*

Chapter
20

Morning came much too soon. After having a good breakfast, Randi asked Kay if she'd like to go to the clinic with her, and her partner quickly agreed. They enjoyed a leisurely shower together, which took a lot more time than they'd anticipated, and were just now getting dressed.

Kay stepped out of the bathroom, brushing her damp hair. "Are you sure you're up to this?" She watched as her partner tucked a white polo shirt into her khaki slacks. She was still concerned about Randi's knee, even though Randi had assured her that it felt fine.

Randi sat on the edge of the bed to put on her shoes. She looked up at Kay while she tied the shoes, grinning at the sight of her lover without a shirt. "Honestly, Kay, I'm all right. It's a little stiff today, but nothing that I'm not used to." Standing up, Randi was careful to put most of her weight on her "good" leg. *No sense in taking any chances.* She held out her arms. "See? Good as new."

"Uh-huh." Not convinced in the least, Kay lightly backhanded Randi in the stomach as she walked by. "That was sweet of Anne to have the papers delivered here this morning, wasn't it?" The contracts for the sale of the clinic and for Randi's loan had been delivered by messenger earlier in the day.

"It sure was." Randi picked up Kay's shirt from the bed and helped her into it. She stepped around Kay and started buttoning the pale yellow top. "It'll be interesting to see if Dr. Wilde will accept the offer or not, though. I'm never too sure about him."

Kay grasped Randi's hands after they finished with her shirt. "It's going to work out, Randi. Just wait and see."

"I hope so." Tired of worrying about it, Randi decided a change of subject was in order. "Say, after we finish at the office, how about going to look at kitchen tables?" She was determined to furnish the apartment so that Kay would be comfortable.

"Are you getting tired of balancing your plate on your lap?" Kay reached up and straightened Randi's collar. She leaned into Randi and inhaled deeply. "You smell good."

Randi bent her head and sniffed. "I used the same soap and shampoo that you do. Or maybe you're just subtly trying to tell me I stunk before." She flinched as Kay poked her in the ribs. "Hey."

"Teach you to pick on me."

"Right. Like you really need a reason to attack," Randi teased. "So, what do you think? Wanna go furniture shopping?"

"That sounds great. Is there any particular style that you've been considering?" She linked arms with Randi and led them from the bedroom.

Allowing herself to be escorted to the living room, Randi couldn't help but laugh. Kay was like her, always up to shopping, no matter what the reason. "I don't know that much about different styles of furniture. As long as it's sturdy and comfortable, I'm pretty agreeable."

Kay stopped before they reached the front door. "You're gonna regret saying that, Doc. I've got lots of ideas for the kitchen." In deference to the chilly morning, she took Randi's coat from the hook and held it out, smiling as her lover obligingly slipped her arms into the fabric.

"Well, let's go see about buying a clinic." Randi picked up the papers from the table and held the door open for Kay.

"Thanks." Kay led the way to the car, a tiny smile on her face.

Randi noticed the look while she opened the passenger door. She hurried around and climbed in behind the wheel. "What's the smile for?"

"I just thought it was nice how you let me help you with your coat. Normally, you won't allow anyone to do anything for you."

"Oh." Randi thought about Kay's words as she backed the Corvette out of the parking space. "I'm sorry, Kay. I never thought about it like that before."

Kay placed one hand on her lover's arm. "You had no reason to, Randi. And you certainly have no reason to apologize. I just enjoy getting to help you with things, no matter how small they are."

"I enjoy it too," Randi admitted quietly. "It's just that in my past relationships, nothing came without a price; and I got into the habit of declining every offer so as not to be indebted." Stopped at the exit from the apartment complex, Randi turned to look directly into Kay's eyes. "You're the first person I've ever wanted to let in, Kay. When you do little things like helping me with my coat, I feel very loved and pampered." She leaned over and lightly kissed Kay's lips. "Thank you."

Kay blinked several times while Randi put the car into gear and pulled out onto the quiet street. "If that's the thanks I get for helping you with your coat, remind me to do it again. Soon."

Benjamin Wilde sat alone in his office, his tired eyes staring remorsefully at the single picture frame adorning his desk. A lovely woman in her late fifties smiled back at him; the smile on her face was one he kept deep in his heart. The guilt he felt over her untimely passing gnawed at his soul; and, just like every day of his life, he sent her a silent plea for forgiveness.

They had scheduled their yearly vacation, a springtime trip to the mountains of Colorado, like they always did. A short flight from Dallas to Denver, then they would take a rented car and drive up to a cabin that they time-shared with another couple. But that last year, Benjamin had wanted to stay behind one extra day to attend a veterinarian's conference, and had sent Ada ahead without him. The mountain pass they normally had no trouble navigating was still covered with snow, and Ada's car skidded off the road into a ravine, killing her the instant it crashed against the frozen ground. He had always felt that if he hadn't been so caught up in his work, he would have been the one driving; and either his wife would still be alive, or he'd be buried alongside her.

One shaky finger reached out to the picture and gently caressed the glass. Benjamin felt his eyes fill with unwanted tears as his heart broke again at the loss. His contemplation was interrupted by a light knock on the office door. Angrily removing his glasses, the old doctor wiped the moisture from his eyes. "Come in," he snapped, upset at being disturbed.

The door opened, and his ex-associate's face peered in through the crack. "Dr. Wilde? I'd like a word with you, if I may."

"Fine, fine. Get in here and get on with it, Meyers. I don't have all day." He motioned to one of the chairs across from him. "Sit down."

Randi stepped the rest of the way into the room and took the offered seat. She could tell that Dr. Wilde was upset, and by the position of the photograph on his desk, she had a pretty good idea why. If she remembered correctly, his wedding anniversary would be coming up within the next week or so, and he always got more depressed around that time. "If this is a bad time, I can come back," she offered, starting to rise from her chair.

He waved an impatient hand. "No, you've already disturbed me. Might as well tell me why."

"All right." Randi placed a stack of papers on the desk in front of the older man. "I believe you'll find everything in order, Dr. Wilde."

"You think so?" He gathered up the papers and studied them carefully. Several minutes went by while he scanned each page, nodding or mumbling to himself every now and then.

Just as Randi thought he'd never finish, the papers dropped to the desk surface. He took his glasses off and rubbed his eyes. Unable to wait any longer, she leaned forward. "Well? What do you think? I believe it's a fair offer."

"It is."

Not knowing whether that was a statement or a question, Randi stood up, angry. "Okay. I can see we're not going to get anywhere today, so I'll just leave those with you." When she reached the door, his quiet plea caused her to stop.

"Wait." Dr. Wilde stood up and held out one hand. "Please, sit back down, Randi."

The defeated tone in the older man's voice and the use of her first name brought Randi back to her chair. "All right. What is it?"

"These last few years have been pretty rough, haven't they?" he asked, sitting back down as well. "But you stuck it out."

Randi frowned. *What is he up to?* She nodded slowly. "I've had better," she admitted.

Benjamin flipped through the contract until he got to the last page, then picked up his pen and started to sign his name.

"Wait. Don't you want a lawyer to go over that?"

The tired old eyes glinted with a long-forgotten sparkle. "Would you try to cheat me, Dr. Meyers?"

"Of course not! But—"

Ignoring Randi's sputtering, Benjamin signed the agreement and set his pen back on the desk. "You've become quite a good veterinarian, Randi. I wish I could take credit for that." He stood up and held out the papers with one hand. "Good luck to you. I'll have my things out in the next few days."

"You...but..." Randi accepted the papers and tucked them under one arm. She shook his hand and took a deep breath. "Believe it or not Dr. Wilde, you helped make me what I am today. Back in the beginning, I learned a lot from you." She released his hand and stepped back, sticking her hands in her front pockets. "There's no rush on you leaving, Doctor. Take whatever time you need." She walked to the door, then turned back, and her demeanor softened. "If you ever need anything, Benjamin, I hope you'll call me. No matter what it might be, or when."

A smile crossed his features as he watched the younger

woman leave the office. Benjamin turned back to look at his wife's picture. "Well, Ada, looks like I've finally done something right." He sat down in the leather chair once again and took stock of the office. "I should have done this years ago. I've just been fooling myself."

Randi walked into the kitchen break room and was met by several expectant faces. Christina, Elaine, Ramona, and Kay sat around the round table. Still in shock herself, she couldn't think of anything to say.

"Well?" Kay asked, standing up and walking over to her lover. "How did it go?"

Waving the stack of papers in the air, Randi grinned. "Does this answer your question?"

Kay squealed. "He signed? Congratulations!" She wrapped her arms around Randi's neck, kissing her partner full on the mouth. Suddenly remembering they weren't alone, Kay blushed and buried her face in Randi's shirt. "I can't believe I did that," she mumbled.

"I can." Randi pulled Kay close. "Thanks." She looked at the expectant faces around them. "Ladies, you're looking at the proud new owner of this clinic." The other women quickly surrounded them, everyone talking at once. "Hold on, folks. Let's not get ahead of ourselves."

Joyce clapped her hands gleefully. "I don't care. This is the best thing that's happened to me since chocolate." She nudged Ramona, who was staring at Kay. "Don't you think so, hon?"

"Yeah, right," Ramona agreed sullenly. She was aware of the relationship between Kay and Randi, but hadn't been prepared for the cold, hard truth hitting her in the face.

Christina smiled at the vet. "So, when do you start?" She laughed at the confused look on Randi's face. "You *are* planning on working here, aren't you?" she teased.

"Of course!" Randi squawked. She looked at the circle of women, suddenly realizing that her dream had just become a reality. "How's business been, lately?"

"What business? You two are the only ones who have come through the door in the last day or so," Joyce griped.

Randi looked at Kay, who nodded. "All right. Everyone be back here on Monday, and we'll get started on bringing the clients back."

The chime on the front door made everyone pause. Christina peeked out through the kitchen door, then turned back to the other women. "Nobody's there."

"That's strange." Randi pushed the door open and walked to
the front of the clinic. She was followed by Kay and the rest of the
women, and stopped when she saw a set of keys sitting on the
receptionist's desk. A short note was under the keys, and she
picked it up to read, holding the keys in her other hand.

Dr. Meyers,
I won't need these anymore. Yes, I know that the sale isn't
final, but I have faith that it will go through as planned. I was sur-
prised to find that there wasn't much to pack in my office, and
took the liberty of "borrowing" an empty box to remove what few
items I had. The desk and chair are yours—consider them an
office warming present.
Thank you for your loyalty and perseverance—I have no
doubts that you'll succeed.
Sincerely,
Benjamin Wilde

"He's gone?" Kay asked. She had been reading over Randi's
shoulder, and was somewhat disappointed that she still hadn't met
the infamous Dr. Wilde. *Looks like I never will, either.*

Randi nodded, looking out into the parking lot and not seeing
the familiar Cadillac. "Looks like it." She felt an unreasonable
pang of sadness at not having had the chance to say goodbye.
Although they had fought bitterly the last few years, Randi could
remember when the old vet was a kind and patient teacher. *Good-*
bye, Benjamin. And good luck to you. "Believe it or not, I'm actually going to miss him," she whispered, glad to feel Kay's calming
touch on her back as one chapter in her life ended and another
began.

"That looks like a good place to start," Kay said, pointing to
a well-known furniture store a block away from where they sat at a
traffic light.

Randi nodded. "Works for me. How's your leg holding up?"

"It's fine."

"Going to kill me for asking you the same question all the
time?" Randi wore a concerned expression on her face. "I'm sorry,
I don't mean to—"

Kay touched Randi's arm. "It's okay, Randi. I don't mind at
all." She shrugged her shoulders. "Kind of nice, to have someone
care enough about me to ask, if you want to know the truth. So,

no, I don't think I'm going to get mad at you for caring."

"That's a relief." As the light turned green, Randi put the car into first gear and started down the street, changing lanes so that she could pull into the parking lot of the furniture store.

Once the Corvette was in a slot, Randi walked behind Kay as her lover navigated the few steps up to the door. She enjoyed seeing how well Kay's jeans fit, and couldn't seem to keep the wolfish grin from her face. *Definitely nice. I think I'm going to like following her around.* The object of her desire turned around and held the door open, ruining her view.

"Do I want to know what you're thinking about?" Kay asked.

Randi walked past her into the store, discreetly patting Kay on the bottom. "Probably not."

They hadn't made it five steps into the showroom when a young man raced forward to greet them. Not much taller than either one of the women, he wore an inexpensive gray suit on his lanky body. With the aid of styling gel, his short red hair stood up in all directions in what he probably thought was the latest style. He walked up to Randi and held out his hand. "Good afternoon, ma'am. My name is Robbie. Is there something in particular that I can help you with today?" He looked past Randi to Kay, studying her with a practiced eye.

Yeah. Don't call me ma'am, you little turd. Randi heard the unladylike snort from her companion when the salesman addressed her. "We're looking for a kitchen table and chairs," Randi explained, resisting the urge to slap the young man's gaze from her lover. "Think you can handle that?"

"Yes, ma'am. We've got formal, informal, glass tops, oak, maple, cherry—"

Randi glared at the young man. "Why don't you just show us where they are, and we'll let you know if anything catches our eye, *son.*"

Robbie pointed to one corner of the store. "Right back there, ma'am." He couldn't figure out what her problem was, but figured that she was just having a bad day. Robbie noticed that her short, dark hair was highlighted with quite a few strands of silver, and he thought she was a decent looking woman. *In her day, anyway.*

Kay grabbed Randi's arm and led her to the back of the showroom before her lover could say anything else to the salesman. "C'mon, ma'am. I'll help you find your way."

With a heavy sigh, Randi allowed Kay to drag her through the store. *I hate being called ma'am. Makes me feel old.* She remembered the look the salesman had given Kay. *Hell, I am old—at least to brats like that.* Her mental musings were interrupted when

Kay stopped in front of a dining room suite.

"Well, what do you think of something like this?" Kay pulled out one of the chairs and sat down. "Seems sturdy enough."

Randi sat down in the chair opposite Kay. "Not bad. I like the color, too." The rectangular-shaped table was made of light oak, with a butcher-block top and six matching chairs. She leaned back in her chair until the front two legs were off the ground. "Yep. Good and sturdy."

Robbie's voice caused Randi to fall forward quickly, almost unseating her. "I see you've found one of our most popular sets," he gushed, sitting down at the table next to Kay. He looked at each woman, then settled on Randi's face. "Divorce, I'll bet, right?"

"What?"

Robbie waved one hand in the air. "I see it a lot in my business." He tried to sound worldly, but came off more like a little boy playing a make-believe game. "You and your daughter must be having to start over in a new place, that's why you're here buying a table and chairs."

"My what?" Randi asked, jumping to her feet in shock. "Did you just say what I thought you said?"

He nodded, oblivious to the severely shortened life span his comments had the potential to bring about. "Now, now. Don't you worry. We've got a really good lease-to-own program for first-time buyers. Starting over won't be as bad as you think."

"I hate to break this to you, Robbie," Kay said, standing up and walking over to her seething partner. She linked arms with Randi and smiled sweetly at the young sales clerk. "This wonderful lady is not my mother. She's my girlfriend."

The look on Robbie's face was priceless. "G...girlfriend? As in..."

"Oh, yeah." Kay gave the young man a very sexy smile. She looked up into Randi's face, which was now struggling to hold back a huge grin. "Why don't we go somewhere else, honey? It's obvious we're not going to be satisfied here." She began to lead a silently amused Randi away, while Robbie looked on in confusion. Loud enough so that he could hear her, she said, "Let's go home, where I know I'll be satisfied."

They were barely out the doors when Randi's laughter broke the silence. "I can't believe you said that." Randi followed Kay to the passenger's side of the Corvette. She unlocked the door and waited until Kay was seated, then hurried around the car and climbed in behind the steering wheel. "I'm sure glad you're on my side."

Kay laughed, proud of herself. Her first reaction when Robbie had mistaken Randi for her mother was to get in the young man's face and yell; but after seeing how upset her partner had become, she decided to defuse the situation with a little fun instead. "I couldn't help myself. That little pissant annoyed me from the moment we walked into the store. He was just asking for it."

"Well, you certainly got his attention," Randi agreed. She realized she had never had a lover stand up for her before. The feeling, although pleasurable, was something she was going to have to get used to.

Her two older brothers were rarely around when she'd needed them, and were often the cause of many of her problems growing up, so she'd never felt comfortable asking for their help. Throughout her life, she had rarely shared her disappointments or troubles with her parents, either. Although they were very supportive of her, Randi had always held her innermost feelings back from them for fear that they wouldn't understand, since she really didn't understand herself.

A quiet child grew into a private adult, and Randi learned quickly that sharing with someone who only claimed to love her brought heartache and pain, especially when that person would throw her words back in her face when it suited their purpose.

The interior of the car was silent for several minutes, both women lost in their own thoughts. Randi glanced over at Kay and realized with startling clarity that she was no longer alone, that the woman sitting across from her would never intentionally hurt her. The feeling was a heady one and brought a lump to Randi's throat. "I can't believe how lucky I am," she murmured, surprised that the words were spoken aloud.

"I'm going to have to disagree with you on that one." Kay turned in her seat so that she faced Randi. Her bright eyes shone with love. "I'm the lucky one."

Randi grinned. "Guess this will have to be an ongoing argument, then. Because I know for a fact that being with you is the best thing that has ever happened to me, and that definitely makes me the lucky one."

Speechless, Kay could only reach across the car and take Randi's hand in hers, pulling it close to her chest while she basked in the love between them.

Soft instrumental music played in the background as Kay glanced across the linen-covered table. Between the dimmed lights and the flickering of the table candle, romance filled the air. Randi had suggested that they go out to dinner to celebrate, and had somehow finagled a reservation at an exclusive, local Italian restaurant. They were seated in a partially enclosed booth in one of the alcoves off the main dining room. Kay was almost afraid to ask what the reservation alone had cost her partner, but knew better than to try and find out. She took a sip of her water and smiled. "This is wonderful, Randi. It feels almost surreal, being in a place like this. Thank you for bringing me."

"You're welcome. You deserve to be treated like this all the time, Kay. You're a very special woman." Randi reached across the table and covered Kay's hand with hers, squeezing lightly. "Thank you for being here."

Wow. She knows just the right thing to say. Kay was so happy, she felt as if her heart would burst. Before she could say anything in response, their waiter appeared at the table, a smile on his face.

"Good evening, ladies. My name is Adolfo," he greeted in a thick Italian accent. "Our chef is anxiously awaiting your decision, so he will know what to prepare for you."

Randi looked up at the young man and laughed. "Adolfo?" His short, blonde hair was slicked back, and the blue eyes that glittered from beneath the pale eyebrows belied his accent. *If he's Italian, then I'm a size six.*

His pale face turned a deep shade of red. "Okay, so my real name is Adam, but most people expect authentic Italian when they dine here, so I'm Adolfo." Gathering his wits about him, Adam nodded at the women's linked hands. "Special occasion? Anniversary, perhaps?"

Caught off guard, Randi stammered, "Uh, no. I mean, yes." Touching Kay seemed like the most natural thing in the world to her, and she didn't even realize she was doing it half of the time. Although normally concerned about appearances, she wasn't very worried about the opinion of a waiter in a restaurant they would rarely patronize. *Besides, she thought after studying the young man closely, he's about as straight as I am.*

Adam obviously decided to let his customers off the hook. Randi thought that he must have realized if he went too far, it would affect his tip. "Would you like to see the wine list? We have some very nice vintages in our cellar."

"No, thank you." Although a glass of wine sounded good to Kay, she didn't want to make Randi feel uncomfortable. "I think I'd just like to have iced tea, please."

"Very good." Adam's demeanor switched back to professional, but without the fake accent. He turned to Randi. "And for you, madam?"

"Tea will be fine." Randi closed her menu and looked across the table. "Everything on the menu looks good, Adam. Is there something you would suggest?"

His eyes lit up. "Oh, definitely. You should try the *Costoletta di maiale con funghi e prosciutto d'oro*. It's one of the chef's specialties."

Randi's eyes widened. "You mind telling me what that is in English?"

"Grilled pork chop with pan roasted garlic, *prosciutto di parma,* roasted mushrooms and veal reduction," Adam recited with a flourish. "But it sounds much fancier in Italian."

Both women laughed, but Kay was the first to speak. "It sounds wonderful, Adam. I believe I'll try it." She turned her attention to her partner. "What about you?"

"Sure." Randi nodded to the waiter. "Go ahead and make that two."

"*Eccellente.* Would you care for an appetizer?"

Randi shrugged. "Surprise us."

Adam's smiled widened. "Oh, goodie. I know just the thing." He took the menus, bowed, and waved to someone on the other side of the room. "Vito will bring your drinks, and I'll have the appetizer out momentarily." Another bow, and he disappeared as quickly as he had come.

"That was certainly entertaining." Kay almost jumped when another young man silently placed two glasses of iced tea in front of them and scurried away. "Do they test them for sneakiness before they hire people around here?"

Randi picked up her glass and took a sip of tea. "They're certainly efficient." She looked up when the same man returned, carrying a bottle of champagne and two glasses. "You must have the wrong table. We didn't order this."

He popped the cork on the bottle and poured them each a glass. "It was sent by a friend of yours," he answered, discreetly indicating another table.

"What friend? We really don't—" Kay paused when she saw who he pointed to. Across the room, an elegantly dressed woman wiggled her fingers in a tiny wave. "I don't believe this."

Randi frowned and also peered across the room. "Of all the nerve." She scooted out of the booth and grabbed the bucket that held the champagne. "I'll be right back." The furious woman stalked across the room, leaving Kay to try and explain the situation to the waiter.

"Hello, sugar," Melissa purred, as Randi none too gently placed the bucket on her table. "What a nice surprise, running into you like this."

"Cut the bullshit, Melissa. What the hell are you doing here?"

Tossing her auburn hair over one shoulder, Melissa continued to smile sweetly. "Having dinner, silly. Did you follow me here?" She reached out with one long fingernail and drew a line across Randi's hand, which was still perched on the ice bucket. Randi jumped back as if she had been burned. In a sultry voice, Melissa said, "I've missed you."

"I can tell you've been pining away for me," Randi bit off sarcastically. "Just our rotten luck that you decided to crawl out of your hole tonight."

"Ouch, that stung." Red painted lips curled into a nasty smile as Melissa glanced across the room. "I see she still hasn't had the sense to dump you." She grabbed the cuff of Randi's shirtsleeve and pulled her closer. "They say those small-town types aren't too bright. It'll probably take her a while to... Hey!" Melissa grimaced as her hand was caught and squeezed in a tight grip.

Randi leaned down to keep from being overheard. "Watch your damned mouth, you obnoxious bitch. One more nasty word about Kay and I'll—"

"You'll what?" a man's voice asked from behind Randi. "Who the hell are you?" He pushed by the angry woman to stand behind Melissa's chair, his hands taking up residence on his date's shoulders. "Is this woman bothering you, Melly?" The well-dressed man brushed the front of his tie and studied Randi closely. He reeked of money, from his designer suit to his expensive haircut and glittering jewelry. Given the gray hair and matching mustache, Randi assumed he was at least fifteen years Melissa's senior.

Melly? Who the hell is this guy? Randi released the hold she had on Melissa's hand and stepped back.

Melissa turned her head to give her companion a fake smile. "No, sugar. We're old friends. I believe she was just leaving." She looked back at Randi and winked. "I'm sure we'll run into each other again, won't we?"

"Not if I can help it," Randi muttered. She spun around and walked back to the booth where Kay sat waiting impatiently. Sliding back into her seat, Randi placed her napkin back into her lap and forced a smile onto her face. "Sorry about that."

"Are you all right?" Kay leaned across the table as far as she could. "Who was that guy with her?"

Scrubbing one hand across her face, Randi shook her head. "I don't know. Probably her latest conquest. She never was particular about which gender she slept with." She noticed that the champagne glasses were absent from their table, and was thankful for Kay's foresight. Although it had been almost a year since she had last had a drink, the confrontation with Melissa weakened her resolve. Her nerves on edge, Randi picked up her glass of tea and drank deeply.

Kay studied her lover with worry written all over her face. Randi looked pale, and Kay saw how her hand shook as she picked up her glass. "Let's go."

"What?" Randi's head jerked up and her eyes bored into Kay's.

"Let's get out of here. Dinner's not worth seeing you upset like this, Randi. We can pick up something on the way home." Kay grabbed her purse and was about to stand up when Randi reached over and touched her arm.

"Wait, please." Not even thinking of how it would appear to anyone else who might be watching, Randi stood up and slid into the booth next to Kay. She turned to face her lover. "If it's all right with you, I'd like to stay." Her face hardened momentarily. "I don't want to give that bitch the satisfaction of us leaving."

Everything faded into the background when Kay looked deeply into Randi's eyes. She brought her hand up to caress the clenched jaw. The protective streak that had just recently emerged came to the forefront in full force. It took most of Kay's self-control to keep from jumping up from the table and racing across the restaurant to slap the redhead for what she had put Randi through, both now and in the past. Even though staying was the last thing she wanted, she could see Randi's point. "Are you sure? Because nothing in this entire world is as important to me as you are."

The gentle touch on her face and the loving concern coming from Kay helped Randi to relax. She leaned into the touch, turning her head to place a soft kiss on Kay's palm. "I'm very sure." Randi's face finally softened. "How's your leg? Think you'd feel up to going dancing, after dinner?"

"My leg is fine," Kay murmured, leaning closer until their faces were almost touching. "But I think I'd rather go home and do some private dancing. Let's take our pork chop dinners and go home."

Oh, yeah. Randi felt that one quiet statement all the way down into her toes. "That sounds like a really good idea to me." Randi struggled to keep her voice normal. She turned and pretended to motion to the waiter. "Check, please."

Chapter
21

"Oh yeah, baby...that's really good," the dark-haired woman crooned. "Mmm."

"You're insatiable." The blonde put her finger up to the other woman's lips. "Here. See if you like this," she offered. "I know you have a weakness for this flavor."

A soft, pink tongue quickly wrapped itself around the extended digit, pulling the finger into her mouth. "Mmm...my favorite." Laughter from across the patio caused Anne to look up and blush. "Well? Can I help it if she makes the best damned barbecue sauce I've ever tasted?" She patted her lover on the rear and walked back over to where their guests were seated. "Just wait until you taste it."

"I'm sure it's great," Kay agreed from her comfortable seat next to Randi. An unseasonably warm Saturday afternoon allowed them all to relax on the back patio of Laurie and Anne's home. Randi and Kay shared a colorfully padded outdoor love seat while they enjoyed watching Anne tease Laurie, who was handling the barbecuing duties on an expensive gas grill.

Anne winked as she sat on a nearby glider. "It's wonderful. Laurie's the cook around here, since I even have trouble with microwave dinners." She tucked one foot beneath her and brushed her dark hair away from her face. "I'm so glad you two could make it today. With both of our schedules, we don't have many opportunities to socialize. Laurie has to stay pretty low-profile at her job, and we hate doing the club scene."

"Are you out at work?" Randi asked, curious. "Or do you have to watch out, too?" She knew that a lot of professional women kept their private lives private, although it hadn't been much of a necessity for her.

"Everyone I work with knows that Laurie and I are a couple," Anne admitted. "I don't go waving rainbow flags or spouting rhetoric, and they pretty much accept us for who we are. She goes to all the company functions as my date, and no one has ever given us a hard time." She looked up as Laurie sat down next to her and put an arm across the back of the glider. "Isn't that right, Laur?"

Laurie nodded. "Yep. I think a lot of my co-workers pretty much know, but it's just not discussed. The good old, 'don't ask, don't tell' bullshit." Her blue eyes twinkled. "But I'm guessing that won't be much of a problem for you, will it, Kay?" The first thing that had been discussed after their guests' arrival was Randi's ownership of the clinic, and Kay's new job as office manager.

"I sure hope not," Kay joked. She tilted her head to look into Randi's eyes. "Do you think my boss will have a problem with me being gay?"

The hand on Kay's thigh squeezed the denim-clad leg. "I think that your boss would have more of a problem if you weren't."

Kay snuggled closer so that her head was tucked against her lover's shoulder. She wrapped an arm around Randi's middle and sighed. "I just hope I don't let you down."

"No chance of that. If you can keep me even partially organized, it will be a miracle." Randi knew from past experience how badly the entire office system needed to be overhauled. Christina had been after Dr. Wilde for years about hiring someone to come in and get everything straightened around, but the old vet had been reluctant to part with the money necessary to fund the changes. "Christina will be thrilled to have you there, believe me."

"Are you sure about that? From what you've told me, she's pretty much run that office for twenty years. If I were in her position, I don't think I'd appreciate some young smart aleck just showing up and taking over."

Randi laughed. "Well, if you were some young smart aleck, there might be a problem. But you're anything but that, sweetheart." The look on Kay's face was so open, so honest, that she couldn't help but lean down and give her a gentle kiss.

"New love," Anne sighed quietly. She turned her head to look into her own lover's eyes. "Remember when we first got together? Seems like a lifetime ago." The emotion that emanated back from Laurie's eyes brought back the memories. It helped her to realize that although they were about to celebrate their twenty-first anniversary in a couple of months, the love and commitment they shared was as strong today as when they'd first met.

"How could I forget? Your first words to me were, 'Get off me, you smelly jock.'" Laurie had been on the college basketball team and had jumped into the crowd while trying to keep the ball from going out of bounds. She ended up sprawled on top of the snooty sophomore business student and the woman that had been her date, and decided with those few words that she had fallen in love. "I thought for sure you were going to have me arrested for stalking you," Laurie reminisced. The junior law major found out what the spectator's name was from a mutual friend, and she began sending Anne flowers, candy, and letters, finally wearing her down. Once they got past the first date, they realized how much they had in common and had been inseparable since.

"I was pretty insufferable, wasn't I?" Anne giggled. She caressed Laurie's cheek and shook her head. "How did you ever stand me?" Soft lips covering hers were the only answer she needed.

Kay was looking over at their hostesses, who seemed to be totally caught up in each other. The two women were almost sitting on top of each other with their foreheads touching, quietly talking to one another. This was something else that was new to her: friends. She had socialized with people she'd worked with, and even some who had gone to school with her, but there had been few women that she felt comfortable enough with just to spend quiet time together. Kay was about to say something to Randi when she felt something heavy brush up against her leg. Looking down, she stared into big, brown eyes. "You must be Clarice."

"That's Clarice, all right." Randi reached down and scratched the big dog's neck. "How are you doing, girl?" For an answer, Clarice lay down at their feet and rolled onto her back, begging for her tumy to be scratched.

"She's a sweetie." Kay watched as her partner knelt down beside the animal and inspected her surgical scar. This was the first time that she had witnessed Randi working, and she was enjoying the opportunity to see how the vet related to her patients. She wasn't surprised by the gentle touch or the soft words of comfort that the vet murmured, especially after seeing the way Randi treated Spike.

While Laurie checked on the grill, Anne crossed the patio to squat down beside Randi. "Is everything okay here?"

Finishing her quick examination, Randi continued to pet the contented animal. "She's doing great, Anne. I'm sorry I haven't been around more to keep an eye on her."

"You have nothing to apologize for. Your receptionist put us in touch with another vet, who even dropped by and checked on Clarice after we brought her home." Anne looked into Randi's eyes and smiled. "Thank you," and then was almost knocked on her rear when Clarice jumped up, shook herself off, and jogged over to sit next to Laurie. Laughing, Anne climbed to her feet and offered a hand to the vet, pulling Randi up beside her. "She may be my dog on paper, but Clarice is all Laurie's."

Randi dusted off the knees of her jeans. "I know what you mean. I used to have a dog, too." She pointed at Kay, who was trying to appear disinterested in the conversation. "But one look from her, and he was smitten." Not that she could blame the animal any. The moment that Randi had seen Kay's face, she was lost. *And I've never regretted a single moment.*

"If you ladies can quit talking about my best girl," Laurie teased from her place at the grill, "lunch is ready."

"See what I mean?" Anne tossed her hands up in the air in mock disgust and crossed the patio to swat her partner on the rear, eliciting a playful growl from Clarice.

Bright flashes from overhead streetlights skipped sporadically into the interior of the Corvette as it sped through the city streets, painting the occupants in muted fragments of gold and silver. Kay was stretched out in the passenger seat, a contented smile on her face as she turned her head to study the profile of her lover. The different shades of light coming from the streets gave Randi a more youthful look by hiding the tiny lines of worry that etched her face. "I had a really good time today, didn't you?"

"Yeah, I did." Randi turned her head long enough to flash Kay a sincere smile. "It's still pretty early. There's a live band down at this little club I know. Want to check it out after we take care of Spike?" She had considered driving directly to the nearby bar, but didn't think it would be right without asking what Kay wanted to do. *Besides, Spike is probably dancing around right now. No sense making him suffer.*

"That sounds like a great idea." For some reason, Kay didn't feel like going home just yet. *Listening to a local band might be kind of fun.* Still trying to learn the area, she was surprised by how close they were to the apartment. "I'm never going to figure out where everything is around here."

Randi chuckled as she wheeled into her assigned parking space. "Sure you will. If you want, I can let you drive and I'll just navigate. That might help you learn your way around better."

She's offering to let me drive her car? Surprised, Kay almost stumbled getting out of the Corvette. She was grateful for the steadying arm that wrapped around her waist as Randi escorted her up the walk. "Did I understand you correctly? You'd let me drive your car?"

"Sure." Barking could be heard from inside as Randi struggled to unlock the door. "All right, all right. I'm hurrying." A turn of the knob, and she pushed the door open and flipped on the light. Spike ran happy circles around the couple, barking to let them know he was glad they were home. Randi grabbed his lead from the nearby table and knelt to clip it onto the excited dog's collar. "Would you please calm down?"

Kay leaned against the door frame and enjoyed the show. She marveled once again at the type of person she had fallen in love with. *Not many people would detour from a night out on the town, just to let a dog outside.* The genuine affection Randi had for Spike reinforced Kay's thoughts on what kind of parent her partner would be. She also knew that was one subject she wanted to broach sometime in the future.

A few minutes later, the three of them returned from their quick walk around the empty field next to the apartment complex. The entire area was well lit, and it afforded Spike the room he needed to run without being hampered by the leash. He sat sadly by the front door as Randi and Kay left, almost causing Kay to cancel their plans out of pity.

"He looked so upset," Kay said, when Randi climbed into the car beside her.

"Of course he did. He's a master of manipulation." Randi started the vehicle and backed out of the parking space. "Don't worry, Kay. He'll have forgotten all about it by the time we get back." The Corvette had just turned onto the main street when Randi cursed and reached up to adjust the rearview mirror.

"What's the matter?"

Randi shook her head, and blinked several times to try and reduce the spots in her eyes. "Damned asshole behind me has his bright lights on, and nearly ran up our bumper." A quick glance in the side mirror showed that the driver behind them had backed off. "Probably drunk or something."

Kay turned in her seat to look behind them. "No wonder he blinded you. That's a pretty big truck." She couldn't make out the color or the model, but could tell that it dwarfed the sports car.

"Yeah." Deciding that it wasn't worth getting upset over, Randi shrugged off the incident and turned to smile at her lover. She wanted to show Kay a good time at the cabaret. "Ready to hear some good music?"

"Ready and willing," Kay assured her, reaching over and

squeezing Randi's arm. "Bring it on."

"The place looks busy," Kay noted as Randi circled the parking lot, finally finding a place on the far end, away from the entrance. "Are you sure we can get in?"

Randi waited until they were out of the car before she answered. "It's a lot bigger than it looks from the outside." Feeling a bit uneasy, she edged closer to Kay until their arms brushed against one another. "It can get a bit rowdy, though. Try to stay close to me, all right?"

"You have nothing to worry about there. I'm going to be stuck to you like glue." They had reached the front door and were about to go in, when it suddenly opened and three drunken men came stumbling out. One of them reached for Kay, but somehow "accidentally" tripped over Randi's foot instead.

The man bellowed and his buddies helped him to his feet. "Wash yerself," he slurred to Randi. Before he could say anything else, a huge man in a tight-fitting black T-shirt opened the door.

"There's your cab, fellas," the bouncer told them, pushing the trio none-too-gently out into the parking lot. He assisted them into the yellow van and gave the driver directions before going back to the bar door. "I'm sorry about that, ladies. Just trying to keep the place—" A large smile broke out on his face when he recognized Randi. "Dr. Meyers! It's been a while since we've seen you in here." He held the door open with a flourish.

"That it has, Eric," Randi agreed. "How's Chester?"

The heavily muscled bouncer's smiled widened. "Friskier than ever, thanks to you. As a matter of fact, I was going to bring him in next week for his yearly shots." Eric was the proud owner of a cantankerous Persian cat he had found near death the previous year. He had brought the animal in to the clinic, and Randi helped nurse the poor feline back to health. When he saw Randi reach into her pocket for her wallet to pay the cover charge, he waved her off. "No charge for you, Doc. Sharon would have my hide, and you know it."

Randi blushed, but put her wallet away. "Thanks, Eric." She put her arm around Kay and pulled her closer. "This is my partner, Kay Newcombe. She's going to be running the clinic from now on. I just bought it from Dr. Wilde, so we'll be changing the name soon."

"Glad to meet you, Kay, and congratulations, Doc." Eric winked, letting Randi know that he wasn't just talking about the ownership of the clinic. "There's probably an open table near the back, if you hurry," he told the women, stepping in behind them as they passed through the door.

Kay blinked her eyes to try and see in the hazy room. Cigarette smoke hung heavily in the air, and the thickest part of the crowd seemed to be gathered around the circular bar that stood in the center of the room. Off to the right was the stage area, where musicians were already setting up microphones and drums. She felt strong fingers wrap around one of her arms as Randi led her around the bar to the far corner of the room, where several tables were set up, a few of them empty. The majority of the people had already moved up to the front of the room to be closer to the band, leaving the back relatively quiet.

"How's this?" Randi asked, motioning to a clear table with her free hand. "Unless you have a burning desire to have your eardrums blown out, this is better than sitting in the front." She held out a chair for Kay, who blushed but took off her coat and sat down.

"This is just perfect, thank you." Kay waited until Randi sat down next to her, then reached under the table to take her hand. "Is it always this crowded?"

Randi shook her head. "Only on Friday and Saturday nights. During the week it's pretty tame."

"What can I get you two ladies this evening?" A waitress in jeans and a black T-shirt had appeared out of nowhere. Her dark blonde hair was pulled back into a ponytail, and she looked to be a bit older than Randi. "Dr. Meyers? Long time no see." She dropped one hand to Randi's shoulder and squeezed lightly. When she noticed the look the other woman at the table was giving her, she quickly removed her hand. "Oh, sorry. What can I get both of you tonight?"

"I'll have a club soda with lime," Randi said, then looked over at Kay with a questioning glance. Surprised at seeing what appeared to be jealousy on her lover's face, Randi swallowed heavily. *Looks like I'm going to have to smooth some ruffled feathers.* "Kay? What would you like to drink?"

Angry with herself for her attitude, Kay tried to smile at the waitress. "I'll just have a coke, please." She wasn't too sure where the jealous streak had come from, but was determined to make amends. Kay held out one hand to the waitress. "Hi, my name's Kay. I'm sorry about earlier."

The waitress took Kay's hand and smiled, showing a mouthful of metal braces. "Don't worry about it, hon. We haven't seen Dr. Meyers in here in pretty close to a year, so I got a little excited." She winked at Randi. "I'll be back with your drinks in a flash."

Kay watched her leave, then looked over at Randi apologetically. "I'm sorry."

"What for?"

"It seems that when it comes to you, I have a rather large jealous streak," Kay admitted quietly, looking down at the table.

Charmed, Randi leaned forward until Kay looked up into her eyes. "So?" Seeing the other woman's confusion, she continued. "To tell you the truth, knowing that you care enough to be jealous makes me feel really good."

"Really?"

"Uh-huh." Randi saw a tall woman pushing herself through the crowd, heading for their table. "Uh-oh."

Kay frowned. "What—"

"Randi! Where the hell have you been?" the newcomer yelled, reaching the table and pulling the vet to her feet. She wrapped both arms around the startled vet and squeezed hard. "Damn, I've missed you."

Looking over her captor's shoulder, Randi noticed the dark look on her lover's face. *I think I've got some 'splainin' to do.*

The late model Ford truck parked two rows away from the yellow Corvette. The driver watched as the two women walked up to the door, and cursed as they stood outside for a few moments and talked to the bouncer. Once they had gone inside, Beth stepped out of the vehicle and slammed the door.

She checked her watch, then tilted the can of beer and finished it off, tossing the empty container on the ground without a second thought. "Lucky for me they came to a bar, since I'm out of beer." The cool night air sent a chill down her back, and she stumbled once before cramming her hands in her denim jacket pockets and hurrying to the door. Before she could go inside, the bouncer stopped her.

"We have a five dollar cover charge tonight," he announced, holding out his hand. "Mainly to pay for the band."

Grumbling, Beth fished in the front pockets of her jeans until she pulled out a crumpled five-dollar bill. She tossed it in the bouncer's face and hurried through the door. "Asshole," she growled, shoving her way through the crowd of people to get to the bar.

"What can I get you?" the bartender yelled, to be heard over the din of voices.

Beth looked around, as if searching for someone. "Beer," she responded. "Whatever you have on tap." After a moment's hesitation, she ordered, "Better make that two."

With a shrug, the bartender filled two glasses and set them down. "That'll be eight dollars."

"You've got to fucking be kidding me," she yelled. "Four bucks a beer? I can buy a goddamned six pack for that." When the bartender reached for the beers, she fished in her pocket and pulled out a bundle of wadded ones. Counting them out carefully, she tossed them on the bar and grabbed her drinks. "Thanks for nothing."

"You're so welcome," the bartender returned sarcastically, glad to see the woman pick up her beers and look around for a place to settle.

Finding a table to the left of the large bar, Beth sat down and began searching the room. *I can't believe they were gone for so long today. Where the hell did they go?* She had been disgruntled when she saw the parking space outside the house empty, and had spent the entire day parked and waiting.

Already through one glass and halfway through the second, she was glad when a waitress stopped by and asked if she needed anything. "Yeah, bring me a couple more draft beers." After the waitress left, she continued to look around. *I know they're here. Where the fuck can they be?* A loud riff from a guitar almost caused her to spill her drink. "What the hell?"

"Good evening, ladies and gentlemen. Thanks for coming tonight. We'll try to make it worth your while, won't we, fellas?" The young longhaired man at the microphone turned back to the band and signaled, and suddenly the room was flooded with loud, rock music.

Fuck. Just what I needed. Why couldn't this have been a country bar? Beth finished off her glass and looked for the waitress, then was surprised to see a woman at the bar staring back at her. *Well, now, this night's looking up.*

Randi struggled out of the larger woman's arms and stepped back, clearly embarrassed. "Um, it's nice to see you again, too, Sharon." She gestured to Kay, who stood up as well. "This is my partner, Kay Newcombe. Kay, this is Sharon Williams, the owner of this fine establishment."

"Nice to meet you, Sharon." Kay held out her hand and was surprised to find herself engulfed in a bear hug.

"We don't stand much on ceremony around here," Sharon told Kay, setting her feet back on the ground. The bar owner was over six feet tall, and her short curly hair was almost completely gray. The woman was easily three hundred pounds, but carried it very well. She looked Kay over critically, then slapped Randi hard on the back. "She's a bit young for you, isn't she?"

Tired of hearing the same old refrain, Kay moved to stand next to Randi. "I'm more than old enough," she insisted, her hazel eyes shooting daggers at the larger woman.

Sharon burst out laughing. She wrapped a companionable arm around Randi and leaned in close. "She's a spitfire, that's for sure. Can you handle her?"

"I refuse to answer that, on the grounds that it may incriminate me," Randi deadpanned. Standing between the two women like she was, she knew better than to say anything to upset either one of them.

"Not to mention making the nights a hell of a lot colder, eh?" Sharon guffawed. She slapped the vet hard on the back, again. Before she could say anything else, the lead singer for the band started talking to the patrons and then the entire bar was filled with a loud rock beat. "I'd better get back to the bar," Sharon yelled to the two women. "Y'all enjoy the show." Another hard pat on Randi's back, and she disappeared into the crowd.

Kay watched the boisterous woman leave, a confused look on her face. *I didn't think Randi would be the type to be friends with someone so...loud.* She sat back in her chair and pulled Randi down beside her. The music was so loud that Kay could feel the beat in her bones, and although the band was good, she didn't know if she could handle too much of the raucous music. The noise was made more bearable by the feel of Randi's arm across the back of her chair, so she leaned back into the warmth and closed her eyes.

Still sitting alone at her table, Beth finished off the next two beers, and was searching around for the waitress when a glass of the amber liquid was placed in front of her. She looked up at the person who had brought the drink over and grinned. The dish standing before her looked stunning in a black halter mini-dress that barely covered her thighs. "Well, hello there."

"Hello yourself," the newcomer drawled. "I don't think I've seen you around here before." She ran one bright red nail across an empty chair. "Is this seat taken?"

Beth kicked the chair out with one foot. "It is now, sweet thing." She waited until her guest sat down, then leaned forward so that she could be heard. "You're too pretty to be in a dump like this, baby. Do you come here often?"

The woman brushed her hair back away from her face and gave a sultry smile. "I used to come here with my girlfriend," her shiny red lips formed into a pout, "until she dumped me."

"That's too bad," Beth commiserated, patting the bare knee inches from her own. *But good for me.* A painted fingertip running along her jaw interrupted her thoughts. "I'm sorry, what did you say?"

"I said," the redhead purred, "that you look very strong. I bet you're good in bed."

"Oh yeah, baby, I'm real good in bed," Beth bragged. "You got someplace close by, I'd be glad to show you." She could feel the excitement pooling in her belly, and forgot the reason she had come to the bar to begin with.

The sexy woman winked. "Oh, sugar, I've got lots of uses for you; but the bedroom's a great place to start." She ran a nail down the front of her new conquest's shirt. "Come on. Let's go back to my motel room and you can show me what you've got." The redhead stood up and left the table, a half-drunk Beth hot on her heels.

Randi had heard about all the music she could stand and had spent the last ten minutes of the band's set looking around the crowded bar. She saw a woman across the room who looked familiar, but had a hard time distinguishing her from a distance, and through the shifting crowd. The woman disappeared before she could point her out to Kay, so she decided it was just her imagination. After the final chord echoed away, Randi could still feel her ears ringing. She leaned down so that her mouth was close to Kay's ear. "You asleep?"

"With that noise? Are you kidding?" Kay's eyes popped open. She yawned and stretched. "They were pretty good."

"Yeah, good and loud. Do you want to stay for the second set?"

Kay shook her head. "No, I don't think so. I'm having a hard enough time hearing right now. One more set and I could be deaf." She watched as the people who had crowded the stage now converged on the circular bar, which left the way to the exit clear. Kay pointed toward the front of the bar. "This might be the best time to make a break for it."

"Good idea," Randi agreed, standing up and helping Kay with her coat. "Even though it was obnoxiously loud, did you have a good time?"

"I had a great time, Randi." Kay linked arms with her and started for the front door. "We'll have to do this again sometime."

Randi nodded to Eric, who was guzzling down a large glass of water near the bar. She waved to Sharon, who was helping the bartender, and was thankful that they were able to leave without another friendly "chat" with the bar owner. *My back's probably gonna have a bruise.* Looking down at Kay's happy face, Randi decided that it was worth anything to see her lover happy. "We'll come back when there's a quieter band," she promised, which elicited a smile from Kay. "Come on. Let's get you home."

Chapter
22

The bright sunlight streaming through the window caused Beth to groan and cover her face with her pillow. She rolled over and found the other side of the bed empty, and uncovered her face to glance around the room. "Hey. Where'd you go?"

"I'm right here," her companion called from the doorway that led to the bathroom. "I was beginning to think you were going to sleep the whole day away." She stretched her nude body, eliciting a moan of another sort from the bed. "See something you like?"

"You know I do," the woman in the bed told her. She flipped open the sheets invitingly. "You look cold, baby. Come on over here and let me warm you up."

After one more full stretch, the redhead raced across the room and jumped onto the bed, landing on top of Beth. "I thought I'd worn you out, sugar."

Beth laughed deep in her chest, rolling over to pin the other woman beneath her. "No chance of that, Red. You obviously haven't had a real woman before." Her head bent and she took a bit of flesh into her mouth, sucking hard.

"Oh, yes!" the older woman cried, raking her sharp nails down Beth's back. "Just like that, sugar."

Sometime later, both women lay panting and sweating, with Beth propped up against the headboard and the redhead nestled against her shoulder. "Damn, but you're good at that," she marveled, running her fingers through the damp auburn locks. This woman's wild ways and enthusiasm were more than Beth had expected. She lay basking in the afterglow, then realized suddenly what was missing. "Hey, baby?"

"Mmm?"

"You're probably gonna think I'm some sort of terrible person, but I don't remember your name." A giggle was the last thing she was expecting, but she smiled anyway. "What?"

Gray eyes looked up mischievously. "You don't remember it because I didn't tell you what it is. Didn't seem to bother you last night." She ran her hand across Beth's chest, latching onto one breast and squeezing it almost painfully. "But, I didn't expect to feel this way, either."

"Feel how?" Beth groaned, her eyes slamming shut at the erotic touch. "Damn, baby. You keep that up, and we'll never finish this conversation."

"Can't have that now, can we?" Sliding up the muscular body, the redhead ran one fingertip down Beth's cheek. "Last night and today were more than just mind-blowing sex," she murmured softly, leaning forward and kissing the other woman. Pulling back, she looked deep into Beth's eyes. "After," she sniffled, biting her lip, "after my girlfriend dumped me, I never expected to feel like this for anyone again." Her eyes filled with tears, which slowly trickled down her face. "Oh, sugar, you're so sweet and gentle, nothing like her."

Beth frowned. "Did she hurt you? Because if she did—" The threat hung in the air.

The redhead nodded. "I was too afraid of her to leave. Why, right before she threw me out of our apartment, I thought she was going to kill me." She buried her face against Beth's chest and cried.

"Sssh," Beth crooned, stroking the auburn hair. "You don't have to be afraid of her anymore, baby. I'll take care of you." Once the woman in her arms calmed down, she pulled her chin up and smiled into the watery eyes. "Do you want to tell me the name of the woman I spent the night with? I'd like to have something to call you besides beautiful."

"Melissa," the redhead whispered. "My name's Melissa." She turned her head to lie down on Beth's stomach, an evil smile crossing her face.

The smell of something cooking caused Randi to slowly open her eyes and look around. A glance at the clock radio told her it was almost noon, and she realized fuzzily that Kay and Spike were nowhere to be seen. *I hope Kay's the one cooking.* Randi rolled over and wrapped her arms around Kay's pillow, inhaling deeply. She could still detect a slight dampness from the night before. They had returned home from the bar and taken a long shower that only ended when the hot water began to run out. She smiled as she remembered how Kay had led her from the shower into the bedroom, telling her not to bother drying off. They'd spent the next several hours cuddling and making love, and Randi was surprised to find that Kay was up before her. *Maybe it's because she's younger.* Burying her face deeper into the pillow, the sated woman drifted back to sleep.

Randi awoke a short time later, this time at the feel of fingers running gently through her hair. She rolled over and opened her eyes. Kay sat next to her on the bed, wearing sweat pants and one of Randi's T-shirts. Randi mumbled, "Mornin'."

"Good afternoon," Kay teased, leaning down and giving Randi a kiss. "I was beginning to worry about you."

"Why's that?" Taking a moment to stretch, Randi yawned.

Kay enjoyed the view, as Randi's stretch caused the covers to fall away and leave her upper body exposed. She unconsciously brushed one hand down the front of her lover's chest. Realizing that Randi had spoken again, she blushed and grinned. "um, I'm sorry. I guess my mind was somewhere else."

"Oh, really?" Normally not that fond of the way her body looked, Randi stretched again, this time leaving her arms up over her head. She enjoyed the way that Kay looked at her, which made her feel like the most desirable woman in the world. *Maybe what they say is true. Love is blind.* She gasped when Kay lowered her head and took one of her nipples into her mouth. *Or maybe it's just extremely horny.* Randi pulled Kay down on top of her and rolled, changing the subject.

Feeling insistent hands pulling at her shirt, Kay sat up long enough for her top to be removed. The look on Randi's face when she realized Kay wasn't wearing a bra was priceless, and Kay resolved to repeat the practice often.

"Oooh. Did we forget something this morning?" Randi ran her hands over Kay's chest, enjoying how her lover's breath quickened at her touch.

"No." Kay allowed Randi to pull the sweat pants down her legs and remove them altogether. She was about to complain about the cold air when she was gently covered by Randi's body. "That feels nice." Her hands came up automatically to wrap around the larger woman's shoulders.

"Uh-huh." Randi looked into Kay's eyes and smiled. "Is this a new side to you, not wearing anything under your clothes on the weekend? Because if it is, I'm all for it." She rolled to the side, pulling the covers up around them both.

Kay kissed the chin so close to hers. "Smartass. I didn't feel like getting dressed, but Spike needed to go." Her hands trailed down Randi's body, causing Randi to moan. "Tell me, why are we talking, when we could be doing more...important...things?"

"Talking? Who's... Oh, God." The hands that had been teasing her suddenly became more serious, and Randi completely lost track of the conversation.

Much later, Randi was comfortably seated on the bed, halfway through her breakfast, or lunch as Kay jokingly referred to it, when the phone rang. Kay stretched across Randi's body to grab the annoying device. "Hello," she answered, slightly breathless.

"Well, hello yourself, Kay. I hope I'm not disturbing anything. It's good to hear your voice."

Kay grinned. "It's nice to hear from you too, Patricia. Do you want to talk to Randi?"

"Not quite yet. Is that daughter of mine behaving herself, or do I need to fly down there and knock some sense into her head? You know how stubborn she can be."

Kay laughed and sat up into a more comfortable position next to her lover. "No, everything's great. She's been nothing but sweet." Kay almost laughed again at the look on her lover's face.

Randi finished her meal and put her plate on the nightstand next to the bed. She rolled over onto her side and propped her head up on her hand, frowning at the conversation that was obviously about her. *I should have known it was a mistake to introduce those two. Now I'm never going to have any peace.* The thought brought a happy feeling into her heart. *Who knew I'd ever get so lucky?*

"Well, that's good. I was beginning to wonder if maybe she had been switched at birth, because I know she didn't get that bullheadedness from either her father or me." The tone of Patricia's voice changed. "Seriously, I don't mean to pry. I hadn't heard from her since last weekend, and I just wanted to see how you two were doing."

"I don't know about her, but I've never been more happy in my entire life," Kay admitted frankly, speaking to the woman lying beside her as much as to the woman on the phone. "And I've certainly never been treated anything like this before. Randi makes me feel so...special."

On the other end of the phone, Patricia sighed happily. "I'm thrilled to hear that, Kay. You both deserve to be happy." Afraid that she would start crying if they didn't change the subject soon, she pursued another tack. "Is that daughter of mine nearby? I'd like to speak to her, if I may."

"Sure." Kay was about to hand Randi the phone when Patricia's entreaty stopped her.

"Kay? Before you go, I just want to thank you for making my daughter happy, and for coming into all our lives and becoming a very special part of our family."

Kay blinked back the tears that the sincere words caused to well up in her eyes. "It is most definitely my pleasure, Patricia. Thank you." She handed the phone to her lover, unable to speak.

"Mom? Is everything okay?" Randi sat up and gladly allowed Kay to snuggle up against her.

"Of course, dear. I just wanted to call and see how you were doing. You seemed a bit out of sorts the last time we talked."

Without thinking, Randi wrapped her free arm around Kay's body and held her close. "Yeah, I think I was. But, things are going a lot better now."

"That's good to hear. Christmas is coming up in a few weeks, you know. Do you two have any plans?"

Christmas? Oh, shit. I completely forgot about it. She looked down at Kay's head snuggled against her. *I've already gotten the best present I could ever ask for.* Her mother's voice broke into her thoughts. "I'm sorry, what?"

"Your grandmother wants to have another get-together at her house. But your father and I were thinking about having a more intimate gathering of just our immediate family here. Do you have a preference?"

"Huh?"

"Randi Suzanne, are you listening to me?" Patricia's voice took on a scolding tone. "Don't tell me you have better things to do on a Sunday afternoon than talk to your mother."

"No, of course not. I mean, well—"

Patricia burst into laughter. "You're so easy to fluster, honey. Anyway, think about what you'd like to do for the holidays. We'd love to see you, either here or at your grandmother's. Talk it over with Kay, and let me know what you decide, all right?"

"Sure, Mom. I'll call you later, okay?"

"You'd better," Patricia threatened playfully. "We love you, Randi. Give Kay our love, too."

"I will, Mom. Love you." Randi disconnected the call and leaned over to put the handset back on the cradle. "Mom sends her love." She resumed her previous position as body pillow.

Kay kissed the bare skin that her face was snuggled up against and looked up into her lover's eyes. "She's sweet."

"Yeah. But, then again, she probably can't help but love you."

"You think so?" Kay blushed, but had a smile on her face.

"Uh-huh. You're just too damned cute." Randi leaned down

and covered Kay's lips with her own. Breaking for air, she pulled back slightly. "She wanted to know what our plans are for Christmas."

"Christmas?"

"Mmm-hmm. She told me that Grandma wanted to have another big deal at her house, but Mom's been thinking of having just the immediate family over to Santa Fe. Got any preferences?" Randi reached down and brushed Kay's hair out of her eyes, thinking again how beautiful Kay was. *If it were up to me, I'd stay home and spend the entire holiday right where we are. But my mother would disown me for sure.*

Kay leaned into the soft touch on her face, closing her eyes at the contact. "I'll happily go wherever you want to go."

Smiling, Randi continued to stroke her lover's face. "What do you usually do for the holidays? Any traditions you want to keep up?"

"No." Kay's open demeanor changed abruptly and a frown covered her face, which she quickly ducked against Randi's chest in an attempt to hide her emotions.

All right. Let's see what this is all about. "Sweetheart?" Randi waited until Kay looked up at her again. "Do you want to talk about it?"

"Not really," Kay snapped. Seeing the hurt look on Randi's face, she relented. "I'm sorry. You didn't deserve that."

"It's okay, you don't—"

Kay covered Randi's mouth with one hand. "Sshh. It's just that I haven't enjoyed Christmas since my brother died. I used to try and make them special for him, but since it's been just me I didn't see any reason to mess with it. The last five years, I'd take a nice floral arrangement to the cemetery and spend a little time Christmas night talking with Jared." She tried to smile. "Of course, then there's my aunt and cousin, who would suddenly be nice to me during the month of December. I think they were trying to make sure they got gifts from me." Removing her hand, she took a deep breath and sat back against the headboard. "So, tell me about your Christmas traditions."

"I'm sorry, Kay. I didn't mean to bring up bad memories." Randi held out her arm. "Can I hold you?" She didn't get an answer, but Kay gratefully accepted the offer, leaning back and closing her eyes. "So, you want to hear about the Meyers' family traditions?" A silent nod invited her to continue. "All right. Well, we normally invaded my grandmother's house every year on Christmas Eve, and the adults would sit around playing cards or dominoes, while the kids all piled up in one of the bedrooms and had a slumber party of sorts. We usually stayed up giggling and playing, until my grandmother would come in and threaten to send Santa a note that there was nothing but bad boys and girls, and he could skip her house."

Unable to help herself, Kay giggled. "She didn't."

"Oh, yeah. Every year, for as long as I can remember. When I was younger, we'd take turns keeping watch out the window for his sleigh. Augie, since he was the oldest, would always take last watch and fall asleep." She laughed. "So the next morning, when Grandma would come to wake us, he'd always get in trouble for being out of his sleeping bag."

"Then what happened?" Kay was completely immersed in the depiction, forgetting what had upset her to begin with.

"Then, we'd all be forced to eat breakfast before we were allowed to go into the family room where the tree and stockings were. You've never seen kids inhale oatmeal and toast like that, believe me. Anyway, after breakfast, the kids would race from the dining room like mad, and then it became a free-for-all when we hit the family room. All of the adults would be seated around the perimeter, and would laugh and watch the kids go crazy." Randi's face took on a wistful look. "I haven't gone back for the last couple of years, so I'm not sure whether that's still how it works, or not. I usually just send my grandmother a gift and call her later on that day."

Kay turned her head to look at Randi. "Why haven't you gone?" She could tell that Randi loved her family and was curious as to why she would miss such an important holiday.

"I wasn't much in a festive mood." Randi took a deep breath and tried to change the subject. "But, I'm feeling pretty damned wonderful, right now. So, what do you want to do for the holidays?"

"Spend them with you."

The look on Kay's face was so serious that Randi almost felt like crying. She couldn't believe how much one person could mean to her. "I'd like that," she rasped, struggling to keep her emotions under control. *This is ridiculous. I'm acting like a moonstruck teenager.*

Kay had heard the catch in her lover's voice, and thought a slight change in subject was in order. "What do you think the rest of your family is going to do? I'd love to see your niece and nephews again."

"That's a good question. I could always call Augie up and see what their plans are before we commit one way or the other." As much as she loved her parents, Randi would much rather have a long drive than a short flight. And like Kay, she would love to see the kids again. For the last few minutes, Kay's hands had been tracing patterns across her skin, making conversation difficult, at best. *I think I'll wait until later to call. We have much more important matters to attend to.* Randi turned so that she was able to kiss Kay, and enjoyed the feeling of her lover's fingers in her hair. *Much later.*

Beth held the car door open, her head and shoulders leaning inside. "So, where do we go from here? I'd really like to see you again."

"I'd like that too, sugar." Melissa reached across the seat and grabbed the other woman's shirt, pulling her back into the car. Her forceful, passionate kiss left them both breathless. "Do you live around here?"

Beth hated to lie, but she didn't think that telling her new lover that she had been following her old lover around was such a good idea. "Uh, no. I just got into town and was looking for a job. Just my luck when I ran into you at that bar last night."

Melissa leaned over again, but instead of kissing Beth, she took her lower lip between her teeth, then licked it to soften the bite. "I'd say we were both pretty lucky, weren't we?" After their marathon sex session, she was sore in places she didn't think existed, but it was a good kind of sore. "What kind of work do you do?"

"I'm a mechanic, but I can also operate a tow truck. I figured the opportunities would be pretty good up here, unlike that pissant little town I came from." Beth had felt a surge of excitement when Melissa nipped at her lip, and was beginning to wish they hadn't left the motel. "Maybe we should go back to your room to finish this little chat. I can follow you over in my truck."

"I tell you what, hon. I've got a few errands to take care of, but why don't you drive back over and get yourself a room? I already told them I was checking out today." Melissa gave Beth her best sad look. "I'm going to have to find someplace less expensive, since my money is running so low." Big tears fell from her eyes. "I've already sold all my other belongings just to be able to eat, and keep from ending up on the streets."

Beth pulled the crying woman into her arms. "It's okay, baby. I'll get a room, and you can stay with me. Are you having a rough time finding a job?"

"Mmm-hmm," Melissa cried. "I don't have any job skills. I haven't worked in years. My girlfriend wouldn't let me. She wanted me to stay home and take care of the apartment," she blubbered, burying her face in Beth's shirt.

Beth waited until she stopped crying, then used her hand to tilt Melissa's face up to hers. "Don't you worry. I'll take care of you." *I can't believe anyone would treat such a sweet, beautiful woman like that. What a bitch her ex must be!*

Melissa fought to keep the triumphant smile off her face. *Hook, line, and sinker. These big burly types are all the same.* "You will?" she sniffled. "I couldn't ask that of you. Why, you hardly know me."

"I know you well enough." Beth used her fingertips to brush the tears from Melissa's face. "Now, you go take care of your errands, and I'll get us a room."

"Thank you, sugar." The redhead paused, then giggled. "I don't know your last name."

"Rogers." Beth had almost forgotten that they had never gotten around to proper introductions the evening before.

"Beth Rogers. I like that name," Melissa murmured. She gave the husky woman another deep kiss, filled with promise. "I'll be back soon."

Beth climbed out of the car. "I'll be waiting." She closed the door and watched as the red sports car raced from the parking lot. *I wonder where she got that car? It looks brand new.* She shrugged. "Probably borrowed it from a friend." The mechanic pulled herself into her truck and headed back for the motel, visions of more nights like the previous one running through her head. She was anxious to reunite with the redhead, and never recognized all the inconsistencies in Melissa's story.

Taking a look into her rearview mirror, Melissa could no longer hold back her laughter. "That stupid little hick! She's going to be perfect for what I have in mind." Her mind whirled with the possibilities. "No one tells me no and gets away with it. That bitch is going to get hers."

After a bit of coaxing from Spike, both Kay and Randi were dressed and now sat on a concrete bench in the nearby park. The small dog ran the length of his lead, barking and chasing imaginary threats. Randi tilted her head back and allowed the warm sunshine to heat her face, enjoying the quiet time. They were only wearing light jackets, and she once again gave private thanks for the mild Texas winters.

Kay sat as close as she possibly could, her leg touching Randi's. She enjoyed watching Spike run around and act silly, and chuckled out loud at his antics. "Sometimes I think he's in his own little world," she noted.

Randi rolled her head in the direction of her lover's voice and opened one eye, too relaxed by the warm sun to expend much more energy. "What makes you say that?"

"Just look at him." Kay pointed at the dog now crouched down with his rear end up in the air, snarling at nothing in particular. "You can't tell me that's a sane dog."

Randi laughed. "He just has a good imagination. Besides, I think he likes showing off for you. He never acted that way just for me." She looked around at the nearly deserted park. "Want to take a walk around the lake?"

"Sure." Kay stood up and offered her hand to Randi, who accepted it and allowed herself to be pulled to her feet.

They walked around the lake in silence, both content to enjoy the day. On the second circuit, Kay stopped and walked down to the water's edge. "What is it?" Randi asked, following her inquisitive partner.

"I'm not sure. I thought I saw something." Kay moved a bit of brush with her hand, finding what appeared to be a dead duckling. "Oh, no." She turned to look up at Randi. "Can you..."

Randi knelt down beside Kay and studied the still creature carefully. Wishing she had rubber gloves, she touched it with one finger, surprised to feel warmth. "It's hard to tell, Kay. If it's dead, it hasn't been dead long." Taking a deep breath, she cautiously picked the duckling up, while Kay held Spike to keep him from getting in the way. The body was still warm and pliable, and Randi thought that she could feel it breathing. "I think it may still be alive."

"What can we do?" Kay asked. "I hate to think of just leaving it here to die."

I am such a sucker. I know I'm going to regret this. Randi stood up. "Let's go to the clinic, and I'll see what I can do."

"Yes!" Kay jumped to her feet and kept Spike in her arms as they walked back to their car.

Randi waited until Kay was buckled into the passenger's seat, then walked around the rear of the vehicle. She unlocked the trunk with her free hand and picked up a towel that she kept for emergencies. After carefully wrapping the bird in the towel, she closed the trunk and walked back around to Kay's side of the car. "Do you think you can hold this and keep Spike away at the same time?"

"I think so." Kay held the dog in her left arm, while letting Randi situate the bundle on her lap. "Thank you, Randi. I know this isn't how you planned on spending the rest of the day."

The vet smiled. "Don't thank me just yet, Kay. I doubt if there's much we can do. He may not even survive until we get there."

"Well, thank you anyway." Kay snuggled Spike to her chest while Randi hurried to climb in behind the wheel. Spike sniffed at the towel, but made no effort to do anything else. "That's right, sweetie. You understand, don't you?"

Randi shook her head as she started the car. *Sometimes I worry about those two.* The link between Spike and Kay was something she was grateful for, even when she complained about it. Since it had been just Spike and herself, alone together for over a year, she had worried that he would be jealous of Kay. Luckily, the miniature Dobie fell in love with Kay almost at first sight. *I can certainly understand how that happened; so did I.* She pulled the Corvette out of the parking lot and headed for the clinic, hoping that Kay wouldn't be too distraught when she couldn't save the duckling.

After doing a thorough examination of the still bird, Randi shook her head. "I don't know, Kay. I can't find anything wrong with him, except that he seems to be malnourished." She hated to be the bearer of bad news, especially seeing the complete look of trust in her friend's eyes.

"Can't you feed it? I mean, if it just needs food, can't we try to do that?" Kay couldn't understand why she was so emotionally attached to the duckling, and why she needed it to survive. She just knew that she wouldn't feel right until they had done everything they could.

Randi shrugged her shoulders. "We can try. I don't think we have any duck food here at the clinic, but there's a feed store not too far from here." That was another advantage to living in suburbs that were bordered by a mainly rural area. Ten years prior, there had been very few houses and a lot of undeveloped land, which had now almost completely disappeared. But Randi was very happy with the laid-back atmosphere of the area and had no desire to relocate. "We're also going to need a brooder."

"A what?"

"A box," Randi told her with a smile. "With a feeder and a water dispenser. It probably wouldn't hurt to use a heat lamp for the next few days, at least until the little guy starts eating well," she murmured, more to herself than to Kay.

"How do you know so much about ducks?" Kay wanted to

know. "You don't see that many here, do you?"

The vet shook her head. "Nope." She reached under the table and pulled out a book, which had a pamphlet marking a page. "I cheated. When you went out back with Spike, I did a bit of quick reading. It's been a while since I've had to know anything about the care of wild ducks."

Kay shook her finger at Randi, trying to keep from smiling. "I should have known it was something like that. You were a bit too eager for Spike and me to go for a walk."

"Yeah, well, I didn't want you to think I didn't know anything," Randi admitted. "Wait here for a minute." She left the room, returning quickly with a box. "I'm going to have to find a bigger box for him, but this should do for now." Inside the box was a clean white towel, where she gently placed the duckling. "Here," she said, handing the box to Kay, "you hold him. We'll take him back to the apartment and see what we can do."

"Thank you." Kay looked up into Randi's eyes. "I just hate the thought of him dying all alone, without someone at least trying to help him." She struggled to keep the tears from flowing down her face, but judging by the look Randi was giving her, she wasn't being too successful.

Silently holding the door open for Kay, Randi followed her out to the waiting area, where Spike was curled up on an office chair. She picked up the little dog and held him close. "You'd better be glad Christina didn't catch you sleeping in her chair. She'd have both our hides for that," Randi told him, getting the response she wanted when she heard Kay chuckle.

An hour later and close to one hundred dollars poorer, Randi and Kay were in the apartment setting up the duckling's temporary home. By mutual consent, they decided that the guest bathroom would be the safest and quietest place for the fowl, and placed its box in the bathtub so that Spike couldn't get near it.

The vet stood up and stretched, feeling the ache of muscles that weren't used to bending over tubs for long periods of time. She had attached a heat lamp to the towel bar in the tub, allowing it to shine into the box so that the duckling would be warm enough. "How's it going?" she asked her partner, who was sitting on the closed toilet, feeding the duckling with a syringe.

"Not too bad. He's actually taking some of this in," Kay admitted in wonder. "How much should I give him?"

Randi leaned over and looked at Kay's progress. "Not a whole lot to begin with. We need to start him out slowly." She had a feeder and a water dispenser set up in the box, along with some old T-shirts in the bottom. "We can try and feed him a little more in a couple of hours."

Nodding, Kay wiped the excess off his bill and placed the fowl into the box. "Look. He's sitting up," she whispered excitedly.

"You're right." Randi watched as the bird did sit up, but made no move to stand or open its eyes. "Just don't get your hopes up, okay? He has a long way to go."

"I know. But, at least he's not alone anymore." She partially covered the box with a towel to keep the heat in, and stood up. "I really appreciate everything you've done, Randi. I just couldn't stand by and let it die without at least trying."

Snapping her rubber gloves off, Randi leaned over and scrubbed her hands in the sink, moving over so that Kay could join her. After they were both sufficiently clean, they left the bathroom and closed the door. Randi was halfway down the hall before she realized that she was walking alone. Turning around, she saw Kay standing at the end of the hallway, staring at the closed door. "Kay?"

"Hmm?"

"What's going on?" Randi hurried down the hall and put her hand on Kay's shoulder. "Are you all right?"

Kay wiped at her eyes and shook her head. "I'm sorry. It must be close to that time of the month for me."

"Hey, don't worry about it." Randi used the fingers on one hand to brush away Kay's tears. "Why all the concern over a little duck? I don't want it to die either, but sometimes that's just how it goes."

"No one should die alone!" Kay snapped, pushing by Randi and running into the master bedroom. She slammed the door behind her, leaving a befuddled Randi in the hall.

"Well, that was enlightening." Randi walked to stand in front of the closed door. She was about to knock, when she heard crying on the other side. *Damn. Now what do I do?* The sound of whining caused Randi to look down.

Spike sat near her feet, a confused look on his features.

"What?"

He cocked his head to one side and whined again.

"Yeah, I'm worried, too." Turning her attention back to the door, Randi knocked lightly. "Kay? Can I come in?" She could still hear the sound of Kay's crying, which made her mind up for her. Slowly turning the knob and relieved that it was unlocked, Randi pushed the door open slightly and stuck her head into the room. "Sweetheart? Are you okay?" *Of course she's not okay, you blockhead. She's crying!*

Kay was lying on the bed with her face buried in a pillow. Her deep sobs could still be heard, but she made no move to acknowledge Randi, or even turn over.

Much to Spike's dismay, Randi stepped fully into the room and closed the door behind her. She could hear his whine outside the door, but ignored it to focus on her lover. Unsure of what had caused Kay's emotional outburst, she cautiously sat on the bed near the prone woman and placed one hand lightly on Kay's shoulder. "Kay? I'm sorry if I said something that upset you. Is there anything I can do for you?" Randi sat quietly for several minutes, afraid that she wasn't going to get an answer.

Finally, Kay rolled over and stared up at her concerned lover, her eyes red from crying. "You didn't do anything," she said, her voice hoarse. She gratefully accepted the box of tissue from Randi and blew her nose. "I guess you could say I have some issues that I need to deal with."

"Okay. um, is there anything I can do to help?" Feeling completely out of her league, Randi offered her hand, grateful when it was taken and held. "If you want to talk about it, I can listen. Or, if you just need some space to deal with it alone, I can give you that, too," she babbled, unsure of what to do.

Charmed, Kay couldn't help but smile. She brought their joined hands up to her face and rubbed her cheek with the back of Randi's hand. "You'll probably think I'm crazy."

"I bet I won't."

Kay took a deep breath and sat up, pulling Randi with her until they were both leaning against the headboard. She held Randi's hand like a lifeline and closed her eyes. "You remember I told you about Jared? How he died, I mean?"

"Yes." Afraid of where the conversation was going, Randi willed her heart to stop beating so rapidly. "You told me he was killed by a drunk driver, but didn't go into any details."

"He was riding his bicycle to school one morning, and took a short cut that he didn't usually take. According to the police reports, the driver swerved and went up on the sidewalk, hitting Jared and throwing him and his bike into some thick bushes." Kay's voice broke and she stopped.

Randi pulled her into her arms and held her close. "You don't have to—"

"No, please, let me finish." Kay leaned back into the strong embrace and took a steadying breath. "They finally pulled the driver over a few miles away, and that's when they noticed the blood on his car. He didn't even remember hitting Jared," she cried, turning her head and burying her face in Randi's shirt. "It took them hours before they finally found him. He was dead when they got there."

Damn. Randi's heart broke at the anguish in her lover's voice.

"He bled to death, Randi. Cold, all alone, and hidden from the street. My little brother died without anyone being there with him." Kay finally broke down and cried in earnest. She wept for the loss of her brother and for what would never be. She'd never see him graduate from high school, meet his first date, or attend his wedding. She cried for the pain and fear he must have felt before he died, and for the senselessness of his death.

Holding the sobbing woman, Randi realized that Kay had never allowed herself to grieve for her brother. She knew there was nothing else she could do but hold the woman she loved and offer her emotional support, no matter how painful it was to herself. Randi anguished at the heartache Kay had endured in her short lifetime, and made a silent promise that she would do everything in her power to protect Kay from any more pain. *Don't worry, love. You're not alone anymore and you never will be, never again.*

Chapter
23

There were more than enough parking places in front of the building that was surrounded by apartments, so Melissa was able to chose one partially hidden by the neatly manicured shrubbery. She checked her face in the rearview mirror and carefully applied her favorite bright red lipstick. Blowing her reflection a kiss, she pushed her purse under the seat and stepped out of the sports car. *After all the trouble I've gone to, that asshole had better be here.*

She had stopped by the apartment once already, and then remembered that her quarry normally did laundry on Sunday. *At least, he used to. That's when we'd get together and enjoy the "spin cycle."* With a furtive glance around to assure herself that she hadn't been noticed, Melissa opened the door to the laundry cabana. Her painted lips turned up into a wicked grin when she spotted Ricky alone, folding clothes on a wide table. The skin-tight white T-shirt stretched across his muscular back, and the faded denim jeans hugged his rear and thick legs invitingly. His dark hair was cut close to his head, military style, and the thirty-four-year-old could easily have been mistaken for someone much younger. She had forgotten what a wonderful body the gym instructor had, and she almost felt bad for what she was about to do. Almost. His back was to the door and he was so engrossed in what he was doing that he didn't hear her heels click softly on the yellowed linoleum floor.

"Well, well, lookie who we have here," Melissa drawled, coming up beside the startled man and leaning against the table. "Still haven't found a woman who would wash your underwear?"

Ricky tossed the T-shirt he was folding back into the pile and turned to face the redhead. "That's all you have to say to me? Where the hell have you been?" His dark eyes flashed dangerously. "You didn't even have the decency to tell me goodbye! I had to find out from your obnoxious roommate."

She picked up the shirt and wrinkled her nose. "Puhleez. I

didn't owe you anything. All you were to me was a good fuck. Not a great one, but better than some." Her countenance turned hateful as her eyesight raked down his body. "It's true what they say. The bigger the muscles, the smaller the equipment." She tossed the shirt back onto the table. Melissa knew the burly man's Achilles heel, and wasn't above exploiting it to get what she wanted. "Besides, I figured once I was gone, you'd finally wake up and find yourself some cute little guy to make you happy."

"What?" The weightlifter's face turned a dark shade of red, his hands balled into fists so tightly that his knuckles turned white from the strain.

"Oh, sugar, don't play coy with me. I remember all those magazines at your place that had half-naked hunks on them. You can't tell me that you didn't close your eyes and think of them when we were doing it. That's probably why you liked it more when I was on my knees, wasn't it?"

Out of nowhere, his hand slapped her hard across the face, splitting her lip. "Shut up, you slut! Those are weightlifting and health magazines. I'm no more queer than you are," Ricky yelled, his hands clenched back at his sides to keep from strangling her.

Melissa laughed, even though it hurt and caused her lip to bleed more. "You stupid little prick! That wasn't my *roommate*," she stressed the final word, wiping her mouth with the back of her hand. "She was my lover, asshole! And she was a hell of a lot better at it than you were!"

One strong hand tangled itself into her blouse, while he backhanded her with the other. The next slap was harder and caused Melissa's vision to blur. *Oops. I may have gone a little too far*, she giggled to herself. Shoving him away from her, Melissa held one hand to the aching side of her face as she glared at Ricky. "You're such a big man, hitting a woman. Do you feel better, now?"

"Maybe. What the hell is your major malfunction, anyway? You goaded me into it, you crazy bitch." Now that he had time to think, he began to get worried. Ricky backed up, waving his hands in front of his body. "I don't know what you're up to, but stay the hell away from me."

"Don't you worry, Ricky. I've gotten what I needed." Melissa started to walk toward the muscular man, but gave up when he continued to back away. She shrugged her shoulders. "Goodbye, sugar. Thanks for nothing." With a waggle of her fingers, the redhead vacated the laundry cabana, leaving a very confused Ricky standing alone in the middle of the room.

Kay woke up slowly. She was lying in her lover's arms, and Randi was still leaning up against the headboard, quietly watching her. She looked up into the kind eyes above her and grinned sheepishly. "I don't even remember falling asleep. How long have I..."

"A couple of hours," was Randi's answer. "How are you feeling?"

"Tired, but better." Kay kissed the arm that was holding her securely. "What about you? Have you just been sitting here all this time watching me sleep?"

It was Randi's turn to look sheepish. "Uh, yeah. Pretty much." She was relieved to see the sparkle return to her lover's eyes, and impulsively leaned down to kiss Kay's forehead. Her lips stayed there for several seconds, before she finally relented and pulled back. "I love you so much," she whispered.

"I love you, too." Kay closed her eyes and was dozing off when she heard Randi's stomach grumble. Not certain of what she'd heard, Kay had decided to ignore the sound when another louder, grumble went off under her ear. She opened her eyes and looked up, enjoying the embarrassed look on her partner's face. "Sounds like I need to feed you."

"Nah, it's not that bad," Randi assured her, just before her stomach complained again. *Jeez. This is ridiculous.* She gave a half-hearted shrug. "Guess maybe we'd better get something to munch on, before my body rebels completely."

Kay waited until Randi released her hold, then sat up and stretched. "Were you serious about me driving your car?"

"Sure. Why?"

"I was just thinking that maybe I could run out and grab something and bring it back, while you check on our new little friend." Kay was almost afraid to look in on the duckling herself, for fear of what she might find.

Randi stood up and twisted her head, grimacing at the loud pop. "Ugh." She put her hands on her hips and leaned back, causing her spine to crack as well. "Much better." Taking in the amused look from Kay, she raised one eyebrow. "Find something funny?"

"No, of course not. I'm sure everyone creaks when they get up."

"Uh-huh." Randi looked Kay over and was relieved to see no ill effects from her earlier crying jag. "Are you sure you want to go out? There's probably something in the freezer that I can thaw for dinner."

"I'm sure, but that's all right. Besides, I kind of need to get out for a few minutes, if you know what I mean." She leaned over and kissed Randi lightly on the lips. "I'm just going to run through a drive-thru and grab a couple of burgers or something. It shouldn't take me too long."

Realizing that she couldn't smother Kay, and that her partner needed a little space sometimes, Randi forced what she hoped was a sincere smile onto her face. "All right. You know where the keys are." Kay was almost to the bedroom door when she thought to call out, "No onions!"

Kay giggled as she hurriedly slipped on her coat. *Better get out of here before she changes her mind.* She grabbed her purse and the car keys from the table by the front door. The thought of getting out of the apartment and exploring the area for a little while gave her a thrill. She hadn't been behind the wheel of a car in some time, and the idea of being able to drive the Corvette excited her. *Randi may not get her car back.* She closed the door behind her and jogged to the waiting sports car.

It only took Randi a few minutes to check on the duckling, and she was relieved to see that it had obviously started eating on its own. The tiny fowl was snuggled up in one corner of the box fast asleep, so she covered the box back up and left the bathroom.

Spike stood guard outside the door, and he looked up when Randi stepped into the hallway. She had only taken a few steps and found herself standing outside the guest room. Boxes still filled the room, making it impossible to even get to the computer desk. "Well, buddy, how about we do a little rearranging? I bet Kay would like to be able to go online whenever she wanted. Maybe that would give her a little bit of breathing room around here." She grabbed several of the boxes and moved them into the hall, so that she'd have more space to maneuver in the room.

Maybe if I move the bed, we can take the dresser out of the closet and store the unopened boxes in there. Randi slid the twin bed several feet.

Tired of almost being stepped on, Spike jumped up onto the bed and stretched out in the middle.

"Gee, thanks for the help," Randi grumbled. After several minutes of pushing and pulling, she finally had the bed where she wanted it. Going over to the closet, she struggled to get a grip on the back of the dresser. Not able to get a firm purchase, she moved her hands to the sides and pulled. The dresser was almost too wide to fit through the doorway, and Randi's left hand became pinched between the furniture and the door frame when the heavy furniture slipped. "Shit!" She pulled her hand to her chest, trying to keep from crying.

Once the pain had subsided to a dull throb, Randi examined her hand. There was a wide scrape from her knuckles to the middle of her fingers, and the skin underneath was already beginning to sport a bruise. "Wonderful." She slowly worked her hand into a fist and grimaced. *Doesn't feel broken, anyway.* Sitting down on the edge of the bed, Randi glared at the offending piece of furniture. "How the hell did I get that damned thing in there, anyway?" The answer suddenly dawned on her, and the aggravated woman stood up.

Randi removed the empty drawers and, not wanting to trip over them and break them, placed them in the hallway. *Knowing my luck, that's exactly what I'd do.* It took longer than she'd anticipated because of the ache in her injured hand, but she was determined to have the room finished before Kay returned. After the drawers were removed, it was easy to turn the dresser up on its side and slide it out of the closet.

She had just finished stacking the last box in the closet when the phone rang. Looking at the dog still perched on the bed, she shook her head. "I don't suppose you want to get that, do you?" Randi hurried down the hall and into the living room, leaning over to check the Caller ID box. Recognizing the number, she picked up the phone. "Hello, Augie."

"We just got back from the beach, and I heard your message. What's wrong?"

"Well, hello, brother. It's nice to hear from you, too. Why does anything have to be wrong for me to call you?"

There was silence on the other end of the phone for several seconds, then Augustus Meyers cleared his throat. "All right. I guess I deserved that. But you can't blame me. I haven't talked to you since Thanksgiving, and then all of a sudden there's a message on our machine asking me to call you back as soon as I can. What was I supposed to think?" Five years her senior, Randi knew Augustus took his responsibility as eldest sibling very seriously. Although they had never really been close, he would do whatever was needed when called upon; it was clear that he felt it was his duty.

Randi rolled her eyes and dropped gracelessly onto the sofa, stretching out and propping her feet up on the aged coffee table. "I got a phone call from Mom earlier today. Has she talked to you about Christmas?"

"I think she may have mentioned it, why?"

Asshole. Always acting so superior. "I was wondering what you and Lauren had planned. I know Mom said something about having everyone up to Santa Fe, but I'm not sure if I can afford airfare right now."

"Are you asking for money? Because if you are, I've already gotten—"

"No," Randi snapped. "I would never ask you to part with one penny of your precious money. It's just that if everyone is meeting at Mom and Dad's, I'll probably just stay home."

He contemplated that for a moment. "Oh. I see. Well, Lauren and I haven't actually discussed it, but I figure that we'll be going back to Woodbridge. Her father isn't doing that well, and we don't know just how many more holidays he has." His wife had been his high school sweetheart, and had left her family behind when Augustus' work relocated him to Florida.

"Does Mom know that? Because I think she'd be really upset if she missed out on a chance to see the kids."

"No, she doesn't. But I'm sure you'll tell her, like you always do," he taunted.

Randi closed her eyes and silently counted to ten. "Well, someone has to, since you're always too damned busy," she barked. Softening her tone, she added, "Listen. I'll be glad to let you tell Mom, if you want. But I was going to call her back anyway. Do you want me to tell her for you?"

Accepting the peace offering, Augustus sighed. "Sure, why not? It'll save me from hearing all about their latest trip. So, is there anything else?"

"No, I suppose not. Goodb— " The click on the other end of the line angered Randi, and she was about to throw the handset across the room when the front door opened. Placing the phone back on the base, Randi stood up to help Kay with her coat. "Have a nice time?"

Kay's eyes shone with happiness as she set her purse and the keys on the little table and held up the bag of food. "I sure did. No wonder you love that car. It's incredible."

"I'm glad you had fun." Randi hung up the jacket and turned around. "Do you want to go get washed up while I grab a couple of plates?"

"Sounds great," Kay agreed. She gave Randi a quick kiss and started down the hallway, stopping when she got to the open guest room door. *Wow...someone's been busy.* Kay hurried on to the bathroom, making a mental note to thank Randi, not only for her hard work, but for understanding Kay's need to get away for a little while.

Not wanting to draw any undue attention to herself, Melissa

bypassed the front desk of the motel and drove around the parking lot, searching for Beth's truck. Luckily, very few people were there at that time of day, and she found the vehicle parked alone on the far side of the building. The old motel was single story, and it wasn't hard for her to figure out which room the mechanic had been given. She parked the sports car next to the large truck and checked her reflection one last time in the rearview mirror. The backhanded blow from Ricky had not only given her a dark, mottled bruise over half of her face, but was also causing her eye to swell almost completely shut. The split on her lower lip had closed, but a quick gnash of her teeth re-opened it so it began to ooze. "Perfect."

Beth stepped out of the bathroom, rubbing her hair briskly with the rough towel furnished by the motel. She already had her jeans and bra on and was reaching for a clean T-shirt when she heard a knock at the door. She allowed the towel to drape across her shoulders while she reached for the doorknob. Swinging the door open, Beth exclaimed, "Perfect timing! I thought I'd take you out to—" She stopped in mid-sentence when she saw the condition Melissa was in. "Jesus Christ! What the hell happened to you?"

"Oh, sugar, it was terrible!" Melissa cried, falling into Beth's arms.

Concerned and confused, Beth slammed the door and helped the sobbing woman to the bed. "Who did this to you? Where are they?" She pulled the towel from her neck and used it to gently wipe the blood from Melissa's chin. "Shhh, baby, it's gonna be all right; I'll take care of you, I promise."

"She...I was just trying to...and then she..." Melissa hiccuped between sobs, coming dangerously close to hyperventilating. "I just wanted to pick up the rest of my things," she finally gasped. "But then, she got mad, and—"

"Who the fuck did this to you, baby?" Beth's hands were shaking from trying to control her anger. "It ain't right to hit a lady. Tell me who it is, and I'll go kick her ass!"

Melissa buried her face in Beth's chest to keep her smile from showing. *That's it, sugar, get good and mad.* Her voice took on a frightened tone. "Oh, no," she cried, wrapping her arms around Beth. "I don't want you to get hurt. She's dangerous."

"Don't you worry about me, I can take care of myself. Just tell me where I can find this bitch." Beth stroked the auburn hair gently, wanting to do serious damage to whoever had hurt the sweet woman in her arms.

"Please, just hold me?" Melissa sniffled. "I don't want to be alone right now," she said in a small voice. She gasped when she felt herself being lifted.

Beth stood up, taking her lover with her. She gently placed Melissa back on the bed, then turned to remove the high heeled shoes from Melissa's feet. "Let's just get you more comfortable, okay? We'll talk more about this, later."

"You're too good to me, Beth. Not many people would be so kind to someone they had just met." Melissa mentally patted herself on the back for reading the husky woman so well the night before at the bar. She had been scoping out the bar patrons for the better part of the afternoon, trying to find someone that would fit into her plans. *I can't believe I got this lucky. This woman is an idiot!* She considered it doubly lucky that she got an evening of great sex out of the deal as well.

They were over halfway through their meal when Kay noticed that Randi was holding her hamburger with just her right hand, keeping her left one on her lap. "Randi?"

"Hmm?"

"What's wrong with your hand?" Kay set the remainder of her burger down and reached over.

Randi casually moved the hand, forcing herself to pick up a French fry and pop it into her mouth. "Nothing." The look she received from Kay told her that she hadn't been believed. "Well, not much, anyway." She slowly wiggled the fingers. "See?"

Kay's eyes narrowed as she saw through the evasive tactic. "Uh-huh." She reached beside the sofa and flicked on the free-standing lamp, lighting up the room. "Let's see," she asked, holding out her hand.

Damn. She's worse than my mother. I'm thirty-six years old, for God's sake. I shouldn't have to answer for each little bump or scrape. But Randi quietly obeyed the command, placing her hand gingerly into Kay's.

"Ouch," Kay sympathized, examining the injury. "How did you do this?"

"Smashed it when I was moving the dresser out of the closet." Randi peered down at the hand, which still ached. "It's not that big of a deal, though."

Kay looked up and shook her head in exasperation. "Did you put anything on it?"

"No, but—" Randi's protest was interrupted when Kay moved both of their plates to the coffee table and stood up.

"Come on." Kay's tone brooked no argument. She escorted Randi down the hallway and into the master bedroom. "Sit down on the bed, and I'll bring the supplies in here." She disappeared into the bathroom before Randi could say a word.

Concerned, Spike had followed the two women down the hall and now sat at Randi's feet, cocking his head to one side. When Randi looked down at him, his stubby tail waggled furiously. "What? Well, what are you waiting for? Come on." Randi patted the bed with her right hand, which was all the invitation Spike needed. He jumped up beside her and stood up on his hind legs with his front feet perched on her upper arm.

"Randi, did you—" Kay broke off when she took in the scene before her. "Well, you two look cozy." She walked over to Randi and took her hand, looking at it closely. "It doesn't look that bad in this light."

"That's what I was trying to tell you. It's a little sore, but nothing serious." Randi slowly formed her hand into a fist, opening and closing it several times. "See?"

Mollified, Kay released the hand and unscrewed the cap from the tube of antibacterial medicine she had brought out. "Maybe. But I'll feel better if we at least make a token effort to take care of it."

Randi sighed, but held up her hand so that Kay could place a minute amount of ointment onto the deepest part of the scrape. Once the emollient had been rubbed in, Kay kissed the area just above the injury.

"Thanks."

"You're welcome." Kay kissed the top of Randi's head as well. "Thanks for humoring me."

Watching her lover walk back into the bathroom, Randi couldn't help but grin. She was almost certain Kay had no idea of the swagger in her walk, but was thankful for the view. "Nice, huh?" she asked Spike, who just sat beside her happily.

The hour was late, and with the outside lights shining through the curtains in the hotel room, Beth could still see the damage that had been inflicted on Melissa's face. She was sound asleep, but Beth couldn't bring herself to join her just yet. She wanted to wake Melissa up and find out who was responsible for hurting her, but knew that the injured woman needed her rest. Her hands itched with a hunger for vengeance; she longed to feel Melissa's assailant's blood on them. She looked at her watch, surprised to see that she had been staring at the other woman for over two hours. Removing her clothes, Beth climbed into the bed beside Melissa and lay down facing her.

The movement of the bed woke Melissa and caused her eyes to open, although the injured one was only a slit. "Hey, sugar."

"Did I wake you? I'm sorry," Beth whispered, reaching over and brushing the hair away from Melissa's face. "How are you feeling?"

"I've been better. What time is it?"

"A little after three." Beth started to sit up. "Is there something I can get for you?"

Melissa grabbed one of the mechanic's arms and pulled her back down. "I'm fine, Beth. What were you doing, before you came to bed?"

"Thinking."

I bet that was painful, Melissa's mind teased. She almost giggled at the thought. "What have you been thinking, sugar?"

Beth propped her head up on one hand and looked down into Melissa's face. Seeing the bruising and swelling caused her temper to flare again, and she had a hard time controlling it. "I've been thinking of different ways to make whoever did that to you pay. I can't just sit around, baby. I need to do something, anything, to make this right." She bit her lip in concentration. "What about the cops?"

"What about them?"

"Did you call the cops on your ex?"

Think, dammit. "um, no. I didn't." Melissa rolled over onto her back and began to cry. "I couldn't."

Sitting up, Beth leaned over the other woman. "Why? Is she a cop, or something?"

"No, she's not. But, I couldn't. She'd...she said she would..." Melissa stammered, unable to continue.

Beth stroked the uninjured side of Melissa's face. "Shhh. It's okay, baby. You're scared of her, aren't you?"

Nodding, Melissa continued to cry. "She told me a long time ago that if I ever called the police, or told anyone else, she'd kill me." She sat up and wrapped her arms around Beth, burying her face in her lover's shoulder. "I'm so afraid of her, Bethie. I don't want her to hurt you; and I'm afraid of what she might do if she ever finds out I told you about her."

"Shhh...it'll be all right," Beth crooned, rocking back and forth slowly. "In the morning, you're going to tell me who it is, and where I can find her. She's never going to hurt you again, baby. I can promise you that."

Melissa muttered incoherently, never releasing her hold. Her mind whirled with the satisfaction that by tomorrow, the woman who had scorned her would pay. Dearly.

Chapter
24

The smell of coffee assailed the redhead's senses and caused her to open her eyes, or at least open the one that wasn't swollen. Melissa sat up in bed and groggily took in the room. Beth was sitting at the table under the window, reading the newspaper and quietly munching away on what looked like a box of doughnuts. "What time is it?"

Beth looked up, bits of doughnut glaze stuck to her lips. "Hey, babe. How're ya doing?"

"As good as can be expected, I suppose." Melissa crawled out of bed and stretched. She padded over to the table, naked, having removed the rest of her clothes after Beth had gone to sleep. She accepted the second cup of coffee from Beth and took a cautious sip. *Not bad. I may have to keep her around a little bit longer— she's sweet.* "What are you doing?"

"Checking the Classifieds for a job around here." Beth put the paper down and pulled Melissa onto her lap. She nuzzled the back of the redhead's neck, while her hands reached around to cup her breasts. "Just how good are you feeling, baby?"

Tilting her head to allow easier access, Melissa struggled to control herself. *No, no, no. We've got things to do today.* But the warm hands caressing her breasts were making it harder and harder to think about anything else. "Mmm. That feels good, sugar." She turned her head and crushed her lips to Beth's, crying out when she felt the sharp pain from yesterday's split lip.

"I'm sorry, baby. Let me see." Beth eased Melissa off her lap and sat her down in her chair. She gingerly touched the now bleeding lip with the tip of one finger. "Hold on." Beth hurried into the bathroom and returned with a wet washcloth, placing one edge lightly on the injured area. "Damn. I should have remembered about your face." She traced over the bruise on Melissa's cheek with the other hand.

Melissa forced tears from her eyes, although with the pain of her lip, it wasn't too hard. She took the washcloth, purposely holding it down harder than necessary in order to keep the wound bleeding. "It's okay, really. I almost forgot about it myself."

Not appeased, the mechanic began to pace the room. "No, it's not okay, dammit! The person that did that to you has gotten away with this shit for too long." She stopped in front of Melissa and knelt down beside her. "I want you to tell me where I can find this bitch. You can stay here while I go and teach her the proper respect for a lady."

"No," Melissa cried, jumping to her feet. Realizing that her outburst could be misconstrued, she sat back down. "I can't let you go alone, Beth. She'll hurt you." *Damn! I almost screwed everything up. I've got to see the look on her face when my "protector" shows up and mops the floor with her.* She frowned, thinking. *I wonder if I have any film left in my camera? I'd love to record this for posterity.*

Beth was touched by Melissa's concern. "Take a good, close look at me, baby. Don't I look like someone who can take care herself?" She raised one hand, bending her arm at the elbow in a show of muscle. "Feel that. Hard as a rock. You don't have anything to worry about."

Her head is as hard as a rock, too, Melissa giggled privately. She struggled to keep her mirth from showing on her face. "It's not just that, hon. I need to..." She paused and looked down at the floor.

"You need to what?" Beth asked, using her hand to tilt Melissa's face back up to where she could look into her eyes. "You can tell me."

"No, I can't. You'll think I'm wicked." Melissa jerked her head away from the other woman's touch.

"Melissa, please. I can't help you if I don't know. Please, baby, tell me," Beth asked gently.

Tears fell freely from Melissa's eyes. "I need to watch."

"What?"

"See, I told you," Melissa bawled. She jumped up from the chair and raced into the bathroom, slamming the door behind her.

Beth stood in the middle of the room with her hands on her hips. "Well, shit. What the fuck was that all about?" She walked over to the closed door and tapped on it. "Hey, baby?"

A muffled cry was the only answer.

"Dammit, Melissa, open this goddamned door!" The mechanic pounded harder on the door, then stopped when she realized what she was doing. Taking a deep breath, she lightly tapped on the door again. "I'm sorry, baby. Please open the door."

"You think I'm a monster, don't you?"

Throwing up her hands, Beth stormed away from the door. *Goddamned soft women! I swear that if I didn't like getting laid so much, I'd swear off 'em forever.* She kicked at the bed and then went back over to the door. "Of course not, baby. Please, come out so we can talk about it."

The door opened a few inches. "Are you mad at me?" a tiny voice asked. "You hate me, don't you?"

"No, sweetheart. I don't hate you at all. But, do you want to tell me why you feel the need to watch me kick someone's ass?"

One gray eye peeked out through the opening. "I have to be there, Bethie. The only way I'm going to know that she didn't hurt you is if I'm there, don't you see?"

Poor thing. I bet she wants to make sure that bitch won't bother her anymore, either. She's probably afraid that I won't do it. Beth held her hand out. "Come on out, baby. No one's ever gonna hurt you again, I promise you."

"Oh, Bethie!" The door opened wide and Melissa raced from her hiding place, practically knocking Beth to the ground when she rushed into her arms.

"It's gonna be okay, baby." Beth pulled back just far enough to look into Melissa's eyes. "Now, you get dressed, and we'll go pay a visit to your ex-girlfriend."

Randi stepped out of the bathroom, extremely proud of herself. The duckling that had been so near death the day before was now showing no signs of its previous illness. It even had the presence of mind to snap at her when she reached in to change the water. She sauntered into the bedroom, looking for Kay. Peering into the master bathroom, Randi saw that her lover was nowhere to be found. She heard a tremendous racket coming from the kitchen, and raced through the apartment. "Kay? Is everything..." The sight that greeted her as she crossed the threshold caused her to stop in mid-sentence.

"Don't say it," Kay warned. Several pots and pans were scattered around the floor at her feet, surrounding her.

"Are you all right?" Randi asked, willing herself not to laugh. "I thought we were going to clean out those cabinets together."

Kay rubbed the top of her head. "We were. I was just trying to get one pan down, and the whole damned mess tumbled out." Randi had used a hard-to-reach cabinet to store all her old heavy cookware, unable to part with it when Kay brought in her newer, easier-to-clean pots and pans. They had finally agreed to sort through all the cookware together, and see which items were the best.

"Are you sure you're all right?" Randi stepped around several fallen pots to reach Kay. She moved the hair away from Kay's forehead, which sported a red bump. "Ouch."

"It doesn't really hurt that much," Kay assured her. "But I do feel rather stupid for letting one of them clock me on the head."

Randi studied the knot. "Well, it doesn't look too bad, but you may have a nice little bruise before the day is out." She was bending down to pick up some of the mess, when a whine drew her attention.

Spike stood in the doorway looking at the mess, then at his food dish. He wasn't too sure what his humans were doing, but he figured it wasn't fun. Afraid of what might happen to him if he were to brave the kitchen floor, he sat down and continued to whine.

"You are just the biggest chicken I've ever seen." Randi walked over and picked him up. She couldn't quite understand how he could face down a woman who threatened to kick him, but balked at pots and pans. "Come on, tough stuff, I'll put your food in the living room, just this once."

Kay watched as owner and dog left the kitchen, Randi mumbling quietly. She finished gathering up the cookware and stacked them on the counter. Before she could follow the two out, the phone rang. "I'll get it," she called, picking up the receiver on the wall phone. "Hello?"

"Hello? Is this Ms. Meyers? This is Frank with The Furniture Place. We've got a delivery scheduled for this morning."

Oh, damn. I forgot all about that. "um, yes. Do you have any idea what time this morning?" After the fiasco at the first furniture store, Kay had trouble talking Randi into continuing their shopping trip. With a few sultry promises and a little batting of her eyes, Kay finally talked her lover into trying one more store. Luckily, thirty minutes after entering, they left the store with the salesclerk assuring them of quick delivery.

Frank said, "Well, according to my schedule, our truck should be there between eight and ten this morning. Will someone be there to accept the delivery?"

Randi stepped back into the kitchen and stood by Kay, a questioning look on her face. Kay put her hand over the mouthpiece and whispered, "It's the delivery guys. They're bringing the table and chairs this morning between eight and ten." She rolled her eyes at her lover's shrug, then spoke into the phone. "Yes, I'll be here."

"Fine. Thank you very much, ma'am. Have a nice day."

Kay hung up the phone and sighed. "I guess I'll just take a cab to the clinic once the furniture is delivered."

"No, wait just a second." Randi picked up the phone and dialed a number from memory. "Hey, Joyce, glad I caught you before you left for work."

"Just barely, boss. I was on my way out the door when the phone rang. What's up?"

Randi winked at her lover, trying to assure her that everything would be okay. "I need a ride to work, if you don't mind."

"That old clunker stall on you again?" Joyce asked, laughing.

"No, no. Nothing like that. We've got a furniture delivery scheduled for this morning, and I thought I'd hitch a ride so that Kay would have the car to drive in later."

"Oh, sure. I'm on my way out the door, so it should be just a couple minutes." Joyce hung up the phone without further comment.

The vet placed the receiver back on the phone and turned to look at Kay. "You don't mind driving the car again, do you?"

"I'm sure I can force myself, somehow. Are you sure it's okay?"

Randi pulled her partner into her arms. "Of course I'm sure. There's no sense in you getting a cab when we have a perfectly good car. And Joyce only lives a couple of blocks away. She's always after me to ride with her." They spent a few moments hugging and kissing until a distant honk from the parking lot caused Randi to chuckle. "See what I mean?"

"Well, okay." Kay pulled Randi's head down until their lips were inches apart. "I'll be in to work as soon as I can, all right?" She kissed Randi with an intensity that left them both breathless and shaking.

Randi gasped once they broke free. "Whoo. Damn, you're good at that."

Kay grinned and fanned herself. "You're not so bad, either."

"Ahh, yeah. Okay." Randi shook her head and backed out of the kitchen. "I'll see you later?"

"You can count on it."

Melissa sat in the passenger seat of Beth's truck, mentally reviewing the various possible scenarios of her new lover pumeling her old lover. One of her favorites had the mechanic grab the vet by the head and spin, breaking Randi's neck with a sickening crack. *Oh, yes, this is going to be a wonderful day.* She giggled, then covered up her mistake by coughing.

"Are you okay?" Beth asked, keeping her eyes on the road. "You're not having second thoughts about being there, are you?"

"No, sugar, I'm fine. Just got a little choked up thinking about it, that's all."

Beth spared her lover a quick glance. "Choked up?"

"Um, sure. You know, I still can't believe that you're going through all this trouble for little ol' me," Melissa pointed to her chest. "It just gets me right here." *Like acid indigestion. I swear, these big ol' country girls don't have the sense God gave to a goose. Probably studies for a pee test.* "Turn right at the next corner."

"Sure." Beth followed the instructions, then realized they were getting close to the apartments that Kay lived in. *I wonder if she's home?* Hearing Melissa call her name, Beth turned her head. "Huh?"

Melissa rolled her eye, the other one still being partially swelled shut. "I said, turn left at the light. It's the first apartment complex on the right after that."

Shit. We're going to the same apartments! I hope Katie doesn't see me kicking this broad's ass—I'll never get her back that way. Beth pulled the truck through the gates. "You never told me what your ex's name is."

"I didn't? I could have sworn I told you, sugar." Melissa looked up ahead and saw the Corvette parked in its usual place. *Perfect.* "Her name's Randi. Pretty stupid name for a woman, isn't it? She told me once that she was named after a—" She was suddenly thrown forward when Beth slammed on the brakes. "What the hell is your problem?"

"Randi?" Beth turned to look at Melissa. "An older broad, a bit shorter than me? Drives a classic 'vette?"

The redhead nodded. "That's her. How did you—"

"That fucking bitch! I should have known," Beth yelled, slamming her hands against the steering wheel.

She definitely knows Randi. This is going to be more fun than I thought. "How do you know her?"

Beth glared at Melissa. "She stole my fucking girlfriend, that's how!" The enraged woman shoved the truck into gear and stomped on the gas, causing the tires to squeal.

Melissa couldn't believe what she was hearing. "She what?"

"Probably forced her to move out of town, threatened my poor Katie with God-knows-what." Beth wheeled in behind the Corvette, effectively blocking it in. "Stay here!" she ordered, jumping out of the truck and jogging up the walk. "I'm going to kill that goddamned bitch!"

Kay had just put away the final pot when she heard a pound-ing on the front door. "That was quick." As she started to the door Spike followed her, barking loudly as the pounding continued. "All right, calm down, guys. I'm coming." She opened the door and stood face to face with a furious Beth.

"Where the fuck is she?" the angry woman yelled, pushing by Kay and stepping into the apartment. At the sound of the dog growling at her feet, she looked down and then pointed at him. "Shut that goddamned mutt up, or I'll kill him, too."

"Now wait just a damned minute! What do you think you're doing?" Kay picked up Spike, who continued to growl at the intruder.

Beth walked down the hallway, looking into the bedrooms, then checking the bathrooms. Not finding what she was looking for, she brushed by Kay again and looked in the kitchen. "Where is she?"

"I assume you're talking about Randi?" Kay asked calmly, although her insides were quaking. "She's not here."

"I can fucking see that!" Beth yelled, getting up in Kay's face. She stopped, raising her hand to brush the hair off Kay's forehead, causing Kay to flinch away. "What happened here?"

Kay looked at her in confusion. "What?"

"Your head. What did that bitch do to you, Katie?" Her emo-tions swung completely around, and Beth looked as if she were going to cry at any moment.

"Oh." Kay tried to smile while she raised her hand to touch the red knot. "Some pots and pans fell out of the cupboard this morning, and I moved too slowly getting out of the way."

Her anger spent for the moment, Beth shook her head. "Katie, please, you don't have to protect her. I can help you." She reached out for Kay, but was stopped by a voice at the door.

"What's going on here?" Melissa saw how the mechanic was reacting to Randi's girlfriend, and was worried that Beth had lost her focus.

"Melissa? What are you doing here?" Kay's head was spin-ning from the turn of events. *Does she know Beth? And what is Beth talking about?* "What happened to you?"

Beth walked over and wrapped a protective arm around Mel-issa's shoulders. "Your fucking girlfriend happened, Katie. She's not content to beat up on you, but did this to poor Melissa last night."

"Last night? That's impossible. I was here the whole—" *But you weren't, her mind taunted. She was alone for almost half an hour. And when I got back...* "Her hand," she gasped quietly. Disgusted with herself and her disloyal thoughts, Kay shook her head. "No. Randi didn't do that. She wouldn't do that."

"Are you sure?" Beth asked. "What about your head?"

"I told you, that was an accident. Randi wasn't even in the kitchen at the time." Kay stepped toward the two women. "Now, get out of my home."

A man stood at the door, watching the unfolding drama. "Um, excuse me? I'm looking for Ms. Meyers."

Melissa snorted. "Isn't everyone?" She leaned over and whispered something into Beth's ear, which caused the burly woman to nod. "We'll be back later," she told Kay, allowing Beth to escort her from the apartment.

Staring after the retreating women, Kay motioned for the man to come inside and pointed to the kitchen. "I'm sorry about that. Just bring in the furniture and put it in there. I need to make a phone call."

Outside, Beth was about to get into the truck when Melissa stopped her. "What?"

"Where are you going, sugar?"

"Hell if I know," Beth grumbled. "You said inside that you had an idea?"

Melissa grinned. "Of course I do, hon. I figure that Randi's gone to work and left the little gal home to take care of the house."

"Great. Then all we have to do is go up to that bitch's job and kick her ass," Beth decided, climbing into the truck.

"Hold on, there. We can't go up to where she works. There's too many people there that know her, and would probably never believe us." Melissa tapped her front teeth with one brightly painted nail. "No, what we need to do is get her to come back here."

Beth slammed the truck door then waved one hand at the apartment. "How the hell are we going to do that? Katie's probably calling her already, warning her that we were here." She just couldn't understand how her former lover continued to put up with the abuse she thought was being inflicted upon her. *Maybe she's been brainwashed, like I saw in that movie one time. Yeah, that's it. No wonder she chose that old broad over me.* Satisfied with her conclusion, she waited quietly while Melissa sat thinking.

"I've got it!" Melissa snapped her fingers and hurried around to get into the truck. She turned and looked at Beth, who just sat there staring at her. "Well?"

"Well, what? Are you going to tell me what we're going to do?"

Melissa smiled. "You're going to drive us back to that convenience store we passed on the way over here, and I'm going to make a phone call."

"Okay." Beth shrugged and started the truck, quickly backing it away from the Corvette.

"Meyers' Animal Clinic. How may I help you?"

Kay breathed a sigh of relief when she heard Christina's voice. "Thank God! Christina, this is Kay Newcombe. Are Joyce and Randi there, yet?"

"No, Kay. I'm afraid they aren't. Where are you? I thought you'd be here with her this morning."

"I was supposed to be, but I had to wait for a furniture... Wait! I'm sorry, Christina, but this is important. Could you have Randi call me as soon as she gets in?"

The older woman paused. "Of course I will, dear. Are you all right?"

Kay thought about the question for a long moment. "I will be, once I can talk to Randi. Please tell her it's very important, okay?"

"I certainly will."

The moment she hung up the phone, it rang again. Kay hurriedly answered it, and almost tossed it across the apartment when she found out who was on the other end of the line. "What do you want?"

"I'm worried about you, Katie. That woman is no good for you." Beth was sitting in the truck with her cell phone looking over at Melissa, who was dropping change into the nearby pay phone.

"Dammit, Beth. Get off the phone and leave me alone."

"Not until you listen to me." Beth watched as Melissa dialed the phone. *Keep her on the phone, she says. Easier said than done. The woman won't listen to reason.* "Katie, please. You know I love you, and—"

Kay sighed. "If you love me so much, then you'll honor my wishes and leave me the hell alone."

"I can't do that, Katie. I love you too much. You should be glad, you know."

"Glad about what?"

Beth looked at Melissa, who had turned around and motioned with her hands to keep talking. *Shit.* "um...you should be glad that I met Melissa the other night at the bar. If it weren't for her, I wouldn't know about how that bitch has been treating you."

"For the last time, Beth, there's nothing wrong with the way Randi treats me." Kay looked at her watch and realized Randi would be showing up at the clinic at any minute now. She thought about what Beth had just said and something clicked into place. "What bar?"

"That one I followed you to on Saturday..." *Oh, shit.*

Kay felt the other woman's panic through the phone. "You followed us? Why?"

"Uh, well. You see, I was trying to—"

"Bullshit!" Kay snapped, tired of the game. "You need to get some help, Beth. Get this through your thick skull, once and for all: I don't love you; I never loved you; and I never will love you!"

"You're upset, Katie. I can understand that. And believe me, if you'd just treated me nicer, I would have never gone back to Melissa's motel room with her. She doesn't really mean anything to me, but she's a nice woman, and I promised to help her." Beth was suddenly the epitome of calm, never taking her eyes off the redhead on the pay phone.

Kay felt like throwing the phone across the room. *Dear Lord, she slept with that bitch? And she tells me this while proclaiming her love to me? Beth really is a sick and twisted person.* "If she doesn't mean anything to you, why on earth did you sleep with her?"

Oops. "I was drunk, sweetheart. You can't expect me to remember everything when I'm drunk." Beth watched as Melissa hung up the pay phone with a triumphant look on her face. *I wonder how much longer I have to do this? I hate doing this to Katie, but she'll thank me for it later.*

"Hang up the phone, Beth. I'm not going to ask you again." Kay's voice was deadly calm. "You and Melissa deserve each other."

"Wait, baby, I—" The phone was jerked out of Beth's hand and turned off. "What the fuck did you do that for? I was talking to her."

Melissa tossed the phone into the glove box. "Sounds more to me like you were begging your old girlfriend to take you back." She turned her head away and looked out the window. "I thought we had something, Beth."

Shitshitshitshitshit. Beth scooted across the bench seat in the truck until she was right beside Melissa. "I was just trying to keep her on the phone like you asked, baby. You know I only care for her as a friend."

"Sure," Melissa sniffled, not turning her head. "And all I am to you is a good roll in the hay."

"No, sweetheart. What I feel for you is special. The last two days have meant the world to me." Beth scooted back across the truck and fastened her seatbelt. "Forget it. The only way I can prove to you how much you mean to me is to kick your ex's ass." She started the truck. "Where to now?"

Melissa checked her watch. "Wait about five more minutes, and then take us back to the apartment. She'll be there."

"Meyers Animal Clinic. How may I help you?" Christina asked professionally.

"Oh, dear. Is this where Randi Meyers works?"

The older woman smiled. "Yes, it is. Is there something I can help you with?"

"Actually, I was trying to reach Randi. I live in the apartment next to hers and frankly, I'm concerned." The woman's soft Southern drawl was quiet and refined.

"What's the matter? Is something wrong at her apartment?" Christina asked, worried.

"I'm not sure. I saw her leave earlier, so when I heard a car door slam I knew it wasn't her. Now there's all sorts of arguing going on over there. I've already called the police, but I thought she might want to know, too." The woman hung up before she could be asked for more information.

Christina stared at the phone, relieved when Joyce's car pulled up and the two women stepped out.

Randi and Joyce walked into the clinic, laughing at a shared joke. They quieted almost immediately when they saw Christina's face. Randi frowned. "What's wrong?"

"Kay called a couple of minutes ago, Randi. She asked that you call her back immediately—said it was important. Then, right before you walked in, your neighbor called and said that she could hear arguing coming from inside the apartment. She told me that she's already called the police, but—" Christina moved out of the way while Randi rushed around the desk and picked up the phone.

Her fingers shaking, Randi punched in the numbers while looking at Christina. "What about Kay? Is she okay? Did she tell you what it was about?" *And who would she be arguing with?*

"No, dear. I'm sorry, she didn't. She sounded all right, maybe a bit upset." Christina jumped when the phone was slammed down, hard.

"Goddamn it!" The busy signal caused the nervous flutter in Randi's stomach to expand into a full-fledged attack. She started for the door, then realized that she hadn't driven. "Shit!" Turning to the two women watching her, Randi gave Joyce a pleading look. "Can I borrow your car?"

Joyce tossed the vet her keys. "Of course. Do you want me to come with you?"

"No, that's okay," Randi yelled, running for the door. Over her shoulder she called out, "Thanks!"

Christina picked up the phone and tried Randi's number again. The persistent busy signal hummed in her ears, and she quickly hung up the phone. "I hope everything's okay," she murmured, watching through the window as Joyce's car spun wildly out of the parking lot.

Chapter
25

While they were waiting for a light to change, Beth looked over at Melissa. "There's something that just doesn't seem right to me."

"What's that, sugar?"

"Your ex." The light changed, and she moved slowly through it. "You told me she was this mean, nasty bitch who beat up on women."

The redhead turned and glared at Beth, pointing to her swollen eye. "And? Can't you see by my face what she's capable of?"

"Well, yeah. But, back in Woodbridge, I tried to get her to fight me and she practically ran away." Beth's face scrunched up in confusion. "She acted scared of me, not tough or mean at all."

She picks the worst times to actually think. "Bethie, sweetie...think about it." *Don't hurt yourself, though*, Melissa's thought wryly. "You're more than capable of taking care of yourself. But look at me. I can't defend myself against anyone."

The mechanic nodded. "You're right. And there's no telling what she's put poor Katie through." She turned the truck into the apartment complex's private street.

Randi raced the gray Volvo station wagon out of the parking lot, almost crying in frustration when she was stuck behind several cars at a red light. "C'mon...c'mon, get the hell out of my way!" She tapped a nervous beat on the steering wheel. Once the light finally changed, she used the turn lane to pass the cars, not caring what speed she was driving at.

Her mind raced, wondering what could be going on at the apartment. Her first thought was of Melissa. She knew what an unstable person the redhead could be, and was genuinely concerned for Kay's safety. *Thank God the next door neighbor already called the police*. Seeing the red light almost too late, Randi slammed on the brakes to keep from flying through the busy intersection. "Dammit!"

The next door neighbor? Christina said it was a woman. The vet's eyes widened in worry. *Ron lives next door, and the couple upstairs is out of town*. "Dammit!" The only other apartment was vacant, and with a sick feeling in her stomach, Randi knew that there would be no police. She mentally cursed herself for leaving her cellular phone in the Corvette. Tired of waiting, she checked the intersection, saw that it was clear, and hurriedly took off. The Volvo's tires squealed as she fishtailed through the intersection and narrowly avoided being hit by another vehicle.

Kay had been a nervous wreck ever since she'd talked to Christina. Kay paced the living room, waiting impatiently for Randi to call, and Spike was never more than a step behind her. "She should have been there by now." The dog stopped and cocked his head, appearing as if he understood every word.

Although she wasn't afraid of Beth for herself, the thought that Melissa was pulling her former girlfriend's strings only heightened her agitated state. *I wonder who actually popped her one? Wish I could have been there to see it*. After her split-second lapse of faith, she knew without a doubt that Randi was not the one responsible for Melissa's makeover. "She'd never lie to me." Kay walked over to the recliner and adjusted the afghan that covered it, trying to keep moving so that she wouldn't lose her mind.

"Do you think I need to call the clinic again?" she asked Spike. An urgent pounding at the front door halted the conversation. "That's probably her." Without thinking, she opened the door, coming face-to-face with Beth and Melissa. She tried to slam the door, but was pushed back into the living room when Beth shoved the door open.

"Why did you do that, Katie? I just came back to talk to you." The muscular woman followed Kay into the apartment, with Melissa close behind her.

Spike rushed to stand in front of Kay and growled at the intruders. Melissa laughed, closing the door behind her. "He doesn't have much sense, does he?"

Kay reached down and picked up the protective animal. "He's a lot smarter than some." She glared openly at Beth.

Beth took another step toward Kay, but stopped at the dog's shrill bark. "Dammit, Katie! Either go lock that mutt up somewhere, or I'll wring its noisy little neck."

Not wanting to antagonize the woman any further, Kay carried Spike down the hallway and put him in the master bedroom, closing the door. She didn't actually think that Beth would stoop to such a level, but cared too much for the little dog to put the irrational woman to the test.

Frantic scratching and whining could be heard through the door, until Spike gave up and quieted.

I don't know what Melissa has told her, but it's obviously warped her way of thinking. Turning around, she almost ran into Beth. "Would you please just say what you have to say, and then leave?" She looked over her ex-girlfriend's shoulder and met Melissa's cold gaze. "What about you? What do you get out of all of this?"

"Hopefully, to see justice served." Melissa walked up behind Beth and put her arms around the mechanic, propping her chin on the heavier woman's shoulder. "Isn't that right, sugar?"

Kay backed up until she was standing against the closed bathroom door at the end of the hall. "What kind of justice?"

"Let us take you out of here, Katie. You won't have to be afraid of that woman anymore," Beth pleaded. She held out her hands when she saw the fear in Kay's eyes. "C'mon, baby. I'm not going to hurt you, honest."

"I don't want to be taken out of here, Beth! I know it's hard for you to understand, but Randi and I are very happy. She's the kindest, most gentle person I've ever known." Kay pointed to Melissa. "And I don't know what really happened to you, Melissa, but I know that Randi didn't touch you."

Melissa moved to stand between Beth and Kay. "She's lying, sugar. You know this little slut is just trying to protect that bitch."

The sound of the front door opening silenced them all momentarily.

"Kay?" Randi called, closing the door behind her. "Where are you?" She headed for the kitchen in search of her lover. "Kay?"

Before Kay could say a word, Melissa lunged at her and clapped her hand over her mouth. She nodded to Beth, who rubbed her hands together and started down the hallway.

Kay struggled to free herself from the redhead's grasp, twisting and pulling at the strong hand gagging her. Melissa dragged her forward, then moved around behind her and wrapped her free arm around Kay's middle.

In a hissing whisper, Melissa said, "Want to go up front and watch the fun? I've got Beth so stirred up, there's no telling what she might do to that sanctimonious bitch you're living with." She giggled, shoving Kay forward roughly.

Randi stepped out of the kitchen and was about to head for the hallway when she ran into Beth. "What the hell are you doing here? Where's Kay?" She was caught off guard when Beth grabbed the front of her shirt in both hands and slammed her back against the wall. "Hey!" Randi shouted.

"Shut the fuck up," the mechanic snapped. She pushed Randi harder, enjoying the look of fear on Randi's face. "You like hitting women, bitch?"

"What?" Randi grasped Beth's forearms and struggled, pulling ineffectually at the muscular mechanic's arms. "What the hell are you talking about?" She gasped as Beth pulled her away from the wall, then slammed her back against it, harder than before. Randi groaned and choked out, "Have you lost your mind?"

Beth leaned closer until she was a mere inch away from the vet's face. In an ominous voice, she said, "I should kill you for what you did to Melissa, not to mention poor little Katie." She shoved Randi into the wall again. "What kind of sick asshole knocks around defenseless women?"

From their vantage point in the hallway, Kay and Melissa could see everything. Melissa stifled a high-pitched squeal. "Looks like the action's just getting started, sugar. This is gonna be fun."

Kay screamed, letting out a strangled and muffled sound, from behind the hand over her mouth. She watched in horror as Beth repeatedly slammed her lover into the wall. Unable to escape from Melissa's hold, she bit down with all her might on the hand covering her mouth, while at the same time she stomped on her captor's foot.

"Owww!" Melissa screamed. "You little bitch!" She shoved Kay hard in the back, and the smaller woman catapulted forward and fell to the ground.

Beth turned her head at Melissa's cry, and saw the redhead push her beloved onto the floor. Then Randi's knee came up and slammed into her groin. "Shit," Beth gasped, falling back and then slipping to the floor.

Randi saw Melissa bend over and reach for Kay's hair. "Kay!" the vet hollered as she dove forward to knock the redhead to the carpet. "You goddamned bitch! I ought to kill you!" Randi yelled. She managed to straddle Melissa and block her ineffective blows.

"Hold it! Police!" two voices rang in unison. A pair of uniformed police officers stood just inside the doorway to the apartment, guns drawn.

"Stop it, Melissa," Randi said. "Just stop it," she panted. She continued to struggle with Melissa, finally capturing the elusive hands and pinning them to the floor. Melissa continued to struggle, kicking and twisting.

Kay looked the male officer in the eye and said, "Thank God, you're here." She climbed to her feet. "These two crazies," she pointed toward Melissa and then at Beth, who was sitting up on the floor, "shoved their way into our apartment, and attacked and hurt my partner."

The female officer stepped cautiously forward. "You live here, ma'am?" she asked Kay, who nodded. Noticing the blood on Kay's chin she asked, "Are you injured? Do you need medical assistance?"

Kay wiped at her chin and pointed to the two women still struggling in the hallway. "No, I'm okay. It's not my blood." She watched in satisfaction as the male officer handcuffed Beth. *I can't believe they tried something as crazy as this.*

The female officer looked at Kay and pointed to the living area. "Ma'am, if I could get you to step over there, please."

Two more officers stepped into the apartment. One of them helped Beth to her feet and escorted her from the room. "Break it up," the other officer ordered Melissa and Randi, then he grabbed Randi by the shoulder. The vet twisted and almost swung at the cop until she realized who he was. With help, Randi stood up and staggered over to Kay, wrapping her arms around her. They stood quietly until one of the officers cleared her throat.

The female officer, whose nametag read Delano, led the two women to the sofa and gestured for them to sit down. "We're going to need a statement from you two." She looked at Randi, who had smears of blood on her face and shirt. "Are you hurt?"

"I don't think so," Randi answered, looking down at her body. She looked over at Kay and tried to reassure her. "It's not mine."

Guiltily, Kay looked down at their linked hands. "It's probably Melissa's. I had to get away from her somehow."

Officer Delano leaned forward. "What exactly did you do?"

"I bit her," Kay admitted. She heard a snicker and looked up at Randi, whose smile had grown. "Do you think I need to get a rabies shot?"

Randi laughed, and the officer struggled to keep from smiling.

"Go ahead and laugh," Melissa yelled from the doorway. "This isn't over, Randi. I'll—" She was pulled away from the apartment before she could finish. "You're dead, you bitch!" Melissa shrieked from the front lawn.

"I'm assuming you want to press charges?" Officer Delano asked.

Kay nodded. "You're damn right we're pressing charges. Although in Beth's defense, I think she was heavily influenced by Melissa."

"All right." The officer sat back and flipped open her note-book. "If you'll start at the beginning, I'll try to make this as brief as possible."

Some time later, the last police officer left the apartment. Randi and Kay were just enjoying the calm. The silence was almost deafening. Kay closed the door and leaned back against it. "I am so glad that's over." It had taken well over an hour to make the report and clear their home, and although she was thankful for the timely arrival of the authorities, her nerves had taken a heavy toll from the entire ordeal. She was tired, irritable, and more than a little concerned about her partner. Randi hadn't left her spot on the sofa since they had given their statements, and was now reclined with her head tilted back and her eyes closed. "Randi?"

"Hmm?"

"Are you all right?" Kay sat down next to her lover and touched her arm. Randi had several scratches on her face and neck from Melissa's sharp nails, and it had taken all of Kay's consider-able verbal skills to convince Randi to allow her to clean the minor wounds.

One brown eye opened and regarded Kay. "Uh-huh. I'm fine. How about you?" Although it was only lunch time, after the morn-ing's excitement, Randi was pretty sure that they'd both have trou-ble sleeping that night. *Of course, we don't have to sleep now, do we?* She smiled faintly at the thought.

"That's an interesting smile. Care to share?"

"Mmm." Randi reached out and pulled her lover close. "Wanna fool around?" She nibbled on one of Kay's ears.

Kay shivered. *God, just the sound of her voice excites me.* She turned her head and attacked Randi's lips hungrily. Cool air hit Kay's back as the shirt she was wearing was lifted, and she broke away from the kiss just long enough to allow Randi to pull the top over her head. Warm hands traced patterns across her back, sending goosebumps over her body, while Kay struggled to unbutton Randi's once-pressed shirt. Her hands were shaking too badly to work the buttons, so in a fit of impatience she ripped the shirt open, sending buttons flying everywhere.

"Anxious, love?" Randi teased, while bestowing tiny bites on Kay's throat. She made quick work of Kay's bra and was about to unsnap the slacks, when she was pushed onto her back. "I'll take that as a yes."

After removing Randi's bra, Kay noticed two faint red and purpling bruises on her chest. "What—"

"Must have been where Beth had her hands wrapped in my shirt and shoved me," Randi answered matter-of-factly, looking down at the area. "I'm glad I didn't go with my first instinct."

"Which was?" Kay put the palms of her hands over the bruises in an attempt to somehow heal them with her touch.

"When I first saw her in the house, the only thing in my mind was that she had done something to you. All I wanted to do was punch that ugly face of hers." She put her hands over Kay's. "But she's pretty strong. I'd have gotten my ass kicked all over the place." Randi smiled ruefully.

Kay frowned. "It's not funny, Randi. You could have been seriously hurt." She brushed the fingertips of one hand over her lover's face, careful to avoid the scratches. "As it is, you look like you've been in a battle with a mountain lion or something."

"Melissa's definitely an 'or something.'" Randi reached up and captured Kay's hand, placing a kiss on the palm. "How about we finish this conversation in the bedroom? This damned couch is too little to go much further."

"Bedroom," Kay agreed, then covered her mouth with one hand. "Oh, no! Spike!" She jumped up from the sofa and hurried down the hall. Moments later, she returned with a very perturbed dog in her arms.

Randi sat up. "I was wondering where he was. What was he doing in the bedroom?" She watched as Kay continued to talk to Spike and kiss the top of his head, and was surprised to see tears flowing from her lover's eyes. "Kay? What's the matter?"

"I put him in the bedroom when Beth threatened to hurt him." Kay rubbed her face against Spike's soft fur.

"She what! I should have gone with my first instinct, after all." Randi reached over and scratched the dog behind the ears. "Thanks for watching out for him."

Kay heard the emotion in her lover's voice, and understood exactly how Randi felt. "I'm pretty fond of him, myself." Spike squirmed out of her arms and jumped to the floor, looking at the front door and then back to the two women on the sofa. "I think he's trying to tell us something."

The vet stood up. "Appears so. I'd better take him for a quick walk, before he disowns us." Spike heard the word "walk" and raced over to the front door. He turned and barked, then looked back up at the door. "All right, I'm coming."

"um, Randi?" Kay watched as Randi struggled to clip the lead to Spike's collar. The excited animal bounced around, making catching him difficult.

"Yeah?"

"As much as I enjoy the view, don't you think it would be a good idea to slip on a shirt or something?"

Randi looked down at her body and blushed. "Sounds like a good idea." She went to the bedroom and came back moments later wearing a heavy sweatshirt. "Be back in a flash," she promised Kay, who had slipped her shirt back on and was picking up the discarded clothing.

"If I hadn't stopped you, you'd definitely be flashing." Kay's comment got her a smirk from her friend. She stood and watched until the door closed behind Randi, then shook her head. "I've got it bad, all right."

Kay had just picked up the last button from the floor when the phone rang. With a heavy sigh, she grabbed the cordless receiver before it rang again. "Hello?"

"Kay? Is everything all right over there?" Christina's voice was breathless, and she sounded very upset.

Damn. I forgot all about calling the clinic. Some office manager I am, not even thinking about them. "I'm sorry, Christina. It's been crazy around here, and the police just left a few minutes ago."

"So they did get there?"

"Yeah, just in time, too. Wait. How did you know about the police?" Kay sat down on the sofa and propped her feet up on the coffee table. She held the clothes in her lap, and still had a handful of buttons.

"I called them. Some anonymous woman called right after you did, asking for Randi. She was telling me some strange story about how she was a neighbor and could hear yelling coming from your apartment, and she wanted to make sure that I told Randi."

Her mind whirling with the possibilities, Kay was silent for a long moment. *Melissa! I bet she was making sure that Randi showed up over here, while that damned Beth kept me on the phone.* "Did the caller have a really pronounced accent? Like a Scarlett O'Hara wannabe?"

"She sure did. I thought it sounded pretty fishy, so after Randi took off like her tailfeathers were on fire, I called the police. What happened over there, anyway?"

"It's a long and complicated story, Christina. I'll be glad to tell you the whole thing later, if that's okay." Kay looked up as the front door opened and Randi walked back inside. "Wait, Randi just walked in. I'll let you talk to her." She walked over and handed Randi the cordless phone. "Christina," she mouthed.

The vet took the phone and handed Kay the leash. "Trade you," she whispered. "Hi, Christina. Sorry we didn't call sooner."

"As long as the two of you are all right, that's all the matters, Randi. Will you be coming back up to the clinic today?"

Randi looked over at Kay. Her lover was saying something to Spike, and the two of them walked into the kitchen to give Randi some privacy. She thought about the question. *I don't think I could concentrate on work after this morning's excitement. And, if I'm honest with myself, I'm exhausted.* "No, I don't think so, Christina. Tell everyone they can take the rest of the day off and we'll try again tomorrow."

"I certainly will." Christina's voice quieted. "You sound tired, Randi. Is there anything I can do for you?"

"No thanks. It's nothing a little rest and quiet won't cure." Memories of her frantic drive to the apartment flashed through Randi's mind. *Damn. I forgot about Joyce's car.* "Christina? Is Joyce close by?"

"She sure is. Hold on a moment."

There was a muted thump, and then Joyce's amused voice came on the line. "Hello, Mario."

"Mario?"

"Yup. The way you took off out of here, I could have sworn you were Mario Andretti. Seriously though, I'm glad that everything's okay. Christina told me that you were giving us the rest of the day off?"

"Yeah." Still antsy, Randi walked over to a window and peeked through the blinds. She was relieved to see that Joyce's car was actually parked fairly well and wasn't blocking the driveway. "Thanks for letting me borrow your car. I'll get it back to you in a few minutes."

Joyce paused for a moment. "Hold on, boss." A minute later, she returned. "Christina said that she'll give me a ride over. Now you don't have to go back out today, if you don't want to."

"Thanks, Joyce. I'll have to think of something nice to repay you."

"No need. You can just give us the scoop once we get there. How's that?"

Randi turned away from the window, a smile on her face. She knew how much Joyce loved to talk, and figured it would be easier to tell her than to have to relate the story to everyone in the office over the next few days. "Sounds great. How about I order a pizza and feed you lunch at the same time?"

"That's a great idea! You know I never turn down a free

meal." Joyce's voice took on a serious tone. "Is there anything we can bring you, Randi? From what little I know, it sounds like you've had a harrowing morning."

"No, I think we're okay. But thanks for asking."

"All righty, then. We'll be there in about fifteen minutes or so. Just need time to lock the place up."

The vet's smile widened at the concern of her friends. "Okay, Joyce. We'll be expecting you. Goodbye." Randi hung up the phone just as Kay came back into the living room, alone. "I suppose His Majesty was requesting lunch?"

Kay walked up until she was standing inches away from her lover. "With all the excitement, I didn't get a chance to give him breakfast. But I think he forgives me." She wrapped her arms around Randi's body and rubbed her cheek against the sweatshirt, squeezing hard. "Mmm...I think I needed this."

"I know I did," Randi murmured. Her arms went around Kay without conscious thought, and she tucked her face against her lover's neck.

Feeling the arms around her tighten, Kay smiled. "How's everything at the office?"

Randi pulled back slightly. "Fine. Christina and Joyce will be here in a few minutes to get Joyce's car. I offered to buy them pizza, so that we'd at least have lunch while we told them all about what happened today."

"Good idea." Kay reached up under Randi's sweatshirt, surprised to find only warm flesh, and no undergarment. "Oooh...looks like you forgot something."

"I didn't forget—just didn't want to be bothered with it," Randi rationalized. "But I guess I'd better become a bit more presentable, since we're having company."

Kay didn't like the idea, but she understood it. "Well, I suppose, if you absolutely *have* to." Her eyes took on a teasing glint. "Besides, I don't like to share. No sense in giving Joyce or Christina a thrill, now is there?"

Randi rolled her eyes. "Please. Even if there was something worth seeing, neither one of them would be interested."

"Lucky Ramona isn't coming." Randi looked at her blankly, and Kay shook her head. "You are blind sometimes, my dear."

Randi looked at her quizzically, then wrapped one arm around Kay's shoulders and escorted her down the hallway. "C'mon. You can help me get dressed."

"I'd rather help you get undressed." Kay pinched Randi on the rear, causing her to screech and run. "But, I guess I'll have to behave. Just don't expect me not to rip your clothes off the minute they leave." She relished the sound of her lover's laughter as they raced to the bedroom.

Chapter
26

Christina and Joyce spent several hours at the apartment. Both women had been justifiably outraged at what Melissa and Beth had done, and they needed to stay until they felt that Randi and Kay were going to be all right. It wasn't until Christina noticed the tired set of the vet's shoulders that she made hasty excuses and dragged Joyce from the apartment.

After their guests left, Kay talked Randi into lying down and getting some rest. Now Kay was lying in the comfortable bed, watching her lover sleep. Although too keyed up to nap, she didn't get up and do anything for fear of waking her. Randi stirred often, obviously reliving the day's earlier events. When that happened, Kay would reach over and stroke Randi's brow, or just put a hand on her shoulder and whisper gentle words of comfort until she would settle down again.

Spike stood up from his position on the foot of the bed and stretched, then jumped down and trotted to the door. He looked over his shoulder at Kay and then back to the door, his intent quite obvious.

Rolling her eyes at his apparent sumons, Kay carefully eased herself out of the bed. She pulled on her jeans and then borrowed the sweatshirt Randi had worn earlier. Lastly, she slipped her bare feet into her sneakers before quietly exiting the room.

The walk was shorter than Spike wanted, but Kay didn't want Randi to wake up and find them gone. She knew how she would feel, especially knowing that in all likelihood Beth and Melissa wouldn't stay in police custody long. After peeking into the master bedroom and seeing Randi was still sleeping, Kay decided to take advantage of the quiet time and catch up on her reading.

From her comfortable spot on the sofa, she was barely into the book when the phone beside her rang and caused her to jump. Kay quickly grabbed it, hoping that she had caught it before it woke her lover. "Hello?"

"Kay?"

"Oh, hi, Patricia." She fell back against the sofa in relief. Kay didn't know what to expect when the phone rang, and realized sadly that she would probably jump every time it rang for some time to come.

"Is everything all right? You sound a bit upset."

Damn. Randi's right. She can read minds. When Randi had told her of her mother's perceptive skills, Kay thought she had been exaggerating, but now wasn't quite so sure. "Um, no, I'm all right. I was just reading, and the phone startled me."

"Uh-huh." The older woman didn't sound convinced. "Is my daughter around? I got a call from her brother, and he seemed surprised that she hadn't called before him."

"Actually, she's resting right now. Is there anything I can do?"

"Resting?" Patricia's voice rose in concern. "Is she ill? It's not like her to be napping at this time of day."

Kay realized that she was going to get into trouble, one way or the other. If she told Patricia what had transpired earlier, Randi would probably get upset. But, if she didn't, then Randi's mother would know for certain something was wrong and would worry unnecessarily. "Actually, she was really worn out. We had a bit of trouble this morning—"

"What kind of trouble? Are you two okay?" Patricia sounded as if she wanted to crawl through the phone to check on them personally.

"We're fine, Patricia. Really." Kay paused, not sure how much she wanted to tell. *Might as well get it over with.* "Randi's ex-girlfriend showed up, and they got into it. Thankfully the police arrived and—"

"The police? Just what was that crazy woman up to? I never did like her. As far as I'm concerned, she should be locked up for what she did to my daughter when she left."

Closing her eyes and rubbing her forehead, Kay realized that the conversation wasn't going well at all. "She had...um, somehow hooked up with *my* ex, and then made my ex believe that Randi had beaten her up." Not able to help herself, Kay chuckled. "I don't know how she managed it, Patricia, but the woman had been knocked around a bit. I wish I could have been there to see whoever it was do it."

The older woman sighed. "That one always was devious. She caused all sorts of trouble at Christmas a few years ago—flirting with the men, especially the married ones. I think she was trying to get back at Randi for something, but I never found out what it was."

That figures. It's not hard to believe she'd stoop to any level to get what she wanted. I just can't figure out how she found Beth and talked her into everything she did. Officer Delano had told them that it probably wouldn't take long for Beth or Melissa to get out on bail, and she told them to call the police if they returned. *I don't think Beth would come back, but Melissa's crazy enough to do just about anything. I wish there were some way of just getting Randi away from here for a while, until things cool off.* Her musings were cut short by Patricia's question. "I'm sorry, what did you say?"

"I said, if that woman is causing trouble, maybe it would be a good idea for you two to come for a visit. You know, get away for a little while?"

How does she do that? "That sounds really tempting, Patricia. But I doubt if Randi would even consider it, since she's trying to get the clinic up and running." Kay liked the idea of spending more time with Randi's parents, and if it got her lover out of harm's way, she liked it even better.

Patricia snorted in disdain. "It's almost Christmas, anyway. I don't see why she doesn't wait until after the first of the year." She was silent for a moment. "How would you feel about it, Kay? We could all fly out together a few days before the holiday and still be in Woodbridge for Edna's festivities. And you could see your family, too."

"I'd rather spend all my time with your family. Mine aren't worth the trouble."

"All right." Randi's mother sounded puzzled, but refrained from commenting further. "Have my daughter give me a call when she gets up, will you? I think I have a pretty good argument for our case."

Uh-oh. From the sound of that, I might as well start packing. Poor Randi doesn't stand a chance. "I sure will, Patricia."

"Great! I'll talk to you later, then. Bye." Patricia signed off before Kay could ask what she planned to say to Randi.

Hanging up the phone, Kay looked down at Spike, who was sitting at her feet with a curious look on his face. "Don't ask me." She fell back against the sofa. "But if Patricia has anything to say about it, I bet we'll be taking a trip pretty soon." He seemed pleased with her answer, because he quickly jumped up into Kay's lap and curled up to sleep.

Soft, gentle touches to her face and hair caused Randi to slowly open her eyes. She blinked several times to adjust her vision in the semi-dark room. Kay's concerned face hovered just above her, and Randi couldn't help but smile at her lover. "Mmm...what time is it?"

"Almost seven." Kay continued to stroke Randi's face. "I would have woken you sooner, but I kind of dozed off on the sofa." Spike's insistent tongue along her face was the only reason she got up when she did, only half an hour after she fell asleep.

Randi struggled into a sitting position and rubbed her face. "Damn. With all the sleep I've had, how can I be so tired?"

"I know what you mean. I feel pretty worn out, too. And I wasn't the one trying to keep Super Bitch from scratching my eyes out." With one finger, Kay traced over the three red marks on Randi's face and neck. One ran almost horizontal along her jaw line and the second, deeper scratch started just below her left ear and zig-zagged down to her throat. The third scratch had come dangerously close to one of the brown eyes she loved so much, and she cringed inside when she thought about the damage that could have been done. "We should probably put more antibiotic ointment on these, and then see about getting something for dinner."

"I suppose." Closing her eyes at the light touch, Randi felt an incredible weariness come over her. Although she had barely touched her lunch, the thought of food was totally unappealing. All she wanted to do was cover up and let the day end. *I wonder if I can talk Kay into joining me.*

Searching for something to rouse her weary partner, Kay tried another tactic. "Your mom called while you were sleeping."

Dark eyebrows rose in question. "Is everything okay?"

"Funny, that's what she asked."

"Huh? What do you mean?"

Kay smiled to try to alleviate her partner's concern. "She said that your brother had called, and he was evidently surprised that you hadn't. So, your mom called here to see if we were okay and was concerned when I told her that you were resting."

I bet she freaked over that. Randi's mother had often tried to get her daughter to slow down and "smell the flowers," but Randi would laugh off her concerns, often working to the point of exhaustion. *Probably scared the hell out of her.* "How did she react to that news?"

"About how you would expect. I think she was about to book a flight to Fort Worth to check on you."

"What did you tell her?" Now wide awake, Randi decided that a phone call was in order to assure her mother that she was all right.

Trying to defuse the situation, Kay rubbed Randi's arm.

"Shhh. Everything's okay. I gave her the condensed version of what happened, and told her that you were tired and I put you to bed."

Randi shook her head ruefully. "Thanks, I think." She knew that Patricia had a way of getting people to open up to her, without them fully realizing it. *I didn't want her to know about Melissa coming back, because she'll just worry. But, maybe it's better if it's out in the open. No sense in getting all bent out of shape about it.* Randi ran one hand through her hair in an attempt to tame it a little. "You said that Augie called Mom?"

"Yep. She said he wanted to talk to her about Christmas." *Should I tell her what else Patricia said? How will Randi take it when her mother asks us to go to Santa Fe for a couple of weeks?* Kay hated keeping anything from her friend, but also didn't want Randi to make up her mind before Patricia had a chance to talk to her. *But isn't that what I'm doing, making her mind up for her?* Kay's internal argument kept her from hearing Randi's query.

"Earth to Kay?" Randi waved her hand in front of Kay's glazed eyes. "Hello, anybody home?"

"What?" Kay blinked and shook her head slightly. "I'm sorry, what were you saying?"

Relieved that everything appeared to be all right, Randi leaned back against the headboard on the bed. "I asked if Mom expected me to call her back tonight."

"Only if you're up to it." *What if Patricia tells her what we talked about? Will Randi get mad? Maybe I should...* Seeing Randi's hand wave in front of her face again, Kay frowned. "What?"

"You zoned out on me again. What's going on with you?" Randi was becoming increasingly concerned over Kay's actions. It wasn't like her lover to fade out like she had been doing.

"Let me ask you something."

"Ooo-kay." The abrupt change in subject surprised her, but Randi crossed her arms over her chest and waited patiently.

Kay scooted closer and reached over to take one of Randi's hands. "When was the last time you had a vacation?"

What's going on in that beautiful blonde head of hers? "Thanksgiving," Randi deadpanned.

"That wasn't a vacation—more like a holiday." Kay glared at her companion. "No, what I'm talking about is, when was the last time you took off for a couple of weeks to just relax?"

"um." Randi's forehead furrowed in concentration. She appeared to be deep in thought, which amused Kay to no end.

"Come on, come on. It wasn't that tough of a question."

Randi shrugged her shoulders. "I dunno. Probably about a year and a half ago, when Melissa dragged me skiing. Although, I don't know how much of a vacation that was, since I had the flu the entire time we were there." She grinned. "Boy, was she ever pissed over that one."

Kay was outraged at the thought. "How could she get angry about you being sick? It wasn't your fault."

"She seemed to think it was. Maybe it was because I didn't want to go skiing in the first place. I have no desire to race down icy cold mountains, wearing two thin strips of wood attached to the bottom of my feet." Randi's smiled widened. "It probably didn't help matters when she found a beautiful woman in our room with me."

"What? You mean..."

Laughing, Randi shook her head. "No, nothing like that. Although, that's what Melissa insisted. Actually, the woman was a nurse, and she and her husband were staying across the hall from us. We met accidentally when I had come back from getting some juice and bottled water, and she found me trying to unlock my door." Her smile turned sheepish. "I was coughing so hard, I couldn't get the damned pass card to work. Helen helped me into my room and was just about to leave when Melissa showed up."

"Oooh. I bet that was entertaining." Having been on the receiving end of one of Melissa's tirades, Kay could just imagine how the redhead had behaved.

"Oh, yeah. It took both Helen and her husband to keep Melissa from jerking me out of bed and knocking me around. She got really pissed and slapped Helen. Randi paused, remembering. "As a matter of fact, they had to call Security, and Melissa ended up spending the night in jail."

Kay laughed. "She hasn't changed any, has she?" She sobered at the thought of what Randi had gone through with her ex-girl-friend. "Was she always like that to you?"

"No, not at first. She only got really nasty the last few months we were together." Tired of the conversation, Randi pulled Kay into her arms. "Enough about her. What do you want to do for dinner?"

"Oh, I don't know." Kay snuck one hand beneath Randi's shirt to caress the soft skin. "What are you offering?"

Randi's eyes widened as Kay's hand found a particularly sensitive spot. "Uh, well...we um. I mean, it's that...mmm." Her babbling was cut short by Kay's mouth, which covered her own. *Dinner can wait,* she thought, as her shirt was pulled over her head. *I think we'll start with dessert.* Randi allowed Kay to sit back so that she could pull the sweatshirt off. "Nice," she murmured, using her hands to caress along Kay's ribs. "Looks like you forgot something, again."

"I didn't forget." Kay rolled off Randi and stood up, taking off her shoes and peeling the denim jeans down her legs. "I was in a hurry." She grinned and leapt onto the bed, much to Randi's surprise.

"Oof." Randi caught her and rolled until Kay was beneath her. "You're pretty frisky."

Kay's grin turned sultry. "You have no idea," she whispered, running one hand down Randi's bare chest and stomach, until she found what she was looking for. "But I plan on showing you."

"Ahh," Randi sighed, closing her eyes. She was barely cognizant of being rolled onto her back. "Kay..."

"Mmm..." Kay's mouth attached itself to Randi's throat, then slowly trailed down the same path her hand had taken moments earlier. She smiled to herself when she felt her lover tremble, enjoying the heady feeling of control that Randi so gladly relinquished to her. Kay took a light bite on the skin beneath Randi's ribs and felt insistent hands tangle in her hair. "I love you," she whispered reverently, working her way down the squirming body.

Randi heard Kay's murmur and struggled to answer. "I...oh, God, Kay," she moaned, throwing her head back against the pillows. "Love you," Randi gasped, as her lover's hands and mouth sent jolts of pleasure throughout her body. No more words were spoken, and not even the far off ringing of the telephone could interrupt their lovemaking.

"But, Mom," Randi sputtered as she paced across the living room, "you know that's not it at all." She glanced over at the sofa, where Kay and Spike sat watching her. Both appeared to be amused at her predicament, which only infuriated her more. *She's treating me like I'm ten, for God's sake.*

"Then what is it, Randi Suzanne? Are you afraid that you might actually get some rest? Maybe you're trying to run yourself into the ground before you're forty, like my sister, Eileen." Patricia's youngest sister had been a corporate lawyer determined to make partner by the time she was forty-five years old. Unfortunately, the smoking, drinking and job stresses had become too much for her, and she'd died of a massive heart attack only weeks before her fortieth birthday. Randi's mother saw the same destructive behavior in her only daughter, and was intent on preventing family history from repeating itself.

Randi threw her free hand in the air in frustration. "That's ridiculous. But I have a responsibility to the people who work with me. I can't be running off on a whim."

"A whim? How can you call taking care of yourself a whim?" The older woman's voice had risen until she was almost yelling, and she paused for a long moment to calm down. "Honey," Patricia started, much quieter, "have you thought about Kay? What if, God forbid, that crazy Melissa gets it into her head to get at you through her? Isn't Kay worth anything to you?"

Randi's pacing had brought her to the front window of the apartment, where she peered through the blinds into the night. "She's worth everything, Mom," she whispered, her voice heavy with emotion. Looking out into the darkened parking lot, Randi realized that her mother was right. The thought of Melissa doing anything to harm Kay made Randi physically sick to her stomach; and she decided right then and there that she would do whatever it took to keep her lover safe. "Let me talk to the ladies at the clinic, okay? If they'd all like to take a few weeks off, then I guess you'll be having company."

"Wonderful! Oh, by the way, we've done a bit of remodeling since you were here last, and I think you'll like the new guest room."

"Should I be worried?"

"No, of course not." As an afterthought Patricia added, "Don't forget to dress warm, dear. It's winter here in the mountains, not like those fall-like days you get in Texas."

Randi rolled her eyes. "I haven't even decided for certain that we'll be there, Mom." But Randi knew as well as Patricia did that it was practically a done deal, and that they'd probably be in Santa Fe within the next few days.

"Of course you will. Now call me tomorrow. Your father wants to get your airline tickets, and you know how he is."

"But—"

"Goodnight, Randi. Give Kay our love, and tell her that I'll talk to her later." Patricia hung up, not allowing her daughter a chance to argue.

Glaring at the phone in her hand, Randi turned away from the window. "Damn. She's always doing that to me." Randi hung up the handset and looked at Kay, who had her hand over her mouth in an attempt to fight off her giggles. "What?"

"I'm sorry, Randi. It's just that you sound like a little kid when your mother talks to you." Kay was unable to contain her mirth. She bit her lip as her dejected partner sat down next to her. "Are you that upset about going? We don't have to, you know."

Randi propped her feet up on the coffee table and shook her head. "No, it's not that." With her arms crossed over her chest, Randi looked more like a petulant child than a grown woman.

"Then what?" Kay placed one hand on her lover's arm in concern. "Are you upset that your mom talked to me about it first? I know I should have told you, but—"

"No, that doesn't bother me. I just feel like my entire life is out of my control, and there's nothing I can do to get it back." Randi sighed and dropped her head back against the back of the sofa, closing her eyes. "I hate running away."

Almost feeling the thought slap her in the head, Kay finally understood. "You think that going to your parents' house for a few weeks before Christmas is running away?"

"Isn't it?" Randi still had her head tilted back and her eyes closed.

"I don't think so." Realizing a different tack was needed, Kay mimicked Randi's posture, but kept her head turned and eyes open so that she could watch her lover. "You know, I've never really had a family to enjoy holidays with. This last Thanksgiving was probably one of the best I've ever had, thanks to you and your family."

Randi took a deep breath and released it very slowly, still keeping her eyes closed. "I'm glad. I know that they all enjoyed meeting you, too." She had a pretty good idea where the conversation was going, but wanted to wait and see what Kay had to say.

"I'm really looking forward to Christmas," Kay admitted wistfully. "For the first time in years, I'll be able to share it with people I love."

Damn. She's right. Maybe I've been too selfish about all of this. Why can't I just see this as an opportunity to give Kay something that she deserves: a holiday surrounded by a family who is beginning to love her as much as I do. Randi turned her head and opened her eyes, startled to see Kay's hazel eyes so close. "Looks like we'll be enjoying the mountains of Santa Fe this holiday season."

"Are you sure you want to do this?" Randi asked. They were sitting in the Corvette, in the deserted lot next to the park.

Kay looked down at the covered box that sat in her lap. "You said he was strong enough to go back, right?" At Randi's nod, Kay squared her shoulders and took a deep breath to gather her thoughts. The Internet sites that she had found all agreed on one fact: the longer ducklings were kept in captivity, the less likely they were to survive in the wild. She was torn between wanting to protect the tiny fowl and giving it a proper chance to go back to where it belonged. "Let's get this show on the road."

"All right." Randi climbed out of the Corvette and walked around to the other side. She opened the passenger door and accepted the box from Kay until the other woman was out of the vehicle.

"Thanks," Kay said quietly, reclaiming the box.

The two women walked silently to the lake. Due to the time of day and the cool north wind, they were the only two people at the park. By unspoken agreement, they walked to the far side of the lake, near the place where they had come upon the duckling to begin with. Randi watched as Kay made her way to the shore and knelt a few feet from the water. Although they had only kept the creature for a couple of days, she knew that this was hard on her partner and vowed to herself to try to help any way she could.

As Kay removed the lid and tilted the box, the duckling waddled onto the damp grass and stopped just before he got to the water. Quacking several times, he waggled his tail feathers and leapt into the lake. Kay stood up and immediately felt a warm arm wrap around her waist. She leaned back and accepted the comfort, never taking her eyes from the duckling, which had quickly found another group of waterfowl and joined them. "You think he's going to be okay?"

"Sure looks like it. But we can stop by after work and check on him, if you want."

Kay turned so that she was looking into her lover's eyes. The simple assurance meant more to her than she could voice, so she smiled instead. "Have I told you lately how much I love you?"

"I think you may have mentioned it once or twice this morning." Randi's arms encircled Kay and pulled her close. "But I never get tired of hearing it."

"I'm glad, because I don't think I'm going to stop telling you anytime soon." Kay's eyes closed as she felt her partner's mouth cover hers. Pulling back moments later, she dropped her head onto Randi's chest and sighed happily.

For her part, Randi held on to Kay as if her life depended on it. *Maybe it does. I don't think I could survive without this...without her.* The distant sound of a barking dog pulled her out of her reverie, and she regretfully pulled away. "We'd better get going, before Christina sends out a posse." They had already fended off one good-intentioned phone call that morning, and assured the older woman that they were capable of coming to work.

"Don't want to." Kay reached for Randi, who playfully jumped out of the way. "Hey!"

The vet turned around and took off at a jog. "Last one to the car has to buy lunch," she yelled, laughing.

"I'm going to have to hurt her." Kay took off after her lover.

Christina looked up as the door to the clinic opened, and her delight at seeing the couple was evident by the smile gracing her features. "Good morning, you two." She stood up and walked around the reception desk to embrace each of them. After delivering a firm hug to Randi, she pulled back and looked up into the vet's face. "How are you doing today?" As bad as Randi's injuries had looked the day before, Christina was relieved to see that the scratches were already scabbed over and didn't appear to be infected.

"Pretty good, actually. Is everyone here, yet? I'd like to have a quick meeting before we have any clients."

Christina looked at Kay, who gave her a comforting smile. "Not quite. Ramona is running late, as usual." She didn't know why Dr. Wilde had tolerated the young woman, since she had a tendency to either be late, or not show up at all. Something told Christina that neither Randi nor Kay would accept that sort of behavior. Her thoughts must have shown on her face, because Kay frowned.

"What is it? Is there some sort of problem?" She looked up at Randi, who had patted her arm and started for the kitchen area. The vet pantomimed getting a cup of coffee, and the question on her face caused Kay to nod. "Thanks." Kay turned back to Christina. "Is everything okay with Ramona?"

"As good as can be expected, I suppose." Christina lowered her voice and pulled Kay into the office recently vacated by Dr. Wilde. After she closed the door, she leaned back against the desk and shook her head. "That girl has only been working here for a few months, but she doesn't seem to learn anything. I don't know why Dr. Wilde kept her around, to tell you the truth."

Kay leaned back against the door, unconsciously mimicking Christina's posture. "What was she hired to do, anyway?"

"She was hired on as a veterinary assistant by Dr. Wilde. But after only a few days, she told him that she couldn't handle the 'mess,' and so he had me show her how to do the filing."

Weary from standing, Kay walked over to one of the visitor's chairs and sat down, motioning for Christina to join her. "How are her filing skills? I know it's not a hard job, but it can be a bit time-consuming."

"Well, it would be if she were here more of the time." Christina reached across the area between them and patted Kay's leg. "Now don't get me wrong, she's a nice enough girl, but she's late more than she's on time, and that's when she bothers to show up at all." She hated to sound so bitter, but it was a bone of contention around the office how the young woman was treated differently from everyone else. Christina normally didn't perpetuate office gossip, but since Kay was the office manager she felt she had a right to know.

"And Dr. Wilde actually allowed this? Was he aware of her work habits?"

Christina nodded. "Oh, yes. He was definitely aware of them," she bit off angrily. "But for some reason, he didn't seem to mind. As a matter of fact, he'd get mad at us for pointing out her tardiness or absenteeism." She leaned closer and lowered her voice to almost a whisper. "I can't prove it, mind you, but I think she's got a little crush on Randi, too."

Kay laughed. "Well, she'll just have to get over it, won't she? I don't share." Seeing the serious look on the other woman's face, Kay tried to reassure her another way. "Don't worry, Christina. I'm sure it's just a harmless infatuation. Once she realizes that Randi is happy with our relationship, she'll be just fine."

"I hope you're right."

Unknown to them, the object of their conversation had walked into the clinic and, after looking around the empty reception area, headed to the kitchen with a devious smile on her face.

Chapter
27

Joyce stepped out of the kitchen, almost running into Ramona. With her long, dark hair and dark eyes, the twenty-two-year-old was an attractive woman, until you noticed the spoiled pout that graced her mouth most of the time. "Oh, I'm sorry," Joyce said. "Have you seen Kay or Christina? Randi wants to have a quick meeting of the staff before the day gets started."

"No, I haven't." Ramona swung her head to toss her hair over her shoulder, brushing by Joyce. "I just got here and I need a cup of coffee."

"Well excuse the heck out of me." Joyce decided to ignore the prickly young woman and check the front of the clinic.

Ramona slipped quietly into the kitchen, smiling at her luck. The only other person in the room was Dr. Meyers, sitting quietly at the table. Even though her back was to the door, she appeared to be completely engrossed in her cup of coffee and didn't hear Ramona enter. Realizing she might not get another chance, the younger woman stood behind the silent vet and put her hands on Randi's shoulders, kneading the tightened muscles.

"Mmm...that feels good," Randi moaned, thinking it was Kay behind her. She closed her eyes and leaned back into the touch.

Smiling to herself, Ramona kept up the impromptu massage, reveling in the feel of the muscles beneath her hands. She had longed to make the vet moan in other ways ever since she began working at the clinic, but didn't know if her advances would be accepted. Finding out that the object of her desire was gay made her certain that she had a chance, conveniently forgetting that Dr. Meyers was already in a relationship. She could hear voices approaching the door, so she leaned forward and rubbed her cheek against the dark head below her.

"I'm sure we'll think of something." Kay led the other women into the kitchen. The four of them stopped when they saw the position of the other occupants of the room. "Are we interrupting something?" she asked angrily, crossing her arms over her chest, but not moving any further into the room.

Realizing with a sickening feeling that it hadn't been Kay's hands on her shoulders, Randi surged to her feet and spun around. She glared at the young woman standing beside her, and then back to her partner at the door. "Kay?"

Although she wanted nothing more than to see what was going to happen next, Christina prudently backed out of the doorway, taking the other two women with her. She had a feeling things were going to get a lot worse before they got better. "Come on you two. Let's go make sure everything's ready for the day."

"Just what in the hell is going on here?" Kay took several steps forward until she stood directly in front of the other two women.

"I don't know." Randi tried to put some distance between herself and Ramona, who continued to edge closer to her. "I thought you had come in and—"

Ramona's eyes widened innocently. "I'm so sorry. I didn't realize that you were here," she told Kay. Turning her attention to the confused vet, she took another step closer to Randi and reached out to touch her. "Why would you lead me on like that if your girlfriend was here, Dr. Meyers?" Her hands were almost on Randi's hips when she felt a strong grip on her shoulder that spun her around.

"Back off, Ramona! Are you trying to tell me that Randi instigated this?" Although she was fuming inside, Kay quickly released the hold she had on Ramona for fear of doing something she would regret later.

"That's exactly what I'm telling you." Ramona turned back to look at Randi. "I thought you liked it."

Randi shook her head and backed away, determined to keep as much space between her and Ramona as possible. She was pretty certain that Kay's anger wasn't directed at her, but she wasn't about to try and find out. "Look, Ramona, I'm very happy in my relationship with Kay. I don't know what I did to give you the impression that I was interested in you, but whatever it was, I'm sorry." She looked to her lover for support. "I didn't even hear her come in, Kay. I felt someone's hands rubbing my shoulders and just assumed it was you."

"Maybe I should just leave." Ramona pushed one of the chairs out of her way. She almost ran from the kitchen, slamming the back door behind her.

"Kay, I—" Randi stepped forward slowly, holding her hands

out from her sides.

Kay held up one hand and closed her eyes. "Wait." She rubbed at her forehead in frustration. "I thought that Ramona seemed to have a crush on you, I just never thought it would go this far." She exhaled heavily and sat down in the nearest chair.

"I swear, Kay, I didn't know anything about it." Randi hated hearing the quivering tone in her partner's voice. She stepped closer to where Kay was sitting, until she was able to squat at her lover's feet. "Please, believe me."

Kay opened her eyes and looked into Randi's face. She studied her eyes closely, seeing only distress and worry. Although she had never even considered Randi guilty of any wrongdoing, she realized that her silence must have made it seem as if she did. Upset with herself at the anguish on Randi's face, she cradled the dark head with her hands. "I believe you."

Closing her eyes at the quiet words, Randi swallowed hard to try and keep her composure. When she felt the feather light kisses on her forehead, her eyes opened again. "We're okay?"

"We're better than okay," Kay assured her. A timid knock on the kitchen door caused them both to turn that direction.

Joyce poked her head around the door. "Just wanted to see if everything was okay in here. We didn't hear any screaming or chair-throwing, so I thought I'd better check."

Kay laughed as she helped her partner up from the floor. "Everything's fine, Joyce. But we may need to start looking for another file clerk."

"Really?" Joyce walked further into the room, with Christina and Elaine close behind her. "Where did you hide the body?"

Dusting off the knee of her slacks, the relieved vet couldn't help but smile. "If we told you that, we'd have to kill you."

"We wouldn't want that now, would we?" Christina took several mugs from the cabinet and brought them over to the table, along with the pot of coffee. "I went ahead and locked the front door while we were out there, since you had mentioned something about having a meeting this morning."

"Thanks." Randi waited until Kay sat down, then took the chair nearest her. "There's a few things that have come up that we'd like to discuss with everyone." She looked at Kay for help.

Understanding her partner's reticence, Kay took Randi's hand in hers. She looked at the expectant faces around the table and smiled to alleviate any worry. "What kind of plans does everyone have for Christmas?"

"Christmas?" three voices asked all at once, then fell silent. Joyce saw that no one else was going to say anything, so she decided to forge ahead and be the first. "Well, Roland and I discussed going to Lake Tahoe. His brother lives there and has invited us out to go skiing." She shrugged. "But, that was before you took over the clinic. I wasn't sure what the holiday schedule would be."

Christina nodded. "I know what you mean. My sister has been trying to get me to come visit her for months." She looked to the vet, who was still silent. "Are we going to be open on Christmas Eve, like last year?" She had no intention of trying to fly out the night before Christmas, if that was the case.

"Well, that's sort of what we wanted to talk to everyone about," Randi said. "I was thinking that you might want a few more days off than that."

"How many more?" Elaine looked at Kay. "Are we talking a long weekend?"

Kay took a sip of her coffee before answering. "What would you say to a couple of weeks? Maybe close down tomorrow, and not come back until after the beginning of the year. We're all going to have a lot to do to get this place into good shape. Dr. Wilde let a lot of things go, business-wise, and I'm going to need everyone's help in getting everything organized. We thought," here she smiled at Randi, "that maybe it would be a good idea to take the next few weeks off to recharge, so to speak."

"What about our salaries? Would this be with, or without pay?" Elaine asked.

"I know that Dr. Wilde had cut everyone's vacation time down to two weeks, with no sick pay." Randi and Kay had talked about this very subject last night after they had gone to bed. Although it would make money tight for a while, they both agreed that the women who worked in the clinic deserved more than they had been given the past few years. "This would be treated as a paid vacation, with everything starting over January first. That includes accrued sick days at the rate of one per month."

Joyce waved her hand in the air. "Let me get this straight. You're trying to tell us that not only are we all getting a long, paid vacation, but we'll be getting sick days out of the deal, too?" She looked at Elaine and Christina, who both wore similar shocked looks on their faces. "Can you afford to do this, Randi?"

"We can, as long as the clinic brings in the kind of business that it did before Randi...left," Kay explained. "I figure that it'll take about two months to get everything entered into the new computer database, which will save us time and money in the long run. We just have to make sure that we work together to make it happen."

"Well, give me a paid vacation for Christmas, and I'll do whatever you want," Joyce joked.

Randi laughed. "I'm glad to hear that. Because I'm going to need all your expertise in helping with our clients, until we can afford to bring in another vet."

Making a show of rolling up imaginary sleeves, Joyce stood up. "Well? What are we waiting for? Let's get this place ready to lock down. I've got a ski trip to plan."

Chapter
28

Kay smiled fondly at the peaceful expression on her lover's face. The previous two days had been filled with frenzied packing and phone calls back and forth between Randi and her parents. Kay was pleasantly surprised at Samuel's generosity. The retired executive not only sent two plane tickets by messenger, but secured them places in First Class. Since the Santa Fe airport only handled commuter airlines and private aircraft, they would make the journey from Albuquerque to Santa Fe by car. It was hard to believe that so much had been arranged in such a short amount of time, but here they were: in the air and on their way to Santa Fe.

The plane had barely cleared the tarmac when Randi yawned and leaned against her window and dozed off. She had warned Kay before they boarded that she wouldn't be very good company on the flight, admitting sheepishly that she couldn't stay awake once they were airborne.

She wasn't kidding. Shifting her legs to get more comfortable, Kay was careful not to kick the carrier beneath her seat that Spike traveled in. Evidently used to the mode of travel, the dog offered only a token whine before settling down and falling asleep, much like his human. Kay spared another glance at her sleeping partner. The ugly scratches that marred Randi's skin were slowly fading; yet every time Kay saw them, her anger at the woman responsible for the injuries surged again. *It's a good thing that Melissa has kept a low profile since she was released from jail. If I ever see her again, she'll wish she were still behind bars.* Although not normally a violent person, there wasn't any doubt in Kay's mind that she could do serious damage to Randi's ex-girlfriend.

Kay settled back with a book and read for almost an hour. No longer interested in the story, she closed the volume and sat thinking about how much her life had changed. The pilot's voice over the speaker jarred Kay from her thoughts. Announcing that they were on final approach to Albuquerque International, he notified the passengers that it was partly cloudy and thirty-three degrees, and added a jovial admonition not to forget to zip up their coats. Kay shook her head and chuckled along with most of the other people on the plane. Hearing their pilot sound like a mildly scolding father was refreshing, and she shared a smile with the woman sitting across the aisle from her. Kay turned her attention back to her sleeping lover. The announcement hadn't disturbed Randi at all, and she looked so peaceful that Kay was loath to waken her. Feeling the plane dip slightly, Kay realized that it wouldn't be much longer before they were on the ground. She reached over and without thinking, gently caressed Randi's cheek. "Randi? It's time to wake up."

"Mmm." Randi tried to snuggle deeper under her black leather coat, which she was using as a blanket.

Smiling at the reaction, Kay spared a glance back across the aisle. The woman she had shared a look with earlier turned away quickly, embarrassed. *Oops. Guess I forgot where we were.* Kay ignored the woman's brush off and twisted around to face her partner. Leaning in to keep from being overheard, she whispered, "Wake up, honey. We're about to land." The hand that once again caressed her lover's face was captured by Randi's, which had snaked out from beneath the heavy coat.

Brown eyes slowly opened and blinked several times. The vet looked around for a moment to ascertain her surroundings, then a sleepy smile worked its way onto her face as she looked into Kay's eyes. "Hey."

"Good morning, sleepyhead. I thought you might want to get your wits about you before we land."

Randi rubbed her free hand over her face and yawned. "We're here? Feels like we just took off." She sat up more in her seat. The plane dipped lower, and she peered out through her window to see the ground getting closer. "Damn." Randi turned her attention back to her lover. "I'm sorry, Kay. I was hoping to stay awake this time."

Patting Randi on the shoulder, Kay couldn't help but smile at the remorseful look on her partner's face. She picked up the book that lay in her lap. "You have nothing to apologize for, Randi. I actually got a bit of reading done." The sudden lurch as the plane touched down caused Kay's eyes to widen. "Whoa."

"You okay?"

"Yeah." Kay was somewhat embarrassed by her reaction. "My stomach always does a little flip-flop when we land. I guess it's the sudden change that does it." The whine from beneath her seat caused them both to smile. "Sounds like I'm not the only one." Kay leaned over and put her hand in front of the carrier, receiving a tiny lick of gratitude from Spike. The plane finally came to a stop in front of the terminal, and contrary to the announcement requesting that they remain in their seats, people were already standing in the aisles waiting for the doors to open. "Shall we?"

"Sure." Randi stood up and slipped on her coat. She accepted Spike's carrier from Kay, turning the crate around and looking inside. "Bet you're ready to get out of there, aren't you, fella?" Spike's answer was another quiet whine and an attempt to lick her face through the square bars. She looked back over at Kay and caught the woman standing beyond her staring, and then the stranger quickly looked away. In Kay's ear, Randi whispered, "What's *her* problem?"

Kay looked behind her to see who Randi was talking about. The other woman pushed by several people to get away from them, which caused Kay to shake her head. "I'll tell you later."

"All right." Randi followed Kay into the aisle, smiling her thanks at the gentleman who allowed them to step in front of him. "Let's go see if Mom has driven Dad crazy yet."

Randi hefted her carry-on more securely on one shoulder and took a firmer grasp on her wheeled suitcase. She looked at Kay and bit back her offer to help her with her bag. Randi had made that mistake at their port of departure and didn't want to have another discussion with Kay over her capabilities. They were heading toward the outside doors when they heard a woman's voice call out to them over the din.

"Randi! Kay! Over here!" Patricia Meyers stood just inside the next doorway. Randi's mom waved her hands over her head in an attempt to be seen, almost knocking the gray cowboy hat from her husband's head.

Samuel grabbed his hat and shook his head. "They see you, Pat. If you keep flapping your arms like that, you're going to end up flying out of here."

Before she could offer a retort, Patricia watched as her daughter broke through the crowd. Meeting Randi halfway, Patricia waited until she set down the luggage to wrap her arms around her. "I'm so glad that you're here." She pulled back and looked at Randi's face. "What happened to you?"

"Uh, well..." Randi looked behind her at Kay for help.

Kay stepped up beside her lover and smiled widely. "Patricia,

Samuel, thank you so much for inviting us here on such short notice." She dropped the bag she carried and hugged the older couple one at a time.

"We're just thrilled you're here." Samuel reached down and grabbed Kay's bags. "How about you let me get these for you? We're parked pretty close by."

Randi started to warn her father about Kay's stubborn refusal of help when she was shocked into speechlessness by her lover's words.

"That's so sweet, Samuel. Thank you." Kay kept her arm around Patricia and looked at Randi. "Are you okay?"

Why does she let him help, and argue with me? This relationship thing is going to be harder than I thought. Randi realized that everyone was staring at her. "What?"

Samuel winked at his daughter, having a pretty good idea what was going through her mind. *It's nice to know that not even women understand women. Makes me feel much better.* "Come on, kids. Your mom has a roast cooking, so we'd better make tracks."

The trip from Albuquerque north to Santa Fe passed quickly as Randi and Kay brought the Meyers' up-to-speed on the recent events. Patricia was outraged and threatened to fly back to Texas and turn a certain redhead over her knee, much to everyone else's amusement. The miles seemed shortened by the comfortable trip in Samuel's black Ford Explorer 4x4, and it wasn't long before they were driving through the streets of the oldest capital in the United States.

Kay peered out her window in awe. "I just love the architecture around here." She turned to see Randi looking at her with an indulgent smile on her face. "Well? Don't you?"

"Sure. But I'm having more fun watching you enjoy it."

Blushing, Kay ducked her head. She was saved by Samuel's excited voice.

"We're coming up to the house, Kay. Look out your window at the view."

Built outside the city, the um home was nestled in forty acres at the foot of the mountains, and the winding drive off the main road offered a view of the natural vegetation and scrub brush that covered the area. After five minutes of driving, the road opened up and the house came into view.

The two-story dwelling was made of adobe, with the round arches and windows reminiscent of the pueblos that dotted the landscape centuries before. Samuel pressed a button on the head-liner of the truck, and a large garage door opened to allow them entry. He glanced in the rearview mirror at Kay's expression, smiling at her unblinking awe. "That's the same way I felt the first time I saw it."

"Wow. It's incredible." Kay turned to look at Randi, who was opening her door to get out of the vehicle. "And you were hesitant to come here? Are you out of your mind?"

"No, she's not out of her mind, Kay. Just stubborn as a mule." Patricia grinned at her daughter's discomfort as the four of them gathered up the bags, then stepped from the garage into the house.

The door from the garage opened into the spacious kitchen, causing Kay's eyes to widen once again. "This place is beautiful." She felt she would run out of adjectives before the tour of the house ended, but decided it was a chance she wouldn't mind taking.

After a thorough tour of the home, the three women were all seated comfortably in the living room, while Samuel gladly showed Spike around the outside of the house. Randi took a place next to Kay on the leather loveseat and stretched out her legs. "You know, it's not that long of a flight, but it sure wears a person out."

"I don't see how you can be that tired." Kay leaned back and smiled as Randi's arm automatically went around her shoulders. "Especially since you slept the entire flight."

Patricia laughed. "You still do that, Randi? I thought you would have outgrown that by now."

Kay looked at Randi, then at her mother. "What do you mean?"

"Mom—"

"As a child, she always fell asleep on family trips, no matter how long, or what mode of transportation. Why, one time we accidentally locked her in the car at a rest stop, because she was asleep in the floorboards. Scared us half to death, when we couldn't find her anywhere."

Randi rolled her eyes and sighed. "Mom, please. I was six years old." She turned to see her lover's delighted smile. "What?"

"I bet you were a cute kid." Kay stared into Randi's eyes for a long moment before turning her attention back to Patricia. "Was she?"

"Oh, yes. She was a doll." Patricia grinned and stood up. "As a matter of fact, I have several picture albums around here somewhere that I think you'd be very interested in seeing."

"Mother!" Randi's eyes went wide in panic. "Not the photo

albums."

Kay leaned over and kissed Randi's cheek, quite comfortable in Patricia's accepting presence. "That's okay, honey. I'll ask to see them later, when you're not around."

Great. If these two ever get together and exchange notes, I'm dead meat. Mother will tell Kay every embarrassing story in my life. Randi threw up her hands in resignation. "I guess I can't stop you, can I?"

"Nope."

Randi stood up and dusted imaginary specks from her jeans. "I think I'll see if Dad needs any help with Spike." She bent down and bussed Kay quickly on the lips before hurrying from the room.

Patricia watched her daughter interact with Kay, feeling a great weight lift from her heart. In all the years Randi had lived with Melissa, not once had she ever displayed any hint of familiarity in front of anyone else. But within five minutes of sitting down, she had shown a completely different side of herself. *I think that my girl is finally happy. Looks like we'll be seeing the two of them together for a long time to come.*

After being chased out of the kitchen by her mother, Randi decided to take Kay for a short walk around the property. The first time she had visited her parents at their new home, she'd found a perfect place to get away from the noise and pressure of the family gathering. About two hundred yards up a trail from the house was a thirty to forty-foot hill, which Randi had discovered was perfect for watching the sun disappear over the Rocky Mountains. She and Kay stood on the hill for several minutes, neither one breaking the silence.

Kay leaned back into the arms that held her tight as she watched the sky be painted with glorious bursts of gold and orange. They were both sporting heavy coats because of the cool evening, but Randi's was open and Kay could feel the warmth from her lover's body. She had never felt more at peace, and decided now was as good a time as any to bring up a subject that had been on her mind for weeks. "Randi?"

"Hmm?" Randi stood just above and behind Kay, and her chin rested on her lover's shoulder.

"I know we haven't been together very long, and you may think I'm crazy for even thinking like this, but..."

Randi turned her head slightly so that she could kiss Kay on the cheek. "What are you thinking?"

Kay turned around and wrapped her arms around Randi's

waist. "I'd like to have a commitment ceremony, with your parents as witnesses."

Did she just... "Are you asking me to—"

"Marry me?" Kay looked up into her lover's eyes, which had grown wide. "Yes, I am. What do you think?"

Randi blinked several times and tried to speak. When nothing came out, she cleared her throat and tried again. "I think you're a hell of a lot braver than I am, that's for sure."

"Well, I wouldn't say that, exactly. It's just that..." Kay looked down at the ground, embarrassed.

"Yes."

"What?" Her head snapped up, and Kay was greeted with the largest smile she had ever seen.

"Yes." Randi leaned down closer until they were almost sharing the same air. "That was a yes or no question, wasn't it?"

"Uh, y...yeah. Yeah, it was."

"Good." Bending forward another inch, Randi's lips covered Kay's. Finally pulling back enough to get air into her lungs, Randi noticed the sun beginning to drop behind the mountains. She turned Kay around and pulled her against her body until there wasn't any space between them. "I love you," she whispered into the ear next to her mouth.

Kay held Randi's arms tightly, feeling an overwhelming burst of emotion. "I love you, too."

Locked together in love, their arms tightly around one another, they watched as the golds and oranges in the sky faded into dark blues and deep purples, just as the pain and loneliness of their lives before they'd met each other had given way to the promise of a wonderful future. It was the perfect beginning to their new life together.

Other Carrie Carr books available from
Yellow Rose Books

Destiny's Crossing

(Destiny's Crossing contains two stories)

Destiny's Bridge

Rancher Lexington (Lex) Walters pulls young Amanda Cauble from a raging creek and the two women quickly develop a strong bond of friendship. Overcoming severe weather, cattle thieves, and their own fears, their friendship deepens into a strong and lasting love.

Faith's Crossing

Lexington Walters and Amanda Cauble withstood raging floods, cattle rustlers and other obstacles to be together...but can they handle Amanda's parents? When Amanda decides to move to Texas for good, she goes back to her parent's home in California to get the rest of her things, taking the rancher with her.

ISBN 1-930928-09-2

Hope's Path

In this next look into the lives of Lexington Walters and
Amanda Cauble, someone is determined to ruin Lex. Attempts
to destroy her ranch lead to attempts on her life. Lex and
Amanda desperately try to find out who hates Lex so much that
they are willing to ruin the lives of everyone in their path. Can
they survive long enough to find out who's responsible? And
will their love survive when they find out who it is?

ISBN 1-930928-18-1

Love's Journey

Lex and Amanda embark on a new journey as Lexington redis-
covers the love her mother's family has for her, and Amanda
begins to build her relationship with her father. Meanwhile,
attacks on the two young women grow more violent and deadly
as someone tries to tear apart the love they share.

ISBN 1-930928-67-X

Strength of the Heart

In the fourth novel of the Lex and Amanda series, Lex and Amanda are caught up in the planning of their upcoming nuptials while trying to get the ranch house rebuilt. But an arrest, a brushfire, and the death of someone close to her forces Lex to try and work through feelings of guilt and anger. Is Amanda's love strong enough to help her, or will Lex's own personal demons tear them apart?

ISBN 1-930928-75-0

These and other Yellow Rose Books available at booksellers worldwide.

Other titles to look for in the coming months from
Yellow Rose Books

Passion's Bright Fury
   By Radclyffe

Thicker Than Water
   By Melissa Good

The Light Fantastic
   By LA Tucker

Tomorrow's Promise
   By Radclyffe

Twist of Fate
   By Jessica Casavant

Rebecca's Cove
   By LJ Maas

Thy Neighbor's Wife
   By Georgia Beers

Destiny's Bridge
   By Carrie Carr

Faith's Crossing
   By Carrie Carr

Carrie is a true Texan, having lived in the state her entire life. She makes her home in the Dallas/Ft. Worth metroplex with her partner AJ and their teenager daughter, Karen. She's done everything from wrangling longhorn cattle and buffalo, to programming burglar and fire alarm systems. Her spare time is spent writing, traveling, and trying to corral the latest addition to their family, a Chihuahua named Nugget. Check out her website at www.carriecarr.com for information such as merchandise, personal appearances, and personalized bookplates for her books.

Printed in the United States
1062100003B/107